Praise for

WAKING NIGHTMARE

"Sharper, I want you to meet Caitlin Fleming, a consultant for the sheriff's department. She's with Raiker Forensics."

The inflection in the man's voice imbued his last words with meaning. But it was his earlier words that had Zach halting in disbelief. Tipping his Julbo sunglasses down he looked—really looked—at the woman approaching.

The mile-long legs could be right. And she was tall enough; only a few inches shorter than his six-three height. The kiss-my-ass cheekbones were familiar. But it was the thick black hair that clinched it, though shorter now than it'd been all those years ago. He didn't need her to remove her tinted glasses to know the eyes behind them were moss green and guaranteed to turn any breathing male into an instant walking hard-on.

His voice terse, he turned his attention to the deputy and said, "Is this some kind of a joke?"

Barnes blinked. "What the hell are you talking about?"

"He's talking about me." The voice was smoke, pure sex. He'd never heard her speak before, but he'd imagined it often enough years ago in his adolescent fantasies. "Probably recognizes me from some of my modeling work, isn't that right, Sharper? A long time ago. If you want me to believe you've changed from a sweaty hormone-ridden teenage boy who undoubtedly used one of my posters to fuel your juvenile wet dreams, then you'll have to credit that I too grew up and moved on. I want a firsthand look at that cave. You're going to take me there."

WAKING THE DEAD

THE MINDHUNTERS

KYLIE BRANT

BERKLEY SENSATION, NEW YORK

THE BERKLEY PUBLISHING GROUP
Published by the Penguin Group
Penguin Group (USA) Inc.
375 Hudson Street, New York, New York 10014, USA
Penguin Group (Canada), 90 Eglinton Avenue East, Suite 700, Toronto, Ontario M4P 2Y3, Canada
(a division of Pearson Penguin Canada Inc.)
Penguin Books Ltd., 80 Strand, London WC2R 0RL, England
Penguin Group Ireland, 25 St. Stephen's Green, Dublin 2, Ireland (a division of Penguin Books Ltd.)
Penguin Group (Australia), 250 Camberwell Road, Camberwell, Victoria 3124, Australia
(a division of Pearson Australia Group Pty. Ltd.)
Penguin Books India Pvt. Ltd., 11 Community Centre, Panchsheel Park, New Delhi—110 017, India
Penguin Group (NZ), 67 Apollo Drive, Rosedale, North Shore 0632, New Zealand
(a division of Pearson New Zealand Ltd.)
Penguin Books (South Africa) (Pty.) Ltd., 24 Sturdee Avenue, Rosebank, Johannesburg 2196,
South Africa

Penguin Books Ltd., Registered Offices: 80 Strand, London WC2R 0RL, England

This is a work of fiction. Names, characters, places, and incidents either are the product of the author's imagination or are used fictitiously, and any resemblance to actual persons, living or dead, business establishments, events, or locales is entirely coincidental. The publisher does not have any control over and does not assume any responsibility for author or third-party websites or their content.

WAKING THE DEAD

A Berkley Sensation Book / published by arrangement with the author

PRINTING HISTORY
Berkley Sensation mass-market edition / November 2009

Copyright © 2009 by Kim Bahnsen.
Excerpt from *Deadly Fear* by Kylie Brant copyright © by Kim Bahnsen.
Cover art by S. Miroque.
Cover design by Rita Frangie.
Interior text design by Laura K. Corless.

ISBN: 978-0-425-23114-2

BERKLEY® SENSATION
Berkley Sensation Books are published by The Berkley Publishing Group,
a division of Penguin Group (USA) Inc.,
375 Hudson Street, New York, New York 10014.
BERKLEY® SENSATION and the "B" design are trademarks of Penguin Group (USA) Inc.

PRINTED IN THE UNITED STATES OF AMERICA

10 9 8 7 6 5 4 3 2

For Carly, who already felt like a member of the family
even before it became official. We love you!

Acknowledgments

One of the most intriguing parts of writing a novel is the research that goes into it, and many people contributed to this book. First off, thanks are owed to Alan Mayer, for describing the cave you found on the face of Castle Rock. It turned out to be perfect for my villain's needs. ☺

For all things bone related, much is owed to Alison Galloway, Ph.D., D-ABFA F-AAFS, and Laura C. Fulginiti, Ph.D., D-ABFA. Your information was as fascinating as it was appreciated!

Thanks to Bud Jillett for the details on the care and feeding of dermestid beetles. Your book was a big help, too!

A big thank you is owed to Wally Campbell, Laboratory Manager of the GBI-DOFS Coastal Regional Crime Lab in Savannah and Tammy Jergovich, Trace Evidence Section Manager, GBI, Division of Forensic Sciences, Decatur, Georgia, for your help regarding collection and analysis of trace evidence, comparison and reference samples, and infinite other nagging problems I sent your way. As usual, all mistakes are mine and mine alone.

A very special note of thanks goes to Kelcie and Guy Santiago for hauling me around to the Oregon caves and through the forest, and answering my endless questions. I had a blast! The area around McKenzie Bridge, Oregon, is one of the loveliest I've seen and is unlikely to house the sort of criminal activity found in this story. The beauty of writing fiction is the ability to change anything that doesn't fit into the plot. Hence some site names, directions, and distances between points, among other things, have been altered to suit the needs of the story.

Prologue

The way through the forest was familiar, so the lack of a moon didn't bother him. With the aid of the flashlight he made his way surely, avoiding fallen logs and low-hanging branches from memory. The large bag he carried on his back added nearly another twenty pounds, but that didn't slow him either. His strength was as sure as his sense of direction.

He carried a shotgun in his free hand and a machete hung from his belt. Not because he expected trouble, but because he'd lived in and around the Oregon wilderness long enough to be prepared for it. There were elk, bears, and cougars in the forest. Any number of poisonous snakes. And sometimes there was danger of a two-legged variety. It didn't pay to leave anything to chance.

His Sweetie would say once he had an idea he implemented it with the precision of a storm trooper. But for a long time now, it'd been Sweetie with the ideas and he who carried them out. That was all right with him.

The path he took wasn't an easy one as there was no trail to where he was going. Just across his backyard and into the forest that fringed it. Walking miles through brambles, salal, and thickets of blackberry bushes. Over outcroppings of lichen-slicked rocks and down through a creek that changed from a trickle in the summer to a rushing torrent when the mountain snows melted in the spring. Then the real test would begin at the base of Castle Rock. He'd have to stow the flashlight and shotgun. Switch on the camper's light he wore over his Oregon Ducks cap. And climb eight hundred feet to his hidey-hole.

He always fasted for a couple weeks before he made this trek. The first time he'd found the chamber in the small cave on the face of Castle Rock had been over ten years ago. He'd bulked up since then. Each time he belly crawled through it there were a few bad moments when he'd get stuck and have to work himself loose. He wanted to make damn sure he was able to do so.

But when he got close enough to see the lights, he slowed. Taking shelter behind the trunk of a large fir, he reached for the night vision binoculars he wore on a strap around his neck and held them up for closer observation. What he saw sent a jolt through him. Looked like he wasn't going to be making the climb tonight after all.

The place was flooded with cops.

There were spotlights illuminating the edge of Castle Rock like a rooftop at Christmastime. Plenty more at the base, shining upward. Dotting its face. His initial thought that the locals had busted a meth lab was quickly banished when he saw that some of the lights came from climbers hanging like spiders in front of his hidey-hole.

Well, fuck.

Sweetie might be the brainy one, but he was smart enough to figure out that his secret hiding place was no longer a secret.

As if to underscore that thought, one figure on a line leaned forward to the cave's mouth to grasp at something coming out of it. Something long and black. Something not so different from what he carried on his back right this moment.

He continued to watch as he pondered his options. He'd

been busy with preparations for the last couple days and hadn't left his place. And Sweetie was on that trip with the kids, so there hadn't been any warning of the discovery, the news of which must be sweeping the area. Their dump site might have been found, but there was no way anything in it led back to them. They'd made sure of that.

He watched for a while longer, wishing he dared get closer. *CSI* was his favorite show. It was the worst kind of luck that he didn't dare hang around and watch the cops work. Not that the locals would be much to see. Hell, most of the deputies were dickheads. With a force like that, Sheriff Andrews was going to be chasing her tail from now until doomsday.

Grinning, he lowered the binoculars and faded back into the forest. Nope, he had absolutely nothing to worry about.

Nothing except finding a new hiding place for the bag of bones he was carrying on his back.

Chapter 1

Seven stainless steel gurneys were lined up in the morgue, each occupied by a partially assembled skeleton and a large garbage bag. The bones gleamed under the florescent lights. At the base of the last gurney was a heap of stray bones that had been found lying separately. Caitlin Fleming's first thought was that they looked forlorn. Deprived of their dignity, until they could be rejoined to form the remnant of the person they'd once belonged to.

Her second thought was that without the skulls, the chances of identifying those persons decreased dramatically.

"What do you think?" Sheriff Marin Andrews demanded. Her booted feet sounded heavily as she walked from one gurney to the next. "The bones were pretty much loose in the bags, but the medical examiner made an attempt to reassemble them. We brought out the bones scattered on the bottom of the cave floor in a separate body bag. Recovery operation was a bitch, I'm telling you. The cave branches off from the original vein, gets wider and higher. Then it drops off to a steep chamber about seven feet down. These were probably dumped from above into that chamber." She must have caught Cait's wince, because she added, "We had an anthropologist from the university supervise the removal process."

Cait nodded. She was rarely brought onto a case in time to help process the crime scene. But that didn't stop her from questioning what might have been destroyed or overlooked in the recovery. "I'll want to see the cave."

Andrews's expression first revealed shock, then amusement. "Fortunately for you, that won't be necessary. It's on the face of Castle Rock and not easily accessible. Either you climb down from the top, or you scale upwards nearly eight hundred feet. There are trails, of course, but they could be tricky for an inexperienced climber. We don't need an injury on our hands before we even get started."

"I'm not inexperienced." Cait knew exactly what the sheriff saw when she looked at her. It was, after all, the appearance she'd cultivated for well over a decade. But her days on the runways of New York, Milan, and Paris were long behind her. She was as comfortable these days in a room exactly like this one as she was hiking in the Blue Ridge Mountains.

The other woman shrugged. She was probably about fifteen years Cait's senior. Her looks were nondescript. A sturdy build filling out a beige uniform. Close-cropped light brown hair and hazel eyes. But Cait knew better than anyone that appearances could be deceiving. Marin Andrews had a reputation for being an excellent, if ambitious cop. And that ambition, along with her father's millions, were rumored to be priming her for a chase to the governor's mansion.

Cait's help in solving this case would provide a stepping-stone to that end.

"Figured you'd want to see the area, anyway. That forest fire in the eastern Cascades has depleted the personnel at the forestry stations, but we've hired Zach Sharper to stay available during the course of the investigation. He's the outdoors guide who found the bodies. Said he was preparing for a client who wanted to spelunk some out-of-the-way caves, so Zach explored a few off the beaten path. Thought he'd discovered a new one when he stumbled on this." Andrews waved a hand at the skeletons. "He runs an outfitting company. Rafting, kayaking, mountain climbing, hiking, that sort of thing." The assessing look in her eyes said better than words that she didn't believe Cait's assertion of her outdoor experience. "He's also on the search and rescue team when campers and hikers go missing. He's got some rough edges, but he's supposed to be the best in the state."

"I can handle rough edges." Cait walked around the gurneys to peer more closely at the nearly identical junctures where the skulls had been separated from each skeleton. She looked around then, spotted a magnifying loupe on a set of metal shelves in the corner, and retrieved it before continuing her examination.

"The guy from the university said it looked like a knife or saw was used to decapitate them."

Cait moved to another gurney to peer at the vertebra. "I'd say a saw. With luck I may be able to narrow the type down for you." Straightening, she scanned the remains lined up on the stainless steel tables. "You've got four men and three women, but I suspect the medical examiner told you that."

"He did. He also tried, and failed, to find a cause of death for any of them. But this thing is way out of his league and he knows it. He's a pathologist, not a forensic anthropologist. When I saw what we had here, I immediately thought of Raiker Forensics. Adam Raiker assures me you're the best in this field."

Cait used the loupe to take a close look at the femur of the second skeleton. The guy had suffered a fracture to it at some point in his life. It had knit cleanly, suggesting certain medical attention. "I am," she responded absently. She looked up then to arrow a look at Andrews. "My assistant will be arriving at dawn tomorrow with our equipment. Will this facility remain available to us?"

"It will. The building is less than a year old and state of the art." The look of satisfaction stamping the sheriff's face told Cait better than words that the other woman had been a driving force behind the new morgue. "Anything you need, talk to the Lane County medical examiner. His name is Steve

Michaels. You'll have to meet him tomorrow." Cait followed the direction of the woman's gaze to the clock on the wall. Eight P.M. And she'd left home at six in the morning in order to catch her flight from Dulles. Weariness was edging in, warring with hunger.

"I've arranged two rooms for you and your assistant at the Landview Suites here in Eugene. You've rented a vehicle?"

"Picked it up at the airport." The compact SUV looked perfect for the ground she'd be covering in the course of this investigation. "I'd like all the maps you can provide for the area. Roads, forests, surrounding towns . . ." A thought struck her then and she looked at the other woman. "And thanks for arranging for the weapon permit so quickly." Raiker refused to let any of his consultants work without one.

Andrews lifted a shoulder. "Your boss made it clear that condition wasn't up for discussion. I doubt you'll need it. These bones may have been in that cave for decades. Even if foul play is determined, the unknown subject is probably long gone by now. The threat should be minimal."

"Maybe. Maybe not. It certainly doesn't take decades for a corpse to be reduced to a skeleton. In some climates it'd be a week if the body were left out in the elements. In Oregon it'd take several weeks or months, depending on where the body's dumped, the season, the temperature, insect and ani-mal access. Maybe you're right and these bones have been there for that long. But not necessarily."

When she saw the satisfied gleam in the sheriff's eye, Cait knew she'd read the woman correctly. Whatever the outcome of this case, Andrews was going to use it to vault her political career. And solving a current crime spree would make for a lot better press than some old murders that had happened long ago.

But the woman only said, "I've got a copy of the case file for you in the car. You'll be reporting directly to me, but in the field you may be working with my lead detective, Mitch Barnes. You can meet him tomorrow, too."

Cait's attention had already returned to the skeletons. There was a lot of preparatory work to bc done on them, but it would have to wait until tomorrow when Kristy arrived. Although she'd be supervising the lab work, these days Cait was an investigator first, a forensic anthropologist second. And she was anxious to get a look at the secondary scene.

"I'll want to get my assistant started first thing tomorrow morning. Have Barnes meet me here at nine and tell Sharper to stand by. We'll head up to . . ."

"Castle Rock," the other woman supplied.

". . . and he can show me how he happened to discover the remains of seven people." She shot a glance at the sheriff as they headed to the door. "How did Sharper react to the find? Is he pretty shaken up?"

Andrews gave a bark of laughter, real amusement showing in her expression. "Nothing shakes up Sharper, unless it's people wasting his time. He'll be steady enough, don't worry. But he won't win any congeniality contests."

Cait shrugged. "I don't need congenial. I'll be satisfied with competent."

Andrews led the way out of the morgue, the echo of her booted footsteps ringing hollowly. "I may need to remind you of those words after you meet him."

———

Her first stop had been an office supply store. The next was a fast food drive-through for a grilled chicken salad with definite wilting around the edges. Cait had eaten in between setting up her work area in the motel room. The crime scene photos were tacked to the white display boards sitting on top of the desk. A collection of labels, index cards, markers, and Post-it notes sat neatly at the base.

Now she sat on the bed leaning against the headboard, the contents of the fat accordion file folder scattered across her lap and on the mattress. The photographs from the cave chamber had been taken with a low-light lens, but they were still darker than she'd like. While she was able to easily make out the bags' proximity to one another, it was more difficult to read the plastic numbered evidence markers that had been set in front of each to tell which one was which.

There was a preliminary report from the ME, Steve Michaels, and it appeared to be solid work. Measurements of each set of bones were included, as was a thorough examination for evidence of trauma. None of the skeletons showed recent signs of injury. Perhaps the missing skulls would. Or maybe the deaths were the result of poison. Cait narrowed her eyes, considering. She found herself hoping for the victims' sakes that the decapitation had been enacted posthumously.

Had the skulls been removed to impede identification of the victims? To prevent investigators from detecting the method of death? Or were they kept by the perp as trophies?

Taking a look at her watch, Cait began gathering up the materials and replacing them in the file. But it occurred to her that if she could answer those questions, she'd be a long way toward profiling the UNSUB they were searching for.

Kristy Jensen was a full foot shorter than Cait at four-eleven, a wispy ethereal creature with an otherworldly air. Slap a pair of wings on her, and with her elfin features and blonde wavy hair, she'd looked like a fairy in a kid's storybook.

Once she opened her mouth, however, that notion would be dispelled forever.

"There is no fucking good way to get to this fuck dump of a town, you know that, don't you?" Kristy sipped at her Starbucks coffee and aimed a gimlet stare over the rim from cornflower blue eyes. "Charter plane, my ass. Eight fucking hours it took me from Dulles. I could have walked faster. I could have parachuted half way here, hitched a ride on a mother-fucking migrating duck and still gotten here before that damn plane."

"So the plane ride was good?" Cait laughed as her diminutive friend gave her the finger as they entered the morgue. "And you owe me four bucks. I'm giving you a pass on the 'damn,' and the one-finger salute because at least that's silent."

"We aren't even on the clock yet," Kristy complained. But she was already digging in her purse to pull out the money. "I think we should change the rules so it only counts during work time."

"Tough love." Cait snatched the five from the woman's hand and dug in her purse until she found a one for change. "You wanted help cleaning up your language. Can't change the rules midcourse."

"Why not? Nothing else has changed, except for my disposable income. I'm still swearing like a one-legged sailor."

They showed their temporary ID to the clerk at the front desk and headed down the long hallway to the room where Andrews had brought Cait the evening before.

"Discipline," she chided. But there was no heat to the word. She could care less whether or not Kristy swore like a seasoned dock worker, as long as she did her job to Cait's exact specifications. And since Kristy was the best tech she'd ever been assigned, Cait was satisfied. "Anyway you'll cheer up quick enough once you see what we have to work with." She paused in front of the door at the end of the hall before opening it with a dramatic flourish.

"Sweeeeet," Kristy breathed, when she got a glimpse of the remains on the gurneys. "What do we have, mass burial? Mass murder," she corrected as she got closer and noted the lack of human skulls attached.

"I suppose we have to allow for the possibility that someone stumbled upon that cave long before the guide did," mused Cait. The thought had occurred belatedly, once she'd gone to bed, her mind still filled with the contents of the files. "Someone with a sense of the macabre who took the skulls as souvenirs."

Kristy was practically salivating as she walked between each gurney. "So I'll double-check them, right? Make sure the right parts are with the proper skeleton?"

"I want you to start a photograph log first," Cait corrected. "I need a notebook kept of images of each skeleton throughout each step of the process." It would be easier to correct mistakes that way, especially in the tricky process of reassembling the full remains of each, which was often a matter of trial and error. "The ME should be around somewhere. Get him to give you a copy of the measurements he's done." She'd left her copy in her case file back at the motel.

"But you'll want me to do my own."

Cait sent her a look of approval. "I doubt he had a caliper to do the measurements with. Then you can ensure each bone is with the right remains." And when Kristy was done, Cait would go over them carefully again, just to be certain. "We've got assorted bones on the last gurney that will have to be matched, as well. Then we'll see exactly what we've got here."

"What should I do in my spare time?" But her sarcasm was checked. Kristy was hooked by the enormity of their task, just as Cait was. Anticipation was all but radiating off her.

"I heard voices." At the sound of the newcomer the women turned toward the door. The man approaching them was average height, with hair as dark as Cait's. He wore blue scrubs, shoe covers, and a slight smile that faded as he got closer. Then his face took on that slightly stunned expression that was all too familiar. He stared from Cait to Kristy and back again, with the look of a starving man surrounded by a steaming banquet. "Ah . . . Michaels." He held out his hand to each of them in turn, visibly wrestling to get the words out in proper order. "Steve. I am, that is."

He looked chagrined, but Cait spared him no slack. "Well, Michaels Steve, I'm Cait Fleming." She jerked a thumb at the other woman. "My assistant, Kristy Jensen. I've got your preliminary report. Appreciate it. Kristy will be working down here most of the time. I've been assured that whatever she needs, she can come to you."

While she spoke the man seemed to have regained his powers of speech. But twin flags of color rode high on his cheeks and his dark eyes still looked dazed. "Certainly." He dragged his gaze away from Cait and fixed it on Kristy. "Certainly," he repeated.

"Then I'll leave you to get started." She didn't know if

Barnes would be here yet, but she wasn't anxious to spend any more time with the ME who looked like he'd just cast them in a low-budget porn fantasy involving a threesome and a stainless steel coroner's station. She started out of the room, throwing a look at Kristy over her shoulder. "Keep me posted."

As she headed through the door she heard her assistant say sweetly, "So Michaels Steve, why don't we go out to the truck and you can help unload the mother-fucking equipment."

A smirk on her lips, Cait decided to let it slide. Nothing was more guaranteed to shatter a guy's X-rated fantasy than a pint-sized angelic blonde with a mouth like a sewage plant. She almost felt sorry for him. Would have if she weren't still annoyed at his all too common reaction. As it was, she figured he was going to get exactly what he deserved working with Kristy.

When she stepped out of the morgue doors she saw the Lane County sheriff patrol car pulling up to the curb a full fifteen minutes early. Her good humor restored, Cait rounded it to approach the driver's door. A stocky deputy got out, extended his hand. "Mitch Barnes, Ms. Fleming."

Belatedly, Cait realized she was still wearing the morgue temporary ID. She snatched it off with one hand and she offered him the other. "Looking forward to working with you, Mitch."

The man came to her chin, had receding blond hair and brown eyes that were pure cop. And it'd been her ID that drew his attention rather than her face or figure. She liked him immediately for that fact alone.

"Sheriff says you want to head up toward McKenzie Bridge. Over to Castle Rock."

She nodded as she dropped her ID into her purse. "I'd like a look at the dump site. Get a feel for it."

"You got the pictures?"

Understanding what he was getting at, she nodded. "Still want to see it."

Shrugging, he leaned into his front seat only to withdraw

a moment later with an armful of maps. "Andrews said you asked for these."

"I did, thanks." She took the stack from him. "If you want to lead the way up to the McKenzie Bridge area, I'll follow this time. That way you don't have to wait around while I go through the cave if you don't want to."

"Sounds good. It's about a forty-five minute drive. I'll call Sharper on the way and let him know we're coming by." A smirk flashed across the man's otherwise professional demeanor. "He'll be thrilled to take you to the cave."

Coupled with the sheriff's comments the night before, Cait had the distinct impression that the guide they kept mentioning was light on social graces. The thought didn't bother her nearly as much as it would if he were another ogler like the ME.

Men like that rarely brought out the best in her.

———

How the hell had he gotten into this mess?

Fuming, Zach Sharper threw another look at the rearview mirror and the empty ribbon of road behind him. The answer was swift in coming. Ever since he'd reported his findings from that cave, Andrews had had him wrapped up like a damn trick monkey. First he'd had to lead law enforcement to the place. Hang around while they did their thing. Then there'd been the endless questioning.

And now he found himself forced to be at the beck and call of some consultant hired by the sheriff's office. Playing glorified nursemaid to a cop—or close enough to it—promised to be worse than the biggest pain-in-the-ass client he ran across from time to time. At least he had a choice when taking on the clients.

Yeah, not being given a choice here rankled the most.

He saw the county car headed toward him. Zach put on his sunglasses and got out of his Trailblazer. Damned if he'd been about to travel down to Eugene and then back again once he'd heard what the consultant wanted. And he sure as hell wasn't going to arrange for the cops to meet him at his place. Whispering Pines was his getaway. His refuge. Guests were rarely invited.

A navy SUV pulled off the road in back of the sheriff's car. He was unsurprised to see Mitch Barnes get out of the lead car. The way Zach heard it, Barnes did most of the grunt work for Andrews while she got all the glory. He'd been the first of the cops to follow Zach into that cave. The sheriff sure hadn't gone in, though she'd been present, running things on top Castle Rock while her people had hauled the bones out. If Barnes wanted another pass at the cave he sure as hell didn't need Zach. He knew where it was located.

Made a guy wonder if this was just one more way for Andrews to yank his chain, show him who was calling the shots.

He walked toward the deputy, who was approaching on the shoulder. The driver of the SUV got out, too, but it was Barnes Zach concentrated on. He wasn't a bad sort, for a cop. Maybe he could talk him into a change of plans. Zach was resigned to the fact that he wasn't going to get out of this forced alliance with the sheriff's office. But Andrews wouldn't necessarily have to know whether he was the one playing nursemaid or if one of Zach's employees fulfilled the duty.

Although he wasn't sure he had an employee he disliked enough to saddle with this job.

"Barnes," he said by way of greeting. The other man gave him a nod. Wasting no time, he continued, "Maybe you and I can reach an . . ."

"Sharper, I want you to meet Caitlin Fleming, a consultant for the sheriff's department. She's with Raiker Forensics."

The inflection in the man's voice imbued his last words with meaning. But it was his earlier words that had Zach halting in disbelief. Tipping his Julbo sunglasses down he looked— really looked—at the woman approaching.

The mile-long legs could be right. And she was tall enough; only a few inches shorter than his six-three height. The kiss-my-ass cheekbones were familiar. But it was the thick black hair that clinched it, though shorter now than it'd been all those years ago. He didn't need her to remove her tinted glasses to know the eyes behind them were moss green and guaranteed to turn any breathing male into an instant walking hard-on.

His voice terse, he turned his attention to the deputy and said, "Is this some kind of a joke?"

Barnes blinked. "What?"

"I mean are there going to be TV trucks and cameras following our every move?" Christ, what a clusterfuck. He could already imagine it. TV channels were filled with so-called entertainment featuring desperate cultural celebrities and he could anticipate what was going on here. "I'm not about to get involved in a reality TV show or whatever the hell she's part of. You can tell the sheriff the deal is off." Andrews had threatened to jam him up with the constant renewal of permits needed to take his clients camping or kayaking. But maybe he could bribe someone at the permit department to circumvent her meddling. He was willing to take his chances.

"What the hell are you talking about?"

"He's talking about me." The voice was smoke, pure sex. He'd never heard her speak before, but he'd imagined it often enough years ago in his adolescent fantasies. "Probably recognizes me from some of my modeling work, isn't that right, Sharper? A long time ago. If you want me to believe you've changed from a sweaty hormone-ridden teenage boy who undoubtedly used one of my posters to fuel your juvenile wet dreams, then you'll have to credit that I too grew up and moved on. I want a firsthand look at that cave. You're going to take me there."

Somehow when he'd imagined her talking decades ago it had been without that tone of withering disdain. His disbelief dissipated, the skepticism remained. He slanted a glance at the deputy. "Seriously, Barnes. *This* is the department's consultant?"

The man's manner was stiff. "Like I said, she's from Raiker Forensics. *The Mindhunters*. That might not mean anything to you, but in law enforcement circles it carries a helluva lot of weight."

Caitlin Fleming as a cop. The implausibility of it still rang in his mind. But then he gave a mental shrug. Most people in these parts used to be something else. Many were reluctant to talk about their pasts. Including him.

Especially him.

He looked her over again, noting the jeans, tennis shoes, and long-sleeve navy T-shirt. "Either we hike down Castle Rock or climb up it. Either way, it's not a walk in the park. Mitch here can tell you that. You might want to rethink visiting it in person."

Instead of responding, she looked at the deputy. "You coming along?"

He shook his head. "Once was enough for me. I've been stopping in at the forest service stations in the area to look at the citations they've issued in the last few years. There might be a pattern. Maybe some common names."

She nodded. "I'll be anxious to hear what you find. See you back in Eugene, then. This will probably take most of the day." She walked back to her SUV and pulled a pack out of the back end. Then she locked it and headed back to where they stood waiting for her.

"We'll use your vehicle, Sharper. I'll want to explore both approaches to the cave." She headed toward where he'd left his Trailblazer parked on the shoulder of the road. Her voice drifted behind her as she walked away. "I'd already been warned you were an asshole, so your attitude isn't much of a surprise. But it'll be up to you to convince me that you're as good at your job as I've heard. Right now, I've got to say, I have my doubts."

Chapter 2

Caitlin Fleming was worried about *his* qualifications.
With dark humor, Zach silently drove east on Highway 126.
Obviously he'd pissed off a major god in a former life.
Though there were plenty who'd claim he'd pissed off his
share in *this* one. Whatever his sins—and he was willing to
admit they were numerous—he was going to be doing serious penance during the course of his work with the sheriff's
department.

Andrews was going to owe him big time, and not just his
fee.

He drove in silence, and the woman beside him didn't
make any attempt to fill it. Point for her. If there was one
thing that got on his nerves, it was a chattering client. She
was poring over a map of the area like she was intent on
memorizing it. Either she didn't trust him to get her to Castle
Rock in one piece, or she was doing her homework before
getting there.

"What's in your pack?"

"Why?"

"Because I have to know whether I need to swing by home and pick up extra equipment or whether you came prepared." Already he was taking mental inventory of what he had in his garage. Most of the gear was at the store in Eugene, of course. That was their headquarters from where they took bookings and sent out guides with clients, whether for kayaking, rafting, or hiking. But he had stuff at home. He tried to think whether any of it would fit her.

"I'm set for the climb and the cave. I don't have line, though. I assume you do."

He grunted. "You'll need a flashlight. Batteries. Proper shoes. Gloves. Hard hat . . ."

"Like I say," she responded coolly without lifting her gaze from the map, "I'm good except for the line. They brought the remains out this way, right?"

A shift of his gaze and he saw she was indicating the top of Castle Rock. "Rappelled over the edge," he affirmed. "Lot easier to haul the bodies up rather than down, and it allowed them to continue their work once night had fallen."

"They worked at night?"

He couldn't help wondering at the note in her voice.

"Yeah. Had the outside lit up pretty good, but inside the cave . . ." He shrugged. It didn't much matter once you went in if it were day outside or night. The only illumination was artificial.

"How'd you get to the cave the first time you discovered it?"

"Climbed up."

"I'll want to see the top of Castle Rock, but let's approach the cave from the bottom first."

Curiosity got the best of him. "Any reason why? It's actually easier coming down from the top. The trail on that side is through the forest, but it's a switch back. Going up the front involves more climbing."

"I'll want to see the back side, too, but first we go up from below. From the maps I studied, it seems more plausible that the UNSUB carried those bones up from the bottom than down from the top."

"UNSUB?"

"Unknown subject. Whoever dumped the bodies, if in fact that's what happened."

"You mean the killer."

"Murder hasn't been established. And even if it is, the two people aren't necessarily the same."

He subsided with an inner sigh. Great. He'd have to follow her up the face of the cliff, shouting instructions about finger and toe holds and be ready to catch her when she slipped, which she inevitably would. Even having a close-up view of her world-famous ass during the climb wasn't going to make the process any more appealing.

His mood, not sunny to begin with, soured further. And there was no more conversation for the next fifteen minutes, until he pulled off the highway onto an old logging road. He didn't expend any energy to avoid the deep ruts. From the corner of his eye he saw Fleming jolt strongly with the lurching of the truck before slapping a hand on the dash to steady herself.

He cut the engine. "We'll have to walk in." He nodded to the forest that surrounded them. "Head east until we get to the bottom of Castle Rock. Then I'll try to select the easiest climb, but I'm not going to lie to you. It will be a climb."

"So you've mentioned." She was already slipping out of the truck and opening the back door to reach in for her pack.

He did the same, although he was going to shed the pack before entering the cave. It was a tight fit. The first time he ended up leaving his pack at the entrance before belly crawling his way inside and he'd still gotten caught a couple times. He wasn't anxious to spend a lot of time wiggling around trying to get unstuck this time. Not with the woman following him.

Digging in the pack he pulled out a khaki ball cap emblazoned with his business logo, OREGON OUTDOORS, and tugged it on. Everything else could wait until they drew closer to the cave. He hesitated, looked down at his black T-shirt. It was plenty warm in the sun, but the temperature cooled a bit in the forest. And he'd want more protection for the climb. He ducked his head in the backseat of his Trailblazer again, rooted around until he found a long-sleeve tee to match the hat, and jammed it in his pack. Then he slammed the door and rounded the vehicle, prepared to wait for the woman. *Caitlin Fleming.*

But she was already prepared to move out. She'd pulled her hair back into a ponytail, and the tail was looped through the opening in the back of her ball cap. Fingerless rock-climbing gloves covered her hands and a pair of expensive-looking mini binoculars hung from a strap around her neck. His quick once over ended at her shoes.

"You'd do better with boots."

She picked up one foot, turned it over to show him the grippers on the bottom. "I like these better for low-level climbing. And for caves."

Shrugging into his pack, he gave up arguing. She'd come equipped, but she still was likely to be unprepared for what was ahead of them, and it would be his job, unwilling or not, to get her through it. "We've got a hike ahead of us. Give a holler when you need to rest or take a leak." He started off for the forest entrance at a good clip, pretending not to hear her muttered remark behind him.

"If I feel like taking a leak you can bet yours will be the first name on my lips."

Because his mouth threatened to smile, he deliberately firmed it. And considered it just as well for the boy he'd been all those years ago that her poster hadn't been accompanied by voice.

There was no telling the damage that might have inflicted on his tender young male psyche.

———

Cait's legs were nearly as long as Sharper's so she didn't have much trouble keeping up with him. Which was lucky, because he seemed to spare no thought about whether or not she was falling behind. He made his way steadily through the forest without a backward glance.

She knew from experience they could have started from

tougher spots. They weren't having to hack their way through brambles or scrub brush, the sort of barrier that sprouted so easily in less well-traveled areas in a forest. Which made her think that if they discovered the bodies had, in fact been dumped, the offender wouldn't have entered this way.

The old logging road was easily accessible to the highway, for one thing. There was too much risk someone would notice a car turning off this way. Too many questions to answer if they did.

Of course, she thought, as she jumped nimbly over a rotted-out fallen tree, the cover of darkness would offer protection against detection regardless.

The forest floor was dense with understory vegetation in some spots, barren but for pine needles in others. The trees were mostly firs, interspersed with some deciduous species, and towered overhead in a fifty-foot canopy. But the spindly trunks allowed brilliant slants of light through. She could think of far worse ways to spend a day than quiet hours strolling through the forest.

But her mind wasn't on enjoyment. Nor was it on the man walking surely several yards ahead of her.

It was on the UNSUB who might have followed a very similar path.

"How did you happen to find that cave?"

"I've given my statement to Andrews's office," Sharper said shortly. His pace didn't slow. "I'm sure Barnes will show it to you if you ask."

Rough edges were one thing. No one was this abrupt without design. Rather than following him over a pile of rocks, Cait detoured around it. Maybe he was the sort who didn't trust cops. It was a common enough feeling among people she encountered in the course of an investigation. And most of them had a reason for that distrust. She couldn't help wondering what had caused Sharper's.

"How long have you been a guide in the area?" She didn't bother telling him that his statement had been included in the case file Andrews had given. Given the opportunity, Cait preferred to ask her own questions, in her own way. Sometimes that elicited different details.

"I grew up around here. Came back and started Oregon Outdoors five years ago."

She kicked her foot free of a tangle of ferns. "So you know the area well. Yet your statement said you'd never explored this cave before."

He turned around so suddenly she had to apply the brakes to avoid running into him. Whipping off his sunglasses, he regarded her, his expression grim. "I've noticed the opening before, yeah. Never bothered finding out if it went anywhere. I'm not into caves myself. And when clients want to go cave exploring, they're usually satisfied with Sawyer's Ice Caves or the lava tubes over in Bend. But this client wanted something different. I thought of the place I'd noticed before in Castle Rock and decided to give it a closer look."

She studied him calmly, despite the hostility emanating from the man. He wasn't the type to cultivate that stubble on his lean jaw for effect, so she assumed it was just carelessness on his part. It went with the slightly shaggy sun-streaked brown hair. Was emphasized by the golden lights in his whiskey-colored eyes, which were surrounded by absurdly long lashes.

Eyes that were shooting sparks at her right now. "If you're suggesting that I hauled seven skeletons up to that cave, dumped them, and then called the cops on myself, you should have stayed with modeling. At least that didn't require thinking."

She could drop him right there, Cait thought grimly. One well-placed shot to the balls would be adequate payback for that crack. But as satisfying at the action would be, she needed him upright. At least until they got to Castle Rock. "I'm not suggesting you put the remains in the cave." Yet.

"Yeah? Well then you're one up on Sheriff Andrews. She grilled me about it for so long I think she was outfitting me for prison blues."

"Once I age the bones we'll have a better idea of how long they were down there." She didn't bother telling him that part of her job would be by far the most difficult. "Who knows? If you've been absent from the area for a number of years, my findings may clear you."

"*You'll* be aging the skeletons." He regarded her skeptically. "In between scaling Castle Rock, leaping buildings with a single bound . . ."

Her smile faded. "My qualifications aren't your concern, Sharper. But if I were you, I'd be hoping I discovered something to suggest you couldn't possibly be involved instead of intentionally pissing me off."

The tension in his expression eased. The flint in his eye didn't. "It's not intentional, it's natural. And I could care less what you do, as long as it doesn't suck up my time." He turned then and began walking again.

"I understand you're being compensated for your time."

"I prefer to choose my own clients."

And somehow Andrews had forced his hand with this duty. Cait could imagine the scene that had elicited his reluctant help. She just didn't much give a damn one way or another. So she finished the hike in silence, ignoring, as much as possible, the broad-shouldered man in front of her. And when her muscles began to burn from the workout, it suited her to blame that on Sharper, too.

A couple hours later she was leaning against the huge pile of rock outcroppings at the base of Castle Rock, scanning the face of it through her binoculars. "Which one is it?"

She lowered the glasses to note the direction Sharper pointed, raised them again to follow the direction with her gaze. Difficult to see from down here whether the indentation in the rocks actually led anywhere. A person would have to be a determined climber, with an avid curiosity to scramble up and check out each shadowy opening in the cliff.

Most would lead nowhere, of course. She knew that from experience, too. She did her share of climbing in the Blue Ridge Mountains, although she wasn't a huge fan of caves. Some would plunge inside the cliff only a few feet before hitting rock again. The one documented in the police report was an exception rather than the rule.

"Any sign of animal life inside?"

Sharper shrugged as he lifted a water bottle to his lips and guzzled. Lowering it, he said, "No snakes or bats that I saw. Plenty of spiders, but didn't see any poisonous ones. Doesn't mean they aren't there, though."

Cait dropped the binoculars and reached for her own water bottle. She drank, still eyeing the face of the stone wall, plotting her approach. "I'll go in first. I want to take the branch to the chamber, and from the description in the report there's not room in there for both of us at the same time."

"Your party."

Because that was true enough she made no comment. She took a few moments to finish drinking, and then found a private place nearby to relieve herself. When she returned Sharper was exactly where she'd left him, and there was no surprise in that either. He'd exchanged his shirt for a long-sleeve one and had replaced his ball cap with a collapsible hard hat. She reached into her bag and withdrew a similar one, the kind recommended for spelunkers with a battery-operated light on the front. She'd rammed her head on stones jutting down from the roofs of caves often enough to not need a reminder to use one. The binoculars went into the pack. She didn't need them swinging and hitting the rocks as she climbed, or worse, catching on something and strangling her.

Then she packed her bag up and shrugged into it again. Without a word, she strode toward the face of Castle Rock. She heard Sharper's voice behind her.

"Best way up is to start over here to the right of the opening. Then when you're about two hundred feet away start making your way over."

Cait forged ahead. Minutes later, a hundred feet in the air, she was ready to admit that Sharper and Andrews had been right. Oh, it was hardly an effort worthy of hard-core climbing enthusiasts. But it was more of a workout than the rock-climbing wall at the gym she frequented. She found herself glad she had as much experience as she did in the wilderness.

She was even happier to see no snakes on the way up.

The sun was warm after the relative coolness of the forest, and the pack made for an extra layer of insulation. She was sweating before she was half way. If not for Sharper's infrequent commands behind her, it would feel like woman against nature. An exhilarating, isolating process.

She began moving toward the left to the cave opening, and the way got a bit trickier. One toehold gave beneath her foot, and her fingers scrabbled, gripping fiercely while her feet swung for a moment, unsupported. In the next moment she found another jutting rock to push off from and regained her stability. And continued climbing despite the fanged hollowness in her stomach.

"You want me to follow you in."

Sharper's words were more statement than question as she hauled herself up on the narrow ledge before the yawning darkness of the cave. Cait reached up to flip on the light of her hard hat. She took a moment to slip out of her pack and withdraw a flashlight before shrugging it back into place. "Be easier," she called over her shoulder belatedly. "Just make sure I don't miss the turn off."

With that she plunged inside. Although she started off crawling she quickly had to drop to her stomach as the ceiling of the cave pinched in. Cait wasn't claustrophobic, but there was nothing as absolute, as impenetrable as the darkness in a cave. The slight sunlight from the opening behind her was lost once she rounded the first bend. And she was fervently glad for both lights she had. The one on her hard hat offered glimpses of where the ceiling dipped and curved. The flashlight in her hand shone on the surface she was currently flattened against. Lit up fingers of rock jutting out from the side that could catch and snag at her clothing or pack. Spotlighted the spiders and cave crickets skittering along on the walls beside her.

It felt more like a tunnel than a cave, but there was plenty of room for her to move as long as she remained on her belly. She had a feeling Sharper wasn't faring as well. An occasional muttered curse drifted forward to her ears. The width of his shoulders would make this a tight fit. She could see why he'd shed his pack at the entrance.

The stone beneath her, to the sides of her were cool but dry. Not smooth by any means, but not so ragged that she'd have to worry about bruises and lacerations when she finished. But she was still thankful when, twenty or so feet inside, she saw the yawning opening to her right.

"Is this the branch to the chamber up ahead?"

Her voice rang in the cave rather than echoed. As did Sharper's answer.

"To your right. You'll be able to crouch the rest of the way to the opening. For Godsakes, don't fall in when you reach it."

Cait made the jog and rose to her haunches thankfully when the branch of the cave widened significantly. It was about three feet across now, and four and a half feet high. Even with the lights she carried, she moved carefully, unsure where the drop off would occur. And imagined, as she made her way in the near darkness, the offender following this same path.

He'd have carried the bag on his back for the climb, maybe rigged in a harness of some type. But once in the tunnel he would have had to drag it, she thought, as she crept forward. There was no other way a normal-sized male would fit hauling a bag that big.

Although she couldn't discount the possibility that the perp was a female.

The beam of her flashlight caught the yawning blackness ahead, and she slowed, inching forward now. She could hear Sharper behind her. "The chamber is coming up. Be careful. I'm going to be mighty pissed off if you fall in and break a leg."

The thought of having to depend on Sharper to rescue her elicited a burst of renewed caution. Cait stretched out on her belly again, sweeping the darkness ahead with the beam of her flashlight as she crawled.

There was little to herald the fact that the floor of the cave was about to give way. Just a few rocks jutting up from the floor, then nothing. There was a quiver in her stomach when her free hand met that emptiness ahead of her. She moved back a few cautionary inches before turning the beams of both lights downward. Wonder filled her.

The chamber was approximately seven feet down, eleven feet by nine feet in diameter. Cait played her lights over the area. The walls were mostly smooth, with occasional rougher patches jutting out that would serve as toe and finger holds. But once down it would be chancy climbing out without someone waiting above with a rope.

She drew back on her haunches and shrugged out of her backpack. Another light speared the darkness. Sharper had made the turn into the branch.

"What are you doing?"

Turning off her flashlight, she slipped it back into the pack. "I'm going in. Position yourself so you can shine your lights down into the chamber to give me more illumination."

"What's the point?" His voice might be pitched low, but it was easy enough to hear the impatience lacing it. "You wanted to see where I found the bones, you can see it from up here. The police were all over the area. You aren't likely to find anything they missed."

"I need to go down myself." She didn't expect him to understand. But this cave was the closest link they had to the UNSUB other than the bones themselves. Given the nature of Cait's job, she was almost never called first to the preliminary crime scene, even a secondary scene such as this one. She always insisted on visiting the scene in person. It was the best way to get a feel for a case.

She turned, preparing to scale down the wall into the chamber.

"Jesus. Wait a minute." A couple seconds passed, then Sharper loomed before her. "You'll want to keep your hands on those stones sticking up right here. See?"

She nodded. She'd already noted the handholds.

"Once you're over the edge, you can reach to the right and find another hand hold. Move your left hand to this stone here." He leaned forward, his figure shadowy in the near darkness as he pointed. "If you angle your body that way, you'll find a couple footholds on the way down."

"You went down there?" She knew he had. It was in the report. But she wanted to hear his explanation for herself.

"Why else would I have called the cops in?" His tone might have sounded reasonable without that note of insolence in it. "Couldn't see what the hell was down there for sure, other than some trash bags. If it'd been garbage, I'd have figured a way to haul it out. It would have made for a pretty impressive cave to show the client I was planning for. But I doubted it was garbage."

She nodded her understanding. No one would make this climb to dump some illicit litter.

"Figured it was a burglary stash or drugs." The dim light offered from their hard hats left his face shadowed, turning it to all lean angles and hard edges. "We've got our share of both problems in the area. But once I got down there, I saw a few bones scattered around the area. Knew I'd stumbled onto something far different."

For the first time she really considered what it'd been like for him to be standing down there in that deep dark hole. Surrounded by bags filled with bones. "Had to be pretty creepy."

There was a note of finality in his voice. "I've seen worse."

Because it was obvious he wasn't going to say more, Cait turned her attention to the climb down. "I'm going in." She positioned her hands as he'd told her and began to lower her body over the edge.

Her feet scrabbled for purchase on the rippled stone wall. It was another moment before she thought to reposition her hands the way he'd suggested and search for the other handhold. Once she did, she managed a descent that was something short of dignified. When her hold loosened she ended up letting go and jumping the last two feet to the bottom of the chamber.

"Okay?"

The word was more grudging than concerned. "I'm fine." The light Sharper was shining downward spotlighted her, shoved at the darkness in the space. She took the time to get her flashlight out of her bag again and shone it around the space slowly.

The scientist in her was enthralled by the thought of the physical forces that had carved out this area. She didn't know enough about the locale yet to guess whether glaciers, water, or lava had had a hand in its formation.

The cop in her was struck by the perfection of the hiding place. It was as if nature had hollowed out a tomb, waiting for the occupants that had been hauled out of it days earlier.

The air was cool, although not uncomfortably so. She slipped out of her pack, dug around in it for the thermometer. Sixty-one point two degrees. The coolness would have slowed decomposition if the bodies had been dumped here in their entirety. But after making that climb up the side of Castle Rock, it was easy to see why only the skeletal remains had been left.

The walls were smooth in spots, rippled in others. The floor of the area was slightly sandy over the stone. Although Cait played her light carefully around, she saw no other exits from the chamber. Nothing more than a long crack in the stone on one side, about an inch across, which may have been the source of the slight dampness edging that wall.

She also, despite a careful examination of the area, didn't find anything the recovery team had left behind. The knowledge had her feeling slightly more comfortable with Andrews's department. It was always good knowing the evidence she'd be drawing her conclusions from had been gathered through competent police work.

Replacing the thermometer in her pack, she dug inside for some plastic evidence bags and a small pocketknife. She used both to get scrapings from the wall and the floor. After carefully labeling the bags, she stowed everything back in her pack. If there were residue of some sort found on the bones, it would help to have the scrapings for elimination samples.

She found herself anxious to get back to the morgue, where Kristy would have set up the equipment in their temporary lab. Cait wanted to do a more thorough examination of the bags the bones were kept in. She already knew there had been no teeth discovered inside any of them. That would suggest the skulls had been removed prior to dumping the bones. As the remains aged, the mandible jawbone would have separated from the rest of the skull. The teeth would have loosened.

She was growing more certain that some daring explorer hadn't happened on the remains and stolen the skulls. They'd never been here to begin with. But if the sawing had occurred down here, she should find minuscule bone fragments in the samples she'd taken from the floor of the cave.

Cait flipped off her flashlight and stowed in into her pack. Shrugged into it. "Toss me a line. I'm coming up."

There were a few moments of silence. Then a rustle as some rappel line snaked over the edge from above. "Give me a minute." The lights Sharper was holding faded, and she was left in the dark bowels of the chamber with only the light on her hard hat slicing through it.

Cait wasn't easily spooked, but she also wasn't in the mood to linger in the darkness. When the line snaked down the side of the wall, she grasped the line in both hands and waited for Sharper's faint shout to begin her ascent. It was a relatively swift climb up and over the lip, which landed her back in the branch off from the original cave.

Releasing the rope, she dug in her pack again for her flashlight and switched it on. Then she crawled to the mouth of branch where Sharper was crouched, waiting. "I want to see how much deeper the original vein goes before heading out."

"I can already tell you that. It dead-ends about twelve feet from here. At least it narrows enough that even you can't squeeze inside it."

"Then it won't take me long to see for myself." He seemed to be settling in for a wait, so she crawled by him and got down on her belly again for the trip ahead. It took only a few minutes to discover Sharper was right. The cave nipped in beyond the point that any human could squeeze through. And although there were a couple shadowy outcroppings along the way, there were no other sections to explore.

She had to wiggle backward to return to where the man was waiting, around the bend of the branch off, a task that took a bit of dexterity. As it was, she misjudged her distance and hit something less solid than the wall of the cave.

"Shit!"

She felt her foot caught, firmly moved.

"I haven't given up all thought of fathering children, so take it easy, will you, Slim?"

"Sorry." But Cait smirked a bit in the darkness as she cautiously backed into the wider branch of the cave. He deserved at least that after the cracks he'd made prior to their climb. "When we get out I'd like to continue up to the top of Castle Rock. Is that doable from here?"

She could hear his shrug in the low rumble of his voice. "Depends on you. Castle Rock is a popular hiking area for tourists, so there are trails. We can make our way to a ledge that comes down from the top of it. Like I said before, the other side is a switchback through the forest. Not a difficult hike once we get to the top."

"Let's do it, then."

"That'll put us about fifteen miles from my vehicle. Maybe you should wait for tomorrow to do the rest of it."

"I can call Barnes and have him pick us up."

"Hope you brought something to eat." He started out into the cave ahead of her, belly crawling toward the entrance. "I only brought one sandwich and I'm not in the mood to share."

"Given your sunny disposition, that's a real newsflash." She struck out on her stomach behind him. "Don't worry about me, Sharper. I've been taking care of myself for a while now."

But somehow her response lost its intended sting directed as it was to the soles of his boots. There was nothing to do but crawl toward the entrance where sunlight waited.

Chapter 3

"Breathtaking."

Zach shot a look at the woman by his side. The descriptor could have just as easily been applied to her, but her gaze was on the scenery below them. He took another bite of his sandwich, chewed and swallowed. It was hard to take in the view from the peak of Castle Rock without comment. "That's the McKenzie River Valley. Those peaks there"—he pointed across the valley—"are the Three Sisters."

"And on the other side of Castle Rock, toward the east, is McKenzie Bridge?"

He nodded, recalling the time she'd spent in the vehicle studying maps. There was more to Caitlin Fleming than the one-dimensional image that had decorated many a soldier's trunk lid in boot camp. She'd still been modeling then, but that had been over fifteen years ago. He hadn't given her a thought since, but if he had, he sure wouldn't have considered her pursuing police work. Or whatever she'd gone into to be working in the capacity of consultant for the Lane County Sheriff's Department.

But he didn't ask questions because he didn't dig into people's pasts. When he'd come back to the area, he'd just wanted to be left the hell alone. That meant offering others the same privacy he expected for himself. Although it didn't always work that way.

That didn't mean Zach wasn't tempted to break his own rule. He finished off the sandwich, chewed reflectively. He found himself unwillingly fascinated. Not in the way he'd been when he'd been a randy teenager and she'd been the hottest teen model to grace a catwalk. He was willing to admit that her earlier comment about him having her poster had a particle of truth in it. But his interest in it had waned about the time he'd discovered pinning a three-dimensional female *against* the wall was a lot more satisfying than pinning a one-dimensional female *to* it.

"I gather this area is quite a tourist destination."

Grateful to shift his attention to something else, he lifted a shoulder. "For people who enjoy the outdoors, Oregon has just about everything there is to offer."

Cait was scanning the area around them. "But summer's the peak season?"

Wondering what she was getting at, he nodded. "We've got ski resorts. Lots of people snowmobile, cross-country ski, and snowshoe in the winter. But summer and fall are busiest, yeah."

"And Castle Rock is a local attraction, right?" She didn't wait for an answer before going on. "Lots of people hike it, Andrews said. Anyone could have stumbled across that cave, at any time."

Dryly, Zach responded, "You may have noticed, it's not exactly easy to get to. But, sure. It was only a matter of time before someone found what was dumped there. Fact is people were probably in that cave before me. Either they didn't go far enough inside or didn't have the equipment to get down in the chamber and check things out."

She seemed to consider that for a few minutes, lost in thought. And he had the distinct impression she'd managed to forget his existence. So he wadded up his sandwich wrapper and stuffed it into a pocket in his bag. Withdrawing his water bottle, he removed his glasses and squirted some water on the lenses, wiping them clean with the hem of his shirt. Then he took another drink, before glancing back at the woman beside him.

She had her phone out, was punching in a number. But after holding it to her ear for a few moments she flipped it shut and shoved it back inside the pack at her feet. "Barnes isn't answering, but I'll keep trying. Worst-case scenario, we'll start back for the vehicle and he can pick us up on the way."

"You might find him a bit more difficult to manipulate than you're used to." Zach knew he was being a prick and couldn't say why this woman seemed to bring out the worst in him. The reaction annoyed him. It meant she had an effect on him, even if it was a negative one. He didn't like the thought of that at all.

She froze in the act of bringing her sandwich to her mouth. Her voice went dangerously cool. "Care to explain that remark?"

There was no reason in the world for him to pick up the verbal gauntlet. No reason, really, to be such a dick. Yet he heard himself saying, "He's gay. So he's not likely to fall for any of the usual ways you probably use to bring guys into line. If he's busy, we're likely going to have to wait for hours before he can get to us." He shrugged, shoving the bottle back into his pack, and awaited her reaction. It wasn't long in coming. It also wasn't what he expected.

"Well, that's a disappointment."

Her tone was husky enough to have his throat drying out again. He couldn't have prevented himself from looking at her on a bet. And once there, his gaze stayed, transfixed.

She took off her sunglasses, the movement slow. Leisurely. He had a moment to observe that her eyes were the same color as the moss covering one side of the rock they sat on before she reached up languidly and pulled the cap from her head. Loosened her hair and shook it back before allowing it to settle into place around that exquisite face.

He knew when he was being taken for a ride. Knew it, and

was helpless to look away, even as he had to remind his lungs to go to work. The tip of her tongue slicked over her lips before she parted them, just a little. Her eyes went slumberous and her expression . . .

Her expression was pure sex. The come-on as easy to read as neon against a starless sky. And brutally effective. Even knowing he was being had, Zach felt himself harden on cue. Which royally pissed him off.

"Well, my kind is best at seduction, but if that isn't going to work, I guess I won't be able to convince Barnes"—she touched the base of her throat in a way guaranteed to draw a man's gaze—"to do much of anything. Which will be a shame." When her hands dropped to the hem of her T-shirt, his pulse gave a leap like a stallion lurching from the starting gate. She dragged it up over an impossibly slender torso to expose a ribbed tank that clung to curves that had been fashioned by a very benevolent god. "I guess that means I'll just have to"— she leaned forward, giving him a tongue-lolling view of cleavage—"ask him nicely and hope that's enough."

With barely restrained violence, he grabbed for his water bottle again, chugged enough to wash down that boulder-sized knot in his throat. "You do that."

Her voice normal now, she shoved her shirt into her pack, her movements rife with temper. "You are a complete and utter tool, Sharper. It's hard to believe you could build a business that depends on tourism, given your personality. I can only figure that your employees do an admirable job of covering for the fact that you're devoid of any redeeming qualities."

He could have told her that he'd once had a few redeeming qualities. But that was *before*. He wasn't sure *that* Zach Sharper existed anymore.

Instead he remained silent, which was what he should have done before eliciting that little scene. She didn't seem to expect a response. With movements jerky with fury, she was pulling her hair back again, donning the cap and sunglasses.

Shoving the now-empty bottle back into his pack, he followed her lead and got ready to move out. She took off without waiting for him, unerringly taking the path that would lead to the switchback heading down the other side of Castle Rock. He followed more slowly, gritting his teeth against the discomfort from the tighter fit of his jeans.

And knowing he had no one but himself to blame for his state didn't improve his mood one damn bit.

———

"Fast work." Marin Andrews, trailed by Mitch Barnes, paused at the foot of each gurney before throwing Cait an approving glance. "I'm impressed."

The sheriff's reaction helped dissipate a bit of the exhaustion riding her. Cait and Kristy had been working nearly round the clock for forty-eight hours on the remains at the morgue. She was pleased with the progress they'd made, even while she was less thrilled with the growing flirtation between the ME and her assistant.

But Cait was willing to admit that might have something to do with the irritation she still felt when she recalled the time spent with Zach Sharper. Throwing herself into the lab work to be done with the bones had distracted her from the annoyance she felt every time she thought of the man. It wasn't as though she hadn't bumped up against that sort of Neanderthal attitude before. She'd spent years in a career where she'd been seen as little more than a face, a body, a shell to be posed and photographed and stamped with someone else's brand. And it hadn't only been men who had treated her that way.

So it wasn't Sharper she was angry at. Not really. It was herself, for reacting to his baiting in a similarly juvenile fashion. She'd thought she was well beyond behavior fueled by self-indulgence. Although this hardly ranked up there with some of the more self-destructive choices of her past, it still stung to discover she could respond without thought to her position.

And it suited her to share the blame of that with Sharper.

She stepped aside to allow Barnes room to view the bones. "These are definitely human remains," she began. "Anatomical specimens can be purchased from a supply house, but that was easy enough to rule out since the bones don't have amalgam restorations. Fillings," she explained, when she caught the quizzical look Andrews shot her. "Michaels did a decent job of laying out the remains, but not all the bones matched up with the correct skeleton, so there was some reassembly necessary. And of course not all the bones of each victim are accounted for." When she saw the sheriff open her mouth, Cait put in, "I'll go into that more in a minute. Once we aligned the bones correctly, we used calipers and an osteometric board to remeasure them to get more exact approximations. There's also a computer program that we utilized that is pretty effective at calculating stature. Kristy?" She flicked a glance at her assistant, who silently handed the two law enforcement personnel a copy of their findings. "You'll note some differences from Michaels's initial report."

"So we know height and sex. And that the bones are human."

"We know a bit more than that." Cait ignored the sheriff's testy tone. "These weren't discarded medical specimens, either. Generally those would be bleached white, have hardware attaching the bones together, and the bones would have a more polished appearance from excessive handling. Nor have they had prolonged exposure to soil."

"You figure that because they're clean?" It was the first Barnes had spoken since entering the room.

"Partially. Bones will take on the color of the surrounding soil. But the acidity of the soil will also eventually erode the surface of the bone." She indicated the ulna in the specimen closest to her. "That hasn't happened. Not on any set of remains. I've found virtually no trace of sediment on the bone."

"But you can tell how old each individual was at time of death, right?" This from Andrews again. She was moving slowly from gurney to gurney, peering at each set of remains as if to derive the answers she was seeking for herself.

"I can approximate." She skirted around Andrews and Barnes to retrace her steps toward the first gurney. "For purposes of identification at this time we're referring to the remains as female A through C and male D through G. Keep in mind the data is very preliminary," she stressed. Cait was a long way from drawing ironclad conclusions before all the tests were done, but in the course of an investigation, she developed a working set of details that morphed as more information became available.

Judging from the impatience on the sheriff's expression, she was more than willing to get to the conclusions, so Cait wasted no more time. "These are all adults. Without the craniums, I have to rely on examination of the auricular surface of the ilium, the sternal ends of the right ribs three through five, and pubic symphysis. None of the remains appear geriatric. I did find evidence of osteoarthritis in female C and males D and G. With all things considered, ages for the individuals range from late thirties to midsixties."

"Now we're getting somewhere." Andrews's normally stern expression relaxed into a slight smile. "Got specifics?"

"Yes, our findings are documented in a copy I prepared for you." The corner of Cait's mouth pulled up. "I tried to keep it to layman's terms as much as possible. Your youngest victim here is female C, approximately thirty-five to forty. The oldest is male D, who was between sixty to sixty-five at the time of death."

"Can you tell which one's been down there the longest?" Andrews took out a handkerchief and dabbed at the moisture on her forehead. Since the temperature in the room was set at sixty-eight, Cait assumed the woman was having a hot flash. Her face had flushed to a bright shade of pink.

"No. The odds of me being able to pin down the sequence in their deaths are pretty remote. And the trickiest part of this process will be nailing down the age of the skeletal remains themselves."

Barnes and Andrews exchanged a glance. "What about radiocarbon dating?" the deputy demanded.

"That's time-consuming, expensive, and would only give you a calibration date specific to a century." Cait shook her head. "Since we're not dealing with archeological remains, that's unnecessary. I can tell you with a great deal of certainty that at least one of these victims died within the last year to eighteen months."

"Holy shit." Barnes breathed the words, his eyes sliding shut for a moment.

Andrews stopped in the act of putting away her handkerchief. And the leap of glee to her expression made Cait more than a little uneasy. "How can you be sure? You just got done saying aging the remains would be tricky."

Motioning for the others to follow her, Cait strode to stand between the third and fourth stainless steel gurneys. "See the difference in the bone color between these two sets of remains? Male G's bones have a waxy, almost yellowish cast. That means they're fresher, for want of a better word." She indicated the remains on the next table. "When the bones dry out more they become whiter."

"Cause of death?" Andrews's voice was sharp with excitement.

She hesitated, unwilling to relay what was really only a suspicion at this point. "Undetermined as yet. On the one hand we have no fresh fractures to the arms or fingers, which would indicate defensive wounds. But my initial conclusion is that the deaths were unnatural, although there is little hard evidence of that at this point."

"If there's little evidence, how can you be sure?" Barnes's tone was curious. He'd started growing a mustache since the last time Cait had seen him. She wondered if it was a personal choice, or if he'd been keeping hours as late as her own and had cut down on shaving.

"Process of elimination." From the corner of her eye she saw Kristy move to the back counter and begin to assemble the copies of their test results in two folders, one each for Andrews and Barnes. "The method of disposal is suspicious in and of itself. It's highly possible that a death wound was sustained to the skull. As such, we wouldn't be able to answer that question unless and until we recover the craniums. We can be sure there is no evidence of blunt-force trauma, wounds from bullets or knives to the bodies. Discovering whether poison might have been used is a long shot. That tends to show up in hair, nails, and skin. But there's a possibility that cause of death may be broken neck. Several of the remains show a fracture of one or more of the cervical vertebra."

"That could be evidence of a fall," Andrews pointed out. "And if those bags were just dumped in that cave, the injury could have occurred upon contact with the cave floor."

"Maybe if we saw that with one set of remains. But for all of them . . ." She rounded the gurney to stand opposite Andrews. "If you look here"—she indicated the cervical vertebrae—"you'll see breakage between vertebrae three and four. The separation marks occur on most samples around vertebra one or two, although two of the individuals had their skulls separated at a slightly lower juncture. But all have this fracture in nearly identical spots. Can I tell you with complete certainty whether the injury occurred posthumously or if, in fact, it caused death?" She lifted a shoulder. "No. But I find it suspicious."

"The way I see it, we're still a ways from determining violent death," Barnes said mildly. Intercepting Andrews's look, he held up a hand as if to stem her response. "I'm just saying this is pretty inconclusive at this point."

"If you mean we need to continue our examination for definitive evidence, agreed," Cait said. "But I want you to look closely at these specimens and tell me what you see?"

The man looked wary. "I see bones. What am I supposed to see?"

"You see very clean bones," she corrected. "All of them likely underwent some kind of maceration process prior to discovery to get them this spotless. We aren't done running tests, so we haven't done any cleaning. There was very little tissue on any of them, even on the most recent set of remains, male G. We found no intact ligaments, either."

Andrews's eyes had narrowed. Whatever her deputy was

thinking, Cait knew the sheriff was far ahead of him. "What are the possible processes for this maceration?"

"Typically boiling is used these days. It's faster and less troublesome than other methods. But when we use it, we have to cut through joints to fit the skeleton into the container of water. None of the joints on any set of remains show evidence of that." With the exception, of course, of the skull. "Which leads me to believe the bones have been cleaned by dermestid beetles. When we tested them, and the interior of the garbage bags, we found evidence of beetle frass."

"That's their shit," Kristy threw in cheerfully from her stance at the counter. "We also found a few of their exoskeletons, so there is ample evidence of their presence in conjunction with the remains. The only other evidence of etymology was a few exoskeletons of cave crickets."

"These are beetles found in the wild, though, right?" The sheriff squinted, as if thinking. "One of the last stages of decomposition if a body is left outdoors."

"But these bodies weren't left exposed," Cait corrected her. "If they'd been out in the wild, accessible to the stages of animal and insect activity, we'd see evidence of animals having chewed on the bones. Many of the larger ones would be missing. They'd be more weathered from the elements. Nor is the cave a hospitable environment for the bugs. They thrive in temperatures of seventy to eighty degrees. I'd hazard a guess that this colony of beetles is domesticated, probably raised for one specific purpose."

Barnes was looking a little sickly. His pale blue eyes widened incredulously. "You're telling me we've got some psycho feeding people to bugs to strip them down to their bones quicker so he can get rid of the evidence?"

"Don't be a . . ." Kristy caught Cait's warning look in time to amend her words. "Don't be ridiculous. Dermestids don't eat live flesh. They don't much like moist tissue, either. When we use them, we actually remove the organs, deflesh the bones, dry them for a while, and then allow the beetles to do the rest of the work. An active colony is amazingly effective."

Kristy's explanation hadn't alleviated Barnes's expression. But it was Andrews that drew Cait's attention. "You say you've used them?"

She nodded. "Forensic anthropologists might utilize them to strip away excess tissue before examining bones, although as I've said, it's more common these days to boil them. But the method of using the insects this way isn't unusual at all. You'd also see them used in large veterinary schools, museums, by taxidermists . . ." She shrugged. "I've even heard of high schools ordering a colony for their science programs. They're accessible to anyone. You can order them from some universities, although I've seen starter colonies for sale on the Internet."

She shot a look at the sheriff. "Remember what I said earlier about some of the small bones being missing? The insects might have consumed them. Their activity has to be monitored closely. Or they just might have been missed by whoever scooped up the bones to put in the bags."

"So if we accept that beetles cleaned the bones—and the evidence you've found makes that likely," Andrews said slowly, pulling at her bottom lip, "it looks more and more as though someone was trying to cover up evidence of a crime."

"We're a long way from finished with all our tests." Cait rolled her shoulders tiredly. "But based on what we've got so far, I'd theorize that we're dealing with a serial offender."

Barnes's expletive was audible. And Cait found she much preferred his reaction to that flash again of unbridled excitement in the sheriff's eyes.

She tried to give the woman the benefit of the doubt. The services of Raiker Forensics weren't cheap. It was a sure bet that the county budget hadn't been healthy enough to pay for bringing her in. More than likely the woman had tapped her rich daddy to ante up their fee. Couldn't blame her for being glad the expense was justified.

But there was still something a little creepy about a law enforcement officer being so enthusiastic about the prospect of someone in her jurisdiction systematically murdering people and dumping their bodies.

She understood ambition. It had been just that quality that had led Cait to leave the Bureau's labs behind without a backward glance to join Raiker Forensics. She was never going to get a shot from the feds to become an agent. But Andrews's motivation still made her more than a little uneasy.

"We're done with the bags." She indicated the garbage bags the remains had been found in. "Do you want us to check them for prints, or will your department handle that?"

Barnes answered before his superior could. "We'll take care of it." His pale blue gaze was wary. "Sort of outside your area of expertise, isn't it?"

Recognizing his territorial air she smiled easily, although she would have preferred to do the testing herself. "We're equipped for it, but if you want, Kristy will box them up for you. In answer to your question, though, no. All Raiker's employees receive thorough cross training." At his curt nod, she sent her assistant a look, and the woman drew on gloves before picking up the folded bags to place in a plastic evidence container.

"The bags themselves are a useful lead," Cait continued. "Black garbage bags have only been around a few decades. If testing shows the material is biodegradable, for instance, that narrows down the age of them considerably. They might even be able to discover the manufacturer. None of them have degraded much since being put in that cave."

She saw the look exchanged between the two law enforcement officers, but Andrews said only, "We've been promised expedited assistance through the state police crime lab in Springfield." The sheriff gave a small grim smile. "The criminal investigative division of the Oregon State Police has offered their help, as well. I'm hoping with you here, that won't be necessary."

More likely she was hoping that the investigation would be successfully concluded in a manner in which the woman could claim the credit, Cait thought cynically.

But she'd developed diplomacy early in life. It came in handy when dealing with her mother. She said only, "We also found traces of sediment in the bottom of some of the bags. When we tested it, we detected a high sulfur content. The scrapings I took from the cave walls and the chamber don't match those findings." Noting the look exchanged between Andrews and Barnes, she paused. "That obviously means something to you."

"Oregon has several renowned examples of hot springs, many of which are tourist destinations," Andrews explained. She started to prop her palms on the gurney at her side, before appearing to remember the bones at her fingertips. "There are several in the general area. Bagby's one of them. Terwilliger at the Cougar Reservoir. Bigelow. But the closest one is probably Belknap Hot Springs, near McKenzie Bridge."

The words had Cait's pulse quickening. "How close to McKenzie Bridge?" The cave had been only a couple of miles.

"Six miles, give or take," Barnes said, correctly interpreting his boss's glance. "It's sort of a summer resort community, with a lodge, hotel, and cabins. The guests come to enjoy a variety of outdoor activities, but the springs are always a draw."

Cait nodded, already making plans. "Do you know if your county's Natural Resources Conservation Service has a current map of soil samples for Lane County?" The expression on Andrews's face and Barnes's silence gave her the answer. "Well, it's easy enough to call and see. If we get lucky, we'll be able to score a map of soil samplings from the entire county." High sulfuric content would be most likely to occur in areas with acidic soil, which should be indicated on the NRCS maps.

"And then what?" Barnes demanded. "There are smaller springs on private property scattered around the area and throughout the state, too. Even if we could get access to every piece of property around with the right soil sample, what would we be looking for?"

"For starters, we look for the missing bones." Cait rounded the nearest gurney to stand at the head of the third one. "For instance, these remains are minus several of the smaller bones from each hand and a couple for the toes. It's possible the beetles destroyed them. Equally possible that they were missed when the UNSUB was transferring the remains into the garbage bags. If we discover the primary scene for these homicides, chances are we find the offender, too."

Barnes still looked unconvinced. "Do you know how long it's going to take to cover every spring in this part of the state? And we can't get access to those on private property without a warrant, which we don't have grounds for."

Undeterred by his skepticism, Cait addressed the sheriff. "We don't have to cover the entire state, or even the entire county. We start in the area closest to where the bones were found and establish a grid around it, working outwards in each direction. Many of the private homeowners may well allow us on their property. It's a starting point." She cocked her brow. "Unless you have a more pressing lead to follow."

The expression on Andrews's face was answer enough. "Lots of folks in the more rural areas value their privacy. They might not be as cooperative as you think." But it was clear she was considering Cait's suggestion.

"We'll explore other avenues simultaneously, of course." Cait went to get the documents Kristy had prepared and walked back to hand one to each officer. "I'll start feeding preliminary descriptions of the victims, at least height, sex, and approximate weight, into the National Crime Information Center database for missing persons and see what we get for hits."

Seeming to come to a decision, the sheriff nodded and looked at Barnes. "Keep tracking down those with violations listed with the Forest Service. Check out those individuals for criminal records. Cait can follow up on the soil samples. With the forestry agencies busy with that fire in the Cascades, we can use Sharper to get her where she needs to go."

Her satisfaction at the sheriff's words was more than a little dampened at the thought of spending more time in

Sharper's company. But Cait made sure her reluctance didn't show in her expression. It had been a long time since a man had been allowed to affect her in any but the most superficial way.

Zach Sharper would be no different.

Chapter 4

Zach managed to refrain from voicing the questions swirling in his head. He may not like playing chauffer for Caitlin Fleming at Sheriff Andrews's demand, but he told himself it could be worse. He could be forced to spend this much time in the sheriff's company instead. Or be paired with Deputy Tony Gibbs, a horse's ass if he'd ever met one. At least Fleming didn't make him want to punch her.

She did, however, leave him wanting to punch *something*. It would be a welcome outlet for the simmering tension that increased with every hour spent in her company.

To divert himself from the unwelcome sexual attraction, he seized on the curiosity that revved to life whenever he saw her studying a map from the sheaf in her lap. It wasn't one of those available from the forest station of nearby wilderness areas. The initials across the top of the first page gave that away. NRCS. What the hell would she be doing with maps from the soil conservation agency?

Because he knew she wouldn't tell him if he asked—and

damned if he'd ask—he kept his mouth shut. Before the end of the day, he'd figure it out on his own.

Pulling off the highway to the access road, he took the quarter mile drive up to the Springs Resort before coming to a stop. "This is it."

"I may be a while." She gathered up a bag, smaller than the backpack she'd had the last time they'd been together, and went to open the door.

"Listen . . .Caitlin."

"It's Cait." Her backward glance over her shoulder was half wary, half quizzical.

He had a feeling he was going to regret what he was about to say. "I might be more help if I knew what it was you were looking for."

"Thanks, but I can't tell you that." As if in afterthought, she scooped up the maps she'd been studying earlier and got out of the Trailblazer.

Zach studied her retreating figure through narrowed eyes. She was dressed as casually today as she'd been when he'd taken her to the cave. The difference this time was he was pretty sure she was carrying. His time in the military had taught him to spot weapons wherever they might be hidden on a person. Her gun was at the small of her back, beneath her T-shirt. And no matter how many times he told himself to let it go, he couldn't quite stop wondering why Caitlin Fleming felt the need to carry a gun to a popular tourist resort.

Almost as much as he wondered how good she was at using it.

With a hissed-out breath, Zach powered down his window and propped an elbow on the sill. He much preferred action to cooling his heels. Pulling out his cell phone, he spent fifteen minutes checking in with the guides he had on various outings—outings he could have been leading himself if he hadn't received the summons from Andrews last night. Since their reports indicated everything was going fine, he flipped the phone shut and tucked it away again. And checked the entrance of the resort.

No sign of Caitlin. *Cait*.

Drumming his fingers restlessly on the steering wheel, he scanned the drive in front of the resort. Looked like business could be better. The parking lot to the side was less than half filled with cars bearing out-of-state plates. Tourists usually flocked to this place, looking to escape the tedium of their lives by immersing themselves in the natural beauty of Oregon's countryside. He could understand the need. There was something healing about spending time in the forests. In the mountains. On the rivers. Something that could always make him forget for a while exactly what had sent him back here.

Zach actually got a fair amount of business from the Springs Resort. The owners allowed him to display his business brochures and recommended his outfit to their guests. After another five minutes crawled by, he gave a mental shrug. As long as he was here, he may as well check at the front desk and see if more brochures were needed. Grateful for the excuse to move, he opened the door and got out, stretching his legs thankfully. Ducking back inside the Trailblazer, he pulled some pamphlets he always carried from the holder on the visor and headed for the front doors.

He nodded at Jim Lancombe, one of the groundskeepers, who was watering the beds and barrels spilling with flowers. The man was kept busy all summer and fall, but come winter he'd occasionally call Zach for some snowshoe hiking in the mountains. He was good company for two reasons. He knew when to keep his mouth shut, and he was as much an expert in the outdoors as Zach was himself.

A blast of air-conditioning hit him as he pushed open the front doors to the rustic log exterior of the resort. He spotted Cait right away, standing off to the side a few yards away from the front desk, talking to Mona Weston, one of the owners. From the expression on Mona's face, the discussion wasn't going well.

Though Cait's voice was pitched low, he could easily overhear Mona's side of the conversation.

"I just wish you'd wait and talk to my husband when he

comes back. I hate to take the chance of my guests being bothered. People come here to get away and relax. They can't do that with cops tromping around the property." Seeing Zach, Mona lifted a hand in greeting.

Cait turned, her green gaze pinning him with the accuracy of a laser. "If it would make you feel better, Mr. Sharper can accompany me while I take a look around. I promise none of your guests will even know I'm here."

Gail's expression was confused. "Zach? You know this . . . Ms. Fleming?"

Well, hell. Zach gave a moment's thought to turning and walking out the door again. Easier that way to mind his own business. But from the look on Cait's face, he could tell that wasn't going to be an option.

He made his way over to the women. Mona was dressed much the same as Cait, in jeans and a T-shirt, but she had nearly twenty years on the younger woman, most of them spent outdoors. She was a good six inches shorter than Cait, with a strong, capable build that came as much from her work around this place as being the mother of three rambunctious boys.

"Mona," he said by way of greeting. "Gil not around?"

"He went to Eugene for copper tubing. We're having trouble with the hot water in some of the rooms."

"Always something." He flicked a glance at Cait. "Ms. Fleming's business won't take long. I can stick with her, if that makes you feel any better."

The woman sent one last uncertain glance toward Cait before saying, "Well, I don't know what Gil would think of me letting a stranger wander around the springs with the guests, but I guess it's okay if you stay with her."

Something lightened inside him when he registered Cait's expression. Although arranged into a bland polite mask, he was willing to bet that beneath it she was seething. "I'll make sure she doesn't bother anyone."

"Mona." The desk clerk trying to get the older woman's attention grew more insistent, and she threw a glance over her shoulder.

"I'll hold you to that, Zach." Her attention returned to them, and she noticed the brochures he was holding. "Oh, I can use some of those. We're down to our last few." She sent him a genuine smile as he handed the pamphlets over. "We always get rave reviews from the guests who sign on for one of your tours."

"And I appreciate you steering them my way. You go on and take care of things at the desk." He nodded toward the college-age girl who looked to be getting more frantic by the moment. "We'll be all right."

"Thanks, Zach." Mona hurried away to handle whatever crisis her employee was dealing with, and he turned to Cait, correctly interpreting the killer expression in her eyes.

"Not exactly a trusting soul, is she?"

He turned and headed for the doors, and she matched him, stride for stride. "Maybe not. Or could be she just knows trouble when she sees it."

"What trouble are you referring to?" Far from the temper Zach had bet she'd been feeling earlier, Cait's voice was curious. "Me? Or the case?"

A wise man knew when a question was loaded. That one was about as innocent as a minefield. Expertly, he skirted it. "Well, discovering seven human skeletons is hardly the norm around here." He headed back toward the Trailblazer. He'd have to park it in the lot before they headed out toward the springs. "No one wants to look out his window and wonder if his neighbor is the one guilty of murdering people and stashing them in a cave."

"No one said anything about murder." Her objection sounded automatic as she got in the vehicle and he pulled around to the parking lot.

"You don't say much," he agreed, wondering why he found that so irritating. Normally he considered that a bonus in a woman. It was vexing to recognize that he had a healthy share of interest in what she wasn't saying. Only natural, seeing as he was the one who'd found the bodies.

It'd taken Mona's statement to tip him off that Cait was

interested in the hot springs. For the life of him, he couldn't figure out why.

"The sheriff's office is keeping this whole thing pretty quiet." Unless one counted Tony Gibbs blowing off at Ketchers over beer and pool every night. Zach knew better than to believe everything he'd heard the deputy had been saying, but he couldn't help but think Andrews would have a fit if she knew she had a leak in her department.

He pulled into an empty space in the lot and turned off the ignition. "The fact is, this place has been crawling with media since those bones were pulled out of the cave. Andrews isn't giving them much, so they come sniffing around McKenzie Bridge, Blue River, and every other nearby town in search of gossip. There's always plenty of speculation in the absence of facts. I'd think she'd want to lay some of it to rest by releasing more information."

There was a slight frown on Cait's face, but she said only, "Sheriff Andrews is handling the press. She's probably waiting to establish more details before deciding what information to release to the public."

And what not to release. Zach knew how the game was played. He got out of the Trailblazer and slammed the door closed. Waited for Cait to do the same before using the remote lock. They'd keep something back, maybe something only the killer would know. Play a cat and mouse game with the suspect until they painted him or her into a corner.

It had nothing to do with him. Nothing to do with his business in Eugene. Unless he counted the fact that he was forced to spend way too much time away from it doing Andrews's bidding.

And more time than was wise in Cait Fleming's company.

He nodded at the couple headed toward their car, parked close to the Trailblazer. The woman gave her male companion a sharp elbow jab when he stared at Cait so long he nearly ran into the bumper of a car. Slanting a look at the female by his side, Zach found her with her head down, studying the soil maps again, seemingly oblivious.

Everything inside him jeered at the thought. There was no way a woman who looked like her, one who'd made a career posing for the cameras, was unaware of the effect she had on people. Men especially. When folks around here got a load of her, the bones found in Castle Rock weren't going to be the only source of gossip circulating in the area. And since he was going to be glued to her side for the duration, that meant that he'd get dragged into the talk, just by default.

The thought brought a scowl to his face. Like he'd said before. She was trouble. "Springs are this way." He paused impatiently as she veered in his direction to join him.

"How big a place is this?"

"Gil and Mona have over forty-five acres of gardens." Once she'd reached his side he started walking rapidly again, waving an arm toward the grounds Jim kept in showcase condition. "I think there's five or six miles of walking trails."

"And the Willamette National Forest all around us." The roar of the McKenzie River grew louder as they walked, though there were only glimpses of it through the heavily wooded area on its banks. "Nice place to get away."

"They do all right." He'd take the solitude of Whispering Pines any day over a place like this filled with desperate tourists fleeing the city. But for those who didn't have access to their own piece of heaven on earth, this resort was a nice little slice of it.

"There are rooms in the main lodge, a few cabins and cottages, and sites for RVs and tents."

Unerringly he headed into the forest toward the springs. And despite his better judgment, fell into tour-guide mode. "There are more hot springs in Oregon than any other state in the country. It sits on the Ring of Fire, a volcanic belt that circles the Pacific Ocean."

"Which also gave birth to the Cascade Mountains."

He shouldn't be surprised. She had her head buried in a map most of the time they were together. "There's super-heated igneous rock and molten magma beneath the surface here. We still have a few active volcanoes. With all the rainfall we get, all it takes is a basalt fissure to release thermal flows into a natural hot tub. Belknap is a good example, but I prefer the less-developed springs myself."

"Because there's fewer people around," she guessed shrewdly.

He skirted a hollowed-out rotted log. "People are overrated."

"And yet important in a business that demands customers to survive."

"A necessary evil." He stopped for a moment to allow the garter snake in his path to finish its journey to the jumble of rocks at the base of a white pine before continuing on. "We sell river and hiking sporting equipment, too, so we're not all about the tours. But they allow me to do what I love most, so it's a trade off." And times spent with days full of chattering tourists made his solitary hours on the river or in the Willamette all the more precious.

Falling into silence, he led the way through the forest surely. It wasn't particularly dense in this area. Zach knew Mona and Gil kept the underbrush trimmed to allow their guests freedom to wander. And the path to the hot springs was a well-worn one. He could easily head back to the vehicle and let Cait do her thing. The fact was, that action held no particular temptation. The curiosity he felt about her purpose here was unusual enough to have well-worn defenses slamming into place. He didn't want to wonder about her. He didn't want to think about her, period.

But that didn't make it any easier to banish the questions that swarmed his mind like pesky flies. He just couldn't quite wrap his mind around the contrast of her former and current occupations. His natural cynicism reminded him that for many, their careers were often owed to who they knew and who they blew.

Unfortunately, that particular visual image of Caitlin Fleming wasn't one easily banished from his mind.

With a muttered curse, he stepped aside and waved an impatient hand. "There are the hot springs up ahead. Looks like you won't be alone." There was a solitary occupant in the pine tub, a man in his midthirties. Unlike some of the more rustic settings for springs in the area, this one had a dress code, so the guy probably wasn't nude.

Cait brushed by him and stepped down the rocky incline leading to the springs while he took up position leaning against a towering pine. He observed the exact moment the guy in the tub noticed he had company. And he'd have to be blind to miss the immediate interest in the man's expression when he caught a look at the woman approaching him.

"Down, cheesedick," Zach muttered. But the guy was too far away to hear him, which was probably a lucky thing. Because he had no business warning men away from Caitlin Fleming. The woman was probably better versed than most in how to get rid of unwanted male attention. If it was unwanted.

Zach's gaze shifted from the guy in the tub back to her. Cait had reached the bottom of the slope and was scanning the ground. She appeared to be looking for something. But even he was surprised when she dropped to her hands and knees, seeming to examine the water's edge where it lapped up against the rocks.

"Did you lose something?"

The pine tub constructed for tourists intent on soaking in the springs was several yards upstream. The man inside it seemed to have lost interest in the sulfuric water in light of the newcomer. He'd risen and was peering over the side at Cait, placing his back to Zach.

"I can help you look, if you want."

"I'm fine, thanks." Cait's voice was businesslike. She'd gotten to her feet again and was walking slowly around the area, still studying the ground intently.

"Water's great. There's plenty of room if you want to join me."

Zach smirked. As pick-up lines went, it was fairly transparent. And it didn't even warrant a response from Cait. She was on all fours again, this time with her pack beside her. Pushing away from his stance against the tree, he took a few steps closer to see what she was up to. But the next few moments provided no real answers. Why would she be collecting soil samples from the area?

Cheesedick was getting out of the tub now and making his way carefully over the rocks to join Cait, still talking. "Whatsa matter, don't have a suit? I won't tell. There's just the two of us, anyway. I promise, if you come in for a soak, it'll be a whole lot more fun than—what're you doing there, anyway?"

"Please stay back." The authority in her tone had the man pausing, and Zach's gaze narrowed consideringly. He watched as she swiftly scooped up dirt with what looked like a tiny trowel and placed it in plastic containers, carefully labeling each.

"You're much too beautiful to be messing in the dirt. Why don't you come on over here and mess with me instead?"

Zach rolled his eyes. But his mood abruptly darkened in the next moment when the man made a grab for Caitlin's arm. She deflected his grasp easily enough by throwing up a forearm and stepping aside. Pushing away from the tree, he was striding toward the couple before he had the conscious thought to move. "You about done down there, Cait?"

The guy froze, his eyes widening at the sight of Zach. "Ah . . . I was just asking her if she needed any help." He gave a weak laugh, his gaze moving between the two of them and back again. "I see now that she doesn't so I'll just . . . ah . . ." He jerked a thumb back toward the tub and inched away.

Zach simply stared until the guy flinched a little. "Yeah. Why don't you do that?"

Cheesedick started to turn but got no more than a few steps before he slipped and began to fall backward. Swiftly Cait took a few steps in the stream toward him and caught his arm to steady him, but the momentum of his fall had her losing her balance, as well. She went down hard on one knee, bracing herself with one hand in the water, but managed to keep the guy semi-upright until he regained his footing.

"Geez, I'm sorry. Really. Are you okay?"

"I'm fine." Cait was on her feet again, wiping her hand on the leg of her jeans.

The guy had turned to her once again, his expression sheepish. "Now you're wet, after all." He nodded to her half-soaked pant leg. "I've got a towel up by the tub."

"I'm okay." Her tone was polite, but she was already making her way back up the slight embankment.

Cheesedick looked like he was about to say something else, but then he happened to glance Zach's way again. "Well, thanks again." He made his way carefully back toward the tub, where hopefully sheer embarrassment would have him thinking twice before tossing lame lines at the next woman who happened by. Zach wondered if the man was capable of realizing that the female he'd just tried to accost likely could have kicked his ass with very little effort. He'd gotten off lucky.

Cait appeared to have already forgotten about the incident. She was back on her haunches taking more soil samples and carefully labeling each clear container before moving several feet away to repeat the process.

Zach found a nearby fir to prop his shoulder against and prepared to wait. And to wonder what hot springs had to do with the skeletons he'd found in that cave.

———————

"Where to next?"

"Terwilliger is closest, isn't it?"

Without answering he nosed his Trailblazer out of the Springs Resort parking lot and headed out of town. Since there wasn't a damn thing to do except drive her around and watch her, he kept his mind busy trying to figure out just what the hell she was doing. She hadn't just taken soil samples in various areas around the springs; she'd waded in, too. Not taking water samples. Just looking.

Problem was, since answers weren't forthcoming, he'd settled on just looking, too. At her. It sure as hell was no hardship.

She didn't exactly downplay her looks, but she didn't do a

lot to call attention to them, either. Her hair was usually pulled back like today, discounting the time she'd loosened it to taunt him. Her casual clothes hadn't been selected to turn heads. Trouble was, she was the type to turn heads regardless, and he couldn't quite figure out whether she was just used to it so didn't pay it any attention or whether she just didn't give a damn. Given her attitude, he was beginning to suspect the latter.

He lifted a hand to return Jodie Paulsen's nod of greeting as the man wrestled a trough into the back of his pickup. Probably had had the thing welded again for Tim Jenkins, the farmer Jodie did chores for. Most people would have bought a new feed trough years ago, but no one pinched a dime tighter than the miserly Jenkins.

As he headed toward Highway 126, he noticed the woman beside him swiping her hand down the leg of her jeans. And the streak it left behind.

"What'd you do?"

With one eye on the road, he leaned over and opened up the glove box. Grabbing a handful of fast-food napkins, he shoved them at her before closing the compartment again.

"Scraped it on a rock helping that idiot out of the water."

One side of his mouth kicked up at her irritated response, but the smile faded when he glanced over again. "Jesus, don't bleed all over my car." Though she'd wadded up the napkins against the wound, it was oozing too fast to be a mere scrape.

"Nice bedside manner, Sharper. Ever consider the medical field? You'd be a natural in a trauma."

Sarcasm he could handle. And it almost, almost pushed aside the images her words had conjured.

The blast of the explosion flinging them backward. The horrible realization that the body parts raining down all around him came from Drummy and Simms.

And Becker . . . there'd been nothing left of Becker but pink mist.

He kicked that mental door shut and brought himself back to the here. The *after*.

The napkins were doing little to staunch the flow. After a

brief hesitation he slowed, pulled over to the shoulder, and put the vehicle in park. "Let me see."

He half expected to see little more than a scratch, even with the copious amount of blood staining the napkins. But the wound in her palm—a palm she relinquished only grudgingly—was about two inches long, and deep. "You did this when you helped cheesedick?"

"Cheese—" Her lips quirked. "Catchy. And oddly fitting. Yeah. I slapped a Band-Aid over it under my glove so I could finish up my samples. But I could use some Steri-Strips." She looked at him hopefully. "You don't happen to have any in your bag, do you?"

"You need stitches," he said flatly. More Band-Aids would be useless, and that's about all he had in the first aid kit in his pack. "I think there's a physician's assistant staffing the medical clinic here most days."

"That'll take hours. Just find me a store where I can buy Steri-Strips, and we can be on our way."

He sat contemplating her, ignoring her discreet tugs to release her hand. It occurred to him that he should have noticed her injury sooner. But after a while he'd just focused on not watching her. Seemed smarter that way.

Reaching a decision, he put the Trailblazer into gear and checked the mirrors before pulling a U-turn to head back into town. "The General Store isn't going to have what you need. Maybe you can talk the PA out of stitches, but the clinic is the only place to get what you need."

"I'm not going to the doctor."

The words sounded like they'd been issued through gritted teeth. Ignoring them, he turned at the corner and drove the two blocks west to the small boxlike building that held the town's clinic. And uttered an oath when he saw the overflowing parking lot.

"Like I said, I'm not wasting the rest of the day. Just forget it." She was bent over the bag she had wedged between her feet and was rummaging through it with her good hand. "I can rig something else up that'll work until I get back to Eugene this evening."

"You need to wash the wound out." Years of experience had taught him the wisdom of avoiding infection. The obvious solution occurred, was firmly rejected. He had what she needed at home, but everything inside him rebelled at the thought of taking her there. Guests were rarely invited. And by no stretch of the imagination did Caitlin Fleming qualify as that.

"I've got some sanitary towelettes in here somewhere," she muttered, her head still bent over the bag. "Just head over to Terwilliger. We've wasted enough time already." She pulled a small wrapper from her pack, ripped it open and removed a couple moist wipes. As she pressed them to her palm, they immediately darkened with blood.

Deliberately, he headed for the highway again. The gash was on the fleshy part of her palm. The wound would ooze heavily, but it wasn't like she was in danger of bleeding out, for crissakes. If it wasn't important enough for her to want to see a doctor, why the hell should he waste time worrying about it?

There was a rustle of paper. He flicked a glance in her direction and saw her taking her wrapped sandwich out of its plastic bag and filling the bag instead with the bloody napkins and wipes.

"Shit," he muttered. There wasn't a conscious decision. He just found himself turning off at the next corner. Heading for the isolated drive a couple miles down the road that would lead to his heavily wooded piece of property.

And he tried to ignore the clutch in his belly that warned him he was about to make a very big mistake.

———

"This is your house?" Vaguely stunned, Cait opened the door of his Trailblazer to jump out and stare up at the mass of angled cedar and glass. The drive to this place had to have been at least a mile long, every inch of it lined with trees that canopied overhead. No fewer than three times Zach had had to get out of the Trailblazer to unfasten a chain blocking the way. It didn't surprise her that he was a man that didn't relish company.

But this surprised her. The home looked like it would pass for a small hotel itself, surrounded by thick stands of firs and junipers as far as the eye could see. There were no curtains or shades at the windows that she noted. Why would he need them? With the woods surrounding him, privacy was practically guaranteed.

"It was my grandfather's property." His voice was brusque as he headed toward the house at a rapid clip. She could tell he was already regretting bringing her. "There was a resort here at one time, before it burned down when I was a kid. He left it to me and I'm rebuilding, on a smaller scale."

Belatedly, she noted the signs of construction in progress. The four-car garage lacked doors, and lumber and power tools were stacked neatly inside. As she followed him up to the planks that served as a walkway to the house, she noticed that only the front had the polished glazed cedar siding, while the other sides were unfinished. There was far more to be done here, but what was completed was nothing short of magnificent.

And about as far removed as possible from what she would imagine for him.

She stopped while he unlocked a side door, pushed it open, and stepped inside. Without waiting for an invitation, she followed.

Things were even less finished here. She ignored his brusque order to stay put and wandered freely around the lower level while he headed toward the back of the house. Obviously the kitchen wasn't a high priority, since he had little more than the plumbing, gas pipes, saw horses dotting the area and a decades-old fridge. But the room was large, with a wall of windows that would open it up to the outside. Make a person feel like they were a part of nature.

The great room was next, and Zach must spend some time there, as it was furnished with soft dark leather couches and chairs and the prerequisite—for a man anyway—big-screen TV. The room ran the width of the house, with gleaming wood floors and two walls of glass on opposite sides. In front of one large window that showed flashes of the river between the dense pines was a card table and chair. Obviously his dining needs were simple. Her gaze lingered on the lone chair. And solitary.

He came out from what must be a bathroom with a handful of supplies, and seeing her farther inside, scowled. "You don't follow orders very well."

"I don't follow orders at all," she corrected absently. At least not Sharper's. But she trailed after him when he went to the card table to dump the supplies he'd gathered and took the wet washrag he handed her. As awkward as it was to work one-handed, she much preferred that to leaving herself to Sharper's tender mercies. Not that he'd offered.

Right now he was surveying her with a closed impassive expression that was all too familiar. No doubt it melted most women into a pile of quaking nerves.

Cait rarely quaked. And it would take more than an illtempered male to make her nervous. She took her time cleaning the wound and applying anti-bacterial spray that—damn him—stung like a bitch. The gash was still oozing sullenly, but once she closed it up, it should be little enough problem, as long as she kept it clean. Hopefully she wasn't going to be doing any more rock climbing in the near future.

When it came time to apply the Steri-Strips, she said, "Help me out here, will you?"

Silently he took the adhesive she was holding and ripped its package. Then, while she held the wound closed he fixed the strips into place. He worked swiftly until he had four strips applied, finally pausing to survey his handiwork. "Slap a Band-Aid over it and you'll be fine. Gonna leave a scar, though."

She picked up a large square Band-Aid from the pile of supplies and used her teeth to open it. "I've got worse." His eyes flared in what she took for interest, but if he was curious he didn't speak it. It occurred to her, not for the first time, that Sharper wasn't one to probe.

Of course, he might just not give a damn. And given his personality, she thought that was equally likely.

After fitting the Band-Aid over the strips, she began picking up the mess. "Thanks for the first aid."

"Leave it," he said shortly. "I'll get it later." Turning, he headed toward the door. Since she had no idea where a trash container might be, Cait set the wrappers down and went to follow him. He couldn't have made it more obvious that he was anxious to get her out of his house.

Trailing behind him, she took one last look around. A person's home often revealed a lot about the individual. Sharper's disclosed only that he liked nature and valued his privacy, neither fact exactly earthshaking.

Nosiness was part of her job. So she blamed that trait for wanting to lag behind and poke around more. After all, Sharper was not only the person who'd found the skeletons.

From her recollection of the maps, there could be hot springs somewhere on this property.

———

The meal wasn't much. Just a cheese sandwich and soup. But he fussed with the tray the way he remembered his mother doing when he was sick. Presentation was everything.

Carefully he headed to the cellar door, shooing Iron Man, one of his Himalayans, out of the way. He set the tray on a nearby shelf while he unlocked the dead bolt, hand on the butt of the pistol tucked into his waistband. He needed to be ready for the remote chance there was a nasty surprise waiting for him on the other side of the door.

But the entrance to the basement was empty except for shadows.

Cheerfully, he flicked on the lights, replaced the pistol to pick up the tray, and headed down the steep steps. At one time, the cellar had been little more than an earthen dugout. But he'd reinforced the walls with cement blocks and poured a concrete floor. Then carefully laid thick insulation to provide further soundproofing. He was good with his hands and details like that rarely escaped him.

He passed through his workroom downstairs and again set the tray down, on his desk this time, his hand on his weapon as he unlocked the door to the inner chamber. The door swung open, revealing his newest guest.

The woman sat slumped in the lawn chair he'd provided, her wrists shackled to the heavy rings he'd drilled into the walls. Of course she was naked. They always were. How else would they relieve themselves, with their hands bound like that?

Because he was a gentleman, he averted his eyes. It had been a long time since he'd been attracted to anyone except Sweetie. A pang of guilt stabbed him, but he nudged it away. The other didn't count. A man had needs. And he and Sweetie . . . well . . . that was complicated.

"Dinnertime." He set the tray on the floor close enough for the woman to reach, but remembered to stay well out of the way of her unbound feet. "You'll have to use the straw for the soup, too. But I'm sure you'll manage just fine. Take just a tiny sip at first. You don't want to burn your mouth." He crossed to the shelves on the far walls, turned on the CD player.

"Please." Her voice was hoarse, and it served her right, with all the screaming she'd done over the last few days. He'd told her—he always told them—that screaming wouldn't help. None of them listened.

He hated to use duct tape to silence them. It seemed disrespectful somehow. Luckily it was rarely necessary. The inner chamber was so well insulated, he could barely hear the screaming when he was working in the very next room.

"I swear if you let me go I won't tell anyone. I promise. Just let me go. I want to go home." Her voice ended on a whimper.

"Are you in the mood for jazz or oldies?" She'd told him her favorites the very first night. They always told him whatever he asked at the beginning. He was a very good listener. Everyone said so. He slipped in a disc of Benny Goodman and turned to smile at her. "I'll empty your chamber pot while you eat. Enjoy your meal."

"Let me go!" The chains rattled as she lunged for him. And he didn't feel a bit sorry when they stopped her progress, yanking her back by the wrists with a force that would surely leave bruises. "You monster! You fucking son of a bitch! Let me go-o-o-o . . ."

He swung the door shut behind him, immune, almost, to her cursing. It was a shame she was upset because her screeching was going to drown out the music he'd arranged for her.

His guests could be so ungrateful. It was enough some days to make him wonder why he bothered.

Chapter 5

"This is fucking lame."

Cait was so preoccupied that it took her a moment to shift her attention from the solution she was studying to the voice of her assistant. Without looking up she murmured, "You owe me a buck."

"Put it on my tab." Kristy's voice held a yawn. "How come you get the sexy work? Detecting latent fingerprints on bone is fucking cutting edge. And what do I get to do? I get to look at mother-fucking dirt."

"Keep it up and you'll be buying me lunch." Cait carefully poured the solution she'd prepared over the pulverized bone fragment she'd extracted from female C. "I'm not going to get around to testing for latents today anyway. These tests will take hours. Although I may be able to get the visual examination done with the alternate light source, so at least that step would be completed."

With the advances made in the missing persons databases recently, she couldn't overlook the possibility that DNA would ultimately identify one of their victims. And samples for those tests had to be gathered prior to testing for fingerprints the UNSUB may have left on the bones or even before cleaning the skeletal remains.

The tests were tedious and time-consuming, but Cait wanted to run them herself. Raiker would make a caustic comment about learning to delegate. But then, her boss was nearly three thousand miles away on the other side of the country. He'd never have to know.

She placed the sample in the centrifuge and, setting the speed and time, prepared to wait a few minutes. Her gaze wandered around their makeshift lab. "Did Michaels balk at giving up another area for our use?"

Kristy never looked up from her work. "*Steve* was an absolute angel about it when I asked." She paused for a meaning-laden moment. "Of course I asked nicely."

Contemplating her assistant, Cait asked cautiously, "How nicely?"

"*Very nicely*," came the smug reply. "I could give details if you . . ."

"God, no." The last thing she needed was a pornographic image of the two of them smeared across her mind. Some mental pictures could scar a person forever. "Spare me the specifics."

"Well, you have to admit, it was well worth the price of a blow job."

Deliberately she turned her back on her assistant and wished she could turn her hearing off as easily. "Gagging here."

Kristy laughed. "I'm kidding. He arranged to have the entire room emptied and cleaned so I could set up. No doubts he has ideas about a suitable reward, but I have as yet to decide whether I'll be delving into that pool of well-defined man muscle. Although you have to admit, I could do worse."

With a noncommittal sound, Cait removed the sample from the centrifuge and transferred the solution to a new tube. "Seemed like a lech to me."

"Well, what guy isn't? But he's sweeter than you'd think,

too. I just might give him a ride. You know how long it's been since my last meat injection?"

Cait nearly spilled the DNA IQ Lysis Buffer she was adding to the original solution. "Uh . . . since the plane ride here?"

Kristy laughed. "I'd call you a bitch if you wouldn't charge me for it."

Which was, Cait acknowledged, a devious way to do exactly that without suffering the consequences. Her tech was getting cagey.

She was also in an unfortunately chatty mood. "Steve doesn't like my swearing anyway, so I should probably work harder to stop. He says people don't take cursing women seriously and that I need to protect my professional image."

"A lech and a chauvinist. More charming by the minute."

"You've said almost the same thing, verbatim, on more than one occasion."

Because Kristy was most annoying when she was right, Cait changed the subject. "Coming up with any matches?"

"No close composite comparisons yet. They all have high sulfur content, of course, but most of the samples you brought have more than twice the amount as the sediment we tested from the garbage bags. The others are closer on the sulfur content but missing the other elements."

Which meant she needed to veer farther afield from the hot springs sources, Cait thought. She'd had Sharper take her to the more touristy ones within a ten-mile radius of the cave. There was no need to expand the grid until she'd gotten samples from the government and private properties shown on maps in the same area.

"So what do you think of Andrews? Personally I found it a little creepy the way she lit up at the thought of some psycho defleshing victims and dumping them in her jurisdiction, but, hey; maybe she's just really enthusiastic about her job."

The words closely correlated with Cait's own thoughts. She vortexed the sample for five seconds before preparing to incubate it. "Yeah, I caught her attitude, too. But she seems like a solid cop. Barnes is a little more out of his element, I think." The deputy seemed sharp enough but slow to accept any conclusions not completely supported by substantiated evidence. Which told her he'd be a skeptic about the profile she'd already started on the perp.

The line the sheriff had given him to follow up on was well within his comfort zone. Cait had found herself vaguely surprised how many of the violators ticketed by the rangers had previous records, however insignificant. He was concentrating on those violators with records before moving on to the rest.

She rested her hands against the counter and leaned her weight against them. The pain in her left palm reminded her of the injury there, and she hurriedly changed position. She didn't want to reopen the wound and risk contaminating the tests. As it was, she had the area wrapped in gauze and covered with two elastic gloves.

"How're you coming?"

Cait lifted a shoulder, a gesture her assistant couldn't see with her back turned. "This is only the third victim. I've got a ways to go." And as always she was worried about the possibility of destroying one kind of evidence in search of another. But there was no help for it. She just had to pray that if a latent was present on any of the victims, it didn't exist on the section of bone she drew the DNA extraction from.

"What's that other guy like? What's his name? Sharper?"

"He defies description," Cait said dryly. And mentally damned her assistant for bringing the man's name up. He'd been successfully banished from her mind since they'd parted ways yesterday. She could only assume he was as grateful for their separation as she was.

"Steve seems to think he's pretty cool. Says there's no one around who knows the area better. Of course, I thought I detected the tiniest hint of hero worship in his voice. Probably because the guy's a decorated war hero and all. Guys get all testosteroney over stuff like that."

She wasn't interested. Other than his usefulness getting her around, Sharper had absolutely nothing to do with the case. But she heard herself saying, "Iraq?"

"Um-m . . ." There was a prolonged silence as Kristy examined her samples. "Okay, this one is another bust. I'll document it and move on. No." Seamlessly, she switched topics to answer Cait's question. "Afghanistan, I think. Some sort of specialist, according to Steve. To tell the truth, I wasn't listening that close. When I'm not in the lab I have a very short attention span. Especially since I was giving serious consideration to jumping his bones. One bone in particular."

Specialist? Or special ops? Cait mulled over the new information even as she gave close attention to preparing the wash buffer. She was willing to bet Special Forces. Sharper had that tough primitive look that came from living through things no one should have to imagine, much less experience.

A look she still occasionally glimpsed in her own reflection, if less frequently with each passing year. And it occurred to her that there might be far more beneath the man's caustic exterior than she'd originally thought.

Maybe he was as adept at donning masks as she was herself.

Recalling the snapped vertebrae on each of the skeletal remains, a shiver worked down her spine. She made a mental note to call Raiker. She'd yet to be in need of intelligence that he couldn't get his hands on. And it might be interesting to see just what sort of information could be found in the guide's military files.

Cait sat straight up in bed, instantly awake but disoriented. There was faint light at the edges of the shades at the windows of the motel room. But it was early. Too early.

Her cell phone rang again on the bedside table, alerting her to what had awakened her. She picked it up, checked the number on the screen, and flipped it open to answer.

"If you're my morning wake-up call, you're a couple hours early."

Adam Raiker's brusque voice sounded. "Thought your email said you were in a hurry for this information."

Cait jammed another pillow behind her and leaned against

the headboard, stifling a yawn. It'd been late when she'd gone to bed. Because the east coast was three hours earlier than the west, she'd thoughtfully used email rather than a phone call to place her request with Raiker.

Although, truth be told, he'd probably still been awake when she'd sent it. She'd often suspected the man didn't sleep.

"So you've got the information for me already?"

"I've got something. Up to you whether you need more." There was the faint rustle of papers on the end of the line before the man started reading. "Zachary Dalton Sharper, age thirty-six, honorably discharged from the Army sixty-two months ago. Served a total of twelve years, ten of them in the Rangers. Several campaigns in Afghanistan and Iraq. Impressive atta-boy file. Couple silver stars, Distinguished Service Cross, purple heart . . . looks like your local war hero is the real thing."

"Any chance you pulled some strings and found out about his training?"

"Figured you want to know that." It was always difficult to tell if Raiker's abrupt tone was due to his disposition or the wounds he'd sustained in the last case he'd worked for the Bureau. Given the hideous scar bisecting his throat, he had to have sustained some internal damage there. But given what she knew of him, Cait figured it could be either one. "Did several years with direct-action operations before becoming a member of an RRD team. Regimental Reconnaissance Detachment. He was a team leader before he left the service."

The title meant nothing to her. "And that is?"

There was a short bark of sound that passed for laughter with her boss. "Twelve of these guys in the whole Ranger operation. They specialize in silent insertion behind enemy lines and intelligence gathering. His actual missions are classified."

"Meaning you couldn't get them?"

"Meaning I need to extend a very big marker to get them," he corrected. "I prefer not to unless you really need it."

"I don't." The missions didn't matter. She knew enough

about elite military forces to know that silent and deadly unarmed combat techniques were part of their training.

Like the ability to snap a combatant's neck.

"How's the case going?"

Cait gave him an abbreviated version of her findings so far, all of which Raiker listened to silently. "And the lab equipment arrived okay?"

"Everything was in one piece. It was just a matter of finding a place to set up." She gave a short laugh. "Luckily there was room at the morgue."

"Jesus. I need to get going on those plans for regional mobile labs."

"So you keep saying." She rolled her shoulders, loosening the muscles. She tended to sleep in a tight ball. "Thanks again for the information."

"Let me know if you need anything else. And keep me posted on your progress." A moment later the line was dead.

Wryly, she flipped her phone shut and considered it for a moment. Raiker was even more curt on the phone than he was in person. She stretched and swung her legs over the edge of the bed. The alarm clock on the bedside read five forty-five. It'd been after ten before she'd left the lab. Well past midnight before she'd finished emailing Raiker and submitting information about individual descriptors for each set of remains into the various missing persons databases, then printing off the results.

She gave a moment's thought to how her boss had acquired Sharper's information so quickly and then put it out of her mind. Better not to inquire too closely about his tactics. His list of contacts were legion. It helped, of course, that the man was a legend in law enforcement circles.

Going back to bed wasn't an option. She'd never been able to fall back to sleep once up. Instead she rose and padded over to the missing persons printouts lying on the table in the corner of the room.

It took over two hours to go through them all. Another fifteen minutes to decide which to follow up on first. The bodies could presumably come from anywhere, but she had to start somewhere, so she'd concentrate first on those persons originating in neighboring states who'd gone missing in the last decade. She jotted down the phone numbers to the law enforcement agencies before checking the time again. Probably still too early to try any of them now. But she could make some calls while she drove.

Rising, she headed toward the shower. She'd planned another long day at the lab trying to lift those latents, but she could afford a detour first.

Because she wouldn't be satisfied until she'd gotten a soil sample from Sharper's property.

———

A fine mist started falling about halfway to McKenzie Bridge. Oregon sunshine, she'd heard it called, but rain was rain to her. She just hoped it stopped before she got to Sharper's place.

She filled her time on the drive calling the various agencies affiliated with the missing persons responses she'd gotten, mostly leaving messages for the case detectives she got routed to who were away from their desks. But she was able to have conversations with a few of them, like Detective Paul Drecker in Seattle.

"Raiker Forensics, huh? Heard of you guys. Met your boss at a conference once when he was still at the Bureau. Brilliant guy. Funny as hell."

Funny? Adam Raiker? The description was baffling. But then Cait hadn't known him until years after the case that had nearly killed him and ended with his retiring from the FBI.

Drecker had already gone on. "Marissa Recinos you said?" She could imagine the man shaking his head on the other end of the line. "Not ringing a bell . . ."

"She was last seen five years ago in December, in Pike Place Market," Cait prodded. "Her mother reported her missing when she didn't show up for the family dinner the following Sunday."

"Yeah, yeah, Recinos. Now I remember that case. Never did find her. I always liked her ex for it, myself. Real asshole, and it was a messy divorce. She's loaded and he felt like he got screwed on the alimony." He snorted. "Ever known a guy to get alimony? Someone should tell my two exes about that. Anyway, he'd made some threats a couple years earlier."

"He was alibied?"

"Airtight. So your remains are Hispanic?"

"All the remains are minus the skulls, so I can't determine ancestry. But I wondered whether she had skeletal identifiers."

"Yeah, guess that description of her tat isn't doing you much good, huh? Well, let me check into it and get back to you. I'll probably have to call her mother. What exactly should I be asking about?"

"Her medical history. Did she ever suffer a fracture and to which bone. How long ago." The remains in question had a fracture to the left wrist that must have occurred within the final year of her life. She paused and thought a moment. "Also ask her if Recinos had osteoarthritis. If her knees bothered her. Any Xrays in her medical files. Anything I could possibly use to validate the remains."

"I'll ask. Can I get you at this number?"

"Yes, or feel free to email me." Cait gave him her work email address.

"Will do. I'll get back to you."

The rest of the calls filled the driving time. After they were finished, her complete attention was required to recall exactly where Sharper's place was.

She had a photographic memory for anything she read. It had certainly made academics a whole lot simpler. But when it came to directions . . . not so much. She'd backtracked several times before giving up and driving to the Springs Resort, and then trying to find her way from there.

She was more successful this time, although she missed the narrow drive to his place once and had to turn around yet again. When she came to a chain barring her approach on the drive, for the first time she considered what she'd do if the guide happened to be home today.

With an eye to the sky, she decided that was a long shot. It didn't look like it had rained here, although the clouds overhead looked ominous. And with all the bitching he'd done about being kept from his business, she couldn't believe that he wouldn't already be in Eugene. It was after ten already.

Grabbing her pack, she locked the vehicle and hiked the rest of the way up the drive, marveling again at the private area. She'd dropped by the Lane County Courthouse before taking off this morning. According to the assessor's office, Sharper's property encompassed twenty-five acres and was worth upwards of a million dollars.

The amount alone was brow raising. He'd said something about inheriting the land from his grandfather, she recalled, as she strode rapidly up the drive. Pretty nice inheritance. And the house he was building wasn't exactly a shack, either.

On foot, it took fifteen minutes before the house came into view. Cait stopped to scan the area. There was no sign of Sharper's Trailblazer. The battered red pickup she'd seen here before was parked in the same spot. The place had a deserted air.

Pulling the NRCS map out of her pack, she studied it for a few moments before raising her narrowed gaze to his property again. If she established a grid and took samples from each corner and random points in the center of it, that'd still put her back at the morgue by one or so. Cait shoved the map back into her pack and continued walking. She'd start in the back of the property and work her way forward.

She was on her fourth sample before she ran across a small hot spring. Compared to the ones Sharper had chauffeured her to, it wasn't much more than a trickle. It was the smell that gave it away. If she were the fanciful type, she'd say it brought images of brimstone. Water erupted from the earth in wide cracks and then disappeared back into the ground after several feet before making a surprise appearance again. She imagined it coursed freely well beneath the surface, and made a note to research the acts of nature that had formed this land. Despite her mother's lifelong efforts to pretend otherwise, she was a science geek at heart, whether she looked the part or not.

She was going to end up with more samples than she'd

originally planned, but she worked swiftly, still intent on making it back to the lab in time to start the latent testing. One moment she was carefully inserting her core sample into a plastic container and labeling it. The next a voice sounded behind her.

"It's a world-class ass. But I still want to know what it's doing on my property."

Shit. Her eyelids slid shut in chagrin. If the voice didn't give him away, the note of derision in it would have. Cait finished placing the sample in her pack before rising to face him.

Temper lent Sharper a lethal air that was all the more chilling for the grim watchfulness in his eyes. Surliness she was used to. But there was more here than she'd observed the other times she'd seen him. He looked like he hadn't slept. He sure as hell hadn't shaved. Given the smell emanating from him, she'd bet he'd spent the time instead marinating in alcohol.

Caution settled over her. Because this was a Sharper she wasn't familiar with. Her mind flashed back to her earlier conversation with Raiker about the guide's time in the military. *Silent and deadly.* Silent, she could attest to. His approach had been soundless until he'd spoken. Deadly . . . if his expression was anything to go by, she was on very thin ice.

Expertly, she skated over it. "I didn't know you were home."

"Guess you wouldn't since you didn't bother to knock." His gaze traveled to her open pack, then back to her face. "I know you have a phone, so that can't be the reason you didn't call, either."

"I figured you'd be at work."

"I'll bet you did," he murmured. Folding his arms across his T-shirt-clad chest, he added, "As a matter of fact, I figure that's why you came. I don't know about the laws where you come from, Slim, but around here we call this trespassing."

The figurative ice beneath her feet cracked a bit. "Be reasonable. Your vehicle wasn't in the drive. You're always harping about the business I'm keeping you from, so I figured you must have a tour." She waited a beat. "Why aren't you at work?"

There was a flash of something in his eyes, there and gone so quickly she might have imagined it, if she didn't make a habit of observing things like that. He bared his teeth. "I was on the Willamette for eight hours yesterday. I spent another four cleaning gear and putting it away. My employees are running three tours today and needed my vehicle. Anything else you want to know?"

Her usual flawless sense of self-preservation failed her. What she needed to know was how to get out of there without losing a limb. But instead she found herself wondering what had put that bleakness in his expression. The one that reminded her of a gaunt lone wolf, howling his pain at an uncaring moon.

"I'm sorry I bothered you." And she was. Sorry she hadn't picked another day, another time to put to rest the niggling suspicion before it could fully form. Sorry she'd seen a side to him that made him all too human. It was far easier to deal with Sharper when she didn't feel a tug of pity for him. She lifted her pack and shrugged into it. "I'll get out of your way and let you enjoy your time off."

Cait didn't get two steps before his fingers closed on the strap of her pack and yanked her to a halt. "I don't think so. Not before providing me with a few answers. And anything else I ask for."

The innuendo was unmistakable. Pulling away from his grasp, she turned to face him, anger pulsing. "Don't be a jerk, Sharper. I haven't hurt anything. I apologize for not getting your permission before looking around. Mea culpa, okay?"

"It's not okay." His voice was silky smooth now, with the slash of temper layered just beneath it. "Not until you tell me what the hell you thought you'd find here."

She hesitated, mentally flipping through her options. She doubted he'd cry foul to Andrews. And even if he did, the most she'd get was a hand slap from the sheriff. But she wasn't willing to share any details from the case, either.

"How about I make it easy for you? I've been carting you around to all the hot springs in the area, and you've been taking soil samples. That map in your pack"—he flicked it with his finger—"shows the location of different kinds of soils. You must be looking for a kind found near hot springs. I've got one on the property, although it's hardly on the same level as the ones you've already visited." He released his grip on the strap and stepped back a pace. "Since the distinctive element in hot springs is sulfur, you must have found sulfur on some of the bones, and that's why you're taking samples from every goddamn piece of land you can access. Legally or not."

Ignoring his obvious exaggeration, she nodded. It wasn't exact, but he was close enough to the truth for it not to matter at this point. "Something like that."

Her affirmation didn't lighten his expression any. If anything, it grew more menacing. "And what? I found the bones, I've got sulfuric soil on my property, so I must be a killer? Sounds pretty thin to me, but then I'm not some cover girl for a cop shop out east, so what do I know?"

He had a knack for igniting her temper. "Very little, from where I'm standing." And sighed inwardly when she saw his eyes narrow. With effort, she reached for patience. "You want to deny me access to your land? That's your right. Want to insist I give back the soil samples? Can't stop you. I'll note that in my report and move on."

His glare would have struck sparks off flint. "Make sure you get permission at the next place, sweetheart. People around here value their privacy."

Cait gave him an insincere smile. "So you've said. I'll let you know when I need your help again. I assume you're still at the sheriff's beck and call?"

It was like baiting a tiger. He had that same still watchful air prior to pouncing. "Caitlin."

Her flesh prickled. How could a man's voice manage to sound silky and menacing at the same time?

"You'll want to be very careful." The first step in her direction was meant to be threatening. The next would have had any woman in her right mind making tracks.

She held her ground, stiffened her spine.

"You're on an isolated piece of property."

She could smell the alcohol again. Not on his breath. More like it was coming out his pores. How much had he drunk? He didn't seem intoxicated. He damned sure didn't appear impaired.

He just seemed lethal.

"No one around to help you." Another half step. Alarm pulsed through her veins. Every muscle in her body tensed. "With a man you really don't know very well."

Coolly, she lifted a brow. "Worried about me? Don't be. I've taken down bigger men than you without breaking a sweat. *Back off.*"

"Or what?" One of his arms snaked around her waist, the hand skating down her spine. Lower.

"Sharper, if you don't take your hand off my ass, you're going to be picking your teeth out of the dirt."

"So you've had training to take men down hard. Think that makes you tough? Lots of us had training." His words filtered through her anger, piquing her interest. But that interest was fragmented by the recognition that he hadn't moved his hand. And his face was far too close to hers. "Here's the thing about toughness, though. No matter what you think you're prepared for, there's always something that smashes everything you think you know to hell. Everything you think you can handle."

"I'm warning you, Sharper." But even she heard the shake to her voice. His words were summoning a memory she'd spent a lifetime locking away. The darkness eeked out. Swirled through her mind.

"You find out how tough you are when you're dodging men's body parts after an IED detonates." The edge to his voice was razor sharp, each word nicking skin and drawing blood. "Or when you inhale the pink mist, all that's left of the guy who was the closest to the explosive. One of the toughest guys I knew swallowed his gun last night because, hey, guess what? Toughness didn't mean shit when they sent him home minus his legs and half his face. Ever see what's left of a guy who eats his gun?"

The past sprang forth like a great fanged beast, snarling and tearing through the gauze of the present.

She was eight again. Fingers in her ears. Cowering under the desk until the weapon went off. Choking back strangled sobs as she crawled out. Did what she had to do.

Just get the gun. Remember what I told you. Don't look at anything else. Don't look.

But of course she had. How could she not? And the image had been seared on her retinas, branded across her memory ever since.

"Blood spatter everywhere. Bone fragments in the chair cushions. Caught in the drapes. Gray matter on the desk. On the gun."

The gun she'd had to pick up. The one she'd had to hide in the special place he'd shown her.

She wasn't sure how much time stretched out before she became aware of the change in Sharper's gaze. On his expression. It was another long moment before she realized she'd spoken the words out loud.

Mortification warred with panic. She wrenched herself from his grasp. Easy enough since he'd dropped his hands, stepped away, still surveying her carefully.

"Cait."

"I have to get back."

With swift movements, she straightened the straps on her shoulders and turned. Began striding rapidly away. And slowed, her steps faltering. Looking over her shoulder, she found him watching her. "I'm sorry about your friend."

Then she headed toward her vehicle, leaving the man behind to stare silently after her.

Chapter 6

"Cait, where are you?"

"Coming up on the morgue, why?"

Barnes's voice held a note of excitement she didn't recall hearing before. "Good. I'm already there. See you in a few minutes."

Disconnecting the phone's blue tooth, she gave a shrug and turned off into the morgue parking lot. She drove to the back of the building, the area closest to the lab accommodations.

It had started to mist again on the outside of town. Which mirrored her current attitude to perfection.

Her mood dark, she got out of the vehicle, loaded down with pack and purse and computer bag. Locking the door behind her, she jogged to the building.

Barnes started speaking as soon as she was in the door. "One of our deputies found this in the forest wrapped in a towel, about four miles from Castle Rock."

This turned out to be a saw. Flecks of blood still marred the stainless steel blade. And, she peered closely, there were splinters of what would surely turn out to be bone embedded in the towel.

"Looks like an E-Z Saw. The kind used for splitting the pelvic bone of large game." She looked at Barnes. "Did the officer happen to notice a blood spill near the site where he found this?"

The deputy shook his head. "That's why I brought it to you. He said this was wedged under some rocks. It's a long shot, but I figured you could test it. At least see if the blood is human."

Mentally readjusting her schedule, she nodded. "We can do that and have results by tomorrow. We already know some sort of saw was used to decapitate the victims. I need to examine the marks on the vertebrae and try to identify the family of instruments they came from anyway. I can do that before testing for latents, I guess."

"If I know the specific tool, I can start looking at purchases made around here recently. Maybe we'll get lucky and find the perp that way."

She smiled, saying nothing. Cait had a feeling things weren't going to be quite that easy, but Barnes was right about one thing. The tool marks were going to be valuable information. Once they found the offender, they could link him to the crimes if he still had the saw in his possession.

"Kristy," she called.

Her tech showed up in the doorway of the other room. Cait blinked once. Beneath her lab coat, the woman was clad in an eye-popping shirt of electric blue and fuchsia. "Bad lighting when you were getting dressed?"

"Bite me," Kristy suggested cheerfully. "Steve bought it for me. We went to a country fair last night outside Springfield. He said it matched my electric personality."

"Were you by any chance sticking a screwdriver in a light socket at the time?"

The finger extended only halfway before the woman caught herself, tucking her hand chastely back at her side. "Since my first response is both unprofessional and unladylike, I'm going to forget you said that."

Cait gaped. She couldn't help it. If the ME was helping Kristy break a bad habit where—let's face it—she herself had failed, more power to him. But the fact that he'd managed to do so only because he possessed a Y chromosome and her assistant had the hots for him was a bit hard to swallow.

Shaking off the reaction, she indicated the saw and towel on the counter Barnes had brought with him. "Deputy Barnes needs the blood tested for species identification."

"Sure." She strolled into the room to survey the instrument before looking up at Cait. "Do you want me to run the Ouchterlony or crossover electrophoresis?"

"Run the Ouchterlony test. If I'm not here in the morning, call me first thing to let me know whether you have results yet."

"You got it." The tech picked up the materials with her gloved hands and headed back into the adjoining room.

Barnes's gaze followed the woman until she disappeared. Cait didn't blame him. Few people knew what to make of Kristy.

"So what else do you have so far?" Mentally she was calculating how long it would take her to examine the saw marks on each set of remains. All day, she realized with a sense of resignation. Which would push her latent exam back until at least tomorrow or later. But this was probably a better use of her time. Whatever tool had been used to decapitate the victims would have left certain evidence. The same couldn't be said about whoever had handled the bones prior to their being found in those bags. Finding a latent on the skeletal remains was going to be a long shot.

The deputy's attention returned to her. "It's been slow going with the ranger stations. Most of their help is on the other side of the state, fighting that forest fire."

She nodded grimly. Whenever the TV was on, local news was providing updates. "So the stations are short-staffed."

"I've got officers at various stations helping with the file review. And I've been following up on the offenders myself." He itched his upper lip as if the newly grown mustache was bothering him. "Been concentrating on locals or those who live in the state for now."

"It's a starting point. Let me know if you want help."

"Will do." He pushed away from the counter.

As the deputy headed toward the door, she stashed her purse, then dug out her cell phone and put it on the desk in the corner of the room. If the detectives she'd contacted today started to return her messages, she didn't want to miss their calls.

Then she took her pack into the next room and started to withdraw the soil samples. "I have a present for you."

Kristy glanced up from her work. And immediately groaned theatrically. "No fucking way. I just got caught up on the other ones!"

"These are special." She shied away from the memory of the scene earlier that day with Sharper. "But they can wait until you finish the plates and treat the long bones in each set of remains with Acryloid B-72." The preservative would give the bones an artificially glossy nonporous surface suitable for dusting for latents.

Cait looked through the contents of the shelves on the other side of the room until she found a pair of magnifying goggles, which she set on the nearby cart holding the stereo-microscope and scanning digital camera. "You owe me a buck, by the way. Two if you don't want me to tell Michaels Steve about your lapse." Carefully she began pulling the cart across the room. That was the pain of temporary lab quarters. Nothing was ever where she needed it.

Though her back was to the other woman, she heard the smirk in her voice. "Turns out he has a love-hate relationship with my language. When it's dirty talk, accompanied by a little soft bondage . . ."

Cait hurried her pace a bit. "I'm not listening."

". . . he has a surprisingly high tolerance for it. As a matter of fact, he asked me to say . . ."

"La-la-la-la-la . . . can't hear you." She escaped with the cart into the other room while Kristy was still laughing.

She manipulated the cart over to the first gurney, which

held the remains of female A. Adjusting the goggles over her eyes, she switched on the lights on either side of them and then picked up the camera to scan in digital pictures. When she was finished, she'd hook the camera to the stereomicroscope and use it to display the pictures with maximum resolution on the monitor.

At least her time spent with the victim would elicit nothing more risqué than the secrets behind the saw marks on the severed vertebrae.

That was infinitely preferable to hearing the details of Kristy's love life.

————

At five minutes to eight, Cait followed the hostess through the restaurant to the table for two in the corner. Marin Andrews lowered her menu as Cait approached. "I'm glad you could make it. Hope you like Thai food." She paused, did a quick once-over of Cait's figure. "And that you eat."

Stifling the quick flare of irritation, Cait picked up a menu. "My starving-model days have been behind me for a decade."

The sheriff grunted. "You won't be sorry. The chef here is excellent."

Several minutes passed before Andrews put down her menu, signaled the waiter. Cait held off until after he'd scribbled down their orders and hurried away before asking the question that had been plaguing her since Andrews's call a couple hours ago. "Your call sounded urgent."

The sheriff raised her brows over the rim of her water glass as she drank. "Didn't mean for it to. I wanted to talk to you before tomorrow morning and thought dinner would give us the time and privacy we need." It was obvious she'd come from the office herself. She was still in uniform.

"What's going on tomorrow morning?"

"Press conference."

Of course. Cait sat back in her chair, a measure of cynicism rising. Sharper had said something a couple days ago about how little information had been released to the media.

She'd been surprised at the time that Andrews had restrained from regular press updates.

It was another reminder that the woman was no fool. And that she had a plan that reached far beyond this case.

Whatever her reasons, the sheriff's restraint so far pleased Cait. There was nothing worse than a press-hungry law enforcement officer spilling details that she'd prefer not being made public.

When Andrews began speaking, her words mirrored Cait's thoughts closely. "I've been talking to the press regularly, but putting them off with any real details until we could be certain what we were dealing with." The expression in her eyes was shrewd. "I don't want to make something public that will later be proven untrue. But media speculation can be just as damaging, so I want to be careful. I'll share some of the facts, and your expert opinion. So we need to separate out the information we have so I can decide what's safe to go public with."

Cait leaned back as the waiter returned with their soft drinks. When he'd moved away, she said, "I assume Deputy Barnes updated you about the discovery he delivered to the lab today." At the woman's nod, she went on. "The species identification results won't be available until tomorrow, but I can tell you unequivocally that the saw your officer found isn't the instrument used to decapitate these victims, although the instrument used was a bone saw."

If the sheriff was disappointed at the news, it didn't show. "You're sure of that?"

"Absolutely. I conducted saw mark analysis on the serrated areas of the bones. When I examine the characteristics of the kerf walls and floors in the bones, I'm able to get a fairly accurate estimation of the size, shape, set, power, and direction of a saw." The sheriff was leaning forward, listening intently. "The tool used is hand powered. Ten TPI—teeth per inch. A rectangular blade. The perp is right-handed. And here's the good news." Cait paused, reliving the satisfaction she'd experienced when she'd made the discovery. "The same blade was used on all of the victims. There's a slight imperfection on one of the teeth."

"So if the UNSUB has the saw in his possession, it links him to the murders."

She nodded. "But that isn't information you want to release to the public."

"Of course not." The sheriff broke off as their food was delivered. Then she picked up her fork and started in on her seafood curry. "Neither are the beetles. So let's talk about what we can safely release."

"The cave's a secondary scene." Cait tried her stir fry, found it delicious. "The newest set of remains was probably put there sometime in the last several months. The manner of disposal has your department treating the deaths as suspicious." She'd had plenty of experience over the years putting together case information for press releases. Unfortunately, her advice was often ignored. Law enforcement officials had to deal with local politics, which sometimes edged out caution when it came to releasing facts to the public. "The deaths are connected, and you're following up on that link as vigorously as possible. You don't feel the residents are in immediate danger, but they should remain cautious and report any suspicious activity to your office, yada yada yada."

Andrews chewed thoughtfully. "That isn't going to be enough to satisfy them."

She was right. But then, nothing would be enough to satisfy a press corps hungry for details about the most sensational case to hit the area in decades. The trick was to keep them from realizing just how sensational it was before the investigators knew themselves. "If pushed, I suppose you could tell them we're matching the remains with persons reported missing, and every attempt is being made to identify the individuals so they can eventually be returned to their families."

Reaching for her glass, the sheriff nodded. "That should do it. Now why don't you tell me about your progress along those lines."

Cait filled her in on the phone calls she'd made that day, adding, "I've talked to three detectives so far. All have promised to get me identifier information that might help me match the missing person to one of our remains. When I get to the point where I think we're close to doing so, I'll ask for DNA samples to compare with the ones I took."

The other woman paused in the act of bringing her fork to her mouth. "You can get DNA from bones?"

"If they aren't too degraded." One corner of her mouth pulled up wryly. "One thing we have to thank our offender for. He left us specimens in excellent condition."

"And went to a lot of trouble to do so," Andrews said, chewing slowly. "The question is, why? Why not bury them? Or chop them in smaller pieces and drop them in a lake or river somewhere? This process you described, the one where he has the beetles cleaning the bones . . . why bother? There have to be quicker ways. Easier ways. He goes to a lot of trouble."

"Burial is a lot of trouble if you're digging a hole deep enough to keep animals from getting at them," Cait pointed out. "The process he follows may be due to easy access or experience. Or it may be part of a ritual that only makes sense to him. It does go a long way in helping me establish the basis of a profile for him."

Andrews wiped her mouth with her napkin, the action surprisingly dainty. "I could write the basis of a profile myself. If everything you say is true, we already know that this UNSUB is one sick son of a bitch."

The next morning, while Kristy put in a call to Deputy Barnes with the results of the Ouchterlony and the saw-mark analysis tests, Cait began to dust the preserved bones of each set of remains with black magnetic fluorescent powder, using a magnetic wand. She fitted her protective goggles into place before picking up the handheld ultraviolet lamp and flicking off the lights.

She'd just snapped on the lamp when she heard her assistant call, "Don't you dare start without me."

"Bring in some black backing cards," Cait called back. She began to shine the alternate light source over the dusted bones.

Kristy all but skidded into the room, slapping the cards on the counter with one hand as she pulled up her set of goggles. "Didn't I tell you not to start without me? You don't listen very well."

The words were eerily similar to ones she'd heard a few days earlier.

You don't follow orders very well.

The stray thought brought Sharper to the forefront of her mind, after she'd done a decent job for the last several hours of not considering him at all. "You never said . . ." Slowly she examined the ulna. "What'd you discover with those soil samples I brought you yesterday?"

"Well, a couple were certainly the closest matches you've brought so far."

Her hand holding the lamp jerked slightly. Drawing in a deep breath, Cait steadied her grasp and strove for a level tone. "Is it within the statistically significant range?"

"No, they were still higher in sulfur than the element percentage in the sediment found in some of the bags. Just not nearly as high as the first ones I tested. Sample one was the closest of them."

Sample one. Cait searched her memory. That would have been taken from the southeast corner of Sharper's property. Nowhere close to the spot she'd found the springs, right before Sharper had discovered her. It was looking more likely that her first deduction was a bust. The match for the soil sample in the bags was acidic, but wouldn't be found in the immediate vicinity of a hot springs.

"What's that?" The woman crowded closer, pointing with one gloved finger.

"Just a smudge, probably from our latex gloves. Without the skull vaults, our chances of finding latents reduce dramatically," Cait cautioned her assistant. The long smooth surface of the craniums was a perfect deposit for fingerprints. But it remained to be seen just how clever this UNSUB was. His hiding spot had, after all, been discovered. He would have needed to get those bones out of the beetles' enclosure. To deposit them in the bag. Common sense would have him using gloves, but anything could have happened. A bone could have been nearly overlooked. Picked up and slipped in the bag when he wasn't thinking.

Seven victims. Chances were he'd made a mistake with at least one of them.

But the first set of preserved bones was minus even the smallest partial latent. So was the second.

By the time they'd moved to the third gurney, Kristy's enthusiasm had visibly dampened. "If we don't find anything on these bones, we could try others, right?"

"Yes. But the smaller the bone the less surface area for a full print. Or even a useable partial. Better cross your fingers."

Hours later Cait straightened for a moment working her shoulders wearily. It'd be tough to choose whether her back or her feet ached more, and they still had two sets of remains left.

Kristy spoke around a yawn. "You were sloppy with that magnetic powder on this one. There's some clear up on the upper tip of the scapula. See?"

"I see it." Automatically, Cait moved the UV lamp to the area her assistant had indicated. "But there's no powder there." There was, however, definitely fluorescence. Clicking off the UV lamp, she strode over to the cart holding the digital scanning camera and spectrometer. "Turn on the overhead lights, will you?"

She brought up the pictures she'd taken yesterday, and found the set of remains in question. Exchanging her UV goggles for the magnifiers, she flipped through the images until she found the spot in question. Magnified it as much as she could without losing resolution.

The two women studied the monitor silently. "I don't see anything," Kristy finally admitted.

"Me, either." Adrenaline spiked as she reached for her UV goggles and lamp again. "Get the lights."

Once Kristy had switched them off, Cait retrained the lamp onto the spot they'd found. "Might be brush marks on the surface." What the hell? She crouched down and looked at the smudge from different angles. With gloved fingers on either side of the scapula, she turned the bone over. And froze.

"Holy shit."

"Fuck a duck," Kristy breathed. The two of them stared, nonplussed. "What the hell *is* that?"

"Some kind of picture. Drawings," Cait corrected herself. "You brought the UV lens for the digital scanning camera?"

"Yeah." But the other woman didn't move right away. Both of them were rooted in place, peering at the miniature scene in green and blue that they'd uncovered. "Is that some sort of new fad, a bone tattoo?" Kristy sounded only half kidding. "I mean, I've got a tat on my left ass cheek, product of a misspent youth, but this . . ."

"It'd be sort of a bitch getting it." Cait didn't know what exactly this was. Had never run across it before. But it ripped wide open the tiny window she'd previously had of the perp's mindset.

She couldn't stem the flood of excitement at the thought. "Get that UV lens." Without waiting for her assistant's return, she turned to the next gurney. Gingerly flipped the scapula over and aimed the lamp at it.

The pink and yellow images on the bone sprang into relief. Similar technique but different pictures this time. A feeling of urgency had her moving to the next gurney. And the one after that.

"I've got it." Several minutes later, Kristy hurried back in the room, words tumbling from her lips. "Was afraid for a few minutes there that I'd forgotten it, but I found it behind the . . . What'd you find? Did you check them all?"

Cait rose, still slightly dazed. "Yes." Her mind was still reeling with possibilities. "And each set of remains has a different scene painted on the posterior of the scapula. Except near the inferior angle of each, there's the same image."

Kristy crowded closer for a better look. And Cait found it difficult to tear her own gaze away from the tiny skull painted at the base of the bone.

Chapter 7

"Okay." Barnes was the first to speak in the darkened lab. "What is it exactly we're looking at?"

The deputy, Andrews, and Cait were grouped around the computer monitor. It was past nine o'clock. Cait had shooed Kristy from the lab hours earlier. There was no reason the woman should have to hang around until the sheriff could get there.

Using the remote, Cait clicked to the next set of images on the screen. "We found these when we were testing the remains for latents."

"You found them?" Andrews glanced at her. "Where?"

"These are scanned pictures of the painted images located on the back of the right scapula—shoulder blade—on each victim." She stopped, waited for the reactions of her audience.

But both stared at her in stunned silence. Barnes found his voice first. "What the hell—you just turned the bone over and found a little mural on it?"

"It was a bit more involved," Cait said dryly, "but yeah,

something like that. Wait. I'll show you." Swiftly she handed out two pair of UV goggles, turned on the lamp, and demonstrated for them with the scapula from male D. "I'd done a thorough visual examination prior to beginning the latent testing. Nothing could be seen with the naked eye, not even with the help of an ALS. We wouldn't have caught this at all, but I prefer working with the fluorescent magnetic powder in latent exams."

"Fluorescent . . ." The sheriff still seemed to be searching for words even as she stared at the scapula with rapt attention. "You're saying these pictures only show up under a black light?"

Cait switched off the UV lamp and nodded. "I spent a couple hours researching it. Didn't know whether the substance was ink or paint at first, but I tested it, and it appears to be paint. There are several online sources for this kind of thing. It's billed as invisible paint because you only see evidence of it under certain types of lighting. They use it for black light posters, haunted houses, that sort of thing. By mixing the paints, it's possible to achieve any color desired. There are a slew of manufacturers, but the paints have varying degrees of transparency, which is the element that renders them impossible to detect without a UV light."

She peeled off her gloves as she spoke. "The most common of the samples would allow you to see a black-and-white picture or design with a light source, or at least in sunlight, and the colors only become apparent under a UV lamp. But there are also several outfits that sell invisible paint that is impossible to detect with the naked eye." Collecting the sets of goggles, she laid the equipment on the counter next to the computer cart. "We should be able to trace the manufacturer of the product after I run comparison samples. The problem will be in acquiring their customer order list. A couple of the sources are overseas."

"Putting them outside the scope of any warrant we could get," Andrews said grimly.

"We may get lucky. The perp could have bought the paint in a store here in the US," Barnes interjected.

Nodding, Cait said, "Or he could have ordered online from a domestic company. At any rate, I placed orders with each place and should have samples of paint coming in a couple days."

"Damn good work." Andrews's gaze had returned to the monitor. "And the pictures are different for each victim?"

"There are similarities, but the only identical image is the one at the bottom of each." Rapidly she flipped through the images on the screen, pausing at the last one.

"A skull." The sheriff gave a tight smile. "Coincidentally, the body part missing from each set of remains. The bastard is taunting us. Could it be a sequential scene of what led to each victim's death? Maybe he stalked them first. Learned their habits. And each pic he painted represents a separate point in that process."

"Maybe," she returned slowly, studying the image again. She'd had the same thought. Especially given the gleaming skull that concluded each set of images. "Certainly there seems to be a sequence to the images. They're magnified on screen. Much harder to make out on the bones themselves. It's also possible that the progression doesn't refer to the final days or weeks before their death, but to their life." She felt both sets of eyes on her. "I can't be certain until we identify some of the remains. But see here . . ." She pointed at the monitor. "This looks like the Golden Gate Bridge. And then there's a ball and bat." She traced the images on screen. "And this . . . I looked this symbol up. It's the mascot for UCLA. And here's a tiny wedding cake. See the bride and groom on top?"

"Christ." Barnes sounded shaken. "It's like he researched each victim. Knew everything about them."

"Or the major points in their life." Cait cocked her head, still puzzled by the next picture. "That book . . . it could represent anything. A hobby, a job . . . I'm not sure. But this one . . ." she tapped the screen. "I can't quite make it out. Maybe it's an animal? Or a monster?"

"Which could represent the perp," the deputy said with dark humor.

"I still think this is more apt to depict the last few weeks of the victim's life," Andrews muttered. "But that would still allow for the perp being the monster."

"Then I'd expect to see that image in each scene, but the only commonalities in the pictures are the skulls." Cait traced the next image. "Here's some sort of small boat. A kayak or canoe, looks like. Then a . . . what? Skyscraper? Condo? There are eight images in all, counting the skull on each set."

"Maybe this means the offender and victim knew each other," suggested the sheriff, kneading the back of her neck. That the woman kept long hours was apparent. Regardless of the hour, she was always still at work when Cait contacted her. For the first time Cait wondered if she had a family at home, or if her job—and the one she had her eye on after this—consumed her life.

"What I don't get is, why bother?" Barnes moved away from the screen to pace. "This proves the bones were cleaned prior to dumping." He sent a quick look toward Cait. "I know you've said that all along, but now we can be sure. He goes to a lot of trouble." Unconsciously he repeated the same thread of conversation she and Andrews had had just the night before. "What's the point? Because you can be damn sure it means something."

"All you can be sure of right now is, whatever his reason, this is about him, not the victims. He's not paying them tribute, he's not acknowledging them as individuals. These images might describe things from the victims' lives. We won't know for sure until they're ID'd. But even if they do, the motivation for the pictures ultimately lies with him." She was as yet unsure what the action told her about the UNSUB, but she was far closer to establishing a profile now than she'd been prior to the discovery of the paintings.

"They may go a long way to helping you establish identity if the images do depict the victims' lives in some way," the sheriff pointed out.

Cait nodded. She'd already thought of that. "Even if I can't find a living relative to provide a DNA sample for testing, I may be able to tentatively match the remains to the history of the missing persons in the database." It would be a

DNA match that would provide a major break in the case. But the images would give them another strong basis for identification purposes, if a less certain one. "When I talk to the detectives again, I'll describe the paintings on the remains matching their missing person and see if we've got any points of intersection."

"What about the latents?" Barnes was still roaming the area, although he was careful not to touch anything. "Anything show up during your examination?"

"Not even a partial."

"But you can test other bones, right?" Andrews glanced at the watch she was wearing. Cait wondered if she had plans for later this evening or if the woman was finally planning to call it a day.

"It would likely be a waste of time. The best deposit points are on the cranium and the long bones. We tested all the long bones today. Anything smaller than that and the likelihood of finding a latent decreases drastically. But there's still the possibility that they'll find a latent on the garbage bags. Any word yet from the crime lab?"

"I'll give them a nudge tomorrow," the sheriff promised.

"Any chance there are more of those"—Barnes nodded at the screen—"anywhere else on the bones?"

"We checked thoroughly. The images on the scapulas were the only ones we found."

"So I guess you'll be busy with stuff here tomorrow." There was a note in Barnes's tone that alerted her.

"Nothing Kristy can't handle. Why?"

The man's look encompassed Andrews, too. "We've been tracking down violators who have been issued tickets by the forestry service. Illegal camping, dumping, whatever. I've run criminal crosschecks on the names on those lists. Came up with a couple roamers I'd like to check out."

Cait looked from one of them to the other. "Roamers?"

Frowning slightly, Andrews answered, "Basically homeless people who use the forests to camp year-round. They move around a lot to stay ahead of the forestry agents. They don't have permits, of course, and they aren't fussy about where they set up camp. We occasionally get calls from Roseboro—the lumber company—or private parties to chase one off their property. There are areas of the forest though where no permits are required. That's usually where you'll find them."

"And the roamers in question had criminal histories?" she asked Barnes.

Taking a notebook from his back jeans pocket, he flipped it open, scanned for the information in question. "Stephen Kesey. He's got a few bumps in county jails on his sheet over the last dozen years or so. Assaults. Breaking and entering." He glanced up to meet Cait's gaze. "He's had no fewer than a dozen forestry violations in the last five years." Returning to study his notebook, he continued, "And then there's Bart Lockwood. Dishonorable discharge from the military for drug use. Convicted for manslaughter and served sixteen years in Folsom before being paroled six years ago. Given the dates of his forestry violations, he's been around ever since."

Drumming her fingers on the counter, Andrews muttered, "From the looks of our call logs, we've got a hell of a lot more than two roamers in the area."

Barnes nodded. His mustache, Cait noted, was taking its sweet time to thicken. Right now it bore a sandy-colored resemblance to Hitler's. "But none that have anything more serious than pot possession on their record."

The sheriff lifted a shoulder and glanced at Cait. "You say you're free here?"

"There's nothing Kristy can't take care of for now."

"Good." The woman started moving toward the door. "Mitch and his men will continue going through the violations list. We need to start a search for Kesey and Lockwood. I'll have Deputy Simms try to round up a forestry agent to form another team. He can get in touch with Sharper to split the area each team will cover. I'll arrange to have Sharper meet you at the General Store at McKenzie Bridge around eight A.M. That work for you?"

Despite the abrupt sink to her stomach, Cait replied, "That's fine."

"Give you a chance to collect more soil samples." The sheriff's expression went grim as she looked at her deputy meaningfully. "And none of this gets out." She waved toward the computer screen. "Can you imagine the press if they got hold of this story? For right now, Cait's most recent finding doesn't leave this room." When the man nodded his understanding, her gaze went to Cait. "Your assistant . . ."

"Is well versed in the need for confidentiality," Cait assured her levelly. "But I'll remind her."

"Good." She started to move away, then paused, looking at the paintings on the computer screen again. "Never seen anything like it. Have you?"

Cait's eyes returned to the image. "No. I've never seen anything like this."

———

Just look at them.

Indulgently, he watched his pets cover the dried roadkill deer carcass as they went to work. Such simple creatures, really, born only to feed and reproduce. But they did their job with such chilling thoroughness he could never help but be fascinated.

The large box he'd built for them was framed, with three sides of Plexiglas. The top of the structure was made of screen, with another sheet of Plexiglas laid on top that he could move to regulate the humidity inside the enclosure. He added to the substrate on the bottom frequently to give his pets a place to pupate. He estimated his colony at several hundred thousand now, because when he loved something, he took the best of care of it.

He could spend hours, his face pressed up against the glass, watching their progress. He fancied they worked as a tiny team, legs and mouths moving in unison to achieve a common purpose. People should demonstrate that level of cooperation. That sort of single-mindedness.

But it had been his experience that most people disappointed in the end.

Take his guest in the cellar. He tapped gently on the corner to encourage a beetle crawling there to return to the feast or miss out. The woman had grown really quite unpleasant. He'd never gotten used to the foul language used by some women these days. His mother had always been a lady, minding her tongue and only opening her mouth when she had something kind or helpful to say. She'd died when he was nine, but he remembered her perfectly.

Not like the childhood memories he worked so hard to forget.

He checked his watch. Sometimes he lost track of time watching his beloved pets. Hours would pass like minutes. Rising, he gave one last look at the beetles and moved reluctantly away. He'd check their progress in the morning, first light. He had to return to his workroom. Finish inking the drawing he'd started for the nasty lady in the next room. The sooner it was finished, the sooner he could be rid of her.

She wasn't deserving, of course. Few of them were. But there was a right way and a wrong way to do anything, and unfortunately, the right way often took the most effort.

Swiftly he crossed the yard and entered his house through the back door. He locked it behind him before heading toward the cellar. But before he even got across the room, there was a knock at the door.

Picking up the pistol, he shoved it in his waistband at the base of his back, beneath his shirt. Then he hooked the curtain over the window of the front door with his finger, peeked outside.

His heart stopped. Then it started again like a locomotive picking up steam, barreling down the track. He unlocked the door, swung it open. "Hey, long time no see." The tone just right. Casual. No telling who could be listening. Watching. "C'mon in."

But when Sweetie walked in the door and after it was closed and locked, he opened his arms wide. "Gimme some sugar, baby."

"We need to talk." The words were muffled against his

mouth, but the lips, those soft wonderfully curved lips, were eager under his. Minutes later, much too soon, the two of them parted.

"What's this?" Sweetie's hand tapped the pistol in the back of his pants. "Expecting trouble?"

"Mm-hmm. Found it, too." He couldn't keep the idiotic grin off his face. Unexpected surprises like this were the best kind. "How long can you stay?"

"Not very."

Disappointment lodged in his throat. But he didn't voice it. Sweetie always got emotional when he asked for more. *Someday*. The oft-repeated promise sounded in his mind. *Soon*.

"God, when I got back to town and heard about the cops hauling those bodies out of Castle Rock, I totally freaked. What do they know? What have you heard?"

"I watched the press conference today. Don't worry, the cops don't have any leads. I didn't leave them anything to go on."

"So you say."

The words wounded, but he knew there was no malice in them. Sweetie was the excitable sort. He was the calm one in this relationship.

"How was the trip with the kids?" He had to ask. Had to pretend that he cared, that every moment Sweetie spent away from him wasn't torture.

"Oh, you know what kids are like on vacation."

He didn't actually, but gave a smile anyway. He tried to be satisfied with the stolen moments they could have together like this. But it was knowing that someday they'd be together forever that sustained him.

Sweetie slipped away and walked into the living room, falling onto the couch heavily. "I'm exhausted. It's been a very long day. And I'll be missed in another half hour or so."

"Poor baby." He wished he had something to offer, even a beer. But he hadn't been to the store for a couple weeks. He was kicking himself now. This was no way to entertain the love of his life.

"No skulls, I heard." There was an unmistakable note of worry in the words. "I know I've always left the disposal to you, but why didn't they find any skulls?"

His gaze slid away from the expectant look fixed on him. "Insurance. It's much harder to identify a skeleton without the skull. Trust me on that."

"They aren't going to find the heads later, are they? I hope there won't be any other surprises cropping up?"

His attention snapped back. Was that disapproval in Sweetie's tone? "No. They won't find the skulls. It's a bitch that they found the bodies, but there's not a thing on those bones that could lead back to either one of us. I can tell you the whole process if you want. You never wanted to know the details before, but if you've changed your mind . . ."

The slight shudder was his answer. "No. I don't have the stomach for it. You know that."

A rush of tenderness filled him. He did know it. And being the strong one, the one to take care of the messy part, always made him feel protective.

He pushed out of his chair to go to the couch. Sank down on it. "Everything's going to be fine." He lifted his hand to stroke away the concern from the face he loved so much.

"What about the other one I brought you? The news said only seven sets of remains were brought out of the cave."

He gave a moment's thought to the woman in the basement. Sweetie would be livid to know she was still alive. "Everything's taken care of." It *was*. The bag of bones was disposed of and the woman . . . his bugs would be feasting on her very soon. But there was a right way to do these things. He alone knew what it was. Just as he knew that Sweetie would never understand.

"Good." The word was spoken on a stream of relief. "I didn't doubt you. I know you'll never let me down."

"I won't." He leaned forward to press his lips to that soft well-formed mouth and felt a familiar clutch of need in his gut.

"I have to go in a few minutes." But the muffled voice was weak.

And he knew what the words really meant. Didn't he always know what was going on in that sexy mind? Swiftly he undid buttons and zippers and lowered them both to a lying position.

"That gives us plenty of time."

———————

Sharper's vehicle was already in the lot when Cait pulled up to the General Store. But before joining him, she took a minute to dial Detective Drecker's number in Seattle. Unsurprised to get his voice mail, she left a brief message. "Detective, I can't explain now, but ask Recinos's mother whether these items were meaningful to her daughter—ballet, skis, fish, gum, computer, picture frame, and convertible." She rattled off the list without thinking twice. Her memory never failed her. Her sense of direction was another story.

She disconnected, already second-guessing herself. The images painted on the scapula of female C were pretty generic. They could have meaning for a lot of people without it signifying a connection to the bones they'd found.

But they'd all have to have more than a superficial meaning for the victim, unless the pictures held symbolism for only the UNSUB. And the sooner they found out which, the quicker she could finalize her behavioral profile.

Locking her SUV, she strode toward Sharper's vehicle. Her pace was in contrast to the reluctance pooling in her gut. After their last meeting, she wasn't overly anxious to see him again.

She was even less anxious to let him know he'd gotten to her. On any level.

Yanking open the passenger door of his Trailblazer, she climbed in and buckled up. "Sharper," she said, by way of greeting.

He barely grunted in response as he shifted the vehicle into gear and pulled slowly out onto the highway. "This is a fucking needle in a haystack. You know that don't you?"

Irrationally, his disgruntled tone had something inside her

relaxing. "I've been fine, thanks. How about you? Had that chip surgically removed from your shoulder yet?"

One corner of his mouth lifted, but his profile remained steely. "Smartass. Hope you've got comfortable boots on. We're going to be doing a helluva lot of walking. The Willamette Forest covers over a million and a half acres."

"Luckily for you I'm only interested in half of that." She smirked when he gave her a quick sideways glance. "Or less." She unfolded a map to smooth it across her thighs and studied it while he drove. "We'll start with a five-mile radius around Castle Rock. Then we can widen the radius if needed. The way I understand it, there aren't state or national parks in the area."

"No, but there are parks with campsites, which fall under the jurisdiction of the Forest Service."

Which is where Barnes had gotten his information. "We're looking for two individuals who have a long list of violations with the Forest Service."

"You want to track down every single person who's run afoul of them, you're going to have to find another guide. I don't have that kind of time."

Ignoring him, she went on. "From what I've heard, these guys live in the forest year-round. Maybe you've run across them yourself on hiking tours you've arranged."

It was impossible to see his eyes behind the mirrored glasses he wore. "I don't lead all the tours. I've got employees. And most of the ones I do are on the river."

She restrained the urge to grit her teeth, a common reaction when she was with him. "You live around here. You spend a lot of time in the area." But when she told him the names, he merely lifted a shoulder.

"Like I say, this is pointless. There are lots of people who drop out. Who live off the land because they just want to be left the hell alone. And these type of people are transient."

"And you're the best tracker in the area, or so I'm told. Who better to find them?" She folded up the map she was studying and pulled out the one from NRCS. Hopefully she'd be able to combine two tasks and get some soil samples while they were trailing down these two.

"And when we do find them?"

When, she noted, not *if*. "Then I'll have a few questions to ask them."

"Sounds like a stupid idea to me. You can't believe one of these guys dumped those bodies. Who are they going to come in contact with, living the way they do? Locals and tourists." He slowed, and turned right onto an unmaintained dirt road. Another logging road? "If there had been locals and tourists disappearing from the area, don't you think law enforcement would have heard about it?"

His reasoning was sound, as far as it went. She looked out the window, noting the way the trees crowded the road. "If they're living in the forest most of the time, they might have seen something; ever think of that?"

"If they did, they won't want to talk about it." He eased the Trailblazer to the side of the narrow road and turned off the ignition. "These sorts live the way they do for a reason. They aren't your typical Joe Citizen. And they probably aren't going to like cops."

She gave him a blinding smile. "I'm not exactly a cop. And I'm very persuasive." Getting out of the vehicle, she stopped for a moment to shoulder the pack she'd brought.

Sharper shrugged into his own before rounding the front of the car and joining her. "Listen."

His voice stopped her as she was about to plunge into the forest. Quizzically, she turned her head to look at him over her shoulder. His uneasy expression piqued her interest. But his words dampened it even more quickly. "About last time. When I found you at my place . . ."

Her stomach gave a quick violent twist. "Forget it." There was no way she was going any further down *that* road with him. She turned to scan the area, saw what was likely an abandoned logging trail leading into the forest. "I've got old DMV photos of both the men we're looking for. Even considering the aging process, I'm pretty sure I'll recognize them if we find them."

"And what're you going to do then, shoot them?" He lifted a derisive brow at her pointed look. "Think I can't tell when someone's carrying? Lower back, under your shirt."

Cait eyed him more carefully. Special ops, she reminded herself. It wouldn't do to forget that training of his. "Behave yourself and I won't be tempted to pull my weapon."

He snorted, and brushed by her to take the lead. "You ever pull a gun on me, Slim, better be prepared to use it. You won't get a second chance."

His tone held that cocky arrogance she'd so quickly grown to loathe.

Trouble was, she was pretty sure that arrogance was well deserved.

––––––––

Cait wasn't sure how many miles they covered before they happened upon another person. At least three, by her estimation. And he appeared to be a hiker. At least she didn't see a campsite in the vicinity.

The man raised a hand in a halfhearted wave and would have gone by if Cait hadn't greeted him. "Hi. Mind if I ask you a couple questions?"

The stranger turned his head. It looked as though a refusal was on his lips. She noted the instant it turned to something else. She squelched the instinctive flicker of distaste. A good investigator used whatever tool was available to do her job. And that's what her looks had always been, a tool. If they could help her in the course of an investigation, she was ruthless about using them. The same way a big brawny cop used his bulk to intimidate.

So she mustered an easy smile and closed the distance between them, pulling the ID she'd been issued by Andrews from where it was clipped to a strap on her pack. "Cait Fleming. Consultant for the Lane County Sheriff's Department." She flashed the ID, but the man barely glanced at it.

"Doug Gates." He looked at Sharper long enough to give him a nod before returning his gaze to Cait.

"I'm looking for a couple of men who might be in the vicinity." She slipped out of the pack to remove the pictures and handed them to him. "Have you seen either of them around?"

Gates peered at the pictures for a few moments, shook his head. Giving them back, he said, "I've only been in the area since yesterday. My family is camping about a mile west of here. My wife and two teenage daughters." His face took on a pained expression. "I needed a break, you know? Felt like I was drowning in an estrogen pool."

Ignoring Sharper's sound of sympathy behind her, Cait asked, "Pretty spot. What made you choose it? Are you familiar with the area?"

"Oh sure, been here plenty of times. I'm from Salem but grew up in Springfield. Every vacation I can recall when I was a kid involved camping." He sent an aggrieved look in the direction of his camp. "Don't remember bitching the whole time about it, either."

"Guess it takes a lot more these days to keep kids entertained."

But her words seemed lost on him. The man's eyes had gone wide behind his dark-framed glasses. "You're here about those bones they pulled out of Castle Rock, aren't you? I saw it on the news the other day."

"We're interested in talking to everyone who might have been in the area."

Gates grew more animated. Small wonder. The prospect of murder never failed to intrigue the general public. "My wife tried to talk me into going somewhere else after we saw that. 'It's not safe,' she said. I told her, 'Cops are going to be all over that area. What could be safer?'" He paused, as if awaiting her agreement.

"You should be safe enough if you take normal precautions. Enjoy your vacation."

As Gates continued on his way, Cait gave the pictures to Sharper and took a moment to secure her ID on the strap of her pack again. He glanced at them before handing them back to her, his face impassive.

"Driver's license photos aren't the best likenesses to go off of. Especially ones as out of date as these." He started walking again in the direction they'd been heading when they'd met up with Gates.

Interest hummed in her veins. "Maybe not. But you recognized them, didn't you? At least one of them." She'd identified the infinitesimal flicker in his gaze when he looked at the second photo. He knew the guy. Even if he'd claimed not to when she'd mentioned their names.

"What makes you say that?"

Cait grabbed his arm to halt him. And it irritated her to note that he stopped only because he chose to, not because her action slowed him appreciably. "I could tell. Quit making everything so damn difficult. Tell me how you know this guy." She held up the second photo again. The one he'd hesitated over.

"I don't know him." He stepped easily around the pile of moss-covered rocks, his gait swift and sure. "But I've seen him before."

"The second one?" she pressed. "Lockwood?"

"We haven't been formally introduced," Sharper returned testily. "He's usually around the area. Sometimes I'll see him over the course of the summer and fall a couple times. He's not always fussy about where he sets up camp."

Cait dodged the low-hanging branch of the fir in front of her. "Meaning you've found him on your property?"

Sharper turned to fix her with a look. "Trespassers can be a pain in the ass." His meaning was clear enough. He hadn't yet forgiven her uninvited visit to his land. "Campfires can get out of control, and I don't open the area to hunters, either. But people don't always know they've left the forest and passed over onto private property. Once they're told they're usually good about moving on."

"And you've moved Lockwood on before?"

"Once. A couple years ago. You're wasting your time. He's just the type of guy who wants to be left the hell alone."

And Sharper, Cait reflected as she slipped the photos in the zippered compartment of her pack, sounded as if he understood that desire. "These areas you've seen him in. Are they around here?"

He stared at her for a moment, his whiskey-colored eyes narrowed in annoyance. "Like I say, it's a waste—"

"It's less of a waste of time if we have specific places to look than if we just canvass this entire part of the forest," she pointed out. "Of course, maybe you've decided you'd rather spend time with me than with your business." She sent him an innocent smile, one he returned with a glower.

"There are a few specific places I can think of."

Spying a large flat rock, Cait halted. "Take a look at this." By the time he'd turned and come back to her she had the soil map spread out before her. "These areas I've marked with red are in the same general vicinity of our location, right?"

He bent down to study the map for a moment. "Within a few miles anyway."

"Good." She folded the paper back up and shoved it into her pack. "I'll want to get soil samples from those places as we come upon them."

When she was ready to move out again, he remained still. "Because of the sulfur. You said you found sulfur on the bones."

She had, in fact, been very careful not to say anything at all. "Did I?"

The familiar impatience was back in his expression. "Well, did you or didn't you? You're also looking for sites where there are hot springs, right?"

"Not necessarily." At least not anymore. She was going to turn her interest to acidic soils without hot springs in the vicinity and see if they provided closer matches.

His gaze narrowed. "A few of these people who camp year-round will sneak onto campgrounds and use the water and facilities. But most of them, though, don't care much about those kind of niceties."

She nodded her understanding, wondered where he was going with this. "I suppose they could always clean up in the river if they have to."

His smile was genuinely amused. It softened his face. On a less irritating man, it might change his looks from merely attractive to devastating. "Doubtful. The McKenzie is usually forty-five to fifty degrees. But there are plenty of smaller hot springs on the edge of the river. Less well known. Tourists wouldn't go looking for them, but lots of locals might know about them."

"And so might roamers," she murmured, consideringly.

He looked impatient with her interruption. "What I'm saying is, you might want to check out springs closer to the river. An isolated spot at river's edge would be a good place for a kill."

Chapter 8

Zach didn't note Cait's reaction. Not then. An all too familiar sense of detachment had settled over him. "You get close to the water, preferably where there are animal trails leading down to it. Shows there will be traffic when they come down to the river to drink. The news didn't say how the victims were killed, but a blood spill is messy. Where better to do it than at water's edge? What blood you aren't able to wash away, the animals would clean up. The rain would take care of anything they missed. Wash it right into the river."

It wasn't until he caught her expression that he considered how his words would sound. Dark humor twisted through him. If those soil samples Cait had taken from his property matched whatever the hell she was looking for, his words would sound pretty damning.

But chances were if those soil samples had been a match, the gorgeous model-turned-consultant would have returned to Whispering Pines for another unannounced visit. This time bringing a search warrant and cuffs.

Her expression had eased, shifting to mere interest. "An

intriguing possibility. But he'd still have to transport the body to that cave on Castle Rock."

He gave a short laugh. Wondered if she were used to dealing with morons or if her reaction was specific to him. "Who do you think you're talking to? I've made that climb, remember? More than once. It's highly unlikely that anyone did that trip no fewer than seven times with a body on his back. Not to mention then having to haul it into that cave and to the chamber. Those bodies were bones before they ever got dumped there."

Her smile was grim. "Given this a lot of thought, have you, Sharper?"

Soberly, he nodded, still surveying her. "Not much else to do when the whole thing is screwing up my routine. Still can't figure why the killer would move the bodies after they'd decomposed. Seems like a lot of extra unnecessary effort."

She was good. Damn good. Her expression didn't change a fraction. Maybe she'd had practice holding a mask in place all those years spent before a camera.

"How would you have done it?"

He shrugged and turned to move again. "I wouldn't have bothered with the cave. What's the point? If it'd been me, I'd have buried them. Deep enough that the animals would leave them alone. There are lots of isolated areas of the forest. But the killer didn't do that. So maybe he found a place close to the water, like I said. Gutted the victims and stripped the flesh off the bones, leaving it for the animals to carry off."

"Interesting theory." Her tone gave away nothing.

Zach scanned the area for a moment before choosing a direction away from the trails in the area. She was decent enough at keeping up, he thought grudgingly. Okay, more than decent. But she was going to find the men she was seeking in out-of-the-way areas, far from other campers and tourists.

"So in your scenario, what happens to the skulls?"

He kicked aside a pinecone as big as his foot and slanted a look at her. "I'm not sure. Makes sense that he'd want to slow identification." This climate was far removed from that of Afghanistan, but he thought the same general principles would apply.

However, it seemed smarter, under the circumstances, to refrain from going into detail. "Maybe hiding the skeleton separate from the skull is just a way to be careful. Because people like you"—and it still blew him away that she'd acquired this sort of skill—"you can reconstruct a face from a skull, right? So it makes sense that the killer would do what he can to prevent that."

"You're thinking of forensic artists," she said dryly. "But yeah, I've been involved in the three-dimensional facial reconstruction process several times. Any other thoughts?"

He doubted she was all that concerned with his ideas about her case. She'd certainly been closed-mouthed about it. But something made him say, "Yeah. Dumping the bones in that cave makes me think this guy is local. Or else he used to be."

He felt her eyes on his back, like a green laser heating the skin beneath his black T-shirt.

"Why do you say that?"

Smooth. He had to give her that. Asked a lot of questions but damn sure gave no information away. Zach gave a mental shrug. She could keep her secrets. All he cared about at this point was getting this time over with so he'd no longer be on Andrews's leash.

"I can see someone dumping a body far from home. But if I were driving across state, or even from a neighboring town, I wouldn't go to so much trouble to get rid of the bones. I'm already going to believe they can't be traced back to me. Dump them in a remote area and let the animals carry them off. If I hear on the news that they've found some of the bones, choose another remote area in the state. God knows we've got plenty of them."

She said nothing to that and he made no further move to fill the silence. He'd already said enough as it was. Too much when you considered she'd been on his property, uninvited, trying to match the soil samples to whatever the hell she'd found on those bones.

Jesus. And to think he used to be known as the man with the knack for being in the right place at the right time.

Nothing about discovering those bags in the cave came close to qualifying as good timing.

They walked for well over four hours. After he told her that camping was allowed in some of the campgrounds for up to two weeks, Cait insisted on speaking to all the people in those areas. Which gave him time to relieve himself, but didn't pay off in any other way, from what he could tell. He cooled his heels while she spoke to everyone in the area, including the camp host. Showed the pictures around. And learned nothing of value.

Not that the process didn't generate some excitement. He watched derisively as the men in the area tripped all over themselves to be cooperative. Teenage boys were just as bad. Worse, probably, given the way the two punks in muscle shirts were edging closer to where she stood.

But she handled them, he noted reluctantly. Men and women alike were subjected to the same questions, delivered in the same crisp professional tone. Because he had no better way to pass the time, he watched.

She was an enigma. One that grew increasingly fascinating the more time he spent with her.

———

Cait's feet were weeping by the time Sharper pulled into the parking lot of the General Store and slowed to a stop next to her vehicle. It was after seven. They'd continued their trek the last couple hours after Zach had called one of his employees and given him a pick-up location.

"Same time tomorrow?" She slung her pack over one arm and looked across the seat at him. Five o'clock shadow shaded his jaw, but if he shared her bone-deep exhaustion, it didn't show.

"We can make it earlier if you can get up here from Eugene sooner in the morning. Cover more ground that way."

She was certain her smile was pained. "Maybe I'll stay in

the area tonight." She'd brought some changes of clothes thinking it was time to start mixing in a bit with the locals. Asking some questions. Listening to their conversations. But her major motivation at this point was to shave her commute time. The trip from Eugene was forty-five minutes. That was three quarters of an hour longer she could stay in bed.

"Good luck."

She arched a brow. "Why do you say that?"

He lifted a shoulder. "Reservations fill up around here fast with tourists. Chances are you won't find a room."

"I won't know until I try." She eyed him speculatively, wondering if it were her imagination that made him seem anxious to be rid of her. In the next moment, he put the vehicle into gear, providing her answer.

"Whatever. See you here at six A.M."

Wincing inwardly, Cait nodded and got out, heading to her car. Once she found a room, she'd soak her feet for an hour. Becoming aware of a twinge in her thigh, she mentally recalculated. She'd use that hour to soak her entire body. She could place a call to Kristy first and get an update before contacting Barnes.

Then she'd go out and mingle with the locals. There was a time for asking questions, and a time simply to listen. There was often insight to be had by hearing the locals' perspective on a case.

———

"You're lucky." The woman behind the front desk of the McKenzie Motel wore a nametag with Nancy written on it and a tired smile. She handed Cait the key to her room. "Usually this time of year we're booked up, most every day of the week."

"So you've been getting some cancellations?"

The woman blew out an exasperated breath. "Are we! Seems like all I've done today is answer the phone. And that press conference yesterday didn't help. Now that everyone in the state heard about what's being going on around here, we're going to get even more cancellations. Most aren't that interested to come to a place where they're liable to trip over human bones."

A few of the campground hosts had said much the same. The sites were at half vacancy, rather than the nearly full occupancy that was the norm. Cait offered her a commiserating smile. "Well, once this is over the tourists will be back."

"Maybe. But we can't recoup the business lost, can we?" Nancy shook back her shoulder-length dark hair and leaned forward to whisper conspiratorially, "I can't even really blame them. I haven't been in the forest since I heard about what the sheriff's department brought out of that cave. It's scary, you know? I make my husband drive over and pick me up when I close the front office at ten, and we live in the rooms at the end of the motel lot. That's how creeped out I am."

Which maybe meant she wasn't going to be able to speak to as many residents as she'd hoped, Cait thought. When people were spooked, they tended to stay inside with the doors and windows locked. "So is the town going to be pretty well rolled up early tonight?"

"Might be fewer people around, but the businesses are still operating as usual. Do you only have the one bag? Need any help with it?" When Cait shook her head, Nancy seamlessly switched back to her earlier topic. "JD's seems to go strong, regardless. That's a combination bar slash Internet café slash restaurant. Nothing special on the menu, just bar food, but it's pretty good. Mullens and Tito's are two nicer restaurants here on Main Street. Just steer clear of Ketchers's tavern. It can get pretty rough after midnight."

"Thanks." Cait sent her a smile and picked up her bag. "I'll remember that."

The room was small and plain, but it boasted a full tub and plenty of hot water. She soaked for half the hour she'd promised herself before dragging herself out of the tub and hurriedly getting dressed. A meal could wait. There was still enough daylight to get a look at the town. Her stomach protested the plan as she slipped out the door and headed down the hall. The veggie sandwich she'd packed for lunch was a dim memory.

As she walked out of the motel, she pulled out her cell and called Kristy. The tech answered on the third ring.

"Where are you? Do I need to send a search party?"

"Not necessary." Cait got into the SUV, started it, and pulled out of the lot. "I'm spending the night in McKenzie Bridge. That way I can get an earlier start tomorrow."

There was a moment of silence. Then, "You're spending the night . . . alone?"

It took less than a minute to find Main Street. Cait pulled over to the curb and got out, locking the door and heading for the sidewalk. "Of course alone. Who else would I be spending it with?"

The main thoroughfare was lined with shops and restaurants. Although there wasn't much traffic on the street, there were people still moving about, making her wonder what exactly was opened at this time of the evening.

"Well, you did say you'd be with that guide all day. Sharper. I thought maybe you decided to scratch an itch while you were up there."

Cait held the phone out in front of her and contemplated it for a moment. It frequently astounded her how brilliant her tech's mind could be in the lab filled as it was with constant thoughts of sex. Resuming the conversation, she replied dryly, "The only itch I'm likely to encounter will be related to poison ivy. So far I've successfully avoided that." She stepped aside so the young couple walking toward her strolling a toddler could get by on the sidewalk.

"Oh." There was a pout in the woman's voice. "So what's the town like?"

Cait looked around before answering. "Picturesque." Surrounded as it was by hills blanketed by forests, it was scenic. The bridge she'd driven over to get to the motel was quaint, its sign proclaiming that the site had been served by a covered bridge since 1890. It looked like a place only minimally touched by outside influence.

It didn't look like a town that housed a serial killer.

She was reminded of Sharper's words.

Dumping the bones in that cave makes me think this guy is local. Or else he used to be.

It was odd to hear him verbalize the same thought she'd voiced to the sheriff. Of course she'd been going on the UN-SUB's familiarity with the area. Sharper had added a different twist; why the offender had bothered with the cave in the first place. It had been an intriguing idea and one that bore further contemplation, especially as she began developing her profile.

". . . and so then I thought, what the heck and I just threw all the bones in for an overnight chlorine bleach soak."

Her focus snapped back to her cell phone conversation. "What?"

"Thought that would get your attention. You called me, remember?" Kristy complained. "The least you could do is listen."

"I'm listening now." Cait walked briskly down the wide sidewalk, looking into store windows. Of course her tech knew better than to bleach the bones. But she'd found a jarringly effective way of jolting Cait's attention back to her.

"I got four of the specimens cleaned today. First I went over them all one more time with the UV lamp to be sure we didn't miss anymore artwork from our creepazoid. I can get the rest of them done tomorrow."

"You'll be happy to know I'll be bringing you more soil samples when I return."

"Whatever."

Cait's brows rose at the woman's careless remark. "You've changed your tune." She strode swiftly by the Hair Emporium, a place called The Sweet Shoppe, and an antique store. Of the three, only the hair salon was still open.

"I want to stay busy," Kristy corrected her. "And tomorrow when I finish cleaning the bones I'm going to be at loose ends."

"Don't forget to update the photo log. And I'll try to find a way to get the samples to you tomorrow. You haven't heard any more about the lab tests on the garbage bags, have you?"

"Are you kidding? Barnes doesn't talk to me."

She thought—she was almost certain—that she heard the murmur of a man's voice in the background. Kristy was probably with the ME again. Cait hoped the man realized that he was going to be dropped without a backward glance when this case was over. Kristy was cheerfully promiscuous. She had no interest in forming lasting relationships.

Not that Cait had a better history in *that* particular area.

"Give me a call if anything crops up. Otherwise I'll talk to you tomorrow." Disconnecting, she dropped the cell phone in her purse and continued down the sidewalk. There were several cars around an ice cream shop she passed by, along with diners sitting at scattered tables on the walk outside the store. The requisite storefronts housing local accountants and lawyers. There were more gift shops than she would have believed one small town could sustain, their windows filled with crafts from local artisans, according to the signs. Glassware, pottery, artwork, candles, baskets . . . apparently the area housed many people of talent. Which Cait found more than a little amazing, since the craftiest thing she could do was braid her own hair.

Her interest turned to speculation. If the perp was a local, maybe some of his artwork could be found in one of the craft stores, either here or in a surrounding area. It may be a possibility to follow up on later.

She crossed the street ahead of two young boys barreling toward her on bikes. Their shouts of excitement brought a smile to her face. She'd had a bike once. It had been bright pink with streamers on the handlebars and training wheels on the back. A distant memory flickered, of her father holding on to the back of it as she wobbled her way down the driveway and then back up again.

But once she'd outgrown that one, there had never been another. That was only one of the many changes that had occurred after her father's death. Her mother had been too concerned about possible falls and resulting breaks . . . or worse, scrapes and scars that would limit her chances of attracting a top modeling agent.

Shrugging off the edge of melancholy that accompanied the thought, she stopped dead in front of a storefront that advertised a very different sort of business. A glassy-eyed fox peered out at her, one paw lifted, as if in midmovement. A ferocious-looking black bear stood in the back, teeth bared. There was also a mink, a bobcat, and the full skeleton of what might be an otter.

Adrenaline hummed in her veins. Cait stepped back a few steps, far enough to read the faded splintered sign above the shop. AL'S TAXIDERMY.

She studied the door. If Al kept regular hours, they weren't posted. Still, she could ask around and figure the best way to talk to him. As she'd told the sheriff and deputy, many taxidermists regularly used dermestids to clean their animal skeletons. It would be interesting to discover if Al kept a colony of the bugs.

The storefronts cast long shadows on the streets. Night was edging in. And while there were still occasional cars cruising by, most of the activity seemed to surround the restaurants Nancy had mentioned. Cait headed back toward her vehicle. It'd be full dark when she finished eating. And she was suddenly reminded that she was ravenous.

When she got to King Road, she looked up the street toward the covered bridge, slowing when she saw the man standing before it. He appeared to be holding a sketchpad, his head bent over his work. Without further thought, she veered from her course and headed toward him.

He didn't look up as she approached, and Cait stopped a few yards behind him to observe his progress. It was a better-than-decent rendering of the bridge, but rather than capturing the quaint, turn-of-the-century look, the sketch made it look eerie, somehow. A place of secrets and shadows with a vaguely sinister air.

"So what do you think?" The man never shifted his gaze from the scene and the pad before him, but Cait was the only one in the vicinity. Obviously she wasn't as practiced as Sharper at moving silently.

"I don't know anything about art."

"That, my dear, is a cop out. I asked for your opinion, not what you know. They come from two different places." His hand moved expertly over the page as he added more shading. "One from the gut and the other from the head. Listen to your gut."

"It's . . ." She searched for a description that wouldn't offend him. "Sort of creepy."

He looked up then and sent her a quick satisfied smile over his shoulder. "Exactly. Not the kind of scene to grace the front of postcards. But evocative in an altogether different way, hopefully." He lowered his pencil and turned toward her. "I'm Jeffrey Russo, by the way. And you are the young lady hired by the sheriff's department to help investigate those bones pulled out of Castle Rock. Caitlin Fleming."

The statement caught her off guard. "A psychic as well as an artist. A man of many talents."

He gave her a self-deprecating smile, a twinkle in his hazel eyes. "I wish I could claim to be either one. What I am is a professor of art history, recently retired from the University of Oregon in Eugene. And a conduit for local gossip. Your name and description have been bandied about by some around here in the know."

Cait studied him. If he was retired, he must have done so at a fairly early age because he looked shy of sixty. His hair was gray, as was the short neat mustache whose fullness Deputy Barnes would envy. She wondered if the long ponytail he wore had been grown since his retirement. He was dressed a shade more formally than other locals she'd come into contact with, in crisp khaki pants and a button-down shirt and sandals. She had no trouble picturing him in a tweed jacket with leather at the elbows, lecturing in front of a class of two hundred.

Although she'd very much like to follow up on the source of the information about her, she figured she'd discover that on her own. She had more pressing questions for the professor.

Nodding toward his sketchpad, she said, "If you live around here, I'm sure you have plenty of sketches of the bridge. It seems to be a focal point in the area."

Flipping his sketchbook shut, he inclined his head. "You're right, of course. The trick is to look at a familiar scene in a whole new light. Isn't that what an investigator does when he or she looks at evidence?"

"We try to." It was a bit disconcerting to be greeted with such familiarity by a stranger. "Do you live here in town?"

"Blue River." He crouched to stow his sketching pencil in a leather bag at his feet. "A recent transplant, actually. I promised Candi—my fiancée—a retirement retreat once I stopped teaching. We found a place on the McKenzie that suited us and bought it the day after I handed in my resignation. We're still getting acquainted with the area. She has the idea that she'd like to open a little shop, with unique pieces from local artisans, but that's in the consideration stage at this point." He rose, slung the strap of the bag over his shoulder. "I can't see the point of retiring only to immediately jump into something else that's going to tie us down."

"Well, McKenzie Bridge certainly seems to have several similar stores, so if sheer number means anything, it may well succeed." She nodded to his sketchpad. "Would I find any of your work in the local shops?"

He gave a wide smile that managed to be amused and charming at the same time. "Doubtful. But there is a gallery in Portland that does quite a nice little business for me selling my works. As a matter of fact, I have a showing midfall." He cocked his head, studying her dispassionately. "I don't suppose I could convince you to pose for me."

God, no. She managed, barely, to keep the instinctive response from her lips. "Sorry."

There was a glimmer of regret in his eyes. "That's a pity. Here." He dug in the bag for a few moments until he withdrew a business card and handed it to her. "In case you change your mind."

Although she had no intention on doing so, she took it and slipped it into her jeans pocket. "Are you familiar with any of the artists in the area?"

"A few." He raised a casual hand as a red BMW convertible slowed to a stop near them. "Many of them also display their work at country fairs in the area. We have some quite good amateurs around. A few even better than that, waiting to be discovered. If you're interested in purchasing some artwork, I'd be glad to advise you."

The blonde woman getting out of the car was a good fifteen years Russo's junior. Pretty in a polished sort of way that Cait used to be all too familiar with.

"Darling, I hope I didn't leave you too long." Although her words were directed at her fiancé, her gaze was on Cait as she rounded the hood of the car toward them. "Natasha called and had to tell me all about the summer reading program Maya enrolled her in."

Russo's expression lightened. "Candi, this is Caitlin Fleming." To Cait he explained, "Natasha is my oldest granddaughter. I have three, ages six, four, and two. As a matter of fact, we just finished spending several days with them while their parents were on a business trip. We're still recuperating."

"I can imagine." But truthfully she couldn't. She'd never spent much time around kids. Hadn't been one herself since she'd been eight.

A more pressing thought occurred to her. "How difficult is it to look at a piece of art and identify the artist? Or at least match an artist to another piece of work he or she has created?"

Russo scratched his jaw. "Well, there are experts in the art world whose only job is to authenticate artwork, of course. But it's quite an involved process, from what I gather. There are excellent forgeries floating around. It's always an embarrassment when a well-known auction house gets caught selling one, although that's increasingly rare these days."

Her mind was racing. "But it's possible to find a painting and link the artist to another piece of work he did, isn't it?"

"Oh, of course. There's a body of experts who do nothing else."

"Darling, I so hate to interrupt you . . ." Candi gave Cait a regretful smile. "But we are expected at the Meechums for drinks shortly."

The professor looked at his watch and said with a note of

surprise in his voice, "So we are." He looked at Cait and his smile lit up his eyes. "It was a pleasure, Ms. Fleming. Perhaps we'll run into each other again."

Accepting the hand he held out, Cait shook it. "I hope we do."

He walked to the car then paused, hand on the door handle, to ask, "Can we drop you anywhere?"

She shook her head. "My vehicle is parked down the street, thanks."

Absently she returned his wave as the car pulled away, but her mind was racing furiously. Raiker would have access to forensic art experts, if she happened upon another piece of work done by the UNSUB. Of course, first she'd have to recognize similarities in the work if she discovered it.

It seemed a long shot. But no more so than some of the other leads she was following in this case.

Walking briskly in the direction of her SUV, Cait pulled out her cell and placed a call to Barnes. When she got his voice mail, she left him a message to call her back. It would be nice to find out that his day had been more productive than hers had been.

In the end she chose JD's over either of the other two restaurants because of the throng of cars parked around it. Cait pushed open the front door of the low brick building, looking around curiously.

She was in a small lobby of sorts, with an empty hostess desk. The Internet café was on her right and a bar was on the left. The decorator had relied on a plentitude of polished pine planks, both for the floors and the walls. But the place was well lit, and the noise level wasn't deafening. After a cursory glance at the half-dozen people on the computer stations, she turned into the bar area.

The clack of balls sounded from an unseen pool table in the back corner. A large horseshoe-shaped bar dominated the room. Small tables were scattered in the rest of the available space, with about half of the seats filled. A harried-looking brunette was moving from table to table at a good clip, practiced smile firmly in place as she took orders, cleared away dishes, and mopped tabletops.

Bypassing the tables, Cait headed up to the bar, which was manned by a slight man with blond hair.

"Evening." He left the group of men clustered at the other end of the bar and headed toward her, swiping at the bar top as he went. "What can I get for you?"

"A Coors Light bottle and a menu." She pulled out a stool and sat, ignoring the group of men at the end of the bar who had stopped their conversation and swiveled in her direction.

"Easy enough." His pale blue gaze was friendly and flirtatious as he handed her a menu from beneath the bar and grabbed a bottle, expertly unscrewing it and sliding it across to her. "Kitchen's open until ten, so you have plenty of time to order."

He moved away and she flipped open the plastic menu. A loud burst of masculine laughter sounded from the area where some men were playing pool. She flicked them an absent glance over the top of her menu.

And then froze, when she caught sight of an all too familiar figure bent over the table, lining up his shot.

Chapter 9

Shit. Cait's eyelids slid closed in disgust. True, Sharper hadn't irritated her as much as usual today, but somehow she didn't think it paid to push the issue. With a sense of resignation, she opened her eyes and surveyed him, a bit bemused to find him here. Somehow she hadn't pegged him as a social creature.

He stood out in the cluster of men around the table. Although all were dressed in jeans and T-shirts, a newcomer's eyes would immediately be drawn to him. It was that hardened edge that gilded his appearance, she decided. The one honed to razor sharpness by experiences others couldn't contemplate.

When her gaze would have lingered, she firmly looked away. Unlike her diminutive lab tech, she *was* discriminating when it came to men, although that trait had been acquired the hard way. She didn't date these days unless she met a man who didn't see her as a mirror, someone who only reflected his taste, his position, his social standing. And although Sharper didn't strike her as that sort of man, neither was he the safe, civilized sort she occasionally went out with.

There was something more than a little untamed about him, much like the wilderness he seemed so at home in. Something unpredictable and not quite civilized. He was the kind of man that raised every ounce of self-preservation instincts a woman had, even while he ignited interest of a different sort.

Cait had quite a healthy streak of self-preservation. She might have been a slow learner, but she'd discovered that touching fire invariably led to a singe, at the very least.

Sharper was definitely scorcher material.

Menu forgotten for the moment, she cast a thoughtful eye around the bar. Even if the UNSUB was a local, that didn't mean he'd live in McKenzie Bridge. He could be from Rainbow or Blue River. He could, she thought fatalistically, be from any one of a number of small towns dotting Highway 126.

It all kept circling around to one thing, though. The trouble he'd gone to stash those bones. Sharper had nailed it correctly. Why go to so much trouble if you didn't live in the immediate area?

The perp would be outdoorsy, she mused. In decent shape. The sets of remains ranged in weight from eighteen to twenty-five pounds. Not a particularly heavy bag to carry, but certainly unwieldy, especially when scaling Castle Rock at night. Her gaze traveled slowly around the space. The description would match most of the occupants in the bar. Certainly the group of men playing pool would qualify.

As would Sharper himself.

A shiver skittered down Cait's spine. She knew more about the man than she did anyone else in the area, including the sheriff and deputy she was working with. Knew he had familiarity with the surroundings. That he had knowledge of the cave prior to the discovery of the bodies. That he had acidic soil and hot springs on his property.

And that he very likely had the skills to break a person's neck, thanks to his time spent in the Rangers.

She tried—and failed—to picture him bent over a work-space for hours, patiently painting tiny pictures on a human scapula. It wasn't that she couldn't envision him as an artist, she thought darkly, though it would be a stretch. But she couldn't imagine him possessing the patience necessary for such detail. She'd seen little evidence of that particular trait in the time she'd spent with him.

She continued to scan the room. The two men playing darts in the corner would fit. As would three of the men still stealing surreptitious looks at her from the corner of the bar. Given the girth of one of them, though, he could be eliminated from consideration.

The waitress was slender. Not a likely candidate. Though from the occasional look she threw the bartender, she had the internal fortitude necessary to maim, if not kill.

"Made your decision yet?"

Cait glanced around to find the bartender leaning on the bar addressing her. And realized with a start that she hadn't more than glanced at the menu. "Sorry." She turned on her stool to face him. "What do you recommend?"

He used her question as an excuse to rake her form with his gaze. "You look like a salad type. We do a mean taco salad, but it's late. We use fresh produce, and if I were you, I wouldn't trust the lettuce."

His honesty surprised a smile from her. "Thanks for the tip."

He leaned farther across the bar to tap at the menu. "We do a decent flat-iron steak here. That's most popular. But you can't go wrong with the blackened chicken sandwich. Comes with steak fries or hashbrowns."

"I'll have the steak fries with it." Snapping the menu closed, she handed it to him, shoving aside the splinter of guilt stabbing through her. It had been a long time since she'd stopped counting calories and regarding food as the enemy. But damn if she could order potatoes of any kind without her mother's shriek of dismay sounding in her mind.

Of course, her mother's voice at any decibel had the power

to flay her nerves raw. She'd found putting a continent between them was the only sure way to maintain their already strained relationship.

The bartender scribbled her order down on a pad, then looked up, and raised his voice. "Joanie."

The waitress hurried over, her tone when she approached more than a little annoyed. "You're closer to the kitchen than I was, Del. Honestly." She snatched the order slip from him and sailed off to the kitchen's order counter, still muttering. Cait figured they were lucky not to be able to make out the rest of her words.

Del shot her a look. "You'll have to excuse my wife. We're short-handed, so she had to pull a double shift."

"So this is your place?" Cait tipped the bottle to her lips.

"Joanie's and mine." He made a grimace. "Well, actually her mother financed us, something she'll never let me live down. The Internet café is new, though. Joanie's pretty good with computers. Not everyone around here has Internet access, so we get lots of business, and not just from the resorts." He propped one elbow on the bar while he did a slow lazy swipe of the top with the damp rag in his free hand. "Whereabouts you staying?"

She briefly questioned the wisdom of answering then gave a mental shrug. It wasn't as though it would be difficult for someone to discover. And she wanted to keep the lines of communication open. Bartenders tended to know everything worth knowing about the patrons. It wouldn't hurt to find out what he had to say. "The McKenzie."

For some reason he looked a bit surprised at that. "Really? Well, they don't have access, so if you need it, we have reasonable prices . . ." His palm slapped the top of the bar. "Damn, it just hit me who you must be."

She raised a brow and took another sip from the bottle. "Who must I be?"

"You're the one working with the sheriff's department on those bones they found in the Castle Rock area, aren't you? Caitlin Fleming?" Without waiting for a response, he gave a disgusted shake of his head. "Saw the press conference yesterday." He jerked his head toward the TV behind the bar. "Andrews said they brought in a special consultant from some place out east, and well . . . some around here have been running at the mouth about you since you got here."

"That's odd, since I haven't met all that many people."

"Hey, Del, we need another round."

The man waved in the direction of the shout but never looked away from Cait. "Some have gotten a look at you, and that was enough." A lone masculine dimple winked when he smiled, managing to make his words seem harmlessly flirtatious. "About the most exciting thing that happens around here is when some tourist gets himself lost and a search party has to go out after him. This whole thing has everyone in the area buzzing."

"Del!"

"'Scuse me." His movements swift and sure, he worked the tap and reached for bottles in a manner that spoke of long practice. She watched him load a tray with the drinks, but her mind was elsewhere.

She hadn't seen the press conference herself, but she'd read a transcript of it online. Although the sheriff had mentioned hiring a consultant from Raiker Forensics, Cait's name had never been mentioned.

It was damn sure her description hadn't been.

So where was this information coming from? And did the gossip stop with her or were there more details being bandied about specific to the case? The former was merely annoying. But if it was the latter . . . she may have to let Barnes in on it.

"Blackened chicken sandwich and steak fries." A dinner basket was set before her on the bar. Joanie took wrapped silverware and a bottle of ketchup out of her apron pocket and set it next to the plate. Turning, she swiped the salt and pepper from the closest table and slid that close to Cait, as well. "Is there anything else I can get you?"

"This is fine, thanks." And from the looks of the slightly wilted lettuce leaf peeking out from beneath the bun, she was glad she'd taken the bartender's advice and foregone the salad. She shot the woman a commiserating look. "Long day, huh?"

Joanie's startled gaze met hers for a moment, before she gave a tight smile. "It shows?"

"Your husband said you'd been working all day."

The woman propped a hip against the next stool and nodded, her shoulder-length dark hair swinging with the motion. "I thought three kids kept me busy. I've been running myself ragged today. One waitress is out with the flu and the other just didn't show up. I could never do it on my own if business wasn't slower than normal right now."

"The lady at the motel said it had been slow all over."

Using her order pad to fan herself, Joanie nodded. "It's those old bones they found that's to blame for all this. Which is crazy because they've probably been there longer than I've been alive. What's the fuss? It's not as though there's any danger now."

"You don't think so?"

"Do you know how long it takes a body to be nothing but bones? Years and years. Everything'd be fine if they just stopped talking about it on TV and scaring off the tourists."

Cait said noncommittally, "Once whoever is responsible is caught, tourism should get back to normal."

"*If* they're caught. And lots of people around here depend on a good season to survive." The woman blew out a breath, sending a practiced eye around the area. "I'll tell you one thing, whoever put those bones in that cave? I'd bet a hundred dollars they're long gone. But we're the ones who're left with the fallout. That's why I say if TV stops talking about it and Tony Gibbs stops running his mouth off, the whole thing would blow over and we could get on with our lives."

"Joanie, can you watch the bar? I have to restock the beer." Del fairly flew by them without waiting for an answer, leaving his wife to glare impotently after him. Then, catching Cait's eye, she heaved a sigh and shoved away from the stool.

"Word of advice? Don't ever work with your husband. There's such a thing as too much togetherness."

Cait's mouth quirked. She doubted she'd need that particular information. "I'll remember that."

As the woman hurried around the counter to wait on the men at the end of the bar, Cait ate her meal thoughtfully. Although it brought out the usual number of gawkers, murder had a natural depression on tourism. That fact often was a prime motivator for one of Raiker's consultants to be called in the first place. Local and state politicians got nervous when they saw the prospect of the cash infusion in their town or state dwindling. That was really no more cynical, she supposed, than Andrews wanting to use the successful resolution of this case to pave her way to the governor's mansion.

"Looks good." Sharper appeared at her elbow and reached over to snag one of her steak fries.

"Help yourself," she offered with mock politeness.

Sarcasm was obviously wasted on him. He took another and bit into it, watching her reflectively. "So where'd you find a room?"

"The McKenzie." She nodded her head toward the woman at the tap. "Joanie and the woman at the motel both mentioned the effect news of the murders have had on tourism around here. Have you seen a slowdown in your business?"

He took his time answering, this time dipping the steak fry in ketchup before bringing it to his mouth. "So now the deaths have been upgraded from suspicious to murder?"

Too late she realized her mistake. "You're a pain in the ass, you know that, don't you, Sharper?"

"Zach."

When she merely looked at him, he replied easily, "My name is Zach. Only my friends call me Sharper."

"These mythical friends of yours must be blessed with an infinite amount of patience. Get your damn hand out of my plate." She picked up the table knife. He wasn't quite fast enough to avoid a rap across the knuckles.

"Stingy. You must have worked up an appetite today. To answer your question, no there hasn't been a real slowdown with my business yet, although the referrals from resorts in this vicinity have decreased. But we don't necessarily only book tours in this immediate area, either."

She thought about that. It didn't preclude a local as a suspect, even if his business might be affected by the discovery of the bones. Most UNSUBs didn't plan that far ahead. Didn't consider those sorts of ramifications. Although it might explain the trouble taken hiding them to begin with, she'd expect someone worried about the effect on their business would dump them farther away from here.

She was convinced that the dump site, just like the painting on the scapulas, had little to do with extraneous considerations like local tourism and everything with what drove the offender.

He was taking advantage of her preoccupation by making inroads on her steak fries. It was, Cait thought darkly, as if her mother had paid him to circumvent her poor dietary choices. "Don't you have a pool game to finish?"

Zach jerked a head to indicate the game in progress behind him. "Already beat them all. They're playing for second place now."

Recalling Joanie's earlier words, she said, "Do you know a Tony Gibbs?" Then watched, amazed at how quickly his expression could go wary.

"Why?"

At her cocked brow, he finally relented. "I know him well enough to know he's an idiot. Why?"

"Because some of the people I've spoken to tonight already knew who I was, a feat in itself since this is the first time I've stepped foot in town. Joanie mentioned a Tony Gibbs talking about the case, so I wondered who he was."

If she didn't know better she'd say he was looking distinctly uneasy. "Maybe you should be having this conversation with Andrews."

"Why is that?"

"Because Gibbs is one of her department's deputies. He lives between here and Rainbow, but is in town lots of nights."

She cast a look around. "Is he here now?"

Zach shook his head. "I haven't seen him tonight. He could be over at Ketchers."

"Maybe I'll check after I leave here."

"Not alone, you won't."

Her long level look had him explaining. "It's a rough crowd. Fights break out several times a week, and some of the people that frequent the place go there for that very reason. I'd tell any newcomer to town to steer clear of the place but you especially."

Cait felt a dangerous sort of calm come over her, even as temper was spiking her pulse. "Me, especially?"

"Don't get pissy; you know what I mean. There's not a woman alive who looks like you that doesn't know her effect on men."

Odd, she reflected darkly, how he could make the words sound less like a compliment than an accusation.

"By this time of night the majority in there are going to be shit-faced and their behavior will reflect that. Any strange woman who'd walk in there right now is going to find herself fighting off unwanted attention. The bartender's idea of taking care of trouble is to wade into the crowd with a baseball bat. Believe me, it'd be a bad way to end your night."

Only slightly mollified, she studied him. "Okay, I'll wait until tomorrow night to check it out."

That familiar look of irritation was back on his expression. She found she almost preferred it to the punch-in-the-chest smile she'd seen on his face earlier. Irritation she could deal with. But that pull of attraction that flared to life between them on occasion was far more troublesome.

"You didn't listen to a damn thing I said, did you?"

"On the contrary." She'd finished the sandwich. Given his assistance, the steak fries were nearly gone as well. Cait reached for her purse to fish out money for the bill. "You've convinced me it's a bad idea to go there right now, so I'll wait and check out the place earlier in the evening tomorrow. I want to meet this Tony Gibbs for myself."

"Then call Andrews and arrange it," he said flatly, his hawklike gaze intent. "No use going looking for trouble."

Because it did no good to argue with him, she merely counted out enough money to pay the bill and tip and slapped it all on the bar. "I'll take it under advisement."

"God, what is it with you?"

Since that appeared to be a rhetorical question, she didn't bother answering. Cait slid off the stool. Hitching the strap of her purse over her shoulder, she headed for the door. She was more than a little surprised to hear his footsteps following her. Downright astonished when she felt his arm on her elbow pulling her around.

She gave his hand a long look before shifting her gaze to his face. "Back off, Sharper."

"Are you incapable of listening to reason from anyone, or is there something about me that sets you off?"

"You are more than a little offsetting," she agreed. Heat was licking up her spine. She preferred to blame that on temper. "I said I'd wait. What's your problem?"

"My problem is you shouldn't go there at all. Anytime. It's just asking for trouble and there's no need for it."

She surveyed him more carefully, a bit of her own frustration fading. "Do you have some reason for not wanting me to talk to Deputy Gibbs?"

"I don't give a shit whether you talk to him or not. I'm just saying . . ."

"We're starting over, Sharper. You want in, or is that lover's quarrel gonna take all night?" The raucous shout came from one of the men near the pool table. Looking past Zach, Cait could see all eyes in the place were on them. And she was aware for the first time how close they were standing to each other.

He dropped his hand as if he'd been burned. "Be there in a minute," he called back. When he turned back to her his eyes had cooled. "Do what you want. I'll see you in the morning."

She let him take a few strides away before something possessed her to say, "If you're that worried about the place, I guess I can let you tag along tomorrow night. Call it part of your deal with Andrews."

The look he sent her then had steam rolling off it. But he didn't say another word before rejoining his friends.

Oddly satisfied, she turned again to leave. But not before giving his broad back and narrow hips a last appreciative look.

Because Zach Sharper had a way of filling out a pair of Levis. Just because she now played it smart regarding men didn't mean she was dead.

Once in the vehicle, she checked her cell phone and was chagrined to discover she'd missed a call about one of the missing persons cases. When she returned the call there was no answer, so she left a short message for the man to call her back, regardless of the hour. Playing phone tag with the various detectives assigned to the missing persons cases she'd inquired about was beginning to be a full-time job.

After driving the short distance to the motel, she parked and locked the vehicle before wondering if she'd perhaps missed Barnes's call, too. But there was no record of it in her phone log, and she frowned a little as she unlocked the door to her room. It wasn't like the man to be out of communication for this long. She put another call in to him, but he didn't answer this time, either, so she left another message. Cait set the phone down on the dresser before securing the door, wondering what had kept the man busy all day. And whether it had to do with their case.

She'd changed into a camisole and shorts to sleep in and was scrubbing her face when her cell rang. The deputy still on her mind, she walked in to pick the phone up and answered, "You're working late."

"Well, I certainly hope you aren't, darling. You know what it does to your skin when you don't get your ten hours sleep."

Cait's eyelids slid shut in chagrin. She almost always screened her calls, for precisely this reason. There was nothing worse than being ambushed by a phone call from Lydia Fleming Smythe Regatta.

"Mother." Because she needed the support, she turned away from the dresser so she could prop her hips against it. "How are you?" Her voice was stilted. Formal. They'd never have a close relationship, but she was *trying*, dammit. Shouldn't she get points for that?

"Absolutely exhausted. Every time we fly I swear it will be the last time. When did travel become this excruciating?"

The words struck a familiar chord. Kristy had had a similar complaint upon arriving in Eugene, although she'd voiced it a bit more colorfully. Cait had never heard Lydia utter a four-letter word in her life. She didn't need to. She was capable of using words the way a surgeon wielded a scalpel, performing tiny dissections of the ego in a perfectly modulated voice.

"So you're on a trip?"

"Oh, heavens no. Henri and I have just gotten back to the penthouse this minute."

Henri. Cait's mind went totally blank. Had Lydia gotten married again? Frantically she searched her mental files, came up with the name. Not husband number four, thank God—at least not yet. Her mother's *gentleman friend*. One Cait hadn't met and, if her luck continued to hold, never would.

"Where'd you go?" The question elicited a ten-minute monologue from Lydia on the trials of Paris in the summertime, and Cait closed her eyes and let the words roll off her. The conversation would require very little of her, for which she was grateful. Ten minutes of filler meant only five more to parry the subtle digs and thrusts regarding Cait's chosen career.

A fifteen-minute phone call was long enough for politeness and, on a good day, not long enough to shred her nerves.

"Oh, and you'll never guess who called me. Cee Cee Walker! Of course she asked about you when we caught up over drinks at The Ritz-Carlton."

The name had trepidation pooling in her stomach. Cait straightened, craning her neck to see the clock in the next room. Only ten and a half minutes had passed. Damn. "How is she?" she asked without enthusiasm.

"Well, she looks marvelous. Of course she's had work done, that's a given, but the surgeon was very discreet." Lydia spoke from experience, having had *her* share of work done over the years, as well. Every time Cait saw her, she'd had something new tucked or lifted. In the war against gravity, Lydia was the crowned champion.

"She told me something I found intriguing." Her mother's voice lowered conspiratorially, as if someone else eavesdropping would find the conversation even slightly interesting. "Duran Cosmetics have dropped that dreadful Giselle Hammenstein as the face for their products, and they are actively looking. Cee Cee said she'd sent them several portfolios of models in her agency, but the word is that they're going for a more mature look."

Not tonight. Cait's head lolled as she rubbed the headache that had suddenly taken up residence behind her temples. After a full day of trading verbal jabs with Sharper, she absolutely couldn't have this conversation tonight.

"Of course, I thought of you. If you landed a contract this big, you wouldn't have to work your way back up the hard way again, you'd make a splash, darling! Don't you recall the glamour of our old life? Don't you just miss it?"

"Like a brick to the head," she muttered.

"What?"

"No, Mother," Cait said clearly, striving for patience. "I don't miss it. I've never missed it. I have a career, and it's one I've found far more fascinating than modeling ever was. I'm not going back. I thought we were done having this argument years ago." Thought she'd grown safer with every passing year. Modeling was a young woman's job. And although at thirty-five Cait was hardly ready for a wheelchair, she was past the prime of most top runway models.

Of course Lydia wasn't talking runway. A point she used another six and a half minutes to painstakingly explain. To paint a laughably surreal image of Cait's former career that bore little resemblance to the reality.

Cait used the time to dig in her purse for some pain reliever for the headache that had taken on power-drill proportions. When that search failed, she switched to her toiletry kit. The lone two pills in the bottle were a welcome find.

When she ran water for a drink to wash them down with, the sound almost, *almost*, drowned out her mother's voice in her ear.

". . . and think of the travel involved! When's the last time you've been to Europe, Caitlin? You can't begin to imagine how much has changed, with the . . ."

Apparently Lydia had already forgotten the miseries of travel she'd spent the first part of the conversation regaling her with. Downing the pills, Caitlin shuffled to the other room again to eye the alarm clock on the bedside table. Seventeen minutes. More than enough time to qualify as a polite conversation. When her mother showed no signs of winding down, she mentally recalculated. Maybe a little longer. Could she endure two more minutes of this?

The mental question was abruptly answered in the next few seconds.

". . . the life your father would have desired for you. He'd never have wanted you to end up in his grim world, Caitlin. To see the sights he saw every day. The countless hours away from his family. That job drove him to his death, Caitlin. Following in his footsteps isn't a tribute to him, it's a slap in the face. He'd have wanted better for you. Not to have you embroil yourself in the seamiest side of—"

"You don't know that." Her voice was tight. Sometimes Cait wondered if Lydia's memory of Gregory Fleming was as fuzzy as her own. Conveniently so, since her mother invoked his name to underscore whatever argument she was currently engaged in. "And I'm not a beat cop, so I haven't exactly followed in his footsteps."

The sound Lydia made was suspiciously close to a sniff of disdain. "Don't split hairs with me, we both know how you ended up where you are. If you hadn't given up everything to run off to college, there's no telling what you could have achieved by now. You were headed for the top."

Her mother was wrong. Cait stared blindly at her reflection in the mirror. She knew exactly where she'd be, what she would have become if she hadn't stood up to Lydia and left modeling for good to start college. It had been an ugly series of scenes, concluding with Cait hiring an attorney to end her mother's control of the money she'd earned. During their estrangement, Lydia had married and divorced twice. The husbands had at least kept her focus off her daughter. Maybe if she married Henri it would divert some attention away from Cait.

"Just think about it." Her mother's voice took on an unfamiliar note of pleading. "Not only could this be good for you, but it re-establishes me in the business as well. I did wonderfully by you as your manager, Caitlin. There's no reason I couldn't take on other clients, as well. But at this point, I've been away from the scene for too long. Not that I want you to do this for me. What I did for you I did for love. You don't owe me a thing, darling, and I don't want you to think I'm saying otherwise."

There was more, but Cait had stopped listening. Because Lydia meant just the opposite, of course. There had never been a moment when Cait hadn't been made aware what a burden it had been for her mother to raise her alone. How much she'd sacrificed to get Cait noticed by that first agency, the first art director. What she'd given up to travel with her to shoots and hire personal trainers and acting coaches.

And above all, how much her father would have wanted this for her.

The words rolled over her in a tired litany that Cait had heard thousands of times in the past. How that "unfortunate situation"—Lydia-speak for the drawn out court case and their resulting estrangement—had destroyed whatever chances she'd had to continue her successful career as talent manager. A stretch by anyone's definition, Cait figured, given that she'd been her mother's only client.

"Even if you didn't get the Duran job, we could get you noticed again. Cee Cee would have you back in a minute. You have been taking care of your skin, haven't you? The last time I saw you, I swear you hadn't moisturized in—"

"No, mother." The steel in her voice came in spite of the pounding in her temples. "I left that world over fifteen years ago and I have no intention of ever going back. I'm sure Cee

Cee could get you a client or two to start you out if you want to get into talent management." A fact Cait could hardly imagine, but that wasn't the important point here. "I don't want to hear any more about it. Now if you'll excuse me, I've had a long day and I've got an early start tomorrow. We'll talk later." Long practice had her disconnecting the call without anything further. A proper good-bye would entail another fifteen minutes of pleas turning to icy anger from Lydia. Better to piss her off now rather than later since the end result was the same either way.

She leaned her hands against the dresser, mentally counting to ten. On seven the phone shrilled again. Twice. Three times. Each ring was like a stake battering through Cait's brain. After the fifth time it went to voice mail. She gave it another few minutes before she accessed the message box and deleted the message her mother would have left. There was nothing worse than stumbling across one of Lydia's callbacks when checking for work-related messages.

Cheered slightly by the action, she checked the lock on the door and headed for bed. She knew from past experience that she hadn't heard the last regarding the issue from her mother, but she'd be more careful in the future about screening her calls.

Snapping off the light, she yanked back the covers and slipped under them, gingerly laying her still-throbbing head against the pillow. Useless to wonder what had set her mother off on the career-resurrection pipe dream this time. Perhaps it was the phone call from Cee Cee. Or maybe Henri was proving wary about becoming husband number four and Lydia was reaching the bottom of her settlements from husbands two and three.

Whichever it was, she knew enough to lay low until her mother gave up. She wasn't a child anymore, to be manipulated at will. Nor a teen with a fragile ego seeking her identity in all the wrong places.

Knowing that should have been security enough. But it was the certainty Lydia couldn't realize only a few hundred miles, instead of the usual thousands, separated them that finally lulled her to sleep.

Cait welcomed the time when she finally met up with the perp responsible for killing seven victims and defleshing their bones before painting macabre scenes on their scapulas.

Thoughts of a face-to-face meeting with her mother, however, had dread pooling in her gut.

Chapter 10

The woman had cost him twenty bucks and two games of pool that he could have easily won.

Since his concentration was shot to hell, Zach handed over his cue to the next guy waiting for a game. Heading to the bar to drink the rest of his bottle in peace, he ignored the good-natured ribbing that followed. His mood had gone south in the last hour, and the reason for that could be laid squarely at Cait Fleming's feet.

A position he was sure she was used to having men occupy.

Scowling, he tipped his bottle to his lips and took a long pull before lowering it and sliding into a stool. For a man who liked his women sexy, simple, and short term, he was spending an inordinate amount of time thinking about a female there wasn't a chance in hell he was going to lay a finger on.

Although she had sexy nailed, there was nothing simple about Caitlin Fleming. She was as contrary a female as he'd ever met, and he'd encountered more than a few unreasonable shrews on the job. Those women didn't have much in common with the special consultant, either. Her abrasiveness came from overconfidence rather than sheer bitchiness.

The pain-in-the-ass end result was the same, though.

"Hey, Sharper." Bill Reagen detached himself from the group of men at the other end of the bar and strolled over, taking a seat beside him. "Heard you been spending lots of time with that hot thing that was in here earlier. You screwin' her?"

Slowly he lifted his gaze to level it at the man beside him. Something in it must have warned Reagen, because he lifted his palms placatingly. "Hey, none of my business. It's just that I heard she's working with the sheriff's department and might be around for a while. Didn't want to try my hand with her if I was stepping on toes, you know?"

The thought of the burly Reagen shooting rusty pickup lines to Cait had one corner of Zach's mouth tugging upward. "Go ahead." Might be worth sticking around to watch, if only to make sure the man didn't go too far and get knee-capped for his efforts. Bill was an affable enough sort, if not too bright.

"Sure is a looker." Reagen took a long drink from his bottle. Lowering it, he added, "My brother had a poster of her in our bedroom when we were kids. When I heard she was around here, I thought they were talking about someone else. But after seeing her tonight . . . that's the same lady all right. Wonder what would make a woman like that want to do what she does, look at bones for murders and stuff?"

It was clear Reagen was inviting the sort of philosophical speculation that passed for conversation when someone new arrived in the area. But Sharper found himself oddly reluctant to participate. Not only because he had an aversion to gossip, having been on the receiving end of it most of his life. But he didn't want to talk about her at all.

His silence didn't deter the other man. "Tony Gibbs has been saying how she's some sort of genius with them bones. Can tell all sorts of stuff like how old they are and who they belonged to. That Raiker outfit she works for? Gibbs says they call them the Mindhunters, 'cuz of the work they do catching criminals and stuff. Raiker used to be with the FBI till he got hurt chasing down that killer in Louisiana. Remember that one seven, eight years ago who killed all them kids?"

Zach let the man drone on while he silently finished his beer. The Mindhunters. He recalled Barnes saying something about it the first day he'd taken Cait to Castle Rock. Obviously she was a very big deal in law enforcement circles. At least her employer was. Maybe that explained that attitude of confidence she exuded, even when it would pay to exercise a little caution and good sense.

He gave an impatient roll of his shoulders. Not his business. She was just a job, and in a few days, weeks at most, she'd go back wherever the hell she'd come from and he'd be rid of her. She wasn't responsible for this . . . restlessness or whatever the hell it was that was burning a hole through his chest these days. Drummy's suicide wasn't, either, though that sure as hell had upped the ante considerably.

If this were due to a midlife crisis, it had arrived about a decade early.

"You guys need another beer?"

Del Barton reappeared from wherever he'd been and hurried down the bar toward them. Zach shook his head. Shoving the stool back, he rose. "I'm calling it a night." Two beers was his usual limit these days. The night he'd heard about Drummy eating his gun proving the exception to that rule.

A red-hot poker of pain stabbed through him. Alcohol hadn't helped dull feelings when he'd heard the news of his friend's suicide. It had only brought a tidal wave of memories that he spent far too much time trying very hard not to recall. He wouldn't be making that mistake again any time soon. He'd seen far too many guys try to wash away their failures with booze. He turned and headed toward the door.

"Hey, did I tell you I ran into your dad in Las Vegas?"

Case in point. Zach halted midstride and turned for the inevitable conclusion to Reagen's question. "Nope."

"Yeah, I went with Handley and Miles on one of them red-eye junkets. Ran into him at the Hilton. I recognized him and went up to say hi. He didn't seem to know who I was, so I said I knew you. Funny thing. He looked right at me and said, 'I don't have a son.' Just like that. I would have thought I had the wrong guy, but Miles, he recognized him, too."

Zach smiled humorlessly. "He was right. He doesn't have a son." And he continued out the door. His relationship with his father had always been strained, but the reading of his grandfather's will seven years ago had severed it completely. No big loss. Jarrett Wellen Bodine III was a fuckup of monumental proportions. The best day of Zach's life had been when he'd gone to live with his grandfather for good when he was twelve. The old man had been hard, set in his ways, and difficult to please. But that had been infinitely better than being subjected to his father's erratic behavior and drunken rages.

Letting the screen door slam behind him, he continued down the walk and rounded the corner to the parking lot. Thoughts of his father worsened his mood.

Maybe he just needed to get laid. He gave brief consideration to driving over to Shellie Mayer's place. Thought better of it. A woman who'd called him an emotionally unavailable bastard just a couple weeks earlier probably couldn't be counted on to roll out the sexual welcome mat, even if he'd agreed with her description. *Especially* since he had.

He unlocked his Trailblazer and got in. It wasn't Shellie Mayer on his mind, at any rate. He had a mental flash of Caitlin Fleming's expression before she'd walked out the door. Mocking. Daring him to . . . what?

Zach started the vehicle and shoved it into gear with a bit more force than necessary. It wouldn't do to start reading things into her expression. Into her words. Wouldn't do to start convincing himself that she was the kind of woman he could take to his bed and not end up with a truckload of regrets afterward.

But knowing that didn't stop him from nosing his Trailblazer in the direction of Ketchers. Just to be sure she hadn't done something stupid and headed over to the tavern despite his warning.

He didn't see her vehicle in the rutted gravel lot around the tavern. But as he was passing by, a body flew out of the front door. A stream of men followed, trading blows and curses he could hear through his rolled-up windows. The thought of Cait mixing it up with the lame heads in there was difficult to picture.

What was getting increasingly easy to picture was the image of her stretched out in his bed. Beneath him. Over him.

He shifted uneasily. Because that train of thought wasn't going to make it easier to spend the day with her tomorrow. Wasn't going to make it easier to ignore the way she moved or the unwilling fascination about her lodged in his mind that he couldn't shake loose.

Zach clenched his jaw and drove in the direction of home. He had a feeling sleep was going to be a long time coming tonight.

———————

He'd used duct tape to shut her up, and he didn't feel sorry for it. Not one bit.

There were still faint noises coming from the locked room, though. Metal clanking against stone. She must be using her feet somehow to slam the lawn chair against the wall.

Gritting his teeth, he adjusted the light and peered more intently at the sketch he was making. Barb Haines was a horrible, nasty woman. Unappreciative and foulmouthed. Never had it been this difficult to wait. To do things right. *Respectfully*. She wasn't making things easy for him. For herself.

But the easy way wasn't necessarily the right way. He'd learned that for himself when his mother had died.

Get a shovel boy. Start digging.

He flinched. He could still hear his father's voice. Still feel the sting from the careless blow that had accompanied the words. But the old man couldn't hurt him anymore. Couldn't hurt anyone. He'd made sure of that.

But far, far too late to help his mother.

The memory burned, so he thrust it away. Tried to concentrate on the pleasant fifties melodies on the iPod. His mother's favorite music. When his father wasn't around, they'd listen to the radio for hours while they worked in the garden or did chores. But whenever his father came home, the music always stopped.

The night they'd buried his mother had been a night much like this one. Clouds covering the moon and stars, as if their glow had been doused out of mourning. He hadn't been allowed to mourn. Tears were another excuse for a beating. And digging his mother's grave in the middle of the night had left him too exhausted to feel anything at all. At least at the moment.

When his hand trembled, he paused, took a deep breath to calm himself. He needed absolute steadiness for the close work of the sketches. The sooner he got done, the sooner he could be rid of the woman in the next room.

But the sneaky slivers of memory wouldn't be banished. He was nine again, shivering in the night air despite the sweat that slicked his body. Watching in the dim light let by the lantern as the old man rolled his mother's body into the shallow grave.

Fill it in. And not a word to anyone about this. Remember? What's the story?

The shovel handle had caught him across the back hard enough to leave a bruise that would last for weeks.

She ran off. She ran off and left us.

And uttering those words had been the ultimate betrayal to the woman who'd shielded him as best she could until then.

Don't think about that. He drew in a deep breath. Blew it out slowly. He had all her best qualities. Hadn't she always said so? He was sensitive and artistic and perhaps too compassionate for his own good.

The thought steadied him, so he picked up the pen again. Began drawing swiftly, surely, the final panel for the woman in the next room. It wouldn't do to draw what he wanted, what best depicted his impression of Barb Haines. That would be an image of a she-demon, horned and fanged, complete with monstrous features. It might be true, but it wouldn't be *respectful*.

The drawing soothed him, as it always did. But it would be good to get done with this last guest so he could return to the sketching he most enjoyed. He flicked a glance around at the superhero comics he'd drawn and taped to the wall. An artist needed his space to create. And he never felt closer to his mother than when he was engaged in the drawing she'd always encouraged.

That sound came again. Metal against stone. Faint but unmistakable. And fury bubbled up with a startling intensity.

"Shut up, you fucking bitch! Shut up shut up shut up!" The pen snapped in his grip, and he hurled the pieces across the room to bounce harmlessly off the door. He tried to draw a breath through a chest that had gone tight. His vision had grayed at the edges. He couldn't hear his mother's voice whispering in his ear anymore. But he could hear his old man laughing. Louder and louder until it echoed and rang in the small space, hurting his ears and filling his brain until there was nothing but that painful sound.

Moaning, he clapped his hands over his ears and rocked back and forth, battling to push the noise from his head.

He didn't know how much time passed before the voice subsided and he took his hands away. The silence in his head was reflected in the next chamber. The woman had gone silent.

Calmer now, he got up to gather the pieces of the pen he'd thrown. He liked to keep his area neat. Tossing them in the trash, he sat down at his worktable again. Got out another pen and resumed sketching with a renewed sense of purpose. He'd finish the sketches tonight no matter how long it took him. Then the scalpel would need sharpening. He'd noted that last time but hadn't gotten around to it yet.

Making plans always calmed him. He hummed along with the song playing on the iPod. Something about a car accident and rain and a last kiss.

Barb Haines wasn't going to get a last kiss. She was only going to get a few last hours.

Because when he was done with his work tonight he was going to go into the chamber and snap that bitch's neck.

In a feat of supreme irony, Lydia Regatta managed to get in the last word, after all. At least in Cait's subconscious. Snippets from the past replayed in short Technicolor fragments in her dreams, melding and reforming with perfect accuracy memories she'd never waste time considering in her waking hours.

There was the heat of the lights again, the glare turning her skin to a sheen of perspiration. The excruciating ache of muscles held in one position for hours, waiting for the photographer to get the perfect shot. And always, always, her mother's voice superimposed over every shoot. Every decision.

I want a different photographer. The last time she worked with Paolo he made her look like a cow. He never gets the right angle.

Cait shifted in the bed, burrowing her head deeper into the pillow. But she couldn't shut out the movie replaying in her head. There was a much younger version of herself, jaw clenched, squaring off with her mother in their ongoing battle.

Later, darling. Your tutor says you're excelling on all your class work. There will be plenty of time for school after this. Do you know how many girls your age would kill for the opportunities you have? And this is exactly what your father would have wanted for you.

The figures wavered at the edges. Melted away to form a new scene. Lawyers facing off across a long polished mahogany table. The smell of old books and rich leather filling the air. And her mother's tight expression. Her voice clipped with disapproval.

Your father would be so disappointed in you, Caitlin.

So disappointed.

So disappointed.

Lydia's voice rang like a knell in her head. The dream scene changed. A different office this time. But instead of a table, there was a desk. And an eight-year-old Cait sitting on her father's lap. Inhaling the scent of cherry tobacco and peppermint that never quite masked the smell of the nasty brown stuff in the bottle he kept in his bottom drawer.

You have to be daddy's big helper, Caitie. Can you do that?

His voice raspier, shushing the sobs she couldn't seem to contain. The sense of impending doom that a child's mind couldn't fully comprehend.

Put the gun in the special place I showed you. No one will ever find it there. And Caitie . . .

His hands gripping hard—too hard on her thin shoulders.

. . . you can never tell anyone the truth. Not ever, Caitie. It's our secret. Forever and ever.

It had been their secret. Because she'd done exactly what he'd told her that rainy evening.

And she'd never told a soul.

Her body twisted on the bed, caught in the desperate state between wakefulness and sleep, trying unsuccessfully to shrug off the mantle of slumber.

The scene shifted yet again, a dizzying blur of faces. The detective with the kind brown eyes who'd coaxed her out from beneath the desk. The lady with the old-fashioned dress and pinched-up mouth that'd asked her questions over and over again. The people moving through the funeral home, a parade of sympathetic faces and avid eyes, all speaking with hushed voices.

I heard it was a burglary gone wrong? How terrible for you, and poor little Caitlin.

Such a tragedy . . . why, she could have been killed, too!

Crimes like this are an outrage. No one's safe in their own home anymore!

At least you have Gregory's service pension. And the insurance policies . . .

The scene shifted again. They were in the lady's office. The one with all the questions. Her mouth got smaller and smaller the madder she got. And she was very angry at Lydia.

Surely you're going to get the child some help? After all

she's been through? She needs therapy to get over this. You can't pretend it didn't happen. You can't . . .

The lady's phone was ringing. Ringing and ringing and ringing, drowning out her sharp words as it rang and rang and . . .

Cait's eyes opened to focus on the ceiling above the bed. A giddy sense of relief swept over her. Only a dream. One she hadn't had in months.

In the next moment she turned her head, winced to discover it was still pounding. Her cell phone gave a final jangle before falling silent.

Jesus. Gingerly, she sat up in bed, reached for the phone. Caller ID showed Barnes's number, so she called him back. The clock on the bedside table said five fifteen.

"Yeah, I figured I'd wake you." The deputy's voice sounded in her ear.

"Have to thank you for that," she muttered. With one hand, she swept the hair back from her face. "Did something break yesterday? I couldn't get you or Andrews all day."

"Yeah, it was a real shit storm. But nothing to do with the case."

Now that Cait was more awake, she could hear the exhaustion in the other man's voice.

"We had a domestic dispute. Turned into a hostage situation. Guy finally blew his wife away a few hours ago before giving himself up."

"Hell." She rubbed her eyes. "Kids?"

"No. And that's about the only positive thing about the mess. Anyway I'm just now heading home for some sleep. You have any luck yesterday?"

"None. I'm meeting Sharper to start again in less than an hour."

"Okay, keep us posted. Oh, I almost forgot." The words were spoken around a yawn. "State lab got our results on the bags. We've got one clear thumbprint on one of them. They ran it through IAFIS and came up with zip. We need to do an elimination match on anyone who came in contact with it, including you and your tech."

It was all she could do to keep from snapping at him. She and Kristy were too well trained to touch evidence without gloves. But, she supposed, he'd claim the same for himself and his officers. "All right."

"Get a sample from Sharper today, too."

Her brows rose. Had she been first on the scene when they'd brought the bones out of the cave, she'd have collected elimination prints from everyone working the area. Especially the guide who'd admitted going down in the cave's chamber first. But it would do no good to point that out, so she said only, "Okay. And you'll do the same for the officers who worked the scene?"

There was a pause. Then, "Of course."

She couldn't prevent a huge yawn. And even that movement worsened the pounding in her head. "Anything else about the bags themselves?"

"Just that they're biodegradable, which could be a plus for us. How many companies could there be putting out black biodegradable garbage bags?"

Cait glanced at the clock again. She still needed to shower and talk to the clerk about paying for another night. "Several, I'm afraid."

"Oh. Well, I can continue on that lead. I'm shot. Need some rest before I fall down."

"Go to bed, Barnes. I'll let you know if we come across anything."

Without further urging from her, the man signed off. Cait slipped from the bed, staggering a little as she headed to the bathroom. She hoped the General Store opened early. She wouldn't make it through the day without buying some more pain reliever.

She could deal with a headache or with Sharper. But she was pretty sure she couldn't handle both simultaneously.

———

He was feeling just surly enough to make a comment about her being late, even if it were only by two minutes. But when Cait slipped out of the vehicle and stalked by him toward the store without a word, the caustic remark he was about to make died on his lips.

The shades she was wearing weren't needed to block the sun at this time of the day, and her skin was even paler than usual. Since he knew she hadn't tied one on in JD's last night, or gone to Ketchers, she likely didn't have a hangover. He spent the next few moments debating whether to follow her inside. On the one hand, he was curious. He did, after all, have to spend the rest of the day with her. On the other hand, if this were related to a female thing, he had a male's natural queasiness about too much information.

Pursing his lips in consideration, he decided to see what she was up to. PMS would only make Caitlin Fleming more dangerous. In which case it would pay to be forewarned.

But by the time he stepped inside she was already at the counter with her purchases, a couple granola bars, a hefty-sized container of Tylenol, and a bottle of water. And when she looked in his direction, he could feel her piercing glare behind the shades, even if he couldn't see it.

Ignoring her, he headed to the cooler and got himself an orange juice and then snagged one of the hot breakfast sandwiches from the warmer. When he got outside she was already in his front seat, washing down a handful of pills with a long gulp of water.

He unwrapped the sausage and egg muffin and took a large bite before pulling out of the parking lot onto Highway 126.

"I can hear your arteries slamming shut in protest. They know you shouldn't eat that thing, even if you don't."

Taking another healthy bite, he chewed and swallowed. "Concerned about me? I'm touched. But you're the one who looks like a strong breeze would blow you over."

With slow careful movements she leaned against the headrest. "Why don't you just say I look like shit and be done with it?"

That almost surprised a laugh from him, but he was smart

enough to squelch it. "If I thought that, I would. You don't."
But she did look . . . fragile, somehow. Like she'd shatter under a careless word. An ungentle touch.

Which was absolute bullshit, because from what he'd seen
so far, Caitlin Fleming was about as delicate as a pit bull on
steroids.

"I had one too many beers to sleep last night. What's your
excuse?" He slowed near their turnoff, checking the light traffic
before turning on to the secondary road.

"I had a conversation with my mother. Always conducive
to pleasant dreams."

Zach subsided. As crappy nights went, she probably won.
Not that he had a mother, but just the mention of his father
had been enough to keep him up to the wee hours working
out his frustrations by hanging new sheetrock. And he hadn't
even talked to Jarrett. "How bad's the headache?"

"On a scale of one to ten, with one being the fat opera
tenor singing me lullabies in Italian, and ten being a dozen
demented dwarves jack-hammering in my skull, I'd rank it a
twelve."

Since she was still coherent enough to be sarcastic he figured she'd last the day. But maybe not without making his
absolute hell. "We could put this off a few hours. Let you get
some more sleep."

"I'll be fine."

And maybe she would. If *fine* was synonymous with working herself into full-blown migraine status. It occurred to him
that he was a bit too concerned about the welfare of the
woman beside him, and he scowled. He only cared because
of how it might affect him, he assured himself. He'd made it
his habit since returning from Afghanistan to not give a shit
about anyone. So far it had worked pretty damn well.

"Up to you. But if you do a face-plant while we're hiking
today, I'm leaving you where you fall."

Oddly, the words had her mouth curling. "You're such a
sweet talker, Sharper. How is it I'm not tripping over women
dazzled by your charms?"

"Beats the hell out of me." But despite his threat he found

himself scanning the area for the best way, the easiest way to hike in and continue the grid they'd started yesterday. And that annoyed him enough that he fell silent until he chose a spot and parked the truck off the road.

"I remembered something last night. That second guy you mentioned. Lockwood. He builds a semipermanent place when he finds a spot he likes. A little lean-to with a tarp over the top. Not too close to water because he doesn't like to be bothered by fishermen and tourists."

She turned her head carefully toward him. "You know where his shelter is?"

He moved his shoulders impatiently, already sorry he'd said anything. The guy was probably an old hippie, a burn-out who just wanted to be left the hell alone. The area was full of them. It didn't make him a damn serial murderer. "I know where it was once, but he isn't likely to be in the same spot."

"Let's head to where you last met up with him. It'll give us a place to start."

He drilled a look at her. "And when you find him?"

Her voice was cranky. "I'm going to shoot him in the leg. Christ, Sharper, what the hell do you think? I want to talk to him. Sorry if that offends your innate leave-me-the-hell-alone quality—which is, by the way, so very endearing. I have a job to do here."

Something about her irritability melted away his reservations. He understood ill temper. At least it was honest. It was the damn perpetually cheerful people that he didn't trust. As far as he was concerned, they were either dangerously out of touch or hiding something.

Worse, though, he heard the pain beneath her words and responded to it, despite himself. "Understood. Just remember that these people can be unpredictable. It's sort of like encountering a wild animal."

"Don't corner them. Yeah, I got that. Believe it or not, I have some experience in this area." She walked ahead of him, taking her sunglasses off as she entered the dim light of the forest.

Zach followed more slowly. Because unlike Cait's assertion, he had no experience in this area at all. At least, not where she was concerned.

And he couldn't say he cared for the sensation.

Chapter 11

Of course there was no one at the spot Zach recalled from the last time he'd run into Lockwood. No surprise there. Like he'd told Cait, guys like that weren't known for sticking in one spot long term. Nor did they run into anyone else for the first couple hours. They weren't in the campsite areas or particularly close to the river. And most other folks had more sense than to get up at the crack of dawn to wander around a forest that would still be there at a much more reasonable hour.

If Cait's headache was still bothering her, she didn't show it. She never lagged, never complained about needing a rest. In fact, he was the one who had to finally call a halt since he hadn't seen her take a drink of water since they'd left the vehicle. He slowed, reaching behind him to unzip his pack. Stopping, he withdrew a bottle of water and handed it to her. "Drink. Getting rid of a headache is part hydration."

"I've got water."

When he merely looked at her, she took the bottle with a sigh and twisted off the lid, looking around the area as she took a long swallow. When she'd tipped the bottle down she asked, "I assume you know where we are?"

"I spent my childhood roaming this forest. More than half of it is in Lane County. I could be dropped down in just about any spot, and I'd be able to figure my location, eventually." He barely remembered the time he'd spent in his mother's house in Sisters. He'd been seven when the car accident that had eventually taken her life had landed them both in the Eugene hospital. And after he'd gone to live with Jarrett, he'd taken any excuse to get out of the house. Although not the safest of playgrounds, the Willamette had been his refuge.

Pointing, he added, "We're not that far off one twenty-six actually . . ." His statement trailed off at a series of crackling explosions nearby.

Pop, pop, pop!

There was a split second of déjà vu, when he was transported back to the past. To the mountains of Afghanistan on the rare occasion they'd stumble on a warlord protecting his territory in their quest for their target.

But in the next instant he was returned to the present. Gaze fixed on the woman at his side.

In a blur of motion Cait's gun was drawn and in her hand as she took off in the direction of the sounds.

"Shit. Wait!" But of course she didn't. No surprise there.

The surprise was feeling himself take off after her.

She was amazingly fast. Somehow he hadn't figured on that. He sprinted along, leaping over fallen logs, dodging around piles of stone until he was within a few feet of her. Voices sounded ahead of them. Young. Panicked.

"Fuck, she's got a gun. Run!"

Cait stopped so suddenly that he had to swerve to avoid running her over. Lungs heaving, Zach watched as three teens scattered in different directions, stumbling through the brush and trees at a comical speed. "Did you see a weapon?"

Shaking her head in disgust, she reholstered her gun. And it occurred to him that he'd never seen anyone draw from a back harness as smoothly, as efficiently as she had. Headache or not, there was nothing wrong with her reflexes.

"Idiots. I don't know what they were doing, but those weren't shots."

"From the scent in the air, I'd guess Black Cats. Firecrackers," he explained when she turned to look at him quizzically. "Light a strip and toss them in a cave and they really make some noise."

"They're illegal in most states."

"Well, yeah." He brushed past her to approach the area the kids had vacated. "Doesn't make them impossible to get. I think you can still buy them some places in Washington." She'd fallen in step beside him and he cocked a brow at her. "Didn't you ever get your hands on M-80s when you were a kid? Toss them under a bridge when a semi was heading over it and the driver would think he'd blown three or four tires."

"Delinquent." Clearly she was unfamiliar with those particular delights of childhood. Her brow furrowed as she scanned the area. "So you're saying there are caves in this area?"

"Sawyer's Ice Caves. Forestry service has chained off the entrance from the road, and I don't think they're on the current maps. But they're not strictly closed to visitors. Just not publicized." He stopped and slipped off his backpack, taking out a flashlight. "Here." He switched it on and led the way to the small crevice sheltered by an outcropping of rocks. "See this?"

She took the light from him, dropping to her knees to peer inside. "How deep is it?"

"Not very. There's a larger one and a couple small ones like this. They're considered lava tubes, though you'll find much bigger ones near Bend. But there's ice on the floor of the caves even in the hottest summer temperatures." The last thing he expected was to see her shed her pack, unzip it, and withdraw climbing gloves. "If you didn't bring a hard hat you're going to end up with a far worse headache than you started with today."

"I'll be careful." Remaining in a crouched position, she started into the entrance.

With a mental shrug, he remained where he was. He'd crawled the caves as a kid, but he practically had to bend himself double to get inside now, and damned if he was willing to do that. So instead he got comfortable on a rock and watched Cait's shapely ass as she made her way inside. There were, he reflected consideringly, far worse ways to spend a morning.

"There's ice on the floors!" Her excited voice drifted outside to him.

"I believe I mentioned that. There are also small stalactites on the ceiling, too, so watch your . . ." He heard a muttered curse and broke off the rest of the warning. Luckily she was the most hardheaded woman he'd ever known. She was going to need it.

In a few minutes she was crawling out again. "You said there's a bigger one?"

Silently he got up and led her to the largest of the caves and climbed down to its entrance. "You won't need the flashlight until you get deeper inside."

She followed him curiously. "Why is it so light . . . ah." Looking up, she saw the natural skylight in the forest floor above. "Have to watch where you're walking up there." He lingered in the opening while she explored the depths of the cave. This time she was gone longer than he would have expected. And her expression, when she finally came out, was thoughtful.

"They wouldn't have been good places to hide the bones."

Her quick sideways glance told him better than words that he'd guessed her thoughts correctly. And when the hell had he developed that knack? Irritated, he began heading south to get back to the area they'd been exploring earlier.

Striding beside him, she asked, "Why do you say that?" She was peeling the gloves off her hands and stuffing them back inside the pack before slipping her arms through the straps. The Steri-Strips, he noted, were still in place.

And the fact that he'd observed that detail at all just made impatience stream through him. "The caves are too well-known. That ups the chances of someone stumbling on them before now. There are tons of bigger, roomier caves in eastern Oregon."

"Like near Bend."

"They would have been even worse choices, for the same reasons. Some of those caves are under the lease of a private company that arranges daily tours. Others are banned from tourists because of erosion or bat habitats, or whatnot." He lifted a shoulder. Oregon was nothing if not environmentally friendly. "Your guy would have been risking exposure to use any well-traveled tourist destination as his dump site. Many of these are also routinely maintained by the Forestry Service."

She was silent for a long time as they walked, and this time he didn't have a clue what she might be thinking.

But his mind was stuck on one thing. With the exception of his years in the Army, he'd spent his whole life in the region. It was clear that whoever put those bodies in the cave in Castle Rock was someone familiar with the area. Which meant it could be someone he knew.

Afghanistan had stripped away any illusions he might have once had. He realized people were capable of unspeakable atrocities.

But it was still hard to believe there was someone living in the area capable of this.

———

It was a couple hours and an undetermined number of miles before they happened upon a makeshift shelter that didn't appear abandoned. Cait walked around the small campsite, taking in the rotted log pulled close to the ring of stones that served as the fire pit. It would function as seating, she supposed, if one wasn't too fussy about comfort. And the current occupant of this site, although absent, didn't appear overly concerned with niceties.

"Fire's still smoldering." Zach stared into the distance, his mirrored sunglasses making it impossible to see his eyes. "Someone used it this morning."

She poked around in the three-sided tarp strung between two pines that served as a shelter. There was a dented kettle stacked with some serviceable metal dishes in one corner on the ground. A battered can of Folgers, half empty. A rolled up sleeping bag in another corner. A backpack, dingy and torn, laid half beneath it.

Ducking out of the shelter, she started, "Whoever lives here, he doesn't have much in the way of . . ."

"I've got a gun pointed right at the woman's head."

The unfamiliar voice was gravelly, as if from lack of use. She stilled, her gaze scanning the area for the person it belonged to.

"Both of you get out of here. Leave my stuff alone and find your own site before I put a hole through her."

She glanced at Zach. Saw him jerk his head slightly to the right. Peering hard over his shoulder, she had to focus for long moments before she could make out a shadow in the underbrush several yards away.

"We're only here to talk to you. We don't want your things." Cait began to edge for the nearest fir. If there really were a weapon trained on her, she'd need the protection. She tried to catch Zach's eye, but the warning she'd intended was unnecessary. He was already moving in the opposite direction, splitting the man's focus.

"I've got nothing to say to you. Now both of you get the hell out of here before I start shooting."

"That's a shame. Because I'm paying fifty dollars for cooperation. Just need some questions answered, that's all. How long you been set up here? A couple months?" She figured the answer was far shorter than that. "You might have seen the person I'm looking for."

There was a long silence. Then, "You got a lost hiker? I might be able to help you with that. I know this forest better than most."

"I have someone here who knows this area." She could no longer see Zach. Had no idea if he had taken shelter or if he was circling around to position himself in back of the owner of that disembodied voice. "I'm not interested in having a conversation with you hidden in that brush. If you want the money, come out here and talk to me."

There was a rustling noise and then a figure emerged. And

once Cait caught sight of him, she was no longer worried about a weapon. The tattered flannel he wore was open to reveal a ripped black T-shirt beneath. In his left hand he held a dead rabbit by its ears. The long sleeve of the flannel was pinned up on the other side nearly to the shoulder.

A lot of life had happened to Stephen Kesey since the dated motor vehicle photo she had in her pack.

He tossed the dead animal toward the fire pit. "Where's the guy that was with you?" he asked suspiciously.

"Here." Zach moved into her line of vision. But he didn't come any closer to them.

Kesey shot him a cautious look before glancing at Cait again. "So it's not about a lost tourist? Seems to me they're the ones people kick up a fuss about. What's going on then? What do you want?"

If she hadn't seen the man's identifying information she'd have had a hard time determining his age. His long brown hair and untrimmed beard were liberally streaked with gray. Deep lines fanned out from faded blue eyes. He looked at least a decade older than his fifty-four years.

"How long has your camp been set up here?"

"A couple days, that's all. I like to move around a lot."

She suspected he was lying. There was no reason to break camp unless Forestry Service or a private property owner demanded it, and according to what Zach had told her earlier, the land they were currently on had no camping restrictions. So where had he moved from? "Any reason for that?"

The man fell silent, his gaze shifting. Cait pressed, "Seems like a lot of trouble involved in moving. You travel light, but there's still finding the right place. Somewhere you won't be bothered, either by forestry or people happening by all the time."

Still he said nothing. She dug in her jeans pocket. Hoped there was a fifty among the bills in there. "You ever see anyone around here at night?"

"Get a lot of fisherman before dawn when I'm near the river. Not in these parts, though." His eyes flickered when she withdrew some bills and peeled off a fifty to hold it up to show him.

"So you've been here a couple days and haven't seen anyone at night during that time. What about earlier? Where were you camping before you found this spot?"

"Couple miles west of Castle Rock." He gave a short bitter laugh and flapped his empty sleeve. "I can admit that, can't I, 'cuz there's sure no way in hell anyone would suspect me of hauling those bodies up it to dump them."

Cait smiled easily, but her mind was racing. He might not have hauled the bones to the cave, but that didn't mean the man couldn't pose a threat. He managed to set up camp and take it down, pack, and travel around the forest, all one-armed.

Or he could have seen something, someone suspicious in the forest. There was no way the UNSUB could dump remains seven times and not be noticed once, was there?

"How'd you hear about that?"

"I've got a radio." He jerked his shaggy head toward the shelter. "Battery operated. So I can know when bad weather's on the way. When I heard about the commotion on Castle Rock a couple weeks ago, I knew it was time to go. Too bad, too. Left a real sweet spot."

"Why'd you leave it?" At his sharp look, she smiled innocently. "Like you said, no one would believe you had anything to do with the deal at Castle Rock. So what was the point?"

"No reason. Just felt like it." His eyes sharpened when Cait took the bill she was holding and proceeded to shove it back into her pocket. "What's the deal?"

"The deal is you're lying. The fifty bucks is for telling the truth." She drilled him with a gaze. "Why'd you move?"

His faded blue gaze never left her pocket where she'd secreted the bill. "Didn't feel safe no more. There was a guy came by. Middle of the night. Passed fifteen, twenty yards from my shelter. He had a shotgun. There are all kinds of crazies out here. I didn't need him coming back. Maybe surprising me sometime when I was sleeping."

"So you saw someone in the middle of the night who scared you?"

The man's beard waggled as he shook his head furiously. "Didn't say I was scared. Just careful. Careful enough to get up and follow him a ways. He was heading east until he just stopped. Never left the forest at all. Then he turned back and headed my way again, so I had to hide so he wouldn't see me."

She suspected the stranger he'd seen had been lucky to be carrying a shotgun. Kesey had probably had more in mind than caution when he'd followed the man. "What night was this?"

"Like I said it was a couple weeks ago. I heard on the radio the next day about the cops hauling bodies out of a cave on Castle Rock."

"You're sure about that? This occurred the night before the newscast?"

"The night before I first heard about it anyway. So like I said, he goes by me again and I figured he might've been out doing some poaching. 'Cuz he's carrying this bag on his back, right? So I followed him a bit farther from a distance to see where he was going. I lost him for a while, but after fifteen minutes or so he came heading back my way, still carrying the bag. I was behind some rocks and he stopped all of a sudden like he knew I was there. Couldn't have, of course. But it spooked me all the same."

Cait pulled her hand out of her pocket again with the bill and he eyed it avariciously.

"The next morning I started thinking I'd best just move out of the area. In case he really did know I'd been spying on him and came back some night."

"What exactly did he seem to be carrying?" When the man didn't answer she said, "Was it a backpack?"

"Couldn't tell for sure. Something dark, that's all I know."

"How long had you been at that campsite? The one near Castle Rock?"

He pondered that question for a few moments. "I don't really know. Months anyway."

She made a production of smoothing the bill between her fingers. "How many months? Two? Six?"

Kesey just shrugged. "Closer to three, but I can't say for sure how long."

"And you never saw anyone else around your site at night in all that time?"

"Kids sometimes. They come out in the forest to screw around. Drink beer and stuff. Otherwise I only saw that guy I told you about, and him just that once."

She slid her bag off her shoulder and crouched down to unzip it. Pulling out a pad and pen she rose and approached him, extending the fifty. When he snatched it out of her hand, she casually offered the notepad. "Can you sketch the area where you were camping at the time?"

He looked at her like she was crazy. "Can't even draw a straight line with my left hand. Not that I was ever much better with my right."

"How long ago did you lose it?" She inclined her head slightly toward his missing arm.

"Two years ago." Now that Kesey had the money he was plainly in a hurry for them to leave. He was inching closer to his shelter. Away from her. "Got infection in a cut and the doctor amputated the whole damn arm. Fucking butcher."

Cait could imagine the condition the arm was in before he'd sought treatment. But she couldn't prevent a surge of pity for the man, nonetheless. "Just do your best with your left hand. I want a general idea of what your campsite looked like. Any focal points that might have been in the area."

Obviously humoring her, he drew a very rough drawing of fir trees and something that looked like a rock. A squiggly line that could have been a road or the river. Then he handed the pad back to her. "Best I can do unless you have a map."

"I do, actually." She sent a look to Zach, who had been standing by silently during the entire exchange. When she unfolded the map of the forest, he approached and squatted down next to Kesey while she studied the drawing.

The stranger was right. He was no artist. And while it was possible he'd deliberately made it appear like he had the abil-

ity of a talentless kindergartner, she was more inclined to
believe that he lacked the capability of painting minute scenes
on human scapulas.

————————

Three hours later Cait's headache had subsided but for a
nagging throb. They'd stopped for lunch and she sat cross-
legged, leaning on her pack, which she'd propped against a
pine. She had no idea where they were. But when she asked
Zach to check off grid-lined sections they'd covered on the
map, he never hesitated. Which was oddly fascinating, because if he disappeared at this moment, she'd be screwed.
Except for the occasional outcropping of rocks or charred
tree, most of the area they'd traveled that day looked pretty
much alike.

The granola bars she'd purchased this morning looked
neither tasty nor filling, but she needed the fuel, so she
chewed unenthusiastically. Sharper was silent as he ate . . .
she leaned over for a closer look. "Peanut butter?" The discovery brought a smile to her lips. "What are you, ten?"

His brow rose. "Peanut butter's a good source of protein.
Besides"—he wadded up the plastic bag he'd taken it from in
one hand—"I didn't have any food in the house. Closest decent grocery store is in Eugene, and it's not like I've been to
town lately."

There was no rancor in his words, but she felt a tug of
guilt anyway. "I have to get to Eugene tomorrow morning myself for at least a couple hours." She hadn't yet gotten those
soil samples to Kristy, and she'd promised Barnes she'd get
latent samples for the elimination match, as well. "That re-
minds me, I'll need to get a fingerprint sample from you
sometime today."

He stilled in the act of shoving the wrapper back into his
pack. And the look he sent her was sharp. "What the hell
for?"

"We have to . . ." Her cell rang then and she stopped to
pull it from her pack. It took a moment to recognize the
number. But once she did, the blood pumped a little faster in

her veins. Rising to her feet in one smooth motion, she answered, "Detective Drecker."

"Fleming?" The Seattle detective's voice sounded in her ear. "Sorry this took so long, but Recinos's mother was hard to track down. Apparently she was on vacation. I did get some information from her to pass along, though. Recinos didn't have any arthritis that her family knew about, but she had broken her left wrist six months before her disappearance. Tripped over the cat, or something."

Her mind racing, she paced a distance away from Zach, although he couldn't help but hear her end of the conversation. It was possible the signs of osteoarthritis apparent on the remains hadn't caused the victim any particular problem before death. Also possible that her mother wouldn't know about every ache and pain her daughter had had. "And she wasn't adopted? This is her biological mother?"

"Yeah, they're blood relatives. What are you thinking, DNA match? Can you do that without tissue?"

"I took a sample from the bones. If you can get the mother to a lab, a sample can be taken and the results faxed to us. If that's not possible, I'd be glad to run the test myself, if she could make her way down here."

"What have you got, your own private lab facility?" The man's laugh was liberally laced with cynicism. Cait knew what he was thinking. Too often evidence gathered in police investigations languished in the state labs for months, some not being processed until well after the trial.

"Yes."

Her short answer had the detective pausing. "Well . . . hell. I almost forgot who you worked for. You might be the first break I catch in this case. I took another look at the case file, after you called last time. I told you I liked the ex for it, right?"

Supremely aware of the man standing only yards away, Cait replied, "You mentioned that."

"I had one of our forensic accountants take a look at the path the money took when I first caught the case. All I know for sure is someone didn't want the money trail traced. There were so many transfers and phony fronts that it would take him weeks to unravel it all. Time he wasn't willing to spend since we didn't have evidence of a crime, y'know? The ex claims that Recinos frequently talked about wanting to get far away from everybody and everything and start over, but I figure he came up with the story because I was leaning on him pretty hard. Her mother and friends all dispute that. No one else thought she purposely disappeared."

His words went muffled then, as if he'd partially covered the phone. "Hey, can I get a cup of that coffee over here?"

Cait considered the possibilities. The remains of female C showed signs of a fairly recent fracture of the left lunate. Marissa Recinos broke her left wrist in the last six months of her life. She also matched in the areas of stature and approximate age. It was enough for her to be damn pumped about running the DNA tests. "I don't suppose you were able to look closer at the finances of the ex. Or even the mother or acquaintances."

"None of them seem to have changed their lifestyle from a sudden infusion of cash, but like I say, no evidence of a crime. I had jack shit to go on here."

"Yeah, I get that." She turned to see Sharper leaning a shoulder against a tree, regarding her enigmatically. "You think the mother will cooperate?"

"There's no doubt she will. She's desperate to get information about her daughter." There was a pause, before he went on. "Guess linking her to bones found in a cave in Oregon won't be exactly the news she's hoping for, though. Oh, and I asked her about that list you gave me. Ballet and picture frame and stuff."

Nerves tightened in a ball in Cait's stomach. "What'd she say?"

"I wrote it down here somewhere. Just a minute." There was a rustling noise as if the man were shuffling papers. After a moment he spoke again. "Marissa took dance lessons for about ten years when she was a kid. Liked to ski. She worked from home designing websites for charitable foundations. One of her hobbies was matting and framing pictures she took. The other was speeding along the Pacific Coast Highway in her Dodge Viper."

Excitement sprinted along her veins. She struggled to rein it in. "Anything about the gum? Or fish?"

"Yes, and no. She was the sole heir of a fortune left to her by her great-grandfather who made his loot in—get this—chewing gum. Recinos couldn't think of any special meaning for the fish, though."

"She was last sighted in Pike Place Market," Cait said slowly. The famous Seattle attraction hosted a fresh fish company where the employees threw fish for the enjoyment of the tourists. "You might want to ask Recinos if that was a favorite spot for her daughter. And if she continued her love of ballet as an adult."

"What's this all about, Fleming?" The detective's tone was curious.

With a flash, Cait's gaze went to Sharper standing only yards away, his gaze fixed on her. "I can't go into that right now. But if we get a match with the DNA sample . . . I'll give you a full accounting on all the details."

"You'd better." The man sounded faintly disgruntled. "Because I have a feeling you're going to get a match. When I went through Marissa's credit card statements again, I found some charges made in Oregon about eight months before she went missing."

Cait went still. "Charges for what?"

"Apparently she stayed in that area for a few days. A place called Springs Resort." He rattled off the dates. "There's another charge to River Adventures, out of Springfield. Her mother said she went up there with a group of friends for a long weekend, even though it wasn't exactly her cup of tea. Apparently she wasn't the outdoorsy type." The man paused for a moment. "If those remains turn out to be hers, maybe she came to the killer's attention on that trip. Which would blow my theory on the ex and make it more likely that we're looking for a local up there."

"That's still a big 'if' at this point." The cautionary words were as much for her as they were for Drecker. But it was difficult to tamp down the flare of excitement she felt. "You might want to check the ex's background. See if he's familiar with this area."

Drecker's laugh held real amusement. "I'll do some digging, but I wouldn't count on it. That guy is more the martini and manicures type than a nature lover."

After eliciting the man's promise to make the arrangements for the test immediately, Cait hung up. And took a moment to still the vortex of adrenaline swirling inside her. If the DNA profile showed the elder Recinos was a blood relative of the remains of female C, the entire case took on a whole new light. Possibly provided motivation, if the money angle panned out. It would certainly give Drecker the justification to dig further into the money trail.

But it also just might blow her tentative profile of the UNSUB all to hell.

The thought had her frowning as she rejoined Sharper. Money was an all too common motivation for murder. But an offender who took the time to paint tiny scenes on bones was definitely outside the norm. It could point to affection for the victim or ego on the part of the UNSUB. The former was far more likely in the case of a serial offender.

Regardless, she needed another briefing with Andrews to update her on the latest development. She stopped a couple feet away from Sharper and pressed the speed dial number for the sheriff. "We need to talk," she said without preamble when she got the woman's voice mail. "Get back to me as soon as you can."

When she'd finished, she squatted to tuck the phone back in the zippered front pocket of the bag, pretending not to notice Zach's intent stare. "I'm ready to head out."

"You get a break in the case?"

She slanted him a glance. Sharper wasn't directly involved in this investigation. The information she gave him had to be guarded. But he wasn't stupid, either. He was going to draw his own conclusions based on what he observed when they were together. What he overheard. And there was little she could do about that. "Maybe. We'll see." She stuffed the wrappers into the bag and rose, shrugging into the straps. "Ready to move?"

The intensity of his stare was its own answer. "Sharper, I can't discuss it. You know that."

"Sure." Unsurprisingly, there was an edge to his tone. "But you can damn well discuss why you need a fingerprint sample. That involves me, right? We can agree on that?"

"We need elimination prints," she said calmly. But she recognized the storm brewing inside him. Wondered at it. "If it makes you feel any better, my assistant and I have to be printed, as well as the officers from the sheriff's department who were at the recovery scene."

Something in his expression eased a fraction. "So . . . what? You got a print from one of the bones? Because I didn't touch any of them. I told Andrews that when I reported them."

Skirting his question, she started walking. "The more people we eliminate, the closer we get to finding the suspect." A hand on her elbow stopped her. Her gaze lingered on it for a moment before lifting to his face.

"So you're saying whoever left that print doesn't have a record. Because there's a national database for that, right? If this guy was in the system, you'd already have a name."

He was, she thought ruefully, entirely too shrewd for her peace of mind. "I guess that's what I'm saying."

"Christ." He dropped his hand but didn't step away. "Easier to believe it's some big-city bad guy with a sheet a mile long. But this means it could be anyone. A person no one would suspect. Isn't that how it usually goes?"

"You said once you thought the killer was local." It was looking even likelier after what Drecker had told her today. And although they were a ways from determining that for sure, she was growing increasingly certain he was right.

He gave her a grim glance and began to head out. "Almost has to be. At least from the area. Walterville, Vida, Nimrod, Blue River, McKenzie . . . someone had to have lived in this area for a long time to know it as well as this guy does. I've lived around here all my life and I never knew that cave existed. Maybe he moved away after living here as a kid, but I doubt he went far. Unless . . . you don't think all those bones were dumped there at the same time, do you?"

She matched him step for step and tried to keep up as easily with the direction of his thoughts. "No."

"So the guy made multiple trips. Probably at night. Could have camped somewhere around here. Brought the bones with him, then struck out at night to dump them. But campsites mean people, and that'd be a risk. No, chances are he came in alone, left the same way. How far is he going to drive to get rid of them? Not far, I'm guessing. Not more than a couple hours. Can't risk being stopped and having human skeletons found in the car."

So engrossed was she in his litany that she narrowly avoided being smacked in the head by a low-hanging branch he'd let go of after dodging beneath it. As it was, the twigs on the branch caught her hair, and she stopped to release it. "First you say he lives around here, then you say he might be two hours away. Which is it?"

He turned to shoot her an impatient glance, saw her dilemma, and relented. Swiftly he walked back toward her and batted her hands out of the way. "You're making a mess of it. Let me."

His hands were quick and curiously gentle as he worked the strands free, but there was no trace of gentleness in his expression when he released her to step back. "Put your hat on," he said gruffly. While she dug in her pack, he seamlessly switched topics. "What I said was, he had to have lived here for a while at some point. Although I guess we shouldn't assume the killer is a man. Those bags weren't that heavy. Someone in shape, someone like you, could probably have made that climb up Castle Rock carrying the bag. But whoever it is, they knew this place. The way I know it. The way Jim Lancombe, the groundskeeper at the Springs Resorts, knows it. They're familiar with every square inch, same as me. Which makes using that cave as a dump site even worse, in my mind."

It may have been the longest speech she'd ever heard him

utter. It was easily the most impassioned. "Why?" Because he'd turned and started walking again, she fell in step, too. But she wanted, needed, the answer to her question. "Why does it make it worse?"

Minutes passed. Long enough for her to think he wasn't going to answer. But finally he said, "It seems like a desecration, I guess. This is one of the few truly peaceful places I've found on this earth." He sent her a quick sidelong glance. "I don't expect you to understand."

But she thought she did understand. At least a little. She headed for the mountains and forests in Virginia at least monthly, if the job allowed. Immersing herself in the tranquility found there never failed to ease her stress.

She had no illusions about the sort of missions he'd taken part in while in Afghanistan. What all those commendations and medals listed in his military record must have cost him.

A man like that, she reflected as she hurried to catch up with him, would be in dire need of peace.

Chapter 12

Sheriff Marin Andrews paced the length of Cait's motel room at the McKenzie, puffing on a cigarette with short staccato pulls. "And this detective ... Drecker ... he suspects Recinos's ex?"

"Yes, but if Marissa Recinos turns out to be our female C, Drecker has to be wrong about that. Her ex certainly didn't have motivation for killing all seven of the victims."

"Where are you on the profile of the UNSUB?"

The woman was as agitated as Cait had ever seen her. She'd been chain-smoking since she arrived here, and Cait had never seen her with a cigarette before. It made her glad she'd taken the time to complete the profile after she and Sharper had parted ways that evening.

Crossing to the desk, she picked up the file folder lying on it and handed it to the sheriff. "This is only a preliminary," she stressed. "It will evolve quickly if this lead pans out."

Andrews took the folder but didn't open it. "Why don't you give me the highlights?"

Unsurprised, Cait complied. "Without factoring in any of

the unknowns about Recinos, I'm guessing our guy is a native to the area. Possibly still lives around here." She thought for a moment of Sharper's assessment. He, at least, seemed convinced that was true. "Early to midthirties. In good shape. Either he lives outside city limits, or he has access to a place outside of town."

Andrews squinted at her through the smoke. "Because of the beetles?"

"Not necessarily. I've known people who keep them in their garages, but not our guy. Before the bones are ready for the beetles, he has to deflesh them. That's messy and there's going to be a distinctive smell. No one's going to do that in town and not have neighbors know about it. It's going to take a well-ventilated area, and he needs privacy and time. I'm guessing he's marginally employed."

The sheriff snorted. "You just described about fifty people in these parts that I could name personally."

Cait was half thinking out loud. "I just can't quite figure out what he does with the tissue once he defleshes the bodies."

"We can be sure he doesn't bury it, right? Or else he'd bury the whole body, bones and all."

"Those paintings on the scapulas . . ." Cait paused, the images flashing through her mind. "Those are likely the reason for his method of disposal. Not the act of using the dermestids. Not the cave itself. It's all about those paintings. He has to mark the victims in some way. Maybe they're a way to brand them as his." Serial offenders were often bizarrely possessive about their victims. "The method he uses will have something to do with his experiences, his ego. It symbolizes something for him. Power, maybe. Affection. Even remorse."

"If this victim does turn out to be Recinos, all those images are about her. Symbols of her life. And death," the sheriff added.

Understanding that she was referring to the last image of the skull, Cait nodded. "But I'm talking about why he feels the need for the drawings in the first place. It makes more sense if they depict his hunt. If he stalks them first, I could understand him painting symbols of things he'd learned about the victim in that process. It's an exciting time for the hunter, on the trail of his prey. In that case, the images would be more a tribute to his cleverness than having much to do with the victim personally."

Andrews dropped her spent cigarette into the water glass Cait had given her to use as an ashtray. "You said affection. Does that mean he knows the victims?"

"It's possible, but I doubt it. At least if he's acquainted with them it's only in the manner by which they came to his attention in the first place. But it's not unusual for the offender to feel emotionally close to the victim at the time of death." Seeing the shock in the sheriff's stare, she lifted a shoulder. "The act of murder is often seen by the offender as intimacy. Perhaps the most intimate act he or she is capable of."

"But you don't think these crimes had to do with rape?"

"There's no way to tell with only skeletal remains, unless the rape was violent enough to result in a fracture. But it would be unusual for a serial rapist to target both males and females. A sadist, maybe. Someone motivated by the deliberate affliction of pain. Problem is, without tissue—"

"—we can't verify whether the victims were tortured, either." A flicker of frustration crossed Andrews's face. "I'm beginning to wonder if defleshing and decapitating them are both merely part of his MO. They help him enact the crime and avoid detection."

"It's possible." It was important when establishing a profile to remain open to other ideas. Each new piece of evidence they acquired could morph the document to a degree. Cait nodded at the file folder the woman still hadn't opened. "But as I wrote in there, I'm guessing if we find the offender, we'll find the skulls."

"Because he's the type to take trophies?"

"Because he's expended so much time and energy on them. Not to mention talent. And it just defies imagination that he disposes of the skull, flesh, and bones all in different ways."

Andrews rubbed her eyes with the heel of one palm. She looked, Cait thought, the way Barnes had sounded on the phone . . . was it just this morning? Like she needed to sleep round the clock.

"All right. Let's plan on briefings each evening, at least by phone. But update me more regularly as you get details on the Recinos angle. What's on your plate for tomorrow?"

"I've got to take some soil samples to Kristy. I'd promised to get them to her today and never got the chance."

"Don't worry, Mitch has been keeping her plenty busy." Although the temperature in the room was comfortable, the sheriff's face was flushed. She fanned herself with the file folder. "He spent the day researching which manufacturers make black biodegradable garbage bags and sent a couple deputies to pick up different samples found in the area. Picked up the bags from the crime lab without latents, and she's logging reference comparisons on them."

"Well the fluorescent paint we ordered should be here tomorrow, at the latest. I'll probably spend the day in the lab and run those tests."

"How soon can we expect that DNA sample from Recinos's mother?"

"It depends on how quickly Drecker can get her to a lab. Day after tomorrow at the earliest, probably." Forestalling the woman's next comment, Cait said, "I'll compare the DNA profiles the minute it comes in."

Giving an abrupt nod, the sheriff moved toward the door, the file folder still clutched in her hand. "Sounds like a plan." Her hand was on the knob before Cait halted her.

"I've got Sharper's elimination prints here, too. And mine." She crossed to the desk and picked up the ten print cards she'd labeled and put in evidence bags. Handing them to Andrews, Cait tried not to think about the awkward moments spent lifting them. Zach's mood had bordered on dangerous when she'd reminded him, after they'd returned to her vehicle, about the need for the prints. But he'd cooperated as she'd led him through the process of inking each finger and pressing it to the card. Hadn't, in fact, uttered a word the entire time. Had just fixed her with a smoldering stare that had made her movements unnaturally clumsy.

After cleaning his fingers with the wipe she'd handed him, he'd walked away. Climbed back in his Trailblazer. Pulled out of the lot. And left her with a vague sense of guilt, the memory of which still annoyed her. There wasn't a man alive who would be allowed to make her feel guilty about doing her job.

At least there never had been before.

Andrews slipped the bags inside the folder she carried. "Great. I'll get these to the regional lab myself." She gave a cynical smile. "Helps to keep the Stateies at least marginally involved in case we need something from them later. They're none too happy about not being invited to help with the investigative end of things on this case."

The statement explained a lot. Cait had wondered why the latent work on the bags had been parceled out, when she and Kristy could have handled it. And she wasn't surprised the sheriff was territorial about the case. She'd want all the credit for the successful resolution of this case.

"We've got all the staff's prints on file, so we've run those for the personnel who were at the scene. Got elimination prints on the civilians we used, too. We still need to get your tech's."

"I'll do that tomorrow," Cait promised. She'd go through the motions as a matter of procedure, but she knew neither her assistant's nor her prints would match the one left on the bag. They'd been too careful.

"With any luck we'll discover that leaving that print was the first mistake the UNSUB made," the sheriff said grimly. "And once we catch him we'll be able to use it to nail his ass to the wall."

It would be a critical piece of evidence tying the UNSUB to the crime, Cait agreed silently. But first they had to catch him.

Another thought occurred. "Oh, and we found Kesey today. One of the roamers Barnes discovered with a record?" The woman looked at her inquiringly, and Cait gave her a quick rundown of her findings.

Andrews was philosophical. "Not much chance he's involved, if he's only got one arm. You think he's telling the truth about seeing someone around at night that once?"

"Fairly certain." Cait snuck a look at the alarm clock on the bedside table. She wanted to get a look at Ketchers sometime this evening. "He was motivated by the money. I figure if he thought there was more in the offing, he'd have spilled everything he knew."

Nodding, Andrews opened the door. "They usually do."

———————

An hour later Cait was feeling fairly human again after a thirty-minute soak in the tub. She was even feeling marginally friendly toward her hiking boots. After the ground they'd covered the last couple days, a less-than-perfect fit would have had her feet in agony. But they'd been well broken in before this trip.

That didn't mean, however, that she wasn't looking forward to a break from them while she did some work in the lab tomorrow.

As she dressed, she put in a call to her assistant and got her voice mail. Grimacing, Cait pulled on a green tank and denim shorts. It didn't take much imagination to figure out where Kristy was. Or at least whom she was spending her time with.

Her cell rang almost the moment she set it down, and she picked it up again to look at the screen, expecting her assistant.

But recognizing the number that appeared there, Cait dropped the phone into her purse, unanswered. This would make the third time her mother had called back since their conversation last night. And she'd delete this message the same way she had the others, without listening to it.

Distractions were something she could ill-afford in the middle of a case. And Lydia Regatta redefined the term *distracting*.

She took her weapon from her holster and placed it in her purse. Not because she credited Sharper's warning of trouble at the tavern, but because Raiker drilled into each of his investigators the need to be armed at all times. It was easy to guess where his insistence came from. All of his employees had heard the story of his final case with the Bureau. After her boss had been caught by the serial child killer he'd been trailing, he'd been imprisoned and tortured for three days before finally freeing himself and killing the man. He bore the scars as a haunting reminder. He regularly insisted on a concealed permit for his operatives before he ever accepted a job from a law enforcement entity.

Finally ready, she went to the door, unlocked it, and pulled it open. Then jumped back, startled. It was difficult to say who was more surprised—her or the man on the other side of it.

"Sharper. What are you doing here?"

He'd used the intervening time since they'd parted to shave and change clothes. He must have a never-ending supply of jeans and T-shirts, since she'd seen him in nothing else. Or maybe, she thought consideringly, he knew exactly how well they suited him.

"You're going to Ketchers tonight, right?" Without waiting for an invitation, he brushed by her to enter her motel room and immediately shrunk it with his presence. "Thought we decided last night that you weren't going alone."

It took a moment longer than it should have for her to recall the conversation he was referring to. Turning to watch his progression in the room, she let the door swing shut behind her. "This isn't necessary."

He raised a brow. "Are we really going to have that argument again?" Digging into his jeans pocket, he withdrew a white wrapper. "Figured you probably needed to change those Steri-Strips by now, too. Might as well do that first."

Taking advantage of her momentary speechlessness, he ripped open the package and sat on the corner of the bed. "C'mere."

The sight of him on her bed scattered her thought processes even further. Given his mood when they'd parted after she'd fingerprinted him, there was a definite Alice-in-Wonderland feel to the entire scene. "I'm perfectly capable . . ."

"Yeah, I know. You've got the whole Superwoman thing nailed, okay?" There was a glint in his eye that could have been amusement. Or she might be imagining it. There was something more than a little surreal about this. "But the sooner we get it taken care of, the sooner we can get to the tavern. Believe me, the earlier we get there, the better."

Her feet seemed to approach him of their own accord. "It's not that I don't appreciate the thought," she began. Then winced a little as he yanked the strips off her palm. He wasn't exactly angel-of-mercy material. It occurred to her that maybe he'd come to exact a bit of payback for taking his prints earlier.

"Looks like it's healing all right." He rubbed his thumb over the wound.

Lowering her gaze, she inspected it critically. "It'll be okay." It hadn't slowed her down much, and she was doubly glad she'd resisted getting stitches. She'd never been overly fond of needles, and doubted she could have gotten any better results if she'd allowed him to haul her into the clinic. Because it would have seemed churlish to pull her hand away at this point, she waited awkwardly for him to finish replacing the strips.

"You've got hidden talents," she said lightly, inspecting his handiwork when he was done. "Where'd you get your medical training?"

He smiled, slow and satisfied and devastating. "Actually I got all my skills from playing doctor."

Something in his expression had her heart stuttering. It ought to be a crime to give a man who looked like him the weapon of a smile that powerful. It was all the more effective for being so rare. She was certain it could shred hearts of unsuspecting females at ninety paces.

And right now she'd feel a lot safer if there were that much distance between them. If she weren't close enough to notice his eyes were alight with tiny golden lights that flickered like wicked flame.

If she weren't close enough to be tempted, just a bit, to pick up his unspoken invitation and be wicked with him.

She took a deep breath. And then another. Cait didn't make reckless decisions these days based on need and sheer self-indulgence. If there was one thing she'd learned over the years, it was that every act had consequences. Some had come at a price she was still paying, decades later.

"You wanna stay in tonight and play doctor, Slim?" Zach's eyes were intent. His voice raspy.

"No." Her answer shouldn't be tinged with regret. But she was lucky to have forced it out at all. Her lungs felt like they were slowly strangling in her chest. "Something tells me you already have a specialty in that area. But once I figured out what lousy taste I had in patients, you could say I gave up my practice." She took a step away. The next step was easier.

His expression was arrested, and she knew immediately that she'd said too much. "Uh . . . exactly how long has it been between 'patients'?"

She was immediately sorry she'd let that information escape. "None of your damn business, Sharper. Unless you're willing to answer the same question."

"Two weeks."

"Two . . ." her voice tapered off as his meaning became clear. "Well, no surprise there." For the first time she found herself wondering if his commitment to the sheriff's department was putting a crimp into his social life. "After this case is over, you'll be able to get back to your normal . . . interests. Whatever they might be." And whomever they might involve.

His gaze was sober. Searching. "After this case is over, the only woman I'm interested in will be gone."

It was surprisingly difficult to draw a deep breath. "I'm not that interesting, Sharper. Unless you've got a thing for women with stratospheric IQs and abysmal taste in men." It'd taken her a long time to recognize that she consistently chose males who didn't see *her*, only their own reflection in her. Once she'd figured that out, she'd started to regain a measure of her self-respect. And she'd kept it all these years by removing the revolving door to her bedroom.

But she'd be lying if she said that Zach Sharper didn't present the most temptation she'd faced in years.

He rose and approached her. Cupped her jaw in his hands and lowered his head to whisper against her lips, "Turns out that's exactly what I'm interested in. And I'm not sure which of us should be more surprised." His kiss then was hard and much too brief. And while she was still reeling from the effects, he pulled away and walked to the door.

"I'll drive."

———————

Ketchers was everything she'd been led to believe . . . and less. Cait looked around at the dim interior curiously as they stood in the doorway. A row of booths lined one wall, opposite the scarred bar. There were a couple dartboards hanging on the wall, and the area around them looked as though the participants weren't too skilled at hitting the target. Two pool tables were jammed into another corner, and the center was filled with what looked like plywood-topped tables. The floor was concrete and the drinks were served in plastic cups.

Cait had the distinct impression that the owner purposely kept things low rent. Given the clientele, that was probably wise.

Zach's next words echoed her thoughts. "Place has burned down three times in the last eight years." With a hand in the small of her back, he nudged her farther into the interior. "Every time Kenny Smalley rebuilds, he goes more and more no frills."

"No frills is one thing," she muttered, aware that all eyes in the place were on them. "But isn't the exterior tin?"

"Aluminum. No insulation, either. Place is an igloo in the winter. Hey, Jodie." He spoke to someone who'd hailed him from a nearby table of card players.

"Hey, Sharper, you want in this hand? I gotta take a leak."

When Zach shook his head at the offer, she cocked a brow. "Go ahead. I won't tell the sheriff that the owner is running illegal gambling from his establishment. I'll even bring you a beer."

"No reason to tell her." He continued to propel her through

the crowded floor. "The guy offering me his chair is Gibbs, one of Andrews's finest."

Cait turned to look over her shoulder. Tony Gibbs was tall and lanky, with close-cropped dark hair, a predominant nose, and large ears. He was leaned forward over the table, talking quickly to the other men playing cards. With a flash of intuition, she knew that she was the topic of conversation.

Thoughtfully, she continued to wend her way through the tables, ever aware of Zach right behind her. If the waitress at JD's could be believed, the deputy also had more to say about her and this case than was probably wise for someone in his position. She was more eager than ever to speak to the man, if only to see how well apprised he was about the details of the investigation. Stopping at an empty table, she looked at Sharper. "This one okay?"

"First the drinks." His hand exerted light pressure at the base of her spine. She could feel the heat emanating from his flesh through the thin fabric of her top. "This place doesn't run to wait staff. If we want something, we have to get it at the bar."

"I don't really need . . ."

He leaned closer, the low timbre of his voice rumbling in her ear. "You're a stranger, and everyone in the place is wondering what the hell you're doing here. A beer will help you fit in."

Without argument, she continued moving forward and found a spot at the bar. He was right, of course. And she shouldn't have needed the reminder. It suited her to blame her unusual lapse in judgment on the excitement of the day. That was more comfortable than to think that his words to her in the motel room had rattled her too much to think clearly.

"What'll you have?" The bartender was the polar opposite of the man she'd encountered at JD's last night. His gleaming bald head was the color of toffee, and when he ducked down to speak to her, she could see a large winged dragon tattooed on his dome. His arms were bare, save for full sleeves of tattoos twining up them. His hands were as scarred as the heavily pocked tables and bar top. She recognized the prison tats on his knuckles. Wondered how long it'd been since he'd gotten out.

"Coors Light."

"Budweiser." Zach's voice sounded behind her.

There was a woman to Cait's right, one of only three females in the place. She gave Cait a quick once-over before shifting her attention to Sharper. "Gonna introduce your new playmate, Zach?"

"I'm Cait." She handed the huge bartender a ten and took the cups he set down in front of her, passing the beer back to Zach. Her attention returned to the woman next to her. "Do you live around here?"

The woman lifted a shoulder. "Depends on what you call living, I guess. Rent an acreage about a mile down the road."

She was wearing what seemed to be a uniform of sorts among women Cait had seen in the area. A spandex top with spaghetti straps with a long velvet layered skirt. Soft flat-soled boots, laced up the front. The single brown braid hanging down her back was threaded with gray. She wore no discernible makeup.

"That qualifies." Cait took a sip. "How long have you had the acreage?"

The woman twirled around on her barstool to face Cait. "That particular one? Couple years. I used to live over my shop in town, but my kids needed more room."

"I walked down Main Street last night." Cait studied the woman, wondering which of the stores had been hers. "Most of the stores weren't open, though."

The woman flicked a glance at Zach and gave a wry grin. "Something tells me you wouldn't be in the market for what I sell anyway."

Following her gaze to the man in back of her, Cait noted that Zach looked amused. "You never know," she responded mildly. "Which shop was yours?"

"Al's. You probably didn't notice it."

"The taxidermy shop." She studied the woman with renewed interest. "You're right. I wouldn't have expected that one to be yours."

"Kathy has been doing the bulk of the work there for what . . . six years?" Zach's voice sounded behind her.

"More like ten. Al sort of lost interest long time ago. I was always around. I'd done his books and answered his phone seems like forever. Sort of moved into helping him with the work, and before I knew it, I was taking over for him when he retired."

The bartender set a drink in front of the woman and cleared away her empty without any signal from her. And it didn't escape Cait's attention that in the act he managed to brush his hand against Kathy's.

She smiled easily at the other woman. "You have a unique occupation. I saw the full skeleton in the window of . . . an otter?"

"I can't take credit for that." Kathy sipped at her mixed drink. "It was Al's. I wouldn't have the foggiest idea how to go about reassembling an animal's skeleton. I do a few animal skulls for people, but I always boil them." She wrinkled her nose. "Al used to use beetles to clean them, but that was way too gross for me. Those bugs gave me the creeps. He used to think it was hilarious to drop one in my hair." She shuddered. "He could be a jerk sometimes. I made him get rid of them when he decided to retire. I'd much rather boil the skulls than deal with those damn bugs."

"Do you know what he did with them?"

"Don't know and don't care. Gave them away, probably. Couldn't take them to Arizona. That's where he went, wasn't it Zach?"

"Couldn't say," Zach responded laconically. "I wasn't around at the time."

"Oh, that's right." Kathy gave him a wink. "I've gotten so used to seeing your pretty face around here, I forget you were gone for a bit."

"Twelve years." His tone was bland. "I can see how that might have escaped your mind." Their give and take had the easy banter of long acquaintances.

"Kathy, you need anything else?"

The woman looked at the bartender askance. "I just got a

fresh one a couple minutes ago, Rick. Did you forget already?"

"We're going to grab a table." After making the pronouncement, Zach took Cait's elbow in his hand and steered her to the table they'd passed earlier en route to the bar.

Once they'd sat down Cait said, "I came here because I want to speak to some locals." And to hear what they had to say about this case.

"You'll get your chance." He lifted a hand to return a newcomer's wave as the man made his way up toward the crowd at the bar. "Everyone here has seen you talking to Kathy, so they know you're accessible. Within a half hour, they'll start heading over here, one by one. At least the bravest among them."

She raised her brows. "You think talking to me requires an act of bravery?"

"Woman who looks like you can be intimidating." He managed to make the statement sound matter of fact. "But alcohol dulls common sense, so like I say, give 'em a half hour."

Since it was difficult to tell whether she should be offended or not, Cait decided to change the topic. "They seem like an unlikely couple."

Zach's hand stopped in midmotion as he was bringing the cup to his mouth. "Who?"

She gave a slight nod in the direction of the bar. "Kathy and the bartender."

His gaze followed hers. "Rick Moses. How'd you know they were together?"

"I'm a trained observer, Sharper." Enjoying his surprise, she sat back and let her gaze wander around the area. Caught more than one set of eyes on her in the process. "And he was jealous that she was talking to you. That's why he interrupted us there at the end. When'd he get out?"

He continued the act of bringing the cup to his lips. Took a drink and grimaced a little. "I hate draft beer," he muttered, setting the cup back on the table. "Get out of where?"

"He's been in prison. They aren't married." Kathy hadn't

been wearing a ring, and the furtive touching of hands seemed more like lovers. "I'd guess he's been free for a couple years, at least." There was a look convicts had fresh out of the system. Paranoia underlying a sort of jumpiness. The man had been out long enough to lose some of that edge, but not long enough for the prison tats to fade.

"Four years. Maybe five."

"What was he in for?"

"I don't know." His nonchalance was deliberate. "Not my business."

"And you're all about minding your own business." She saluted him with her cup and took a swallow. Then silently agreed with him about the taste.

"More people should feel the same." He shifted in his chair and stretched his feet out, as if settling in. "Half the world's problems would be solved if people just left each other the hell alone."

"Ever thought about becoming a hermit?"

He gave a slow nod in mock seriousness. "I would. Haven't figured out how to factor in sex on a regular basis, though."

She laughed, amused. One thing that could be said about the man, he was genuine. No one would ever have a doubt where they stood with Zach Sharper. That trait of his made her wonder how he'd fared in boot camp with a drill sergeant shouting at the top of his lungs. Did becoming a soldier mean so much to him that he'd swallowed his innate sense of self-reliance for the chance to accomplish his dream?

"What else?"

His question jolted her attention back to their conversation. "What else, what?"

He jerked his head toward the people huddled around tables surrounding them. "Let's hear some more of your observations. I'll tell you how close you are."

She let her gaze wander around the area for several minutes. "Guy over there to the right of Gibbs works on a farm. The blonde sitting in the corner, wearing the gray pullover? She's an addict. Just starting to come down from something. The short guy on the far left of the bar is the likeliest one to start a fight. The one with the red bandana playing darts would be the last one standing if one did break out."

"Present company excluded, of course."

She inclined her head. "Of course." It didn't take any special observational powers to conclude that Zach Sharper was the most dangerous person in the place. Even with no prior acquaintance with the man, she would have figured that within a minute of entering the tavern. There was something about his still watchfulness that would mark him as such to anyone with a normal amount of caution. Something that warned this man would be good to have at your back in a fight.

And a risky one to cross.

"Not bad." The expression of respect on his face would have been more satisfying if it weren't accompanied by surprise. "Jodie Paulsen does chores for Tim Jenkins, who lives between here and Blue River. Beth Swenson's drug of choice these days is meth. Tyler Babcock is more mouth than brains." He turned his head slightly, considered the man at the dartboard. "I don't know the other guy. Logger, probably. Not sure I agree on him."

"Bet you twenty bucks he's got a knife concealed in his boot."

He took another quick look. "You're on. How do you expect to find that out?"

With a smile of satisfaction she said, "Leave it to me. I've got a . . ." When her cell phone rang she dug in her purse, looked at the screen. Not her mother. It was ridiculous to feel this overwhelming sense of relief. But it wasn't a number she recognized, either.

She rose as she answered it, striding toward the door. "Fleming." The background noise in the place would make it impossible to hold a conversation inside.

"Caitlin Fleming?" The voice on the other end of the line was female. "This is Detective Cindy Purcell, Las Vegas PD. Got your message about my missing persons case in a pile of a hundred others when I got back on the job yesterday."

"Thanks for the call back." Shoving out of the door of the bar, she nearly ran into a couple on their way in. Neither gave her as much as a glance before brushing by her. "I've got seven sets of skeletal remains, and so far none of them are identified."

"Well, I'd sure like to be able to close this case on Mark Chastens. Been missing for two years, and every lead I had fizzled." There was a pause, as if Cait's words had just sunk in. "You've only got skeletons?"

"That's right." Although she didn't see anyone in the vicinity, she remained guarded in her responses.

"Chastens was in a bad car accident ten years prior to his death. Had screws and plates put in his right hip." The detective's voice was hopeful. "That match with any of the remains you've got up there?"

Faintly deflated, Cait said, "No." She stared across the lot to where bugs were flying in crazed circles around a security light mounted on a pole and encased in wire. "That doesn't match any of the victims."

"Damn." The word came out as a sigh. Then, "You're sure? I mean maybe the screws came out or something."

"I'd see evidence of their placement in the bone. I've got four sets of male remains. None of them sound like your guy. Sorry." And she was. So far of the detectives who had returned her repeated calls, this made three of the missing persons who could be dismissed out of hand. Which had her even more excited about receiving the DNA profile on the elder Recinos. Their best chance of solving this case lay in their ability to identify the victims.

"Well, thanks anyway. Good luck with your investigation." The woman's tone grew wry. "With seven sets of remains, you've got a lot bigger problem than my missing persons case."

And that, Cait thought as she hung up the call, was an accurate and all too depressing summary of their predicament. There was no denying it. A DNA match right now was going to be the one thing that would propel this case forward.

Chapter 13

Cait heard the crunch of boots on gravel a moment before a voice sounded. "Was that about the case?"

Turning, she saw Deputy Tony Gibbs approaching in a slouched shuffling stride. Slipping the cell in her jeans pocket she surveyed him with a critical eye. "Just a lead that went nowhere."

Hooking his thumbs in his jeans, he said, "Barnes had me running all over yesterday shopping for garbage bags. Said you were going to try and match them to those we hauled out of the cave, so I was surprised to see you here."

With an insincere smile she asked, "Is that what you told the men in there tonight?"

The flicker of surprise across his expression was its own answer. One he denied an instant later. "My buddies and me have an understanding. I can't share details of department matters with them. Our jobs depend on confidentiality, yours and mine. It isn't easy sometimes being the one everyone looks to for answers, is it?"

She managed, barely, to avoid rolling her eyes. "It's a burden."

He took a step closer, lowered his voice confidentially. "The thing is, Barnes isn't utilizing me as fully as he could. I know this area and the people in it. Be the easiest thing in the world for me to be conducting interviews on persons of interest in these parts. They trust me. Some won't open up to strangers, but they would to me."

Until they could come up with something solid establishing the killer as an area resident, there was no real reason for the interviews, but she didn't tell him that. She already knew him well enough to realize it wouldn't be wise to tell the man much of anything.

"You should speak to Mitch about that."

"Mitch has let this lead investigator thing go to his head." It was plain that Gibbs was disgruntled. A faint whine had entered his voice. "All he does is issue orders. We don't even have daily briefings updating everyone on the progress of the case. Just do this, do that. I know damn well he's not telling us everything. If you ask me, he's priming himself for a run at Andrews's job."

"Seems like a solid cop." The door swung open and a man stumbled out of the bar, made his way in a haphazard fashion toward his truck.

"He's got no imagination," Gibbs corrected. He reached up a hand, scratched his prominent nose. "His type's got no business being top cop of Lane County. Problem is, this is Oregon. He just might get himself elected."

Cait studied the deputy more carefully. Although he danced around the subject, she didn't think it was Barnes's qualifications he objected to as much as the man's sexual orientation. Whichever, she no longer had to worry about mentioning Gibbs's penchant for gossip to the chief deputy. He'd already limited the information being passed to this man.

She'd be lying if she said she hadn't already had a half formed opinion of Gibbs before this meeting. But her initial impression hadn't been too far off. He was a man whose job afforded him the only sense of importance he'd ever had in his life. And one he wielded to get respect, even if it meant sharing far more than he should about issues that should remain confidential.

"Everyone's efforts on this case are appreciated." She eyed the tavern. No more could be garnered from this conversation, but there were still people inside she'd like a chance to speak to. Cait began to inch away.

Gibbs grabbed her elbow when she would have passed him. "But that's just it! My *efforts* are being underutilized."

Her gaze dropped to his hand before rising slowly to regard him. "You're going to want to move your hand."

He released her and stepped back with far more alacrity than Sharper had when she'd leveled a similar order at him, only the night before. But then, Gibbs wasn't in Sharper's league. Few men were.

"Sorry. It's just that I can do more." He shoved a hand through his short-cropped hair in frustration. "Just wanted you to know that, because I heard you were taking soil samples on properties that have hot springs on 'em. Most of the private property owners in this area aren't going to let a stranger go tramping around, because they got things they don't want law enforcement knowing about. Maybe growing a little weed on the side, but hey, that's got nothing to do with the case, right? But they might let me on because they trust me. They know I won't jam 'em up over something like that." He paused expectantly. When she didn't respond, he continued, "So if you run into trouble getting access to some places you'd like samples from, could be I can help you out with that."

His words had her stomach plummeting. Barnes had taken measures to stem the leak in the department too late. If Gibbs knew that much, chances were all his buddies inside Ketchers knew it, too. And by extension, so would untold other members of the nearby communities. The deputy couldn't know that she'd veered in a slightly different direction with the samples, but that didn't matter. The damage had already been done.

"I'll keep that in mind." A car pulled into the lot much too fast, and they both stepped out of the way of the gravel sprayed in its wake. It didn't appear to occur to Gibbs that he'd just revealed he was willing to turn a blind eye to his friends' illegal activities to retain their trust. Cait was inclined to believe that her original assessment of the man was valid.

She was headed toward the tavern door when he stopped her again. Not by touching her this time, which meant he had at least some measure of good sense. But his voice had grown diffident.

"Uh . . . I was wondering . . ."

Turning toward him, she cocked a brow inquiringly.

He shifted his weight a bit. "Saw you come in with Sharper. But if you want to go somewhere quiet and discuss the case . . . maybe talk over some possible leads . . . I'm available." His shoulders seemed to hunch even more. "I was on my way out anyway."

"I appreciate the offer." Experience had made her an expert in the art of softening rejection. "Tonight, though, I think I'm going to take a break from the case for a few hours." That wasn't strictly true, of course, since her time spent inside was more about observing than relaxing. But Gibbs seemed to buy it.

"Oh, yeah, of course." He pulled his keys out of his jeans pocket. "I can understand that. Another time, maybe."

"Another time." And when she strode back toward the door he didn't try to stop her.

———

When Cait rejoined Zach, there was someone else standing at the table. Jodie Paulsen, she recalled. The farm hand whose boots bore the evidence of his occupation. But from the easy expression Sharper wore, he was friendly with the man. The same as he was with Kathy. For all his self-avowed solitary ways, it was evident that he was well regarded in the area. Even Sheriff Andrews spoke of his skills, at least, with a measure of respect.

Both men looked up at her approach. Paulsen's face was

puppy-dog friendly. He was around Sharper's age, she estimated. Midthirties, with none of the guide's hard edges and vague sense of menace. Paulsen's plaid shirt was almost an exact match for his gingery-colored hair. And it was clear from his appearance that he'd come to the bar straight from his chores.

Zach's gaze was searching. "Trouble?"

Cait shook her head. "Just business." She gave the other man a smile. "Hi, I'm Cait."

"I know." Paulsen beamed a smile in return. "I've been standing here for ten minutes trying to pretend I wanted to talk to Zach, but really I was just waiting for you to come back inside so I could meet you."

"Careful." A corner of Sharper's mouth quirked. "You're going to hurt my feelings."

"Way I hear it you've got no feelings, Zach."

Cait caught his slight wince at the jibe as she sank back into her chair.

"You've been talking to your neighbor." Sharper tipped the cup to his lips and drank.

"Mostly just listening." Paulsen rested a hand on the back of the free chair in front of him. "Woman scorned. She had a lot to say, and nothing I said in your defense made it any better."

It was difficult to say which fascinated Cait more. The topic of conversation or the look of discomfit on Sharper's face. "Sounds like an intriguing story."

"Not one you're going to hear," he muttered.

She shifted her gaze from him to Paulsen. "Is your neighbor here tonight?"

The man took a huge swallow of beer before answering. "This isn't Shellie's type of place. And I'm just giving Zach a hard time. She knew the score going in. Hell, everyone 'round here knows Zach Sharper is the last person alive who's going the white picket fence route. Shellie's just sore because she thought she . . ."

"Jodie." Zach's tone was pleasant. His eyes flinty. "Shut up."

The man appeared to take no offense. "Shutting up." He took another drink and winked at Cait. Thoughtfully, she considered the man seated across from her as she took a sip of her own now-warm beer. There wasn't a doubt in her mind that Paulsen's assertion was correct. Sharper wasn't exactly the type of man about whom a woman should be spinning dreams of white lace and organdy.

She was also certain that he would have been brutally honest in that regard. And maybe that's what had roused the woman's ire. Some would find his brand of forthrightness abrasive. But few could complain that they didn't know where they stood with the man.

Rubbing at the condensation collecting on the outside of the cup, Cait figured she'd rather deal with a man like Sharper than most of those she'd dated. Men that used gloss and polish to mask their true design. Men who finally convinced her that the instinct she relied on to profile a criminal's motives didn't generalize to her personal life. When it came to taste in dates, she'd long ago concluded her judgment was too frequently flawed.

"So Gibbs says you work for some outfit out east. That you used to be a fed." Paulsen's words were directed at Cait.

Her answer was noncommittal. "I did work for the Bureau, but only in their labs, not as an investigator." And although they'd valued her contribution there, she'd known there was no way she'd be allowed to move out of the lab into an agent slot. Once she'd determined that that was exactly what she wanted, she'd grown increasingly restless. She didn't know how she'd come to Raiker's attention. But she hadn't had to weigh his offer too long. And she'd never regretted making the move. Her work for Raiker Forensics allowed her to utilize her forensic anthropology and molecular biology background while putting her at the forefront of investigations. So far it seemed a perfect fit.

She smiled at the man blandly and decided to do a little pumping of her own. "What else did Gibbs say?"

He seemed to recognize that the words were baited and exerted some belated caution. "Oh, not much." He moved his shoulders uneasily. "No one really listens to him anyway. He's a good guy, though."

"Hey, Paulsen, you in or out?"

Visibly relieved, he inched away. "Gotta go. I'm down five bucks. I make it a habit to break even before I leave the table."

"Good luck with that."

With a slap on Zach's shoulder, the man moved away. Sharper looked across the table at her, his gaze amused. "You must be a terror in interrogation."

"I underestimated him. I figured he'd walk right into that one."

"Jodie's smarter than he looks. Which is more than I can say for Gibbs." He toyed with his empty cup. "You run into him out there?"

She nodded. "Not hard to tell where some of the gossip about this case is coming from. But Barnes is on top of things. I don't think Gibbs is in the loop as far as details in this case go."

"Good thing."

Raised voices at the far corner of the bar drew both their attention. "Might be a good time to leave. These things tend to escalate quickly."

His suggestion seemed overly cautious. As far as she could tell, no one else was paying attention to the short loud-mouthed man and his much larger counterpart. And it was early yet. Far earlier than he'd indicated trouble could be expected.

"I'd like to stay a while longer and talk to some more people."

Sharper rose. "We need to leave."

Irritated, she remained seated. "Go ahead. I can find my way back to the motel if . . ."

A chair hurtled through the air and narrowly missed their table. The bar seemed to explode. Men tumbled from their chairs and waded in, flinging fists and beers with indiscriminate abandon. Zach all but hauled her to her feet. "Grab your purse."

They didn't go more than a few paces before their exit was blocked by the mob of men. And one woman, Cait noted. The emaciated blonde in the corner was beating one guy in the head with the heel of her sandal.

At the sound of a sickening thud, she risked a glance over her shoulder and saw the bartender on this side of the bar swinging a club at anyone within reach. He caught the arm of the logger and knocked the blade he'd drawn out of his hand.

Then she was shoved to her knees with a force that had her teeth snapping together. From the corner of her eye she saw a blur of motion as a pool cue swiped harmlessly over her head and caught Sharper squarely in the chest. In the next moment the other man's head snapped back. His eyes rolled white. And he crumpled, nearly landing on top of Cait.

Zach rubbed his fist, then pulled her up by her elbow. She followed him closely as they made their way toward the door. Out of it.

The brawl seemed to follow them into the lot. They stumbled toward Zach's Trailblazer. Before getting in, Cait looked over her shoulder. Bodies grappled in the shadows and rolled on the ground.

Her door flew open. "Get in." Zach's jaw was clenched. Once she'd obeyed, he engaged the automatic locks and started the vehicle.

"Well." She settled back in her seat and secured her seat belt. "That was interesting."

"That was avoidable," he corrected her tersely. He wasted no time pulling away and nosing the vehicle in the direction of the motel. "I seem to recall telling you the place is a nest of idiots."

He was entitled to an I-told-you-so. She kept her voice mild. "You mentioned something to that effect." There was silence as he traveled the few blocks to their destination. She didn't consider the night a total loss. Just the opposite. She'd wanted to meet Gibbs. She'd planned to talk to the taxidermist. All in all, the time had been well spent. At least until the end when she'd nearly been clobbered.

She looked across the shadowy interior of the vehicle at

the man bringing the SUV to a stop in front of her motel door. The lot's nearby security light splintered the darkness in the front seat. "You owe me twenty bucks."

He threw the Trailblazer into park, incredulity lacing his words. "And how do you figure that?"

"Our bet." When he said nothing she prompted, "The logger? He had a knife at the end. Granted I didn't see him pull it, and you could split hairs and argue that it might not have come from his boot. So to be fair, I guess we could settle at ten."

"Given the fact that I saved your ass back there, let's call it even."

"You saved my . . ." She stopped abruptly, narrowing her eyes. It had been a blur of action, but she hadn't been in any danger. Unless. . . "The pool cue?"

He smiled humorlessly. "If he'd connected, you'd be nursing the mother of all headaches right now."

She'd been shoved to her knees, she recalled. Not by the press of the crowd, but by Sharper. "But he hit you instead."

"Like I need the reminder."

Her gaze lowered to his chest. And remembering the sound the cue had made when it'd smacked him had her feeling a little sick. "Why would you do that?" She was honestly baffled.

"Why would I . . . yeah, I forgot. You're the woman of steel. Did I offend your super-agent sensibilities? Excuse me all to hell." His voice dripped derision. "Next time I'll step aside and let the idiot whale on you."

His sarcasm sailed by her. Cait was still grappling with the ramifications of his actions. Zach peered more closely at her. "Haven't you ever had a man step up to protect you?"

She lifted a shoulder impatiently. It was a nonissue. She didn't need a male to protect her when she was usually perfectly capable of doing it herself. But his question gave her pause. Because she hadn't always had the training she'd acquired in the course of her work for Raiker. And Cait was trying—and failing—to remember a time prior to that when anyone in her life had tried to protect her. From anything.

"I almost got mugged once," she recalled suddenly. The memory was hazy. It'd been nearly twenty years ago. They'd been in Milan. Or maybe Rome. "The man I was dating threw the guy my purse so he'd let us go." She didn't bother to mention that the man had been fifteen years her senior. Some details weren't pertinent.

She was surprised by his loud bark of laughter. "Your boyfriend gave up *your* money? What a prince."

His mockery had annoyance rising. "And what would you have done? Chased the guy down and beat an apology from him?"

"Damn straight."

His verbal machismo wouldn't have been so irritating if she weren't so certain it was accurate.

"I guess you had to be there." It had seemed slightly more heroic at the time. Of course she'd been sixteen. A bit more impressionable than she was now. "My ex-fiancé once gave me a gift certificate to a women's self-defense course for my birthday."

"I have a news flash for you, Slim. The guys you dated were dicks."

The fact that he'd summed up the men in question so precisely when it had taken her months, and one very messy broken engagement, to do the same wasn't particularly flattering. But no one knew better than she that shaking out the men from her past would result in a pile of users, losers, and liars. And that said far more about her than them.

"So . . . I guess you keep the ten then. Like you said. Call it even."

He cocked a brow. "Ten bucks for your life? Seems about fair." He paused a beat. "Of course I also might have saved you some professional embarrassment. If you'd landed in the hospital with a concussion, it would have been hard to explain to your boss."

Amusement stirred. "So now I owe you, is that it?"

"Then there's the pain and suffering aspect. Probably going to bruise where that guy connected." He lifted a hand to brush over his chest. Gave a theatrical wince.

"My tab's mounting."

"Don't worry, though." His voice in the semishadows was pure wicked invitation. "I've got a payment plan in mind."

She'd just bet he did. "Let's keep things in perspective. It's not like you threw yourself under a bus for me."

He tapped his finger against his lips. "One kiss. Just one. Then call us square."

Cait eyed him dubiously. If he was trying for innocence with that expression, she could have told him his effort was wasted. He looked about as innocent as the serpent in the Garden of Eden, offering Eve a bite of that Granny Smith.

And like Eve, she found the temptation overpowering.

She made a production of releasing her seat belt. Noticed his had never been fastened. And slowly, with a great deal of anticipation, leaned over to touch her lips against his.

Their previous kiss had been too brief. Unsatisfying. It hadn't allowed her to test for herself whether there was any softness in the man. To tell if he was all hard edges and steely resolve. Or whether she was fooling herself by believing his tough exterior really masked a depth that she'd occasionally caught glimpses of.

He was motionless, and that surprised her. If he had tried to take control of the depth or speed, it would have been all too easy to stop. To pull away and end the evening with a glib comment and more than a little regret. But since he didn't— since he allowed her to set the pace—she found herself relaxing infinitesimally. And took her time discovering some answers about the man for herself.

Her lips parted slightly to explore his. They were softer than she would have thought. With a firmness that held promise. She scored his lower lip with her teeth, and smiled at his sharply hissed in breath. It would be easy to get used to this. To tease and taste without worrying that it wouldn't lead any further. That it couldn't. To indulge in a fantasy that, if she was honest, had lingered in the corner of her mind like a persistent ghost.

The console between them made it difficult to get closer. To change the angle and deepen the kiss. But she leaned nearer, sliding her bandaged palm over his smooth jaw. And when she slicked her tongue along the seam of his lips, he exploded into action.

His arms sped out to lift her up and over the dividing console so she sat across his lap, all without breaking contact. His mouth ate at hers, pressing her lips apart so his tongue could sweep in, staking a claim.

And she couldn't resist reveling in the torrent she'd unleashed for another minute. Or maybe two.

He was good at this. No surprise there. There was a basic carnal pleasure to be had in the mingling of breath. The clash of lips, teeth, tongues. But when the sensation kick-started need, she mentally clawed for reason. Found it surprisingly difficult to summon.

A man with this much appeal was dangerous on a level she hadn't even contemplated. If he could have her setting aside logic with a mere kiss . . . The thought fragmented when he nipped at her lip. Re-formed as he soothed at the tender area with the tip of his tongue. Then he posed a risk she couldn't afford. And she'd given up her risky behaviors years ago.

With effort, she drew in a breath. Tried to shift away. And found him matching her movement for movement without releasing her mouth.

Against her lips he murmured, "Technically if we don't come up for air it's still only one kiss."

He was nothing if not creative. His hand slid beneath her tank, and she jerked a little at the contact. His fingers spread against her skin, each digit an individual brand. And the sneaky little thought occurred that she could touch him that way, too. Her palms itched with the need to reciprocate.

She slipped her hand under his T-shirt and smiled against his lips when she felt his stomach muscles jump and clench beneath her touch. There didn't seem to be an ounce of spare flesh on him. Just hair-roughened skin layered over muscle. Peaks and hollows where bone met sinew. And she knew in a flash it had been a mistake to touch him this way. Each step brought a greater intimacy. And fueled the need for more.

His palm crept upward to cup her breast, and she could

feel her nipple tighten as he brushed it, behind the lace of her bra. Senses seemed unbearably heightened. There was a growing anticipation as if every nerve ending she had was poised, waiting for a deeper contact. At the same time Zach drew her bottom lip into his mouth and bit down, not quite gently. The dual assault sent little sparks of desire firing through her veins.

As their mouths twisted together, thought receded. There was only the taste of him, dark and faintly primitive. His hands, slightly roughened, that knew just how to touch. Just how to tease and tantalize until she strained against him, begging for closer contact.

And then his fingers slipped inside her bra to cover her breast, and excitement thrummed through her system.

Her movements lacked finesse as she bunched his shirt upward. Skated both palms over his chest, her touch softening when she felt the slight jerk of his body. Fingers skimming tenderly over the area that was probably already bruising. Her eyelids fluttered. But she couldn't drag them open to check. Pent-up need was pumping through her, lending a sense of urgency.

The urgency dimmed the alarm bells shrilling in her mind. Didn't still them completely. They were too well constructed for that. But muted them to a point that made it incredibly easy to ignore them altogether.

There was a surprising pleasure to be found here, pressed closely against him. To feel the leap in his chest when she scraped one of his nipples with her nail. To hear his breathing lose it's steady rhythm and grow just a little choppy. And to feel. God, to feel. His fingers drew her nipple to a tight knot of nerves that shot shocks of desire straight to her womb.

She was used to inspiring desire in men. Desire that had everything to do with how she looked rather than who she was. So there was no reason for the evidence of this man's desire to fill her with a thrilling sense of female satisfaction. No reason for it to amp up her need for him until it threatened to blur common sense. Blind her to consequences.

His thumb flicked her nipple. The sensual rhythm had her

squirming on his lap. "Been a long time since I made out in my car."

She could feel every word formed beneath her lips. One kiss. She recalled the invitation. And he'd yet to relinquish her mouth.

"Do I stay or go, Cait? Your call."

Everything inside her stilled. She was distantly aware that he'd frozen, too, as if in anticipation of her response. Neither of them seemed to breathe while they waited for her response.

A response, that, when it came, took her as much by surprise as it seemed to him.

"Stay." The word was breathed against his lips. For a moment he didn't react. Neither of them did. There was a brief flare of panic as she considered her choice. Then that was diminished, as his breath streamed out of him. And the tethers harnessing his control seemed to fray.

There was a ferocious hunger evident now as his mouth ate at hers. His arms wrapped around her, a tight band that pressed her closer to his chest. A light flickered as he shifted. She felt herself being carried.

By the time she had her eyes dragged open to half mast they were standing in front of her motel door. She blinked, dazed. The man seemed endlessly resourceful. His lips moved to the corner of her mouth. "Key."

"Purse. Outside pock—" Then sighed a little as his lips settled more firmly over hers again. She was dimly aware that he'd hung the purse on the doorknob while he went in search of the key. Mentally congratulated him when the door swung open a few moments later.

Then thought spun away as they were inside the room in two quick paces. She heard a thud. Then the door closed. And with a speed that was dizzying, found herself on her feet and pressed up against it.

There was no teasing in his touch now. Just raw unvarnished need with the slightest sheen of desperation. And that fanned the flames of her own desire to a scorching level. Their mouths twisted together in a kiss that was deep. Wet.

Frankly carnal. Hands battled to unfasten snaps and buttons and zippers.

She wasn't used to this rollicking in her pulse. This fierce compulsion to strip him bare so there'd be nothing but flesh against flesh with no whisper of air between them. To explore every hard angle of his shoulders and chest. The surprising softness of the skin on his sides. And lose herself in a journey of discovery that she didn't want to end.

He released her mouth long enough to divest her of shirt and bra, and she hastened to shove his tee up and over his head. Then moaned a little at that first sensation of skin against skin. His fingers threaded in her hair to cup the back of her head as he sank into another kiss.

Heat, a quick stabbing spear of it, arrowed up her spine. It wasn't enough to run her palms over his arms, down the strong back. She tore her mouth away from his, tried to get her breath. Lost it in the next moment when his hands cupped her breasts. Fingers stroking and lightly squeezing by turn.

She nipped at his shoulder in a savage thirst for flesh. Pushed the jeans she'd loosened down his narrow hips. And gave a purr of satisfaction when his heavy sex sprang forward, hard and ready.

When her hand wrapped around him, his hips jerked, then stilled. But she could feel him quivering in her palm. Straining for release. Her fingers glided down the shaft and back up. Once. Twice. Again. Then faltered in their rhythm as he leaned down to take one of her nipples into his mouth.

Colors fragmented behind her eyelids. And when his teeth scraped the nipple, an edgy blade of need nicked over nerve endings already unbearably sensitized. Her shorts were shoved aside and his fingers, those clever wicked fingers, traced the seam of her leg teasingly before delving inside her panties. Cupping her where she was damp and heated.

Her head lolled, her breath coming in short ragged pants. He took advantage of the position to raise his head and cruise his mouth along her throat, closing his teeth on the sensitive cord there. And when he parted her folds and slipped one finger inside her, Cait's knees went to water.

Sensation after sensation battered at her. Even as he explored her, his thumb pressed and released against her clitoris in a rhythm designed to drive her to madness.

It was a journey she was determined not to take alone.

She traced the length of him with dancing fingers, alternating between a lighter touch and the firmer one his hunger would demand. And had a moment of pure feminine satisfaction when he thrust against her hand demandingly.

The feeling was replaced by satisfaction of another sort, when the first shattering climax ripped through her, graying her vision and startling a cry from deep in her throat.

"Yes." She heard his voice in her ear. Struggled to recover from the eddies of pleasure still battering her. "More. Again."

She shook her head weakly. It was too much. Too soon. She couldn't think. Couldn't tear away the fog of release to climb the slippery slope of desire again.

But he proved her a liar in the next moment. His touch deft and insistent, he had pleasure building again in long lush waves. Helplessly, her hands climbed to his shoulders. Clutched there as her body quaked and followed him up and up and up to the peak he was relentlessly driving her toward.

Then pushed her over it. Ruthlessly using hands and lips and teeth to intensify sensation from a thousand individual pulse points so the implosion went on and on until she was a weak shuddering mass. Grateful for the solid support of the door behind her.

Cait felt him move away, lifted a protesting hand. And had to force open eyelids that seemed weighted. Zach was stripping with quick frantic movements. Digging into his pocket for a foil wrapper that he seemed to have an inordinate amount of difficulty opening.

"Shit."

The edge of desperation to his voice had her smiling. And since feeling was beginning to return to her limbs, she said, "Let me."

"I don't think so. I know my limits." He swore again, savagely, before finally ripping the package and donning the condom.

His choice of words gave her pause. For a man who knew his limits, he seemed dangerously close to the edge of them now. Anticipation pooled in the pit of her stomach. Because she was going to do her level best to tip him over.

Hooking her thumbs in the waistband of her shorts she dragged them over her hips and let them fall to the floor before stepping out of them. Then caught his gaze on her. Heavy-lidded and intent. And impossibly, the blood in her veins turned molten.

The wisp of black panties hadn't been chosen with seduction in mind. But from the expression on his face, they worked admirably in that regard.

He took two quick steps and she was in his arms again. And this time she could feel the tiny tremors coursing through his body. Feel his shredding restraint in the pressure of his kiss. And knew, as a bolt of exhilaration twisted through her, that she'd never caused such genuine unvarnished need. It elicited an answering hunger in her. An appetite for returning every bit of pleasure she'd received and watching it mark him. Change him the way she was very much afraid the experience had altered her.

Without releasing her mouth, he tugged her panties down her legs. And when she stepped out of them, his hand was already under her butt. Lifting her.

Bracing herself with one hand on his shoulder, she wrapped her legs around his waist as he walked them both to the bed.

He was inside her before her back hit the mattress.

They were both still for a moment. Cait was a little stunned. A bit panicked. He filled her with a completeness that bordered on the uncomfortable. She hadn't been kidding about how long it'd been for her. She shifted slightly, feeling surrounded by the breadth of him. Then stopped as she felt the delicate throb of his penis inside her. Felt herself soften as a fist of need clutched in her belly.

She opened her eyes. Found him watching her. And her breath strangled in her lungs. There was nothing shuttered about his gaze at the moment. His eyes looked more gold than brown in the shadows. And in that moment, she knew he thought of nothing but her. Saw nothing but her.

Cait arched her hips, a silent invitation, and one that he met with a long slow thrust. His hand crept between their bodies to cup her breast, while the other remained wrapped under her hips. She could read the urgency in the way the skin pulled tightly across his cheekbones. In his clenched jaw. But still he held back, keeping his movements controlled.

Until she smiled into his eyes. Reached down to touch him where their bodies were joined. And felt him shudder against her as his control abruptly snapped.

Zach surged into her again and again, and this time she met him stroke for stroke. Desire was firing through her veins. The hem of her vision was hazing. But she kept her eyes open. Fixed on his. The night rushed in, crowding their bodies on the bed. She could see nothing but him. Hear only the rasp of their breathing. The slap of flesh against flesh. The beat of her blood, roaring through her veins. Hammering in her ears.

Her heels dug into his back. She was wrapped around him. And still it wasn't close enough. His hips pounded against hers in a primal frantic pace until he surged wildly, and she felt the last little bit of sanity slip away as the climax tossed her up. Spun her dizzily.

And when he followed her into madness, when senses were dimmed and there was only feeling, she imagined she heard her name on his lips.

So Sharper was screwing the consultant. Interesting.

He stared at the closed motel door, mind racing. He'd been watching Fleming's motel room when he had the chance ever since he'd learned where she was staying. Not that there'd been anything of interest to discover. She went in. She came out. Always alone.

Until now. Now she was in there with Sharper.

He sat in his darkened vehicle in the shadows of the motel

lot. Wondered what the information meant. Other than the fact that Sharper was a horny bastard who somehow managed to nail every decent-looking woman around these parts. He'd always been a lucky SOB. Because Caitlin Fleming was as close to perfect as any female he'd seen off the screen.

The thought was purely objective. The only interest he had in the woman was figuring out what she knew. And keeping her from learning more.

Because there was nothing more to see, he started his car. There had to be a way to use this dirty little detail. Knowledge was power. And he was an expert in acquiring knowledge. A few scenarios occurred but didn't hold up under closer consideration.

He put the car into gear and headed for the street, being careful to stay in the shadows. Something would come to him. It always did.

One thing was clear.

It was becoming increasingly obvious that he'd have to get rid of Caitlin Fleming.

Chapter 14

Cait shifted restlessly on the bed, but her movements were restricted. There was a furnace of heat sealed against her back. A weight around her waist, over her legs, that pinned her in place. Her unconscious sounded an alarm and her eyes snapped open. Took an instant to adjust to the dim light in the room.

And in that instant, comprehension filtered in.

She looked down at the hair roughened arm draped carelessly over her. Who would have figured Sharper for a cuddler? Although it was probably more likely that he was simply a bed hog and she'd merely been an obstacle preventing him from claiming all the mattress space.

Eyeing the bathroom door, she wondered how she could go about freeing herself without waking the man. It'd be infinitely easier if she had a shower before facing him. A jolt of caffeine wouldn't hurt, either, but the room didn't run to amenities like coffee makers. Carefully she tried inching away. His arm tightened and she stopped. Tried to turn her head to see if she'd wakened him.

In the next moment it became a moot point. A phone rang.

They sat up in bed simultaneously. Cait looked around for her purse. Saw it lying on the floor inside the door, contents half spilled out.

Zach was rubbing a hand over his stubbled jaw, his eyes drowsy. "Is that yours or mine?"

"I don't know." They both listened for a moment. Heard two different alerts. "Sounds like both of ours."

He swung his legs over the side of the bed and rose to pad across the room, unconcerned about his nudity. Which was just as well, Cait observed, because she'd been wondering how to retrieve her phone without making a production of wrapping herself in a sheet like a Victorian virgin.

She could only imagine the comments *that* would have elicited from Sharper. But she was uncertain that she was up to prancing around the room in front of him wearing nothing at all.

Although the sight of him doing the same wasn't exactly hard on the eyes.

"Here." The purse he tossed toward her almost hit her in the head. She preferred to blame that on early-morning sluggishness and not being hopelessly diverted by the sight of his tight male buns. He was already answering his call while she was still fumbling for her cell.

"Yeah, Tuck. What's up?"

Cait's phone had gone silent by the time she reached it. And looking at the screen, she figured that was a good thing. Talking to her mother could wait until after this case was over. It certainly wasn't something she'd tackle first thing in the morning, on any day.

"Why, what happened?" Silence on his end for a moment, then, "Let me check."

He came back to sit on the edge of the bed, looking at her inquiringly. "What's my schedule today?"

"I . . ." There was a jagged scar on his shoulder. Wide, like too much flesh had been torn away for the skin to heal evenly. And she knew without asking that shrapnel had caused it.

She forced her gaze to his face and mentally regrouped. "I have to go to Eugene. Maybe for only part of the day, but likely I'll be in the lab until evening."

He returned to his call. "Yeah, Tuck, I can take the IK trip. How many rafts? Uh-huh. What's the meeting point?"

It occurred to her that now was as good a time as any to make her escape. So while his back was turned, she slipped from the bed and hurried to the bathroom. And tried not to think of it as fleeing.

Turning on the shower, she waited for the water to warm before stepping inside the enclosure. She might even get lucky and Sharper would have left before she got done. Calling herself a coward for having the thought didn't make it disappear. She'd walked into last night with her eyes wide open. But facing him today was another story. Sex wasn't the only area in which she was out of practice.

She was rinsing the shampoo out of her hair when the shower door opened. Before she could say a word, Zach was crowding inside the cramped space. "Ah . . . I'm almost done here."

"Seems sort of stingy to shower alone when I'm right in the next room." He picked up the bar of scented soap she'd brought and began to lather his hands. "Here in Oregon, we take conservation seriously. We're very green."

"I've already washed, thanks." One-handed, of course, which hadn't gotten any less awkward, as she'd attempted to keep her right hand out of the spray in an effort to keep the Steri-Strips dry. But certainly she hadn't spent the care he was expending as he soaped her breasts. Trailing a path of lather down her stomach. Lower.

"Then you can wash me." Somehow he seemed to loom closer. And there was a glint in his eye as he lowered his head toward hers that had hormones revving to instant life. "You look good wet, Slim. I knew you would."

And when his lips covered hers, Cait realized that this didn't have to be awkward at all.

It could be very, very easy.

"Well, well, well. Look who's slinking back to the lab."

"I make it a point to never slink," Cait responded. She set

a white bakery bag on the desk in the corner. "Bad for the spine. I brought you pastries."

Kristy's expression lightened. "Cream puffs?" She scurried over to the desk, opened the bag, and made a sound of rapture. "It *is* cream puffs! Oh, I love you, Cait. I've missed you."

"Yeah, I could tell by that rousing welcome." She watched in bemusement as her tech lifted one out of the sack and began to devour it with delicate greed. Kristy's appetite never failed to astonish her.

"Called you last night to catch up but didn't get an answer."

The other woman's brows rose. "I went to a movie. Didn't see your missed call until this morning, so if you hadn't come in I would have . . ." She stopped midbite, stared harder at Cait. "You had sex!"

Shock flashed through her. Followed quickly by a ridiculous tug of guilt. "What?"

"You did, I can tell in your face. And your eyes." Kristy pointed the remainder of the pastry at her. "You're all . . . loose and glowing. That's a sex glow. I'd know it anywhere."

It wasn't that she was ashamed of the night she'd spent with Sharper. And the morning, she recalled, remembering their shower together. But damned if she was going to stand here and discuss every detail for her assistant's lascivious pleasure. "If anyone should recognize a sex glow it'd be you. But in your case too much sex has scrambled your brains. I've been hiking forests by day. Dodging bar fights by night."

As usual Kristy was easily diverted. "Bar fights? And you didn't call me?" She finished one pastry and reached in the bag for another. "I'm great in fights. Especially in a mob of guys. Because of my height," she explained around a mouthful of pastry. "I'm just the right height to punch them in the balls."

"That's charming. Really." Because her lips threatened to curve, she firmed them. "Perhaps you could demonstrate when Michaels takes you home to meet his mother."

"I don't do mothers. Meet them, I mean. What would be the point? We'll be done here in a couple weeks, right?"

"M-mm." Spying the workstation her tech had set up for the comparisons on the garbage bags, Cait approached it. "Found anything so far?"

"Outside the more obvious qualities, like drawstring or tie top, the only real points of reference are whether the heat seals are on the sides or bottoms." Because she obviously wasn't done eating, only Kristy's voice followed her. "The two marked are similar to the bags found in the cave. And they're biodegradable."

Cait gave her a sharp look. "Different brand names?"

"Yep." Having devoured the pastries, Kristy balled up the sack to throw it away before going to scrub her hands. "One of the deputies who dropped them off yesterday said he'd bought both samples in Eugene. Don't they need to start looking closer to where the bodies were actually found?"

"Maybe." Depending on the results on the Recinos DNA test they might become very focused on that area. "Barnes already has this information?"

"I don't have his number."

Quickly Cait called the deputy, and when she got his voice mail, apprised him of Kristy's find before disconnecting. He'd put some officers to work calling local businesses in the area, she figured. Discovering who stocked the bags and how long they'd done so. He was nothing if not methodical. It was a tedious thread that would have to be followed up on, but she doubted it'd lead anywhere. They couldn't be sure they were bought in the area, and it's not like anyone would keep records of those sorts of sales. It was, however, one more thing that could tie the offender to the crimes if they found similar bags in his possession. Just like the saw would.

"Before you start work this morning, I need to get an elimination print from you."

"Like I'd be unprofessional enough to touch one of the bags." But Kristy went to the shelves and started rummaging for the materials they'd need. She was obviously more cheerful now that she'd gotten her sugar high. "You got a couple boxes from FedEx this morning. I started stacking them over here. It's that invisible paint you ordered to run comparisons on."

"Nothing on the fax machine yet?" She glanced over at the machine on the desk, as if she could make Recinos's DNA profile appear by sheer force of will.

"Get to work on the paint comparisons," Kristy advised. After washing and drying her hands thoroughly, she inked each finger and pressed it against the cards she'd laid out. "It'll make the time go faster."

"Speaking of time going faster . . ." Cait went to her pack that she'd set just inside the door and unzipped it, withdrawing the soil samples she'd been gathering while she and Sharper were in the forest. It was surely a character flaw that had her enjoying the way her assistant's expression went glum when she saw what Cait was holding.

"Fuck a duck."

"That'll be a dollar. You can pay me after you run these samples."

"Maybe I was wrong about your sex glow." Kristy made a production of turning her back on Cait, but the snippiness in her tone was a giveaway to the alteration of her mood. "Sex typically relaxes people, not make them meaner. At least good sex does."

Lips curved, Cait headed over to the boxes that had arrived that morning. It was nice to have her assistant off that subject even though she did have an urge to tell her just how wrong she was. She was more than a little relaxed. And the sex had been *very, very* good.

It felt great to get back on the water. Though nowhere close to the longest or wildest river in Oregon, the McKenzie had always been his favorite. Maybe because he'd grown up on its banks. He'd been floating it since he was eight.

Zach kept his eye on the inflatable rafts, each manned

with six clients and one of his guides, but his employees were in their element. Kirby Wendall had his people in stitches most of the time, and Pat Swenson was pointing out the flora and fauna while giving a running mini science lesson on the ways lava flows had impacted the river over thousands of years.

He was happy enough to leave the entertainment to his guides as he and another employee, Staci Lannert, acted as safety boaters in individual hard-shell whitewater kayaks. Although their jobs would be to rescue any clients in case of accidents, that wasn't particularly likely on such a calm stretch. He'd spend more time this morning angling close to the rafts and begging for cookies when the snacks came out.

Zach dipped his custom paddle in the clear water, the polished white paint gleaming in the bright sunshine. Its blade bore the red and black insignia of the 75th Ranger Regiment. He'd had new personal paddles made when he'd returned home. It had seemed important, somehow, that he meld his past with his present. But his life in the military never seemed further away than when he was on the water.

He thought Cait would enjoy this. At least she seemed comfortable in the forest, even off the trails where the hiking sometimes grew demanding. And the climb up Castle Rock certainly hadn't fazed her. The unexpected thought of her took him aback. But he couldn't shake the mental image of her on the river with the group, similarly clad in helmet and wet suit.

Which made him a sap any way you looked at it.

At Staci's shout, he followed the direction of her gaze and watched an osprey's flight overhead, but his thoughts were still centered on Cait. Sleeping with the woman didn't change anything between them. It sure as hell hadn't altered the fascination she held for him. A fascination that somehow had grown rather than been depleted after last night.

There hadn't been enough hours to touch her, taste her everywhere he'd planned. Not enough time to discover every soft and secret place on her body and linger over it until she strained and shuddered beneath his lips.

There'd been plenty of straining and shuddering, he recalled, stroking the paddle through the water rhythmically. And it definitely hadn't been one-sided.

There'd be less to worry about if her attraction centered solely around the physical. But he found himself just as intrigued by things she'd said. Things she'd probably wished she hadn't.

Unless you've got a thing for women with stratospheric IQs and abysmal taste in men.

And based on the couple examples of guys she'd mentioned from her past, he was inclined to agree. They'd sounded like assholes.

And then there had been what she'd revealed the time he'd caught her trespassing. The day after he'd heard about Drummy offing himself. He'd been like a wounded animal, he recalled. Hungover and raw, thinking of how his friend had ended things. He'd wanted to strike out. To shock her, and yeah, maybe scare her a little since she didn't seem to have the sense to know when to feel fear.

But he hadn't shocked her by demanding whether she'd ever seen someone blow his brains out. He'd been the one left shaken by her reply.

Blood spatter everywhere. Bone fragments in the chair cushions. Caught in the drapes. Gray matter on the desk. On the gun.

Just the memory of her recitation, her tone flat and emotionless, had his skin prickling. It was probably something she'd seen on the job. On a case.

Hell of it was, her voice had sounded young when she uttered the words. Vulnerable. And the moment between them had forced open an inner door that he usually was much better at keeping locked.

And what the hell was he supposed to do with that? The chatter of the people behind him faded to a distant buzz of background noise as he considered the question. His life was exactly the way he liked it. He had a job he never grew tired of. A home—at least the beginnings of one—slowly taking shape to his exact specifications. When he got tired of being alone, he could drive a few miles to where friends and conversation would be waiting. When he needed sex . . . well, finding a woman was never as difficult as ridding himself of her later. Shellie Mayer was just the latest to discover that he wasn't long-term material.

On the surface, that made Cait and him perfectly matched. After this case she'd be on the other side of the continent. He should be grateful for the ready-made escape clause and try to get his fill of her while he could.

But there was a sneaky little sliver of doubt that told him that might not be possible.

"Otter slide," he called back to the rafts, pointing toward the shore with his paddle. He heard Kirby and Pat relay the info to their clients as he scanned the river ahead. On the weekends it wasn't unusual to run into several other outfitters manning floats on the river, but sometimes the weekdays were slower and they'd have the area to themselves, at least for a while. And according to Tucker's call this morning, they'd had a couple cancellations in this area in the last couple days. Their schedule wasn't hurting, though. They offered trips on several different rivers in Oregon, as well as the Lower Salmon in Idaho, and those remained popular.

He just hated to see this region's tourism take a hit because of all the publicity about those bones.

"We've got nature calling."

Zach looked over his shoulder at Pat's call. "Mimosa Creek's up ahead." He waited as the guide relayed the information, and when he got a thumb's-up signal in response, he paddled closer to shore, looking for a good place to exit the water. On a full-day trip Mimosa Creek would be a natural stopping point for his outfit, but this float was only for morning. There wasn't going to be time to dwell on shore, which was a shame. It was one of the most unspoiled and little-known hot springs in the region and only easily accessible from water.

Getting everyone a place to pull ashore and then up on

dry land took some doing. The rubber suits and booties they provided their clients didn't make answering nature's call an especially easy task.

There were six couples on today's tour, so there was a great deal of bantering about which gender had the weakest bladders. But as Zach and his guides pointed out the most secluded nearby areas, he noted that the men were just as willing to take advantage of the break as the women were. And that was par for the course.

One woman—Marcy, he thought her name was—sent him a flirtatious look as she passed by him. "You can come, too, Zach. Keep me out of trouble." She was a brassy blonde, heavyset, maybe midforties, with a bawdy laugh that had sounded several times so far on the trip.

He grinned at her. "But then who'd keep *me* out of trouble?"

She gave a hoot at that. "Son, with those looks of yours, you've likely been trouble all your life."

Since there was more than a little truth to that, he just gave a shrug. And she and her friends went scrabbling over the rocks to disappear into the woods, seeking some privacy.

"Still having to beat them off with a stick, I see," Pat jibed as he came over and squatted down next to him.

"I usually try to use a bit more finesse than that."

"Oh, so maybe that's where I'm going wrong."

"That, and the fact that you still live in your mother's basement," Staci called from her perch on the edge of the nearest raft.

"A man who takes care of his mother is sensitive," Pat responded good-naturedly. This particular discussion had been long running. "Chicks dig sensitivity."

"You know what else chicks dig? Guys who can stay out past midnight without asking permission." Kirby ducked the rock Pat sent whizzing by him, and popped back up again, grinning like a fool. "You might want to . . ."

The rest of his statement was lost as an ear-shattering scream split the air.

Zach shoved away from the boulder he was resting on and

raced in the direction of the sound. It had been Marcy's voice. He was almost certain of it. Then it was joined by a chorus of screeches as the rest of the women joined in.

Most wild animals were skittish when they smelled humans, so that wasn't a worry unless they had a rabid creature on their hands. But they had their share of snakes in Oregon, a few of them poisonous. He had a snake-bite kit packed in their supplies, but if more than one woman had been bitten . . .

He skidded to a stop to where the women were huddled together at the side of the hot springs. "Is anyone hurt?" His gaze flicked over them. At least they were all standing. But Marcy pointed a shaking finger beyond him. "No. It's in there."

"I saw it, too . . ."

". . . ohmygod, ohmygod, I almost touched it . . ."

". . . I'm gonna puke . . ."

"What's going on? What happened?"

Zach's employees were on his heels. The male clients stumbling through the woods right behind them. He looked around, found a long stout stick. Turned in the direction Marcy was still pointing. Toward the rocks embanking the natural hot springs. They formed a small grotto around the natural pool, which was about five feet deep and would fit about four people. It wouldn't be uncommon for snakes to seek out the warmth on the surrounding stones, but they'd shy away from the hot sulfuric water itself.

Stepping warily, he approached the springs, the scent of sulfur stinging his nostrils.

"There." He heard Marcy's voice quavering behind him. "Stuck in those boulders underwater."

He sent her a quick frown before getting closer to the point she'd mentioned. In the water? Snakes wouldn't . . .

"Jesus." His involuntary step backward had him nearly knocking Kirby and Pat over, they were following so closely.

"Holy shi-i-i-t," breathed Kirby, peering around his shoulder. "Is that . . .?"

"Yeah."

They stared at the bones showing through the partially degraded garbage bag that bobbed and dipped in the water. Sulfur would eat away at the plastic, he thought in a distant part of his brain. Maybe the bones, too, given enough time. Continuous immersion in hundred-degree water was bound to destroy any evidence, wasn't it?

A dull ache spiked through his temples. What had started out as a pretty decent day had just abruptly turned to shit. "Get the satellite phone. I'll have to call this in."

"Seems like you've got a knack, Sharper." Andrews's tone was a little too edged for humor. "You stumble on the damnedest things."

"Yeah, I'm all kinds of lucky." He didn't bother to keep his sarcasm in check. "And I didn't stumble on them. My clients did when they decided to take a quick dip in the springs. You spoke to them, remember? At least twice. And then you let my guides take them home hours ago. And yet I'm still here."

He'd shed his helmet hours ago but was still clad in his wet suit and rubber booties while law enforcement did its thing with excruciating slowness. He hadn't been able to get Andrews when he'd called the sheriff's office, but he'd been routed to Barnes who'd instructed him to herd everybody back to the rafts but not to let anyone leave. That'd been midmorning. Full darkness would descend in another hour or so, and he couldn't tell how close they were to being done. Although there were plenty of forestry and law enforcement personnel on the scene, seemed like some of them were all but tripping over each other as they went about their work.

And Cait seemed oblivious to it all.

Although his view from where he sat on a fallen log away from the scene was partially obscured by a spill of rocks, there were glimpses of her as she knelt for a time at water's edge. Flashes of her when she'd rise and stride to the large bag of equipment she'd brought with her, and after rummaging through it, return to the springs. He had the thought he'd like to be close enough to watch her work. She looked competent, in her element, as she gave instructions to deputies assisting and to the pint-sized blonde who'd accompanied her.

"So how do you think these bones ended up in this particular place?"

He looked at the woman askance. "How the hell should I know? You're the cop."

"I mean," Andrews's voice was testy, "how well known is this place? You said you'd never been to that cave before. Is that true about this area, as well?"

"No. We make regular stops here if we're on an all-day trip on this river. But the last time my outfit had a trip like that scheduled for the McKenzie would have been at least three weeks ago. We wouldn't have stopped today at all except someone needed to take a leak." And part of him wished that urge had occurred another half hour downstream. He didn't need this. Andrews wasn't having him hang around because she enjoyed his company. There was something else on her mind, and it didn't take a rocket scientist to figure out what it was.

"So it wasn't your idea to stop here today."

He blew out a breath, reaching for a measure of diplomacy that too often eluded him. "It wasn't my idea to stop, no. But when my guide said someone needed a break, I'm the one that scouted out the nearest place to put into shore. Happened to be here."

She half turned away to squint toward the area where her team was working. "Never been in this area myself. Is this a well-known place?"

"It doesn't get the traffic you'd see in Belknap or Cougar. But it's more popular with locals. Hard to access it except by water." He nodded toward the dense thicket of brush and brambles and salal that grew up around the trees, providing a shield of privacy around the area.

"So you're saying people in the region would know about it."

"The river rats probably do. And the outfitters who guide

trips on the McKenzie, definitely. As for others . . ." He shrugged. "Who knows?"

"So first we have a secret cave dump site." Her pause seemed deliberate. "And now an out-of-the-way hot springs known only to locals. Seems odd."

"You expected him to dump the bones on Main Street during the Fourth of July parade?"

Her face was flushed. It couldn't be from heat, so he wondered if it was from temper. "I'm asking for your opinion, Sharper," she snapped. Temper it was, then. "Because it's looking more and more damn unlikely that someone could waltz in here and discover these hidey-holes for stashing bodies without more than a little familiarity with the area."

"You're looking for a local," he allowed. Hadn't he said the same to Cait on more than one occasion? "Or at least, someone who used to be local. Someone who spent enough time outdoors in the area to become very well acquainted with it."

"That's exactly what I thought."

He didn't like the gimlet look she fixed him with then. But her next words were the most welcome he'd heard all day. "You're done here. You can head home."

Zach didn't need to be told twice. He pushed away from the log and suppressed the need to rub his numbed butt. He threw one last look at Cait as he circled around the yellow tape the cops had placed around the scene. Found her bent over what looked like a body bag. Then he lost sight of her completely as he headed for the trees that thickened closer to the river-bank.

———————

"What about the paintings? Any evidence of pictures on the inside of the scapulas?"

Andrews was standing so close that Cait bumped into her every time she moved to reach for another bone. "That was the first thing I checked," she said patiently. "The UV lamp and magnifier didn't show any trace of it. The temperature of the water was one hundred five point three degrees. The invisible paints I'd ordered arrived today, right before your call. None of them claim to be water resistant. But given that the remains are minus the skull, I think we can safely assume the same UNSUB is responsible."

"So why would he have bothered with the images if he was going dump them somewhere they'd be destroyed?" Andrews whirled and began to pace the lab. "From what Sharper said, those bones couldn't have been there long. Not all summer. He claims those hot springs are known by locals, who prefer them to the more well-traveled ones in the area. Barnes is following up with other outfitters in the region to see if they've stopped there recently with any of their tours. But if Zach's correct, someone on the river would have stumbled on that skeleton if it had been there longer than a few weeks. Maybe less."

Cait wasn't ready to make a guess at how long the bones had been in the water. Certainly there was already some exposure of the spongy undersurface in some of the smaller bones. "The specimens will have to dry out completely before I can do close examination. And that process can take up to two days." And even then they might be in poor condition and need further treatment.

"You said the paintings on the bones were a major factor in his method of disposal." Andrews returned to her earlier subject as she turned to retrace her steps. "But by submerging them in hot springs, he all but guaranteed he'd erase them. It looks like he's changed his methods."

"His method of disposal maybe," Cait corrected. Gently she continued transferring the wet bones from the canvas body bag to the thick pad of newspapers she'd covered the spare gurney with. "But the paintings are part of his ritual, and he won't vary from that. He would have been compelled to follow the same pattern regardless of how he meant to get rid of them."

"They almost have to have been dumped since we found the remains in the cave," Andrews muttered. Her boots rang hollowly as she continued to roam around the room. When under stress the woman seemed to resort to compulsive behaviors, Cait noted. The pacing she'd seen before. The chain-smoking last night had been new. "The bastard is thumbing his nose at us. And I agree with Sharper. It's someone from the area. Someone who knows the region as well"—she shot Cait a grim smile—"as he does."

Cait digested the information silently. He'd expressed the same opinion to her on more than one occasion. She'd seen the sheriff talking to him before he'd left. From the expressions on their faces, it hadn't seemed like a pleasant experience. Plainly there was no love lost between them.

"So the UNSUB's dump site is discovered. He's forced to adapt. What I find most interesting here is that he didn't bury these bones." And she still couldn't get a handle on that. "In an isolated part of the forest he could have dug a hole deep enough so they wouldn't be found. Hell, he could bury them on his own property." She'd already concluded he had access to a place that allowed him privacy. "I'm beginning to think burial is significant to him in some way. And that it holds a negative connotation."

"And I'm beginning to think that maybe we're overlooking the possibility that the UNSUB is a woman." When Cait looked at her, Andrews held up a hand, as if asking her forbearance. "You've said yourself, the bones don't weigh that much. What, twenty pounds or so?"

The estimate was close enough. "Approximately."

"Woman in good shape can carry that easy enough. And if she's familiar with the area she's just as capable as climbing up Castle Rock as a guy is."

"You're thinking digging a grave is too much work for her, though?" Cait didn't follow the reasoning.

"Maybe."

With exquisite care, she removed a femur from the canvas bag and placed it on the mat. "Whatever the gender, the UNSUB may just have made a miscalculation. Could be he—or she—thought the combination of the temperature and the sulfur would destroy all evidence of the bones, given enough time." If so, that had been a mistake. It would have taken days of submersion in boiling water to break the bones down. The waters of Mimosa Creek weren't nearly that hot.

A thought struck her then, and she looked up, caught the sheriff's eye. "Kesey mentioned seeing someone in the forest in the Castle Rock vicinity the night the bodies were recovered, remember? Someone carrying a pack."

Andrews's stocky frame went still. "Finding out that his hidey-hole had been discovered would have thrown him off his game. But you said Kesey couldn't give you a description."

Cait shook her head. And she was fairly certain they'd gotten all from the man that he knew. "It was too dark. But neither team has run across the other roamer Barnes mentioned. Lockwood. Maybe he saw something."

The sheriff grunted. Began moving again. "Nearly two weeks since we hauled those bodies out of that cave and we still have a whole lot of nothing. I'm getting buried on the publicity surrounding this thing. What am I supposed to tell the press when they catch wind of this latest set of remains we found? That I'm following up a lead on the damn garbage bags? I need something solid."

Although she could have pointed out just how much they'd put together in just a few days, Cait remained silent. She understood the frustration felt by the lead law enforcement officer who'd catch every piece of flack, whether from politicians or the media. "I tested three samples of paint this morning and more arrived while I was gone today. Since there are a limited number of suppliers, I'm confident I'll find a match. And unlike garbage bags, paint is something that can't be kept around for long periods of time." Andrews looked a little more cheerful at the words. "It'd probably need to be reordered, especially if months or years transpired between kills."

"You're right. And if that turns out to be . . ."

The fax machine on the desk began to whir. Cait went still in the process of removing the sternum from the canvas bag, staring in the direction of the desk. Drecker had promised the lab would fax Recinos's mother's DNA profile when it was finished.

Andrews strode swiftly over to the machine, started picking up the pages as they spit out into the receiving plate.

Cait laid the bone on the newspaper and followed the sheriff to the desk. She flipped through the file folders she had in the plastic organizer on its corner until she found the one containing female C's DNA profile. Opening it, she took the sheets from Andrews and laid the profiles side by side, leaning over to peruse them.

The other woman crowded by her side, although to Cait's knowledge she had no scientific background, and the profiles were likely Greek to her. To Andrews's credit, though, she didn't prod, although impatience all but radiated off her.

Cait compared the profiles once. Twice. Again. Finally, she blew out a breath. Straightened.

"Looks like you've got something solid at last. These profiles match at seven markers." She looked up, excitement spurting through her veins. "We can be reasonably certain that we've identified female C. She's Marissa Recinos of Seattle, Washington."

Chapter 15

Barb Haines's carcass would take several more days to dry. He tested the screens covering the shed's loft doors to be sure they were secure. The bits of rotting tissue that still adhered to the skeleton would attract insects if he wasn't vigilant about keeping them away. The industrial sized fan he had aimed at the bones would help dry them out more quickly, reduce the odor, and discourage any insects that might creep in.

He climbed the ladder down from the loft. Before slipping outside to cross the yard back to the house, he checked on his beetles. As always, their busyness enthralled him, but that piece of raccoon roadkill he'd prepared for them wouldn't hold them for long. He had such a large colony that it took him hours every week to keep them in food. Sometimes he thought they were insatiable.

Sometimes he wondered the same thing about Sweetie.

The thought seemed a betrayal, and automatically he shook it off. Sweetie was the planner. The one who had all the ins and outs figured. But first there were only going to be five to kill. Then it was seven. With Barb Haines they were at eight.

And that made him ask himself whether Sweetie would ever really be satisfied. If the promise of a future together would ever really happen.

The thoughts made him angry with himself and ruined the joy he usually took in watching his bugs work. Now was a time for faith. For standing strong together as they outwitted the sheriff and her entire department. It wasn't a time to start entertaining doubts.

Carrying his Maglite, he hurried to the door of the shed and carefully padlocked the structure behind him before continuing to the back door of the house, where he'd left a light on the porch.

Entering the kitchen, he paused to lock the door behind him before setting his flashlight on the counter. He continued through to the living room. And stopped dead in the doorway separating the two rooms when he saw who was standing inside the front door.

Not just inside the door, actually. Sweetie's hand was on the doorknob to the basement door, twisting it this way and that, trying to get it open.

Which made him all the more glad that he'd remembered to lock it the last time he'd been down there. He hadn't returned to it since he'd carried Barb Haines's dead body up those stairs a couple nights ago.

"If you're looking for me, I'll hide in the bedroom."

Sweetie jumped and whirled to face him. And his smile faded when he saw the expression on the face he loved so much.

"They've found another set of bones!"

He stilled, shock radiating through him. "What? That's impossible." He'd been so careful. Given the new spot so much thought. He'd weighted the bag down with stones. Tied the drawstring tight, then secured it again with a twisty before wedging it under larger rocks forming a lip along the lower side of the hot springs. "There must be some mistake."

Sweetie's voice was filled with bitterness. "There was a mistake all right, and *you* made it. Of all the lame-ass moves. What were you thinking?"

What the hell were you thinking, you dumbass? His father had always accompanied the words with a cuff of the head that would have his ears ringing. He'd lie in bed all night nursing his bruises and plotting his revenge. A revenge that had been slow in coming, but had been immensely satisfying.

"I was thinking you asked for my help," he said stiffly, and headed back to the kitchen for a beer. He didn't ask if Sweetie wanted one. Returned to the room where his lover still stood and tipped the bottle to his lips. "I was thinking that since the cave was out of the question I needed to find a new place as soon as possible."

"I'm not blaming you." But they both heard the lie in Sweetie's words. "I just don't understand. There were seven sets of bones in the caves, but I brought you eight. So this is the last one, right?" A dagger of pain sliced through him at the distrust in Sweetie's eyes. "This is the last 'surprise' find?"

"Of course." But his gaze slipped away. Not even Sweetie needed to know that he'd used that cave before the two of them had joined forces.

Barb Haines had only been dead two days. And regardless of what was said here, her remains wouldn't be disposed of until it could be done right. *Respectfully.*

But clearly he'd have to give that disposal some thought. His last bright idea hadn't worked out as well as he'd hoped.

"I didn't show up at your place and demand to know why five wasn't enough, did I?" The words burst out of him, surprising in their bitterness. "I didn't push and pressure you about the decisions you've made, even though you varied from our original plan."

Sweetie took a few steps toward him, before halting. "Now you're mad at me. You don't know what it's been like. I'm worried all the time. Not about Andrews and her crew, but that consultant they brought in. That Fleming. She's got more smarts that the entire sheriff's outfit combined. I hear they have their own lab facility set up and everything. You know what that means? We can't count on a backlog of cases at the state crime lab to hold up results. I'm telling you, the woman's trouble."

He found himself softening a little, but the earlier sting lingered. "They can do their tests and police work. It won't matter. There's nothing that can tie them to us. You worry too much."

"Easy for you to say. I can't sleep. I can't eat. It's all I think about." Sweetie's smile was tremulous. "But this is it, right? There's nothing more for them to find."

"Nothing more," he echoed reassuringly, but his mind was racing. He was going to have to give this last disposal a great deal of thought. Maybe he could get his hands on a wet suit and hide the bones in the river somewhere. Soakers wouldn't find them there; it was too cold to swim in the McKenzie.

But there were fishermen on the river, he recalled in the next moment. With his luck, one would catch a hook on the bag and drag it to the surface.

"I just hope you haven't brought them to our door." Sweetie checked the time. "I'm going to be missed soon."

"Maybe you'd better go." For the first time he was anxious to see the end of his lover. A bitter sense of resentment bubbled up inside him. After all he'd done! All he'd sacrificed! Only to be treated no better than the old man had treated him really. By the one person he trusted more than anyone else in the world.

Sweetie looked at the door, then back to him. "I can't leave if I think you're upset with me. It'll tear me up so I can't think of anything else."

"I'm not upset," he lied. But the kiss his lover brushed over his lips failed to move him the way it usually did. And once Sweetie had gone, the emotions crashed and collided inside him like bumper cars at a carnival.

It had been their first fight. A sense of terror accompanied the thought. He didn't want to live without Sweetie. For once, it seemed as though his life had meaning. A higher purpose. Perhaps he'd been too sensitive. Maybe Sweetie had just been looking for comfort.

But there had been no excuse for name-calling. He took

a long swig from the beer. The comment still burned. And maybe he needed a little bit of comfort, too. A comfort Sweetie hadn't offered.

A comfort he could find downstairs.

He didn't give the thought too much consideration because if he did he'd feel bad about what he was doing. He just dug the key from his pocket. Crossed to the locked basement door and opened it.

Don't think of it as a betrayal of Sweetie. He made his way to the cellar swiftly. It had nothing to do with his lover. Everything to do with a dark and insidious need that had begun growing with the first victim that had been brought to him.

His feet found their way swiftly, surely to the locked cabinet in the corner of his drawing room. Another key to open that. Then that lovely catch of breath as the door swung open. That giddy sense of anticipation as he looked at the rows of gleaming skulls lining the shelves.

So much care had been taken in their restoration. Jaws wired together. Teeth glued back in. Eye sockets drilled out. It was perfectly natural to feel . . . a bit possessive after putting all that effort into the process.

Unerringly his hands went to the skull on the second shelf, right in the middle. He'd be lying if he said he didn't have a favorite. Sydney Schaefer. She'd been everything he could have wanted in a houseguest. Quiet and unassuming. And she'd pled so prettily at the end.

He set the skull and cloth on the desk. Undid his pants and covered himself with the soft cloth before inserting himself into the eye cavity. And gave a low moan. He held the cranium steady in both hands as he began to thrust.

Forget the fight that had been so upsetting. Forget the doubts. The worries about the next disposal site. This made it all worthwhile.

And when he came, it was Sweetie's name on his lips.

———

It was after midnight before the lone figure exited the morgue and headed to her rented SUV parked under the security light. Zach noted the exact moment Cait caught sight of him sitting on the hood of her vehicle. Saw the tension shoot into her muscles. And then watched her body ease again when she recognized him.

"You lost?" she asked when she got close enough.

"I was at the store cleaning gear. Figured you were still here. And that you hadn't eaten." He held out a clear plastic bag with a six-inch sub in it.

"You figured right." She took the bag and joined him on top of the hood. Withdrew the sandwich and unwrapped it. "Interesting choice of locations for a picnic."

He chewed and swallowed the bite of steak and cheese sub before responding. "I knew a nicer spot. Surrounded by nature. Private. Unspoiled. They pulled a bunch of human bones out of it this afternoon."

"Good point." He saw her expression lighten when she discovered he'd brought her an oven-roasted chicken breast. He'd paid attention. "No chips?"

Handing her a napkin, he said, "You don't eat chips."

"I don't?" She bit into the sub hungrily.

"Not that I've noticed. You can have half my big cookie, though. They only had one chocolate chocolate-chip left. A more chivalrous man would give you the whole thing, but . . . I'm not that man. I take cookies very seriously."

Her lips curved, and there was a shrewdness in her gaze that he immediately distrusted. "You're not that man. But you brought me a sandwich because you thought I hadn't eaten."

He shrugged, discomfited. "I was hungry. Thought you might be, too. You need to keep your strength up. Leaping tall buildings with a single bound has got to take energy."

"You're a nice guy, Sharper. This is going to wreak havoc with your go-to-hell image, but deep down, you're a nice guy."

"Yeah, well . . ." He moved his shoulders, oddly ill at ease with the turn of conversation. "Don't let it get around. I actually only worry about feeding whisper-thin ex-models turned scientists who look like a good wind could blow them over.

And only then on the fourth Friday of the month after they've hauled old bones out a hot springs."

"Very specific conditions."

"I'm no pushover."

"No one would ever claim you were." She surprised him then by lying back on the hood, staring up at the sooty fingers of clouds that would hide the stars even if they decided to make an entrance. "There was a breakthrough today. I can't tell you more than that, but . . . we've got a lead. It's solid."

He paused in midbite. Cait was usually so guarded that what he knew about the case came from what he could piece together from eavesdropping on her phone conversations or from news reports. That she shared even this much with him touched him somehow. More than it should have.

"I wouldn't have thought soggy bones would have told you much."

"We'll have to see what they tell me after they dry out." She turned her head and looked at him from her prone position. "Andrews said the women on your tour found them."

"Yeah." He blew out a sigh, recalling the scene. "They figured, hell they were in wet suits anyway, why not test the water. Dumb idea. They would have roasted in those suits if they sat in the springs for any length of time. But they all got in, a bit of a tight squeeze. One of them stepped on the bag. The rest is history."

"A piece of history none of them will forget any time soon."

"Whoever those bones belong to deserves to be remembered. If for no other reason, that makes me glad the women found them. No family should have to wonder what happened to their loved one." At least when his mother had died that night in the hospital, he'd known it. There was no wondering if she'd walk through the door someday and take him home. Away from Jarrett's addictions, his erratic behavior and random mood swings. At seven he'd realized that there was no going back for him. And though brutal, that had been better than living with false hope.

"I agree. I want to get IDs on every set of remains before I'm done with this case. I don't know if it'll be possible. But that's my goal. It'd be hard to believe justice was done until we have names to go with the bones."

He wondered how she was going to manage that but figured she couldn't tell him so he didn't ask. But he thought of her now, bringing closure of sorts to the families who'd lost the people belonging to those bones. And thought they were lucky to have her standing for their loved ones.

"Justice can sometimes be in the eye of the beholder and slippery to navigate." When she remained silent, watching him expectantly, he surprised himself by going on. "My grandfather probably thought his will delivered the most fitting justice to my father by not leaving him a dime. The resort that used to be on the land he left me? Teddy Roosevelt once stayed there, or so I'm told. Local legend had it that the place was haunted. The place burned to the ground when I was three. Although it was ruled accidental, my grandfather let it slip once that Jarrett had done it. Probably high at the time, and wanted to rid it of ghosts." The corner of his mouth lifted. "My grandfather wasn't the forgiving sort."

Especially when the old man had tried one thing after another to make his son grow up and act like a man. Zach himself had been a tool in that attempt. When his grandfather had gotten proof of Jarrett's paternity, it was he who had forced Zach's father to do his duty. Probably had hoped the act would make Jarrett shoulder some responsibility for the first time in his life. It hadn't turned out that way.

"My father contested the will of course. The old man had made sure it was ironclad, but I could have worked a deal. Could have given him at least part of what he thought was his share."

"But you didn't."

"It would have been a betrayal of my grandfather's last wishes. One more reward for my father that he didn't deserve, didn't work for. Wouldn't appreciate." Most of the time he knew he'd done the right thing. But doubts were sneaky little bastards that often preyed on nights when sleep was elusive and memories took hold.

Shaking off the moroseness that threatened at the thought, he finished the rest of his sandwich in silence before lying back on the hood next to her, one knee raised. He turned his head to study her. The dim light of the street lamp silhouetted her exquisite profile. And he surprised himself by asking the question that had been bothering him since they'd first met.

"How'd you get here, Cait?" She faced him, her brow winging upward, and he rephrased. "Not to Oregon, but to where you are. What you do."

A corner of her mouth lifted, but he could discern no amusement in her expression. "You mean how did I go from teen model to a forensic anthropologist slash investigative consultant?" Her gaze traveled past him, and the shadows in her eyes had nothing to do with the darkness hemming them. "Modeling was my mother's dream for me, never really mine, although I enjoyed it for a while. It was hard work, but it was exciting, too." Her shrug was almost indiscernible. "But I'm a geek at heart. I was always getting in trouble for smuggling science texts in bed and reading until three. Used to drive my mother wild because lack of sleep causes shadows under the eyes, and I'd show up for shoots looking haggard and gaunt. Her words."

He snorted. "Like that would be possible."

Her hand brushed his arm, one light stroke. "I decided to leave the job and attend college."

Zach could read far more into what she wasn't saying than what she was. "And your mother?"

"Disagreed. But it was my life and I decided it was time I started living it on my own terms."

That much he could understand. He'd done the same when he'd joined the military. Again when he came back here. He studied her in the faint light, a little shocked at the clutch in his chest when he saw the smudges under her eyes. "At the risk of sounding like your mother, you need to get some sleep."

Her voice was light. "Are you saying I look haggard and gaunt?"

His throat thickened and he strove to clear it. "I'm saying you push yourself too hard. You don't take care of yourself. Maybe because you've never had anyone really look out for you."

Her expression softened. And the slight quiver to her lips had panic streaking up his spine. But her voice when it came was teasing rather than shaky.

"You haven't offered me dessert yet. If you want to follow me back to my motel room here, I'll let you leg wrestle me for rights to the whole cookie."

Feeling on safer ground now, he pretended to consider the offer. "Will you be naked?"

"That can be arranged."

"Then lead the way."

———

The Landview was a step up from the McKenzie Motel, but it wasn't the amenities that held Zach's interest as he followed Cait into the darkened room. A decent man would leave her to get some rest. No one knew better than he did the hours she'd kept today. After very little sleep the night before.

Learning he wasn't that man wasn't the biggest disappointment he'd ever experienced. But he had a feeling leaving her alone tonight might come close.

Hormones, simmering the entire time they'd been together, flared to instant painful life as she snapped on the light on the bedside table. Spending time with her was a balm to nerves that had been rubbed raw by the events of the day. There was more than a little discomfit in the realization that his need for her was owed more than just to the physical.

She turned to face him, found him watching her. And he saw the exact instant when the easy confidence she usually wore turned to something more tentative. He said what was in his head without thought to how it would sound. "I don't think about beauty much, but it catches me by surprise sometimes. The way sunlight hits the water when I'm paddling. The view of a sunset backdropped against the forest." He stopped a moment, considered the way her eyes had gone huge and dark. "When it comes to people, there's just genes, lucky or unlucky. But I don't think I've seen anything as lovely as you tonight, sitting on your car, bathed in moonlight. I thought you should know that."

Her smile flickered a little. "You've got a sure thing here, Sharper. You don't need compliments to win me over."

"I know." Because he had a hunger to touch her again, he strode rapidly toward her. "That's why I waited until now to say it."

Her gaze was widening when his arms closed around her. And it pleased him, somehow, that he'd surprised her.

That first contact, curves against muscle, was briefly satisfying. But his thirst for her ignited, as if it hadn't been quenched only that morning. He pressed his mouth against hers in a slow thorough kiss that had the blood flashing and strobing in his veins. And recognized again just how difficult it would be to get his fill of her.

She gave, more than he would have expected. There was a measure of trust in that, he thought. Hoped. A woman didn't wait between partners as long as he suspected she had only to take a man into her bed lightly. Her lips parted, and when his tongue swept in her mouth, she met it with hers, a long teasing glide. It was enough for a few moments to just kiss her. To allow the flavor of her to kick his system to life. But it didn't satisfy for long. Not when there was the memory of all that sleek skin now hidden by jeans and a T-shirt. The promise of softness encased in lace beneath the functional clothing.

He'd take his time, get his fill. Scoring her bottom lip with his teeth, he had the thought, though his body called him a liar. With one hand he grasped the bottom of her shirt and drew it up and over her head. Then visually feasted, breath held, at the vision she presented.

The lace was ivory this time, covering skin nearly the same color. Her nipples were already taut, and he couldn't resist brushing one lightly, even as his free hand went to the waistband of her jeans. He stripped them down her legs, pausing to remove her shoes before smoothing his lips up the silky expanse of skin he'd revealed. And felt his heart lurch in his chest.

Her matching panties were cut high on her legs, and had a narrow expanse of satin on each side, holding the lace panels together. "My compliments to the maker of your lingerie. He—or she—should be worshiped as a God."

Her smile was slow, and secret, and female. "And here I'd have pegged you for an agnostic."

Going to his knees before her, he cupped her silky calves in his palms, marveling at the toned muscle beneath the softness. She was a lot like that. Steel beneath the surface. A person might underestimate her if the surface was all they saw. He had a feeling if they did, they'd regret it.

Leaning forward, he traced the shadow of her mons where he could see it through the fabric. Felt her legs jerk against him and heard her hissed in breath. The signs of her response pleased him. And feeling totally in control, he leaned forward for a closer contact.

He dampened the lace with his tongue, while his fingers traced the crease of her thighs, making teasing little forays under the edge of the elastic. Her fingers stabbed into his hair and clutched almost painfully. And he could feel restraint eddying away, making a liar of his earlier intentions.

There was a moment when he thought to recapture it. An instant when he really thought it was possible to harness the hunger that snarled and snapped inside him like a wild beast. He drew away just enough to hook the panties with his finger and drag them down her legs before closing the distance between them again and tasting warm damp flesh without the barrier of fabric between them. And knew, as he traced the seam of her folds with the tip of his tongue, the futility of that hope.

He savored and sampled and savaged, while his control teetered alarmingly. She was dark fire beneath his lips, her scent and flavor whipping his pulse to a frantic pace. Every jerk of her hips, every clench of her fingers drove him just a little mad. He was ruthless in his feasting, determined to wring every last sigh and moan.

Cupping her butt in his hands, he brought her closer. It should have alarmed him to discover the woman was like a fever in his blood, throwing everything he thought he knew about himself in disarray. But he relished the hunger that raged through him, the demand for this female. All of her. Everything she'd give and everything she'd seek to hold back. And when she shattered under his lips, when her body trembled and shook, a desperate primal need rose inside him that only she could quench.

Rising, he rid her of the bra. More quickly than he'd planned. With less finesse. And swept her up in his arms and on the bed in two quick seconds before stripping with awkward, clumsy haste and fumbling for protection.

There was a roaring in his ears, a fire in his gut that would only be alleviated by this woman. It surged through his system, trailing heat in its wake. He was trying to feed an appetite that couldn't be assuaged. He couldn't touch her enough. Taste her enough. He stroked and smoothed her trembling flesh, pausing to kiss and nip at her flushed skin. Explore the dip of her waist. The slope of her breast. The curve of her shoulder. And when his mouth found hers again, a primitive sense of possessiveness flared.

This kind of greed was new. The sort that gnawed through every attempt at control until there was only need, edgy and fierce. Their kiss grew more frenzied as his blood lunged recklessly through his veins like an uncaged animal. He tunneled his hand through her hair, used his other to cup her breast, flicked at the nipple that was taut and beaded.

His brain was hazed with desire. And there was a tightening in his groin that warned him that restraint was rapidly spirally away. He could feel her nails on his shoulders, the slight sting fanning the fire that was raging hotter and hotter inside him. The silky glide of her leg along his.

Somehow he managed the strength to tear his mouth away. To open his eyes and try to recapture a measure of control.

But the sight of her in the soft spill of light from the lamp had his hormones howling in a primal quest for fulfillment.

Her skin glowed with an ivory sheen, several shades lighter than his. The long dark hair fell away from the perfect oval of her face. Her lips were full, wet, and slightly parted. And her eyes . . . when she dragged them open were drugged and drenched with pleasure.

Demand pounded through him, wouldn't be denied. He reached for restraint, found it depleted. Eyes fixed on hers, he nudged a knee between her legs to urge them wider. And nearly disgraced himself when her hand settled around him, guiding him to her damp softness.

He gritted his teeth with the effort it took to hold back when all he wanted was to lunge into her. Quick, hard, and deep. Perspiration dampened his forehead. His breath was ragged. He entered her with one long stroke that had them releasing a mingled groan.

And felt, strangely enough, at peace.

But the instant of calm was shattered in the next moment when her legs climbed his hips to wrap around his waist. And the evidence of her urgency reignited his own. He began to move, carefully at first, but then with increasing desperation. He thrust into her, possessed by a fierce intent. To brand himself on her so completely she could never forget.

But as his vision hazed, as the blood pounded in his ears, he recognized dimly that he was caught in his own trap. The need skyrocketed in his veins, matching the pace of his hips as they jackhammered against hers.

And knew, even as the climax ripped through him, that it was he who would never forget.

"It's late."

"Technically, since you haven't opened your eyes yet, you can't possibly know that." Zach pressed a stinging kiss to her throat that made her shudder, before tonguing the sting lightly.

Her back was to the alarm clock. But when she cracked one eye open slightly, she could see the light edging the shades on the window. And gave a mental sigh. It was at least seven, if she didn't miss her guess. Well past the time she needed to be up and moving about, readying for the day.

But the man beside her obviously had other ideas. His erection nudged insistently against her belly. And the way the hand on her waist slipped to her butt wasn't exactly innocent.

"If you're going in to work today wearing the same clothes from last night you're going to have to do the walk of shame." The thought had her lips curving before she pressed them to one of his firm pecs.

"Women do the *walk* of shame." His hand slid to her breast and lightly scraped the nipple with his nail, making her shudder. "Men strut."

She gave an ungentle tug to his chest hair. Was satisfied to see him wince. "Not if their 'strutter' is broken."

"That sounded suspiciously like a threat." With a quick and sneaky move he rolled to his back, bringing her with him and settling her on top of him. His eyes gleamed up at her, filled with sleepy male satisfaction. "Since I know you have a weapon close by and I'm unarmed, I'm obviously at your mercy. Do your worst."

She studied him from beneath lowered lids, duty warring with desire. The battle was unfamiliar. For the last several years duty had always been foremost. First with school, then her job.

But it had been a long time since she'd been presented with temptation the likes of Zach Sharper.

She slid down his body slowly, anticipation thrumming in her veins. She took his shaft in her hands and flicked delicately at its tip with her tongue. "I certainly intend to."

———

It was telling that Cait spent the drive to the morgue trying to figure a way to divert Kristy's attention once she arrived. The last thing she wanted was to have another conversation about "the sex glow" the woman claimed to be able to detect on her face. Because she was very much afraid that she looked exactly the way she felt . . . loose, satisfied, and intensely female.

It seemed that spending a night wrapped around Zach Sharper had that effect on her.

But as she was pulling in to the morgue parking lot, a more pressing concern arose when her cell rang. Reaching one-handed to withdraw it from her purse, she saw the LA prefix on the screen and considered allowing it to go straight to voice mail. It wasn't Lydia's number, but she could be calling from a different phone. She was tenacious when she wanted something and had called almost daily since their last conversation.

All of the messages she'd left had been deleted.

Nudging aside the prickle of guilt at the thought, she took a chance and answered it on the third ring. She couldn't risk missing a job-related call on the off chance that her mother had found a new way to reach out and nag her. "Caitlin Fleming." She parked the SUV and dropped the keys into her purse before getting out of the vehicle.

"Fleming, this is Detective Richard Gomez, LAPD. You left me a message a few days ago about a missing persons case of mine. Sorry about the delay. I just closed a homicide investigation that was sucking up all my time."

Her steps faltered a moment before adrenaline kicked in and quickened her pace. "I did call. You were the detective listed on a case regarding Paul Livingston, three years ago."

"That's right. Guy disappeared one night when he went out to pick up a few groceries for his wife. Never showed up at any store we could discover. No one ever saw him again. You got something on him?"

"Maybe." Quickly she filled him in on her background, the investigation she was working on, and the DNA samples she'd taken from the remains. When she'd wound down, the man on the other end of the line was silent for a moment.

"Raiker Forensics? Why does that sound familiar?"

Releasing a quick breath of impatience, she used her temporary ID card to open the morgue's back entrance and hurried to the lab. "It's headed by Adam Raiker. He was . . ."

"The Mindhunters. Yeah, yeah, I remember now. Read about your outfit not too long ago. Saw something about your case on the news." A new note of respect had entered the detective's tone. "You think you got Livingston in that batch of bones you all pulled from the cave up there? Because I've got to admit, I always figured the guy pulled a fast one and took a hike."

Pushing open the door to the lab, she lifted a hand to acknowledge her assistant's greeting and sat down to the desk in the corner. "You think he disappeared on purpose?"

"Made it look good if he did . . . but, yeah. Thought it was possible. At least that's what I'd have done if I'd been him. Livingston was loaded, but his wife, excuse my language, is a class-A bitch. And he had a no-good son who was bleeding him dry, bailing him out of one scrape after another. If it'd been me, I'd have run fast and far."

If Livingston turned out to be involved in this case, she'd have a name to go with the bones of male E. The approximate age and stature of the remains matched the physical description of the missing man. But they were a long way yet from making that determination. "You wouldn't happen to remember whether he attended UCLA, would you?" The mascot of UCLA had been one of the images on male E's scapula.

"Now how in hell would you have known that from looking at some bones?"

Excitement balled in the pit of her stomach. Gomez went on. "'Course my memory is shit these days, so I wouldn't have recalled that, but I reviewed the case file before calling you back. Got it right here on my desk."

"Could you take a look in it and see if it includes any copies of credit card statements?"

"I had copies made for the last two years before he disappeared. What are you looking for, exactly?"

"Check for a billing to a resort of some kind in Oregon months before his disappearance. The only victim we've identified so far had stayed in the vicinity eight months before she disappeared." She waited, barely breathing, for several minutes as he flipped through the contents of the file on the other end of the line.

"Yeah, okay, here's something." The knot in her stomach tightened as the man began to read. "Payment to a place called Blue River Cabins eleven months prior. Must be some place in the mountains, huh? I remember his wife saying they took separate vacations because he was into hiking and kayaking and she liked the beach. Anyway there's more here. Got a couple smaller payments to places in Sisters. McKenzie Bridge. Some gas receipts, and then one other charge to a place in Eugene. Called Oregon Outdoors."

The reference to Zach's business gave her a jolt. But both of the identified victims had come to the area to enjoy nature. It wasn't surprising that they'd hire a company like his.

Although they had no DNA reference sample match yet, the rest of the details were sounding eerily similar to the disappearance of Marissa Recinos. "How much money did you say was missing from his account?"

"Several accounts, actually. And it was just shy of a million. His wife was plenty pissed about it, believe me. We didn't discover it for several days, and then she was initially convinced he'd taken off, just like I said. But eventually she changed her mind. Said he'd never have been satisfied leaving her the bulk of their money and taking only that much for himself."

"Did you trace it?"

"Tried." She could hear the continuous ringing of phones in the background that reminded her of every visit she'd ever made to a police squad room. "We dead-ended. Bounced us around to one overseas account after another in a half a dozen countries before fizzling."

She thought hard. Cyber theft wasn't her area of expertise. "But if Livingston didn't show up in a bank to wire the monies, they had to be done online, right?"

"Yeah. The banks indicated the money had been transferred with Livingston's personal information, but there was no evidence of the transaction on his personal computer. Whoever planned the transfer was slick."

Cait had heard enough. "Can I get you to fax those credit card statements to me?" She gave him the fax number. "What are the chances you could also obtain a DNA reference sample match from one of Livingston's relatives? Maybe his son?"

"Shouldn't be difficult to get that." Gomez's voice was heavy with irony. "He's serving a ten-year stretch at Corcoran for possession with intent to deliver. His DNA is on file with the California Department of Corrections."

Chapter 16

"Kristy has finished with the comparisons on the garbage bags, with the exception of the one kept by the crime lab. She's got two possible matches. One to the brand name Sowell's, a biodegradable bag that's been on the market for seven years. The other to Caston's." Cait passed out the sheet detailing the results to Andrews and the dozen deputies collected in the conference room at the sheriff's office. "I've included the list of the samples she compared and where they were collected from. I suggest more brands be picked up for testing, and this time concentrating our focus on stores in towns closer to the vicinity of Castle Rock."

Barnes looked at a dark-haired deputy on his left. "Hank, you and your team can continue on that." The man nodded silently.

"We follow every lead, but I want the highest concentration of manpower at the two resorts that showed up on credit card statements for the two victims Fleming has identified," Andrews put in. Just an hour earlier Cait had determined the DNA profile in the database for Raymond Livingston shared five markers with that of Paul Livingston. The remains of male E now had a name. "You pull in every employee for an interview. Show the pictures. It's been years since the victims were guests at these places, so you're going to have to spend some time. Go over employee histories and get the owners to give you a list of any former employees who would have been working at the time the two disappeared."

"Kristy will have the results from the remaining paint samples finished within the hour. I don't doubt we'll have a match for you." Cait had delegated the remainder of the task to her assistant after her conversation with Gomez that morning. "Wouldn't hurt for another team to be ready to track down that lead, as well."

"Sutton, you can stand by and wait for those results. Your men will follow up." It didn't escape the notice of anyone at the table that Barnes had usurped Andrews's role of relegating duties to the chief members of the investigation.

"Now that we've determined at least two of the victims visited the area where their remains were eventually found, we have reason to focus more closely on people in that region." Cait caught the sheriff's gaze. Held it. "If the killer lives in the vicinity, and it's looking increasingly like he does, that focus is going to make him very nervous."

"So he might make a mistake."

"Or feel cornered." She shifted her gaze to encompass all the personnel in the room. "He's killed eight times. That definitely makes him dangerous."

"Understood," the sheriff said brusquely. "Every officer here will exercise the utmost caution. I'll want progress briefings by the end of shift from team leaders."

There was a scraping of chairs as the detectives and deputies departed from the room. When only she, Barnes, and the sheriff remained, Cait said, "What about Lockwood? Do you still have people looking for him?" The roamer had never been found in the searches she and Zach had made. In light of the most recent developments in the case, continuing the search for him didn't seem to hold the priority it once had. But like Kesey, he could have seen something that related to this case.

"Yesterday evening a ranger discovered a body of a man in the forest north of Highway One twenty-six." Andrews drummed her fingers on the file folder in front of her with Cait's most recent report of her findings. "No ID, and the animals and insects had gotten to him, but there's enough left of his face to be fairly certain it's him. He also had a couple items in his lean-to with the initials B.L. on them. The ME figures heart attack or aneurism, some time in the last week."

In the last week. Which meant if they had happened to find him, he would have already been dead.

"All right." She started to rise, but something in the sheriff's expression alerted her. "Is there something else?"

Andrews and Barnes exchanged a gaze. Cait felt all her senses go on alert. "Crime lab contacted me today. They have a match on the thumbprint they took off the garbage bag."

Mystified, she sat back down. Wondered at the edge of tension in the room. "From one of the elimination prints?"

The other woman nodded. Picked up the file folder to fan her face as it began to flush. "The print belongs to Sharper."

There was a viselike squeeze in Cait's chest. It took effort to take a breath, survey the two impassively. "I suppose it's to be expected. He said he'd looked inside one of the bags."

"That wasn't in his original statement."

"In the statement he was asked if he touched the bones." Like anything else she read, details of that document were imprinted on her memory. "He didn't. But no one asked if he'd handled the bags." It had been the sort of mistake made during questioning that Raiker would never tolerate from his employees. "He told me he had when I took his prints."

Again that look of shared knowledge between the two. And it was starting to irritate her. "Climbers wear gloves, don't they?" Barnes asked.

"Climbing gloves don't have fingers in them. They protect the palms while still allowing dexterity for grasping finger holds." Cait's voice was cool. Her pulse was thudding in her ears. Trepidation pooled in her stomach. It was easy enough to see exactly where this was going. And like a train wreck, she was helpless to stop it.

Barnes leaned forward. His mustache had filled in a little, more rusty colored than the remaining hair on his head. His brown gaze was unblinking. "How close do you think Sharper comes to fitting the profile you developed for the UNSUB?"

All those years of donning masks for her photo shoots came in handy now. She could be certain her expression remained professional even as nerves were scampering up her spine. "Superficially, there would be some similarities. Given his time in the military, he may have acquired training in various kill techniques. There's acidic soil on his property, although the sample I took wasn't an exact match for the sediment found in the bottom of a couple of the bags."

"And both of the identified victims went missing in the time he's been back in the area," Andrews put in.

Cait inclined her head. "With another six set of remains to be identified," she reminded them. "But once you get past the superficial qualities—qualities that are probably shared with several others in the region—I don't find him a probable match for the offender."

Andrews sat back, folded her arms over her chest, still grasping the folder. "You don't? What about the fact that he found the bodies in the cave? And that his clients stumbled on the last one? We know he did business with Livingston when the man vacationed in the area."

"What would his motivation be for 'accidentally discovering' them?" Cait argued. "Chances are those bones could have sat in that cave for years longer if he hadn't brought them to your attention. While it isn't all that unusual for an UNSUB to deliberately insert himself into an ongoing investigation in some way, it's hard to believe one would do so when it looked for all intents and purposes as though he was getting away with the crime."

"He may have done it to prove he's smarter than we are." At her look, Barnes lifted a shoulder. "We had that a few years ago. An arsonist was burning places down and leaving us notes. Finally caught him with the help of a handwriting expert."

Irritation was starting to take the place of her earlier panic.

"With an arson, you already had evidence of the crime. In this case the killings could have remained undetected for much longer. This isn't Hollywood. It's actually more rare than you'd think to have serial offenders deliberately engage the police. The act is about *their* compulsion, whatever drives them. It's not about us."

Andrews shrugged, clearly unmoved. "It should be simple enough to check out his alibi for the days the two victims disappeared."

Cait doubted there would be anything simple about providing alibis for dates three and five years ago, respectively. "Obviously you'll want to talk to him. We should follow up with all the businesses in the area that showed up on the victims' credit card statements. But I think you're wasting your time focusing on him as the UNSUB. As a matter of fact, after speaking to Gomez this morning, I'm wondering if we're dealing with more than one offender."

Cait watched the dismayed look pass between the two and wondered if she should have waited before bringing this up. She hadn't worked through all the angles of the theory yet, although it was beginning to make a great deal of sense to her.

"Your earlier profile didn't mention that possibility." Andrews tapped the edge of the folder on the table in a rhythm that immediately set Cait's teeth on edge.

"I said it would be a developing document. It changes as more information comes to light. And if money turns out to be the motivation for the homicides, rather than the act of killing for itself, the picture of our offender changes."

Barnes cocked his head. "How so?"

"Marissa Recinos disappeared from Seattle. Paul Livingston from LA." She raised her brows, but when neither of them commented, Cait went on. "That's a lot of area to cover. Someone has to do the actual kidnapping. The money transfer. The kills. The disposal. Whoever set up the offshore accounts is good enough to have stumped law enforcement in two different states. That suggests a highly evolved individual with advanced training and knowledge in that area. A very different personality type from the offender who disposed of the bodies. The second person is also organized, given the degree of planning that goes into the disposals. But his planning shows signs of being rooted in emotion, drawn probably from a traumatic experience in his past." She paused a moment, because she hadn't completely had time to thoroughly think through the description. "Offender two may also be the one to do the actual killing."

"How can you know that?" Barnes's tone was more curious than questioning.

"When it comes to profiling, very little is *known*." Cait wished she'd brought in the bottle of water she'd bought on her way here this morning. Her throat felt like she'd been gargling with sand. "I'm just drawing conclusions based on the evidence as it presents itself. But supposing there are multiple UNSUBs, there has to be something that draws offender two more deeply into the crime. Offenders that act as a team are often careful to be sure one is just as guilty as the other. An equal division of labor, if you will. It helps build trust that one won't turn in the other. He can't, or he risks incriminating himself, as well. Disposing of the bones hardly carries the same danger as stealing funds or homicide."

"But that inequity is exactly what I would expect to find if, say, it were a man and woman working together," Andrews argued. "It wouldn't be unusual at all for the female in the team to be at lower risk, although she helps somehow in the commission of the crime."

Nodding, Cait replied, "True. But if one of the offenders is female, it's my guess she's the brains. The one behind the money transfers, simply because it's difficult to imagine a woman hauling those bodies up to Castle Rock in the middle of the night."

Stubbornly, Andrews said, "Painting those images seems more feminine to me. But you may be right about there being multiple offenders." She shot a look at Barnes. "I'll want a list of all Sharper's known acquaintances since he's been back in the area."

"He grew up around there," the deputy reminded her. "He likely knows most everybody."

Ignoring his words, Andrews went on, "And see what you can find out about his finances. He happened into a great deal of money in the last few years, I'm told."

There was a quick vicious twist in Cait's gut. "The property he's building his house on is worth approximately a million dollars." She wasn't sure if the shock in their expression was due to the number or the fact that she knew about it at all. "I looked it up in the courthouse records. He said he was the sole beneficiary of his grandfather's will. I'm sure you can acquire details of the probate."

"I'll do that." There was a light in the other woman's eyes that she didn't trust. "I want a go at him before he has a chance to prepare. So I'd appreciate it if you don't let your relationship with the man blind you to his possible guilt. I don't want him tipped off that I'll be talking to him."

Every organ inside her ground to a halt. Brain. Heart. Lungs. Then they restarted with a lurch that had the blood pulsing like a sprinter through her veins. "My relationship with him?"

Barnes studied a nonexistent spot on the wall while the sheriff spoke. "It's come to my attention that you and he may have become . . . closer recently. I have to be sure that isn't going to affect your ability to remain objective."

She welcomed the temper that fired at Andrews's words. It was infinitely preferable to the self-doubt, the all-encompassing fear that had all but paralyzed her earlier. "If you're asking if I've slept with him, the answer is yes. But my brain happens to function independently of my sex organs." The deputy flinched a little in the face of her frank language. But it was the sheriff she was addressing. Barnes may have been the conveyor of that little message, but it was Andrews who was twisting it to suit herself. "I've never given you any reason to question my professionalism. But if you've got doubts now, say so." Even she could hear the dare in her words. She stared at the sheriff, their gazes doing battle. And it was small comfort when, at the end, it was Andrews who looked away.

"Don't be so damn touchy. I was just saying . . ."

"I know exactly what you were saying, Sheriff." Cait stood, more than ready to leave. "You made it clear enough. Rather than focusing on Sharper, you'd do better to run the records on locals in the area. Anyone with a history of violence. I know for a fact that Rick Moses, at least, recently got out of prison."

"We're on that. Moses served time for vehicular manslaughter." Without a breath, the woman shifted back to her original topic. "I thought you could come with me when I talk to Sharper today."

She'd rather chew glass. "There are still a couple detectives I haven't heard from yet. I'm going to contact them again and then interview the owners of the businesses that showed up on the victims' credit card statements." Cait pushed back her chair and rose, seeing the skim of Andrews's eyebrows and not giving a damn. Regardless of the sheriff's inferences, she'd provide any information she had in her possession about the case, whoever it might point to. But she wasn't up to interrogating the man. Not when she could vividly recall the hours she'd spent wrapped around him last night. This morning.

Professionalism was one thing. She gathered up her files and headed for the door. But she'd be lying if she claimed anything in her training had prepared her for getting involved with a man who was a possible suspect in the case.

It was midafternoon before Cait nosed her vehicle toward McKenzie Bridge. She'd checked out the businesses that had shown up on Livingston's statement first, a couple gift stores in Sisters. As she'd suspected, it was nearly impossible to jog people's memories about a tourist that had been a customer over three years ago. Employees at the businesses had come and gone. And none of those she'd talked to had recognized his picture.

It was difficult to believe she'd have any better luck in McKenzie Bridge, but she was determined to conduct those interviews as well before the day ended. She'd wanted to meet more of the locals there anyway, she reminded herself, slowing behind a county dump truck filled with gravel. There was a more urgent need for that now after finding out that Recinos had stayed in the area.

She'd managed to make contact with a Detective Mark Holder in Nevada that morning, and she could now officially discount his missing person case. New evidence had recently come to light, and Gary Smith's wife was now suspected of killing her husband and cremating him in the family's mortuary business. Which was a macabre ending any way you looked at it.

There was still no response from Sergeant Hal Cross of Idaho, but she'd left yet another message. And considered, again, that she was going to have to relook at the list of missing persons she'd formulated. She'd deliberately concentrated first on subjects from neighboring states, but it was time to branch out farther. It was still hard to believe the UNSUB—or, if her newest theory was correct—one of the UNSUBs had traveled hundreds of miles to kidnap the victims. But the offender was proving much more daring than she'd originally believed.

Her cell beeped, indicating an incoming text message. Keeping her eyes on the road, Cait felt around in her purse until she retrieved the cell. It was another minute before traffic thinned enough for her to risk a glance at it.

PICNIC AT MY PLACE TONIGHT. REAL FOOD.

She dropped the phone on her lap as if it burned. Obviously Andrews hadn't caught up with Zach yet. It was doubtful he'd be in the mood to issue invitations after spending a few hours in the sheriff's company. As a matter of fact, Cait had an all too clear mental picture of exactly how he'd react to the questions the woman would be leveling at him.

It was still plenty fresh in her mind what it had felt like to be on the receiving end of the sheriff's interrogation this morning.

Not for the first time that day, she considered Andrews's implication about Cait's objectivity. Without knowing it, the woman had unerringly put her finger on the button guaranteed to elicit all the old self-doubts about her judgment in men. Doubts she'd never considered in the course of her job. In that area, at least, her instincts didn't fail her.

She'd discounted Sharper when she developed the profile. Before she became involved with him. But it was easy to question those conclusions now, with the sheriff's questions still fresh in her mind.

Rather than bothering with a map, she relied on familiar landmarks to find her way back to McKenzie Bridge. When she saw the General Store up ahead, Cait knew exactly where she was. She took the next left toward the small town.

Andrews was wrong about Sharper. And it was professional opinion rather than emotion that told Cait that. Even the evolving theory that they were looking for at least two UNSUBs instead of one ruled him out in her mind. The man was a loner. While it was plain he had friends and was well liked by people in the area, he wasn't the type to join forces with another in something as twisted as the crimes they were investigating.

If Zach Sharper were going to kill eight people, she'd be willing to bet he'd do it alone. And he damn well wouldn't invite the sheriff to his disposal site to show off his handiwork.

Certainty accompanied the thought. Almost enough to completely alleviate the sneaky little sliver of doubt Andrews had unleashed this morning.

Doubt that reminded her that it wouldn't be the first time she'd been wrong about a man. Her track record in that area was dismal. But just because she'd chosen men for years who were interested only in arm candy, didn't mean that this time she'd hooked up with a serial killer.

Cait pulled up to the curb on Main Street and put the vehicle in park. She'd made mistakes in her life. And maybe—a chill broke out over her skin as the echo of that long-ago gunshot sounded in her mind—maybe she'd started the mistakes at an early age. Undoubtedly the trauma when she was eight had factored into a years-long habit of choosing the wrong men for the wrong reasons. But she'd broken that pattern long ago.

And Sheriff Marin Andrews wasn't going to convince her any differently.

The glare from the afternoon sun was still strong, so she kept her sunglasses on as she got out of the vehicle, locked it, and rounded the hood toward the sidewalk. There were people out and about. Little clusters chatting in front of the ice cream shop and the post office. Others loitering outside the shop windows, peering in. Whatever impact the murders had had on the area, business seemed brisk this afternoon, with most storefronts boasting a steady trickle of customers through their doors.

Because it was closest, Cait ducked into the ice cream shop first, her gaze going to the wait staff at the counter. She knew immediately they'd be no help. Both were teenagers, a boy and a girl, and neither would have been working age three years ago when Livingston had been in the area, much less Recinos.

Nevertheless she approached them and waited patiently to be waited on. As it happened she got the girl, who raked her over with her gaze, taking in every inch of her appearance.

"What can I get you?"

She spoke with a slight speech impediment, but Cait decided that was due to the piercing on her tongue. The girl couldn't be more than fifteen, with brown hair in need of a wash, and an unfortunate complexion.

"I'd like to speak to the owner. Is he or she around?"

As an answer the teenager turned away toward a door that led to a back room. "Mom! Someone here to see you."

Obviously feeling like she'd done her duty, the girl walked by Cait to wait on the next customer. Several moments passed before a woman appeared in the doorway, a frown on her face as she wiped her hands on a dishtowel and scanned the interior of the shop.

"You're the owner?" Cait was already reaching for the file folder she carried with the victims' pictures.

"Casey Teames. And you're not a salesperson." Something in the woman's stance eased and she came closer to the counter, leaned both hands against it. "Sorry, but that's about the only people who come in asking for me."

A slight smile curving her lips, Cait pressed her temporary Sheriff's Department ID against the clear plastic backsplash separating them. "No, I'm not here to sell you anything. I just have a few questions. How long have you owned this shop?"

The woman gave the ID a cursory glance before returning her gaze to Cait. "Nine years, I guess. No wait, eight and a half. Steph was in second grade when we bought it, and she's a sophomore now." She slid a quick glance to the girl who was now giggling with the boy working beside her. "Hard to believe."

Passing the pictures of the two victims to Casey, Cait said, "Both of these people have been tourists in the area in the past few years. Recognize either of them?"

To her credit, the other woman took her time studying each, before slowly shaking her head and passing the photos back. "I don't. Sorry. We usually get a lot of people in and out of here in the summer and fall. Is there any reason I should recognize them?"

Ready to move on, she said, "Not really. I'll be hitting as many shops in the area as I can to ask the same question. I appreciate your time."

There was a slightly puzzled expression on the woman's face, but it was clear the majority of her focus was on her daughter and the girl's attention to the boy working with her. "No problem."

Cait vacated the shop and wended her way through the half-filled tables on the walk outside it to move on to the next store, a small crowded space featuring leather goods. The owner, a lean taciturn man by the name of Jacob Beales, spent much less time looking at the photos than Casey Teames had, and much more time pressing his wares on her.

"Finest leather goods in the area, and everyone around here will tell you the same." He picked up a brown suede purse and tried to thrust it into her hands. "Just feel that. Doe skin. You may pay less at a country fair, but then you'd never be able to find the vendor again if something goes wrong. I guarantee everything I sell. Thirty days, same as cash."

The bell on the door tinkled, and Cait took advantage of the diversion to make her escape back outside.

She remembered the gift shop next door. She'd spent a bit of time looking in its windows the last time she'd strolled Main Street. Pushing the door open, she entered to find it crowded with several browsers.

With a quick glance toward the front, she saw one woman with gray braids pinned up on her head manning a cash register and another, a couple decades younger, helping a couple trying to decide between two paintings on whitewashed canvas.

Cait decided to use her intervening time perusing the rows of artwork lining ledges along one wall. But after only a few moments, she decided that nothing on display came close to the images painted on back of the scapulas. Not, she admitted silently, that she would necessarily recognize the style on a bigger canvas. But it reminded her to show the picture she'd brought of close-ups taken of a few of the images, just in case.

"Ms. Fleming. Decide to buy a painting after all?"

The familiar voice had her turning. And smiling when she saw Jeffrey Russo behind her. "Just poking around. What about you? Looking for another place to display your work?"

"Can't paint fast enough to keep my gallery happy as it is." Today he was dressed in creased walking shorts, Birkenstocks, and a buttoned-down shirt. With a flip of his hand, he indicated his fiancée on the far side of the store. "You remember Candi Montrose? She's trying to decide whether to make an offer on this place. It wouldn't be my first choice, but she's the one with the head for numbers. And according to her figures, it's very successful, given its limited inventory."

Cait's gaze lingered on the woman for a moment. There was a certain charm to the shop, but somehow she couldn't imagine Candi spending her days inside it, waiting on demanding customers. She reminded Cait of her mother. Although the women didn't look alike, they shared a similar regal bearing and a vague sense of entitlement. Something that said they were born for better and that their expectations in life had never quite been met.

"And how is your case going? I'll admit to being intrigued enough by the details to listen to every bit of news there is about it. The news of the bones being found in Mimosa Creek was absolutely chilling."

Her attention firmly back on the man at her side, she said, "Have you ever been there? To the springs?"

The elderly man shook his head. "Candi's not much of an outdoorswoman. Are you close to making an arrest?"

The retired professor, she decided, was something of a gossip. "The case is progressing. We have several leads we're following."

"Cop speak," he complained, but his eyes were twinkling. "I've watched enough TV to recognize it."

"Maybe so. But that doesn't make it untrue."

Russo lowered his voice. "I heard some young lovers found the bones when they snuck into the springs au naturel."

"You heard wrong." The man looked so crestfallen that she almost felt sorry for her response. "As usual truth isn't as an exciting as rumors."

"Well, that's to be expected, I suppose." His tone was rueful. "Never believe everything you hear, right? Small-town grapevines are like university campuses. Facts change to become more titillating." He scanned the displayed artwork critically. "See anything that meets your fancy?"

Coming to a sudden decision, Cait took the camera picture of some of the images she'd blown up that had been found on male E. Handing the sheet to him, she watched his expression closely. "Actually, I'm looking for something along the lines of this art work."

His expression went from curious to scholarly. "Shows aptitude, undoubtedly. There's uniqueness to the line movement. The technique is solid. Originality is hard to determine since he or she has chosen familiar objects. But this artist hasn't had formal training." He handed the sheet back to her.

"Why do you say that?"

"Several reasons." Russo slipped his hands into the pockets of his shorts and sent a quick glance at his fiancée before returning his gaze to Cait. "The materials used in the paintings are subpar, for one thing. Garish rather than soft or bold. It's difficult to enter into the work, as the over-specificity of content lacks individualization." Her expression must have been blank, because he explained, "Even in the rendition of familiar objects, something of the artist should be imbued in the work. Whether in the lighting, brushwork, spatial relationships . . . if the objective is to paint exactly what you see, one may as well use a camera."

As if suddenly realizing he may have insulted her taste, his expression became arrested. "But of course if you enjoy this artist's work, if it speaks to you on some level, don't let my opinion sway you. The most important thing about a piece is how it makes you feel."

Dark humor filled her. How these particular images made her feel was hardly appropriate subject matter to be discussing with the professor. But if he was correct about the UN-SUB being untrained as an artist, that, too, helped her get a handle on the offender.

"I appreciate your insight." She tucked the page back into the folder.

Russo began to move away. "Looks like Candi is ready. I hope you find more of that artwork you're interested in."

Cait murmured a good-bye and strolled closer to the ladies manning the front of the shop. Despite the warmth in the shop, the professor's parting words gave her a chill.

Because she found herself hoping exactly the opposite. She was hoping the person responsible for this particular work was finished. That they'd catch him before he "created" again.

It was nearly twenty minutes before she was able to speak to one of the women running the store. It was the elderly of the two who waited on her with a wide smile and a discreet glance that took in the fact that Cait had no store items in her hands. "How can I help you?"

Handing her the two photos, she said, "I'm wondering if you recognize either of these people. Both have been tourists in the area in recent years." She stopped, a bit bemused as she caught sight of the woman's nametag. MOONBEAM. Either the woman's parents had hated her when she was born or she'd changed her name for her own incomprehensible reasons. Whichever it was, the woman was studying the pictures intently.

After a few moments Moonbeam tapped the picture of Recinos. "She has such a tragic aura," she murmured before lifting her gaze to Cait. "Who is she?"

"Do you recognize her?"

The woman shook her head. "I don't think she's been in here this year. Him, either, for that matter. I have a pretty good memory for people. Always recognize our return customers. Some people vacation here every year," she explained, leading Cait a little to the side so clients could make their way more easily to the cash register. "Or at least return for a weekend or two. We get folks from all over the country and every once in a while from overseas. That's why we keep the guestbook. It's sort of fun to figure how many states have been represented here each year."

Spying the large register-like notebook on a table to the side of the door, Cait moved toward it, interest sharpening. She waited impatiently for the girl signing it to finish before moving in front of it and flipped through the pages. "Do you put a new book out every year?"

"No, only when one gets filled." Bending down, Moonbeam opened a cupboard below and indicated the three other ledgers on a shelf.

"Mind if I take a look?"

"Not at all." The woman's smile was wide. "It's a wonderful way to connect with those whose paths have intersected ours as we travel parallel courses on the planet, isn't it?"

Moonbeam, Cait was willing to bet, had smoked a bit of

weed in her day. Or a lot of it. But she was content to flip through the pages, looking for the years Livingston and Recinos had been in the area while the older woman turned to a couple waiting to ask her a question about some stained glass.

The first entry in the register was a couple years ago, so Cait reached for the other books in the cupboard below and hauled them out. Looking at the last page of each, she was able to put them in chronological order fairly quickly. She looked through the next most recent one, finding the dates corresponding to the time Livingston had been in the area. Many customers had not only signed the book with their names and states but also left little messages to the storeowners or about their experience in the shop. The messages were overwhelmingly positive. Cait imagined the people who'd left unhappy didn't feel compelled to linger long enough to write about it.

Livingston's signature wasn't to be found. But she did find Marissa Recinos's near the front of that same register. She stared at the signature for a moment. Wondered at the mood of the woman who'd written it. A woman who'd just gone through a messy divorce and had come to a vacation she was ill suited for with a bunch of friends. There was no message under her name. Just a silent testament that she'd been here. Happy, perhaps. And blissfully unaware that eight months later she'd be dead.

Something compelled her to keep looking. She reached for an older book and began scanning the dates. But even though she was consciously looking for it, she still experienced a jolt when she saw the nearly illegible scrawl dated September, six years ago.

Bill Bentley.

She stared, nonplussed for a moment. Then her heartbeat picked up pace as adrenaline spiked. William Bentley from Boise, Idaho. Disappeared five months after the date on the record, almost to the day.

The missing person in the case Sergeant Hal Cross of the Boise Police Department still hadn't gotten back to her about.

Chapter 17

"Sergeant Cross." Cait gritted her teeth as she left yet another message for the man on the sidewalk outside the gift shop. "This is Caitlin Fleming of Raiker Forensics calling again. I may have a lead for you on the William Bentley missing persons case. The only way to be sure, however, is to return the damn call this time. It's a matter of some urgency."

She disconnected and dropped the phone back in her purse with more than a little impatience. The desk sergeant had assured her the officer was on duty, so there was little reason he couldn't at least reply. But it wouldn't be the first time she'd crossed paths with cops who could be complete jerks. Some of the time she even had to work side by side with them.

And after her conversation with Andrews and Barnes this morning, she wasn't excluding the two from those ranks.

She had no more taken a step when her cell rang. In one quick movement, she grabbed the phone and answered it, hoping, half-expecting, to hear the detective on the other end of it.

"Fleming."

There was a moment of silence. Then, "That's such an unattractive way to answer your phone, dear. Although I suppose I should count myself lucky you answered at all."

Cait's eyes slid shut in frustration. The absolute last thing she needed right now was a dose of Lydia Fleming Smythe Regatta. "Mother," she began flatly, staring blindly at the people strolling by on the street. "I don't have time for . . ."

". . . for your mother? I've been trying to reach you for *days*, Caitlin. After always being there for you, I had the erroneous assumption I could count on you for support."

So caught up was she in the irony of the first part of the statement, that it took Cait a moment to comprehend the latter. "What's wrong?"

She heard her mother's voice hitch. "It's Henri. He's . . . he's . . . *left me*."

With a feeling of inevitability, Cait found an unoccupied bench situated off the sidewalk on a grassy area between buildings. And sat there for long minutes while she listened to a litany of Henri DuBois's shortcomings. His miserliness. His sheer audacity. As a matter of fact, she reflected, as she interjected a few noncommittal sounds into the occasional breaks of conversation, if the man were as bad as Lydia let on, one could ask what she'd seen in him in the first place.

One could. Cait wouldn't. Instead she checked her watch. Eight minutes. "It sounds like he doesn't deserve you." A remark guaranteed to elicit another four minutes of agreement from her mother. And she knew it was mean-spirited of her, but she was grateful that at least this time she didn't have to listen to Lydia wheedle her about going back to modeling.

The stray thought had her feeling petty and low. So she said, when she had a chance to interject a word, "I'm sorry about Henri. After this job, I'll see if I can fly down and spend a couple days." And damned the immediate flood of dread that washed over her at the words.

"That would be lovely, Caitlin. I very much appreciate the thought." Lydia was much calmer now, but then she wasn't the type to lose control. Not really. She might just have finished railing against her faithless lover, but she'd never raised her voice in the process. She could slice and dice a person with no more than an icy tone and a carefully arched brow. "I know you're busy, so I'll let you go now. Please contact me when it gets closer to the time so we can arrange the details of your visit."

"I'll do that. Good-bye, Mother." She disconnected with a familiar feeling of relief, one that was too familiar to feel guilty for. Their relationship was what it was. And accepting the parameters of it was far easier than trying to dissect and reform it into something different. Something it would never be.

She stood, aware for the first time of a man loitering near the curb, giving her a once-over that he was taking no pains to hide. When she caught his eye, he began to grin, then froze at the unblinking stare she fixed him with. Turning, he hurried away.

Wise choice. Getting up, she retraced her steps to the gift shop. There was nothing like the prospect of a visit with her mother that made her want to kick someone's ass.

Neither Moonbeam nor her daughter could shed any light on the sheet of images she'd brought with her, so Cait tried showing the victim photos at the next store lining the walk, The Sweet Shoppe. And topped off her day nicely when she discovered the owner was none other than Sharper's former squeeze, Shellie Mayer. Given the fact that Cait's relationship with Zach had reached Andrews's ears, it was too much to hope for that Mayer wouldn't have heard of it. Needless to say, the woman didn't trip over herself to be cooperative.

The scene didn't exactly improve Cait's mood.

When she left The Sweet Shoppe, she noted Joanie Barton hurrying down the street toward JD's and briefly considered heading that way. But then she saw that Al's Taxidermy appeared open today. And without another thought, she veered toward it.

The shop was old, vaguely musty smelling, although both the door and the windows were open. There was no one at the front, but she heard Kathy's voice call out, "Be right there."

Cait took the intervening time to poke around and give the animals in the window a closer look. Although the fur on the beaver closest to her looked like it had been cleaned recently—Vacuumed? How the heck did they keep the things dusted?—there was dust on the base the feet were attached to. She found herself wondering how many of the animals were leftovers from Al's tenure at the store and how many were Kathy's handiwork.

A woman came bustling out from a door that led to a back room wiping her hands on the white butcher-style apron covering her clothes. Although she was wearing jeans and a man's old denim shirt, Cait immediately recognized the woman from Ketchers the other night.

Kathy smiled widely. "Hey, how are you? Never thought I'd see you in my place."

Returning her smile, Cait said, "You got me curious the other night. I had some spare time, so I've been looking around the town."

"Well, if you're really curious, come on back. I'm in the middle of a project. You can take a look."

She didn't wait for a second invitation. Following the woman through the doorway, Cait found herself in a long narrow room lined with sinks, counters, and shelves. Two long tables shoved together took up the center of the space. Spread in the center of the table was . . . Cait cocked her head. What used to be a coyote, she decided, given the size of the pelt spread fur side down on the table. The windows on the back wall were open, to very little effect. The aroma was pungent.

"Not squeamish are you?" Kathy picked up a medium-sized deflesher and went back to work on the hide.

"Nope." Fascinated in spite of herself, Cait roamed freely around the room. In undergrad courses, she'd practiced technique on animals, and the workroom was a primitive copy of some of the labs she'd worked in. She recognized many of the instruments lining the shelves. Sanders, power-operated fleshers, power saws. The equipment was stacked beside supplies of chemicals she assumed were used for tanning hides and soaking bones. She stopped, disconcerted at the sight of two large clear containers of glass eyes. On one far end of the table was a plaster of paris form of the animal.

"You've got something cooking." She crossed to the old stove set in one corner and lifted the lid on the large pot to reveal what was likely the coyote's skull. "M-mm. My favorite."

Kathy looked up, a quick smile of delight on her face. "Not too many have that reaction when they come back here. Mose doesn't mind, but then, he's seen worse."

Rick Moses, Cait recalled. The bartender from Ketchers. The ex-con she'd just asked Andrews about. "Does he help you out around here?"

"Mose?" Kathy continued to scrape away tissue without missing a beat. "He's around a lot. Actually think he's getting pretty good at this stuff himself. He's good help. Made a run to Eugene for me this afternoon to see if he could get me a cast mouth system for this. Otherwise I'll have to order one online."

Although she doubted it would do much good, Cait showed the photos of Livingston and Recinos to the other woman. Kathy looked with interest at each of them, then shook her head. "Neither of them would have come in here unless they were avid hunters or fishermen. I can go through the old records, if you like, once I'm done for the day. See if maybe we mounted a fish and shipped it to them."

"Why don't you do that." It was highly doubtful that Recinos would have had reason to use Kathy's services, but Cait took a business card out and scribbled her name, as well as Bentley's and Livingston's, and the dates each victim had been in the area. "I'll leave this on the counter up front."

"Sounds good. Thanks for stopping in." A wicked grin crossed the woman's face. "Not many people have the guts to make it this far inside."

Giving a laugh, Cait started for the door. "If bones made me squeamish, I'd be in the wrong line of work."

"Oh, I almost forgot."

Kathy's voice stopped her as she was about to leave the back area. "Al's wife called last night. They're on their way to Louisiana. Or was it Mississippi? Anyway, she just called to nag me about the check—I'm buying this place on contract— and I asked her where Al had gotten rid of the beetles. She said he gave them to someone at the university in Eugene."

"Okay." Of course it wasn't going to be that easy. It never was. "Thanks for checking."

"No problem."

Once outside her cell rang again. This time prior to answering she remembered to check the caller ID. And when she saw the Boise prefix on the number, her heart began to thud. "Fleming." As she answered she dodged a girl walking a Saint Bernard easily double her weight.

"Sergeant Hal Cross, Boise PD." The gravelly voice on the other end sounded like it suffered from too many late nights, bottles of Scotch, and cigarettes. "I'm answering your *damn* call, but it won't do either of us any good. I closed that Bentley case a couple years ago."

"What?" Disappointment pooled in her gut. "How is that possible? He's still in the system."

A shrug sounded in the man's voice. "Maybe I didn't get back into the database and clear it out. God knows his family isn't satisfied. The man still might be missing, but it's a pretty good probability that he's sipping mai tais on a Belize beach somewhere while the rest of us chase our asses."

It wasn't possible, she decided, to take a dislike to someone based solely on his voice. So her reaction to Cross was likely due to the disappointment blooming inside her and not his insolent tone. "What makes you think he's in Belize?"

"Not me, the feds. They waltzed in here about three months after Bentley disappeared asking questions. They didn't care so much about where he went, but they were all kinds of concerned with what happened to the quarter million he moved overseas to various accounts."

Adrenaline spiked through her, sharp and edgy. And with it brought certainty. "So there was money missing from his account. He didn't appear in the banks to transfer it himself. And there's no trace of the transfers on his computer."

"Sounds like you wrote the story. Feds took their sweet

time, but eventually they concluded he'd been laundering money. Couldn't figure out for who and how exactly he was doing it. Or if they did, they never shared those details with me. He must have thought things were getting too hot and disappeared. Happens all the time."

"If they never proved or disproved their theory, how can you be sure the feds were right?" She raised her hand to return Jodie Paulsen's greeting as he slowly drove by with his pickup loaded with what looked like scrap metal.

"It made a helluva lot more sense than someone vanishing into thin air, that's why," he retorted. Something told Cait the two of them weren't going to hang up as buddies. "Hell, people lie all the time. Families lie. Where'd the guy go? They don't know. He had no enemies, everyone loved him. Yeah, okay. Except he's *gone*, right? Maybe he had a mistress he ran off with to Bora Bora. The fact that he didn't want to tell his brother about his plans doesn't mean he's dead; it just means he left."

Or else, she thought cynically, it meant that accepting that story made it easy for Cross to wash his hands of the whole thing and improve his closed-case ratio.

"You might want to take another look at Bentley's case." She watched an old man who looked on the wrong side of ninety step cautiously off the curb as if fearful of breaking a hip on contact with the street.

"And why should I do that?"

"Because I've got skeletal remains here in Oregon that are a tentative match for his age and stature." Ignoring the rude sound he made, she continued, "We've got seven sets of remains all hauled out of the same cave. So far the two sets we've positively identified spent time in this area within a year of their disappearance."

"What does that—"

"I just discovered records today showing Bentley was here six and a half years ago."

That stopped Cross for a moment. "He disappeared about six years ago."

She mentally sighed. "Yes. And a large sum of money went

missing at the same time as the other two victims' disappearance. Is this starting to sound familiar to you at all?"

"Helluva coincidence."

"If you believe in coincidence, Cross, you haven't been in police work nearly long enough." The elderly man had made it safely down the curb and was now proceeding at a snail's pace across the street. "Bentley didn't happen to be a fan of the New York Giants, did he? And an avid whitewater rafter?" Both an image of the New York team and churning whitewater had been depicted on his scapulas.

"I'd have to check the file."

She'd had more than enough. "You do that. And while you're doing it, look for his credit card statements and see where he stayed during his time here. Then contact his brother about getting to a lab for a DNA profile. Got a pencil handy?" She gave him her fax number. "Get those results and his statement to me as quickly as possible, and I can give you a definitive answer about whether I've got William Bentley's remains on a gurney in my lab."

"Feds aren't going to like hearing they're wrong," the man muttered.

"We all have our little disappointments." She disconnected and called Gavin Pounds, Raiker's cyber wizard back at headquarters in Manassas. As she waited for the call to go through, she spared the old man one more glance. He'd progressed about four feet. In the course of his short journey, he'd received, and shaken off, no fewer than three offers of help. McKenzie Bridge was a friendly little town.

Except it hadn't proven so friendly for William Bentley. Or Marissa Recinos. Or Paul Livingston.

———

"So we should check with all the resorts in the area for a guest named William Bentley." Andrews was seated at the desk in Cait's McKenzie Motel room, scribbling on a notepad as she spoke. "What was the date again?"

Cait repeated it, and added, "Don't forget the campgrounds. We can't be sure where he stayed. I don't have access to his credit card statement yet, and I don't know how long I'll have to wait for it." Cross didn't strike her as the sort of guy who would move at the speed of light. "We also need to find out who the Internet provider is for the resorts in the area. At least who it was at the time Recinos, Livingston, and Bentley went missing."

Andrews looked up from her jottings, her expression shrewd. "You think the transfers were generated up here?"

"It's possible. People of wealth caught our UNSUB's attention. But he had to have some way of knowing they had money. Which means he had to gain access to their accounts initially to select his victims. What better way to do that than through their computer use?"

The sheriff frowned. "I'm pretty sure the provider is Lantis. They provide access to a lot of the outlying areas in Lane County. But you're not thinking the company is involved."

"Just an individual. One of their techs. Maybe even a former employee. We'll need them to open their employment records to us, as well as which tech serviced the resorts."

"I've got a couple men in cyber crimes, but I'm guessing if we need to search computers for this kind of evidence, it might be outside the expertise of my department. I may have to contact someone at State Police."

"Eventually, maybe." Cait sat on the edge of the bed. "I talked to Gavin Pounds earlier, Raiker's cyber genius. He said it could be as simple as the IP host capturing cookies or keystroke information. To access their online bank records, the offender just needs the account names and passwords. If they check their email from a computer the offender is monitoring, he can even install spyware on their home computer remotely and continue to get information long after they leave here."

Andrews was staring hard at her. "That easy?"

"I know." She'd been shocked herself when talking to Gavin. "Although years ago it would have been a bit more of a process, recent 'innovations' in the industry have made cyber spying easier. And a state-of-the-art powerful spy system can circumvent many of the more popular anti-spyware software."

"Del Barton has that wireless café," Andrews mused, tapping her pencil rapidly against the tablet.

"He told me it had only been open for a year and a half."

"I think I remember Gibbs mentioning it being fairly recent."

"These victims disappeared three, five, and six years ago. Did he begin the business from scratch or take over an existing one?" In her one conversation with the man, it had sounded like the place had been a fresh start, but they needed to verify that. As the sheriff jotted that down in her notebook, she continued, almost to herself, "Of course, we've got more than one resort in two different towns. Do they both use the same provider? They'd almost have to for this theory to work."

"Easy enough to find out." Finished writing, Andrews looked up again, her mouth a thin flat line. "We got nothing on the photos. No one seems to recall either victim at the resorts. Not much surprise there, given how long it's been since they were here."

"I struck out, too," Cait admitted. She stretched her legs out in front of her and suppressed a yawn. The lack of sleep was catching up with her. "I didn't get to the restaurant that showed up on Livingston's bill here in town. Tito's. You might have better luck sending a few men there to interview everyone on staff. It'll take some time to round up former employees. Any word on the garbage bags or paint?" A brief phone call with Kristy early this afternoon had resulted in the news that the tech had, indeed, found a match.

"Nothing on the paint yet. The garbage bags are sold in several spots within ten miles of here, including the General Store here in town. But other than nailing down accessibility, that lead is pretty much a dead end. We haven't gotten anywhere on the paint yet."

"And that would be easy to buy online, too," Cait admitted. "I think our best lead at this point is the Internet provider."

"Proving anything is going to be a bitch." The sheriff's familiar antsiness was present as she bounced out of the chair and began to pace, slapping the notebook against her stocky thigh as she walked. "Definitely won't be immediate. We'll need cyber experts on it, and with the state lab, no telling how soon I can get results."

"Detective Cross in Idaho mentioned a federal investigation into Bentley's money transfers. Every monetary transfer in the United States of ten thousand dollars or more has to be reported, so the offender stuck with nine-thousand-dollar transfers to multiple banks. Pounds told me red flags would have been raised if those multiple transfers went out on the same day or if they went to countries known for private banking havens, as many of them are on the terrorism watch list. If we get anything at all on this lead with the IP, you should be able to get some cooperation from the feds who looked into it."

Andrews threw her a sharklike grin. "Cooperation from the feds? Isn't that an oxymoron?"

Since there was more than a little truth in the question, Cait responded with a slight smile. "The banking transactions were also looked into for Recinos and Livingston. Those investigations sounded like they stayed local, so we might have better luck there."

Andrews grunted and seemed to come to a decision. "Well, we'll start fresh tomorrow. Maybe those newest bones will tell you something."

Cait hated to tell her that the set of remains they'd taken out of the hot springs were likely to yield the least amount of clues. "I'll go back to Eugene tonight so I can check on their drying progress in the morning. Once they're in condition to be handled, we can at least get them put together and get height and maybe approximate age." It would depend, in any case, on the condition of the bones and whether they were mostly all accounted for. "I don't know if I told you before, but those remains were male."

"So we've got five men and three women." The sheriff looked bemused. "I'd expect it to be the other way around."

"Ostensibly if money is the motivation, it might be easier to find men with bank accounts flush enough to attract the UNSUB. Although you'd think women would be easier to snatch."

"Some women." Andrews patted her pockets as if searching for cigarettes. Cait gave silent thanks when she failed to find any. "Others can surprise you." When her look grew pointed, Cait went tense. "Take you, for instance. You were well and truly pissed this morning. Can't deny that."

"You don't hear me trying to."

The other woman gave a bark of laughter. "I know what you're thinking. That Bentley being killed six years ago eliminates Sharper as a suspect because he was still in the Army then. But that still doesn't necessarily clear him. He could have started killing while home on leave at the same time."

"Sure," Cait agreed with mock politeness. "There's nothing like a little R and R. Fly a few thousand miles home, kill a tourist or two, and then back to the Army for more fun and games. Problem with that is how would he find the tourist if he wasn't here? How would he have the time to track Bentley for five months and then be back here to kidnap him?"

"Way I hear it that was about the time his grandfather died."

"That was seven years ago, not six."

Undeterred, Andrews continued. "I have to do a bit more digging into the exact dates. But if we're looking for two UNSUBs instead of one, he's still not off the hook."

Cait eyed her knowingly. "How'd you come out with him today?"

"He was an asshole, if you must know. Practically invited me to haul him in and charge him. He knew damn well I couldn't, so he threw me off his property. He's a real charmer, that one."

Because her lips threatened to curve, Cait deliberately firmed them. "That's surprising. Most people are more understanding about being suspected of multiple counts of theft, kidnapping, and homicide. Maybe it was the suspicion of money laundering that put him over the edge."

"I'm not going to apologize for doing my job," Andrews said bluntly. But she hesitated then, and her tentative manner instantly put Cait on alert. "I didn't get to where I am by looks or personality."

Even as Cait could feel herself heat, the other woman held up a hand as if to halt anything she'd say. "Not saying you did, just saying that wasn't ever a possibility for me. So I worked harder. Thought harder. Proved myself twice as good as any man. And so if sometimes I'm . . . less than tactful . . . I guess that's why."

It was, Cait realized with a sense of bemusement, as close to an apology as she was likely to receive. And because she could empathize with the woman's experiences to some degree, she felt herself thawing. "Like I said this morning, we'll pursue all leads. See where they take us." But she was as certain as she could be that they wouldn't be leading to Zach Sharper.

Andrews nodded and headed for the door. And Cait let her go, a realization bringing a pool of trepidation with it. Sharper had issued an invitation today. One he no doubt wanted to rescind by now. But she was going to his place, regardless.

She had a feeling that her welcome would make the one Andrews received from him look positively friendly by comparison.

When he ignored her knock, she walked right in. He'd left the door unlocked. Didn't think she'd have the balls to come after Andrews had worked him over today. But if there was one thing Caitlin Fleming didn't lack, it was balls. No doubt she collected them from the men she'd stomped on over the years.

He watched her come through the door and halt when she saw him in the recliner, regarding her over the top of his beer bottle. Thought he saw a jitter of nerves in her expression before she deliberately smoothed it. And that calm composed mask shot his temper from simmer straight to boil.

"Plans have changed." He took a drink, lowered the bottle to give her an insolent stare. "Turns out I'm not in a picnicking mood."

"I think I can guess what kind of mood you're in."

"Shouldn't be hard. Seeing as how you're the cause of it."

Because he was watching, he saw the flash in her eyes. But her movements were loose and easy as she crossed the room to sit on the couch. "You know better than that."

"Do I?" The words burned, so he took another sip. The beer didn't appreciably dissipate the scorch in his throat. The betrayal in his chest. "I knew what to expect with Andrews."

"I couldn't warn you she was coming . . ."

"Don't recall asking you to. As a matter of fact, I don't recall asking you to do much of anything, although"—he raised the bottle in a mock salute—"there are a few things you've thought of on your own that I have to admire for sheer creativity."

A slow flush crawled to her cheeks. And her face may still have been composed, but her eyes weren't. A vicious sense of satisfaction filled him at the sight.

"Fuck you."

"That you did. Up, down, and then . . . over."

"How do you figure me for the bad guy in any of this?" She bounced off the couch, fists clenched at her sides. Dispassionately, he took a moment to note that she looked good with a mad on. There was a twist in his gut at the recognition. Of course she would. "Because I asked some of the same questions of you a few days ago? This is a serial murder investigation. Was I supposed to intervene on your behalf with Andrews? Would it matter to you if I said I did? And she didn't give a shit."

"I don't need your intervention." He shoved up from his chair and crossed the room until he stood before her, his hand tightly gripping the throat of the bottle. "I don't need a damn thing from you. I can handle Andrews. Hell, I have been handling her all along with her half-baked accusations. But I gotta hand it to you, Slim, I wasn't expecting you to arm her with more ammo against me. Didn't see that one coming." He made a gun with his fingers and put it between his eyes. Jerked his head back as if feeling a bullet. "So yeah. Count me as another sap too dazzled by a pretty face and"—he raked her with a gaze deliberately insolent—"a killer body to see what was right in front of him."

She pushed her face close to his. Looked for all the world as if she'd like to take a swing at him. "You couldn't see what was right in front of you if it were written on the end of your nose. I've never seen a man so willfully stupid."

"Stupid? Maybe I'm mistaken. Maybe I misheard Andrews when she said you'd looked into my military record. Used my training . . . my missions . . . and somehow twisted that to make me out to be someone with the skills to snap necks, I'm told." He cocked a brow, the fury pumping through him now, a scalding flood of heat. "See, the sheriff isn't quite as close-mouthed as you are. But then I supposed confidentiality is off when you think you have the prime suspect in hand."

Something in her seemed to ease. "You're not the prime suspect."

"No?" He cocked his head. "Sure seemed like it today. But after you'd fed her that info about my military record, I'll bet she was hard to hold back." He stared at her for a moment, willing her to respond. Feeling like a kid with the strength of the longing. "Or are you going to tell me she was able to dig into confidential military files on her own?"

"No." Her gaze was steady. "I pulled some strings. Or at least got my boss to."

The admission hit him in the chest like a fast right jab. Suspecting it was one thing. Hearing it was quite another. "Well, guess that was faster than sleeping with me and hoping I'd spill my guts after a good blow job."

He caught her wrist before her fist connected. No ladylike slap for her. He'd expect nothing less.

"I didn't ask for details of your missions. I didn't need the information." She jerked away from him and he released her. It wasn't wise right now to be touching her. In any way.

"Right." Like she'd put the brakes on getting too much info if she had an inside channel. Something raw and unchecked was prowling in his chest. He wasn't ashamed of anything he'd done for his country. But back in the States the parameters changed. From a safe civilian distance it was easy to misconstrue the nature of acts half a world away. Easy to pass judgment on the ones making those sort of split-second decisions that had ramifications for entire teams. The thought of Cait sharing those details with Andrews made him want to punch something.

"Believe whatever the hell you want. And Andrews has had that information about your military record for days, so you're blind if you think that knowledge all of a sudden made her want to slap cuffs on you."

He didn't believe her. Why should he? And what she was saying didn't make sense anyway. "Something sure as hell convinced her recently. She was ready to break out the inter-rogation tools." He gave her a humorless smile. "Pretty sure she would have enjoyed it."

Her eyes were murderous. "Believe me, I know the feel-ing. Your prints were on one of the bags, Sharper." His face must have been as uncomprehending as he felt because she went on. "From the cave? Your print came back as a match when they ran the elimination prints. That's what got Andrews hot on your trail. And the fact that I just told you that makes me an even bigger idiot than she accused me of being."

Her movements rife with fury, she wheeled around and headed for the door. And even though her final words had his anger abruptly dwindling, he let her go.

Because he couldn't afford this welter of emotion crash-ing and careening inside him. He was better off . . . far better off . . . when he hadn't cared about a blessed thing. Nothing outside his house. His business.

He was sure as hell better off before he gave a damn whether Caitlin Fleming had sold him out for a case.

————

"I come bearing gifts."

Insects circled the porch light in slow death-defying or-bits. The illumination was the only spear of light in the utter darkness. It haloed around Sweetie, who was wearing the win-some expression that was especially endearing. Spotlighted the white wax paper bag bearing the familiar logo. The Sweet Shoppe.

"You remembered." The pleasure pushed aside the resentment that had pricked at him since their fight.

"How I acquired my nickname? How could I forget?" The bag was lowered. A note of uncertainty entered the voice he loved so much. "I know it's been a long time since I've brought you something special, but am I still your sweetie? Or have you decided you can never forgive me?"

Ever mindful of the eyes that could be watching, he stood aside to allow entry. Waited until the door was locked and closed before pressing that sexy body between his and the front door. And there was a desperation in their kiss. Maybe because of their argument and maybe, maybe fueled with guilt because of his lapse afterward. He'd make it up to Sweetie tonight. They'd make it up to each other.

All too soon, Sweetie slipped hands up to his chest to wedge a bit of distance between them. "Easy. I can stay for a while tonight so there's no hurry."

Pleasure bloomed. Having more than a few stolen minutes with his lover was an even better treat than the fudge in the bag. He slipped an arm around Sweetie's waist and felt a quick burst of excitement when they walked, arms entwined to the living room.

"Cops were all over McKenzie Bridge today." And although Sweetie tried for a matter-of-fact tone, he could hear the concern layered beneath it. "The town was buzzing about it. They were showing pictures of two of them. How in hell did they identify them? I can't understand it. What else do they know?"

"Nothing, or else we'd hear more. There's no way any of it leads back to us. I was careful. So were you."

"I know. Still . . ." Sweetie paced the length of the room, the bag hanging from the long sensitive fingertips. "I don't want to place you in danger. I think we need to consider Plan A."

"Of course." He was still trying to soothe. Still trying to be the strong one. "Someday . . ."

"I mean now. Or at least soon."

He froze, almost unable to comprehend. They'd waited so

long. Sometimes it had seemed as though they would never be together. Like it was all a fool's dream and all he'd have, all they'd ever have, were these moments together.

Sweetie was still talking. Nervous. Pacing with quick driven movements. "It'll have to be the way we talked about. I'll go first. You'll follow. But not in six months. That might be too long to wait. Maybe four?"

"I can say I'm moving to Portland. To be closer to my dad in the nursing home." That story had been told so often sometimes he even believed it was true.

There was a tug of regret at the thought of leaving this place. His old man's fate had been sealed when his sainted mother had been buried in the garden. Without regard. Without regret. Left to the grubs and insects and whatever animal sniffed around to dig and dig and carry off a limb. He'd planned the bastard's death since the moment he'd seen the coyote running off the property with Mother's ulna in its jaws.

"Good thinking. Right. And you remember where we'll meet. And the route you'll take? You can't fly directly there or you'll lead them right to me . . ."

A belated sense of joy eddied inside him. Higher and higher until he felt ready to drown in it. At last. At long last. He crossed to his sweetie and tenderly laid two fingers against those beautiful lips for a moment. "I remember it all. And you remember how to let me know if the plan changes?"

One slow sober nod was his response. "But first you have to take care of Fleming. She's a threat to us. Even if we leave the country, with her help I'm afraid they could find us. She's all that stands between us. The only thing keeping us apart."

Of course she was. He saw it so clearly now. Sweetie was absolutely right, as usual. And there was nothing he wouldn't do to salvage their future together.

"Leave Fleming to me. She'll be dead within twenty-four hours."

Sweetie released a sigh. "I'm depending on you. I always depend on you."

Heart singing, he forgot about Barb Haines's body, still

waiting for the bugs. For the painting. For disposal. Forgot about the worry of not seeing his lover for four—only four rather than six!—months. Didn't consider yet how he was going to do away with Caitlin Fleming. The details weren't important.

He thought only of the beginning of their life together. Soon now. Very soon.

"Let me show you what it will be like. The two of us. Alone. Rich. Blissful."

Slowly he cupped Sweetie's jaw, his breath hitching when his palm was kissed. But he wouldn't be diverted. Not by the buttons marching down that chest he liked to lick and nip and explore. Not by the belt, surely worn to tempt and taunt.

The leather was undone. The snap unfastened. And the zipper inched down one tooth at a time.

When he'd released Sweetie from the clothes, he ran his tongue over the velvety shaft and murmured against it, "Soon, my love," before taking him in his mouth.

And knew he'd never been happier.

Chapter 18

Damn, damn, damn.

Cait fairly flew around the Landview motel room getting ready for the day. She'd overslept, and it suited her to lay the blame for that squarely at Sharper's feet. The glaring numbers on the alarm clock had seemed to mock her throughout the long sleepless night until she'd thrown a pillow over them to block out the sight of the time passing while she'd lain awake. As a result she'd woken groggy and fuzzy headed, a feeling the bracing shower had only partially dissipated.

To make matters worse, she needed to do laundry. She only had one more set of clothes in her bag here, and she had no idea when she was going to find the time. Maybe the Landview offered a cleaning service. Hearing voices in the hallway, she rapidly walked to the door and pulled it open, wanting to catch the maid and ask her.

And then stared with mingled shock and dismay when she saw one of the clerks from the front desk outside her door.

Her mother was beside her.

"Darling." Lydia swept in, kissed both her cheeks before stepping back to survey her critically. "Oh heavens, you aren't going out looking like that are you? You look positively dreadful."

"I'm sorry, Ms. Fleming." The young clerk was wringing her hands nervously. "I wanted to call up first, but she insisted . . . and she is obviously your mother. I could see the resemblance. And . . . well . . ."

Woodenly Cait took pity on her. "It's fine."

"Of course, it's fine." Lydia swept by her into the room, a canvas tote slung over one arm, her purse on the other. "Why wouldn't it be fine? I'm your *mother*."

Cait shut the door. Resisted the urge to bang her head against it. "Why are you here?" And hearing the words, realized they were devoid of the sort of diplomacy that she was usually able to muster. "I mean . . . we just spoke. I said I'd come visit after this case. I'm really not going to have any time to—"

"I think you'll make time. For once, Caitlin, you will do exactly what I say."

Lydia's words, her tone, put all her instincts on alert. Her mother was always self-assured. Always so certain that she could snap her fingers and the world would shift on its axis at her command. But there was something afoot here. Something that had dread licking down her spine.

"How'd you know where I was?"

"You're not the only detective in the family, dear." Lydia lifted a regal brow. "I did my homework over the last few days. Trolled the Internet for every bit of ghastly news going on this country. I suspected you might be working on this case. And yesterday you affirmed it." Cait must have looked as stupefied as she felt because her mother went on helpfully, "You said you'd come *down* for a visit. So I started calling around the area and found people here are really quite helpful. Of course, you're difficult to forget. That helped."

She felt in need of some support. Because there was no caffeine nearby—nor a stiff shot of whiskey—Cait reached out to grasp the back of a chair. "You still haven't answered the question. Why are you here?"

There was a flash of anger in her mother's eyes. "Did you think you could just dismiss me like that, Caitlin? My wants? My needs? I allowed that once and look at you." The flick of her up-and-down gaze stung like a whip. "I never should have let you walk away from the career that brought us both so much happiness. I won't make that mistake again."

"You didn't allow anything, Mother. A judge did, remember?" He'd released her from her mother's parental control and from her management of Cait's money. At seventeen she'd finally been free. And she hadn't spent an instant regretting it.

But it was as if she hadn't spoken. "I spoke to Cee Cee again. Duran Cosmetics is absolutely beating the bushes for the right face. We're going to take Paris by storm, darling. It'll be like a few years ago, remember? We'll be back on top."

The first niggling of concern filtered through Cait's annoyance. "It wasn't a few years ago, Mother. It was more than fifteen. And I'm not going back to it. I told you that."

A dreamy look crossed Lydia's face. "Of course Paris is beastly this time of year, but you'll be busy for weeks anyway with art directors and measurements and a strict diet and exercise program. At least you haven't let yourself go. That's a blessing. Although I swear, if those are freckles on your nose, I'm going to—"

"Mother!" Her tone was deliberately sharp. If they were to have this fight again, she'd welcome it. Anything other than this sick feeling of trepidation that was pooling in her stomach. "You need to go home. We'll talk after the case. But not about Paris. I'm not going to Paris. Neither of us are."

"I knew you'd say that." It was the old Lydia back, in control. And for a moment Cait wondered if she'd imagined that disconnect between past and present. "Knew what it would take to convince you. I didn't want to have to use this, but I will. Because it's for your own good. It's what's best for both of us. Just like before."

She set the tote on the floor and withdrew the dark wooden

box. Cait's breath strangled in her chest. Her breathing sounded like a locomotive in her ears.

The carving on the top was polished. The lid that Lydia opened revealed the soft green velvet-lined interior. But it was the false bottom that had concealed the horrors of her past.

"You'll do exactly what I say. Or the world will know you for what you are. You as good as killed your father. Did you think I didn't know? I always knew. I always covered. You *owe* me for that!"

The words barely registered. They couldn't break the grip of the past.

You have to be my good girl, Caitie. Remember the story. Don't ever tell.

"It was the only way. I understand that, but the authorities wouldn't. You'd be ruined in this profession, so you may as well go back to the life I made for us. It was worth all the planning. All the sacrifice." Her mother's eyes went far away, and she made a motion as if stroking a much-younger Cait's hair. "You mustn't feel guilty, darling. Your father would have allowed his depression to ruin everything. To leave us with nothing. But I was there for you. I always knew how to take care of you."

Ice slicked over her skin. Bumped through her veins. "What . . . how did you take care of things, Mother?" She forced the words out, but she didn't want to hear the response. Didn't want to know a truth that would undoubtedly be worse than the memory she'd lived with all her life.

"He wasn't a stupid man." Lydia's voice was brisk. Almost normal. Except for the sheen of madness in her eyes. "Emotionally weak. But not stupid. I knew if I left you alone in the house with him more and more when he was in one of his funks that he'd plan things out. The insurance would never have paid on a suicide. Your father came to the right decision."

The child that she'd been, the child that still lived inside her, screamed silently in protest. "The right decision? I was *eight*!"

But her mother didn't hear her. When had she ever? "It was a difficult time for both of us. But look at the life I made for us! Children don't comprehend money worries, but there was the portfolio to put together. The head shots. The agency fees. The clothes and the travel before you were picked up by an upper-tier agency. It cost money to get you noticed."

She made a dismissive gesture in a manner that was pure Lydia. "You're not a parent, Caitlin, so you can't know how it can sometimes hurt a mother to force her child to do what's right." She watched numbly as her mother pressed unerringly in the one spot sure to have the bottom of the box sliding open. "But you'll have to . . ."

Lydia gaped at the empty compartment. "What . . . where is it?" Her gaze flashed angrily as she stood, drawing herself up to her full height. "What have you done, Caitlin?"

"The gun's at the bottom of the Grand Canal in Venice." Her voice sounded wooden, foreign, to Cait's ears. Even as a teenager, she'd realized the need to destroy that connection to her past. "But it doesn't matter, Mother." She stood, gently took the box from her hands. "We don't need that. You're right. We'll leave for Paris in the morning."

"Excellent." Her face wreathed in smiles, Lydia accompanied her uncomplainingly out the door. Down the hallway. "Do you still have that green silk Valentino? You must wear that when you meet with Duran Cosmetics. You always looked your best in it."

Out the front doors. Across the parking lot to the SUV. "I remember." She'd been fifteen the last time she'd worn that dress. A lifetime ago. "We can make plans over breakfast."

"An excellent idea. I knew you'd see reason. Oh, let's go to that little bistro on Champs-Éllysées. What's its name? The one with the wonderful crepes?"

"The Athénée."

"Of course, you'll order a yogurt. You'll need to lose at least fifteen pounds before getting in front of a camera again." Lydia got in the vehicle. Fastened her seat belt. "And be careful, dear. You're not used to driving on the right side of the road."

Cait started the vehicle, eyes burning. "I'll be fine, Mother. We'll both be fine."

———————

Kristy's eyes were filled with sympathy. "Oh my God. What'd you do?"

Jamming a hand through her hair, Cait finished the carefully edited version she'd been relaying and said, "Checked her in to the psychiatric hospital. Spent two hours trying to get in touch with that man she'd been seeing recently. The one she told me yesterday had just left her. Turns out they split up six months ago. They hadn't just returned from Paris, the way she'd told me. He had to give me the address of the place she'd been living."

And that fact would continue to haunt her for a long time.

"You couldn't have realized." Kristy was staunchly supportive. "It sounds like she just snapped. There was no way to predict it was going to happen."

She thought of what her mother had revealed about their past. And wished she could dislodge the knowledge. As awful as it had been to carry the secrets of her childhood, somehow this *knowing* was worse. Far worse. "I think it's been a long time in the making, actually."

"You should call Andrews." Kristy got up and brought Cait her purse she'd left on the desk in the corner of the lab. "Tell her you'll be back on the job tomorrow. Jesus, Cait, she can't expect you to work today after what you've been through."

Making no movement for her phone, she said, "I've already called her and said I'd be in late." Holding up a hand to stifle her assistant's protest, she said, "Lydia's doctors kicked me out after giving them what I could of her medical history." But there was one portion of their past she hadn't dared shared. Not because of her fear of the consequences for an eight-year-old's actions. But for her mother's. "I'll let them assess her and then find a place . . ." She stopped, rubbed at the ache between her eyes. "I guess out east somewhere would be best. Closer to my place." A place she was rarely at, given her occupation.

"You don't have to worry about that right now." Kristy eyed her shrewdly. "If I told you I kept a flask in my purse, would you take a stiff belt?"

"Please tell me you're joking."

"Of course I am." But the woman's tone was less than convincing.

Cait considered it for all of three seconds before deciding that Kristy's possible tippling wasn't a subject she was going to tackle right now. It took effort to focus on work. To put her thoughts in order.

"Have you been checking the new set of remains regularly?" Her assistant followed her to the gurney holding them.

"They're progressing but will need another day or so to dry out."

After a few moments of examination, Cait was inclined to agree. "There's no telling how long they were in the springs, but I tend to think it was less than three weeks. And I'm anxious to get some data from them to start referencing with more recent disappearances."

Kristy looked at the remains dubiously. "They aren't going to be in the best shape after saturation."

"They'll bend or break easily," Cait admitted. "So we'll have to be extra careful handling them." But for now it was a moot point. They were still leaving damp spots on the newspaper pads beneath them as the water continued leaking out of them.

"Oh, I forgot." The diminutive blonde hurried to the desk and snatched a file folder from the upright plastic holder on the desk and brought it back to hand to Cait. "This was lying in the fax tray when I got in this morning."

Flipping it open, Cait found a copy of Bentley's credit card statement for a year prior to his death. And another note signed by Cross with a scrawled message.

Brother confirmed WB Giant's fan and rafted for hobby. Will fax DNA profile when get it.

The motel on the statement was one she recognized. It was a trendy establishment on Highway 126, four or five miles from McKenzie Bridge. There were no other charges from businesses in the area, with the exception of gas stations.

Regardless what Andrews had said earlier, positively linking William Bentley to this case cleared Sharper. If she had to she could ask Raiker for a copy of the dates of his leaves from the Army. Cait was convinced they wouldn't coincide with the time Bentley had been in the area years ago.

She told herself that wasn't relief she felt at the thought. After last night, she'd almost think he deserved it if the sheriff had taken another shot at him.

But it wasn't his beef with the sheriff that had kept her awake until dawn. She'd run the facts through her head over and over until her thoughts resembled a rat in a maze. But she'd done nothing wrong. She'd done her job when she'd asked Raiker to delve into Zach's files, but she hadn't asked for more than she needed. And sharing those details with Andrews was her job, too. She wasn't going to apologize for it.

And she refused to feel guilty that he didn't believe her. She was carrying all the guilt she could handle without taking that on, as well.

But knowing that—accepting it—didn't make a dent in the heaviness in her chest.

"I also did a bit of research yesterday after I was finished with the paint samples. Great work with that match by the way," Kristy said in a poor imitation of Cait's voice. Her eyes went wide then and fluttered as she brought a hand to her chest. "Why thank you, Cait, I thought I did it in record time, too." Her voice dropped an octave again. "You're the best fucking tech I've ever had, and I'm going to tell Raiker he should double your pay."

Cait fixed her with an unblinking stare. "Number one, I do *not* talk like a frog with a five pack a day habit, and number two, you're going to need double the salary if you don't stop dropping the F-bomb in every other sentence. Tell me about your research."

"I've cut way back on swearing. Even you have to admit it. Okay," Kristy said hastily, crossing to her purse to dig out a dollar. "It's worth the buck. Steve's constant nagging is starting to get almost as annoying as yours."

Cait stuffed the dollar in her jeans pocket. "Trouble in paradise?"

"Trouble in monogamy," the tech corrected her. She riffled through the folders in the file organizer and selected one before heading back to where she'd left Cait. "One could never confuse that with paradise. Even if he does have the best-looking ass in the northwest. I'm going purely on the laws of probability, there. More's the pity." She switched seamlessly to her original topic of conversation.

"Okay, I ran the rest of the soil samples you brought me after matching the paint samples. Nothing jumped out at me. But there were a few that were at least as close to the sample you brought from Sharper's property. I went down to the NRCS and had a nice talk with one of the guys there. He was pretty cute, sort of beta, but with this totally awesome punk rock thing going on . . ." Catching Cait's eye, she veered back to the subject. "Anyway, he was telling me about the formation of the hot springs in Oregon, and I started thinking about the sediment found in the bags. Maybe we've been focusing on the wrong element in the soil sample."

She had, finally, gotten Cait's undivided attention. "You mean the sulfur?"

"I mean what's missing, I guess. All these springs you were looking at were in and around the forests, right? The samples taken close to hot springs had a much higher sulfur content than our sediment. The one you got from Sharper's property, and various places in the forest were closer. But they had minerals associated with plant decomposition and that was barely discernible in our sample."

Kristy's voice grew animated. It often did when she could combine her two loves, science and men. "But Gary and I put our heads together—that's his name, Gary Neller—and looking at the composite we made of our sample, he suggested that the other trace minerals might have come from animal excrement."

Her mind racing, Cait said, "We knew that. But it doesn't

help all that much. Even the forest would have scat from the wildlife."

"But not in the concentrated amounts you'd have on, say, a farm. Not that our sediment bore concentrated amounts suggesting manure, but he suggested maybe a place that *used* to be a working farm. He even suggested maybe sheep had once been raised near there, because of the level of sulfur in the soil." When Cait didn't immediately respond, Kristy lifted a shoulder. "It's an idea, anyway. If you pass a shepherd up there, you might want to check out his flock."

Cait ignored her tech's euphemism. She'd already come to the conclusion that the main value of the sediment in the bags would be for a comparison sample taken from the UN-SUB's property, but she filed the information away. "At least it narrows down places to focus on if I take more samples." Right now, though, she had better leads. Beginning with the two positives and one nearly certain identification on three of the remains. "I'm going to check in with Barnes and Andrews. Fill them in on the data I got from Cross and get updated on their progress up there."

"Not much to do here right now," Kristy agreed. "Just for shits and giggles, I'm going to do some preliminary measurements of these bones." She raised her voice a bit to stem Cait's response. "I'll be careful, I promise. Did it ever occur to you that you could just call all the resorts in the area, get a list of their guests for the last year, and then feed the names into the missing persons database to see which of them have gone missing? I'm betting we could get this guy's name that way."

She had thought that exact thing. And hoped it wouldn't come to that. "I'm going to send out some emails to detectives with missing persons cases in states outside those bordering Oregon." It still surprised her that the UNSUB had ventured so far abroad. The need for traveling greater distances to snatch the victim upped his risk. "If the bones dry out sufficiently, we can run our tests and hopefully get the same results faster. Check in later today if you've got anything. And that last dollar you owe me will go on your tab."

She heard the woman mutter in an undertone behind her back, "Thought she missed that one." And smiled as she sat down at the desk in front of the computer. It was never boring working with Kristy.

"Make sure you back up all your work on that thing." Her tech's voice was muffled. Her head was stuck in between the shelves as she gathered up equipment. "It quit on me twice when I was typing my notes yesterday. Not sure if it's the software or the computer itself, but you need to be sure the IT guy looks at it when you get back to headquarters."

Cait froze. "What'd you say?"

"You know. What's his name. Calvin. The computer wizard who works for Raiker. He'll have it running right in no time. That man has magic in his fingertips." Her tone went regretful. "I'm sorry to say that I know from personal experience that his *magic* is reserved only for technical equipment."

She'd stopped listening. Reached for the phone. Then hissed out an impatient breath when she reached Andrews's voice mail. She left her a message regarding the Bentley credit card statement and verification on two of the images found on his scapula. Then she called Barnes. "Any progress on the employees for the Internet access provider?"

Disgust sounded in Barnes's tone. "Lantis refused to hand over the records without a court order. Guess civic duty doesn't mean squat to them. The sheriff is at Judge Grayson's office right now getting a signature on the warrant. I'm hoping the bastards have to work all night getting the records together for us. It would serve them right."

"This should have occurred to me before, but you need to call the resorts back and find out who services their computers."

A frown sounded in the deputy's voice. "Lantis, I told you."

"No, I mean who do the resorts call when a computer gets a virus or they get new equipment? Lantis employees might not be the only ones with access to the computers at the motels."

"Huh. Guess I hadn't thought of it. I've had the same computer for seven years and never had a problem with it."

A sense of irony filled her. "You know you've dared the fates just by saying that, right? Take it from me, that's not the case with most computer owners. And as much use as the shared computers would get at the motels, I can guarantee they need regular servicing. Get those names, and we'll add them to the list of employees we eventually get from Lantis."

"I'll do that right away."

She filled him in on the Bentley credit card statement and verification on two of the images found on his scapula while she composed and sent emails to the other detectives on her list with missing persons. New Mexico. Colorado. Nevada. If any of these related to the case, it meant the UNSUB had taken more risks than she had at first believed.

"Three sets of remains identified." She could hear the faint sounds of traffic noises. Barnes was on the road. "We're making progress."

"It's a start. What about the paint? Any hits there?"

"Got an art supply place over in Sisters that sells small cans. 'Course the only records they have are credit card statements, so that's going to take a while. The officer questioned all the employees about a return customer buying that stuff, but seems like it's mostly kids doing stuff for school."

"The UNSUB probably got them online." That's what she would have done. The anonymity would have been appealing. "We can eliminate the aerosols, which should help. But it wouldn't hurt to contact the online companies I gave you to see about getting their client list."

"I'm sure they'll hand that right over," the man muttered.

"How are you coming on talking to the restaurant employees at Tito's?"

"About like you'd expect. They barely remember tourists from a couple weeks ago unless they were big tippers. The photos didn't jog any memories."

So there'd be no use showing Bentley's picture around if he turned out to be one of their victims in the lab. If the people hadn't recognized tourists from three and five years ago, they certainly weren't going to recall one who'd been in the area six years previously.

"I'm going to finish a few emails and then I'll head back up there. Continue showing the photos around at the local businesses."

After disconnecting, she finished emailing the detectives and then turned to Kristy, who had laid out the various sizes of calipers and was squatted down eye level with one femur. "I'm going back to McKenzie Bridge."

"I heard."

"The hospital has my cell number, but I also left this number just in case they couldn't reach me."

Kristy looked up, her gaze sober. "If they do, I'll find a way to contact you."

"Thanks." She regarded her friend for a moment. And the diminutive tech was that, she realized. Cait could think of no one else with whom she would have shared details of that scene with her mother, even as carefully edited as the version had been. "And thanks for listening." She made an awkward gesture with her hand. "I mean earlier."

"I know a little bit about relationships with mothers." She gave a thumbs-up sign. "It will work out."

"Yeah." Cait couldn't quite pull off an answering smile. "It'll work out."

She held that thought on the drive to McKenzie Bridge. Tried to believe it. But a positive outcome of the scene with Lydia was difficult to fathom. She'd been demanding and frantic by turn when Cait had had her admitted. Shifted with dizzying speed between the past and present, from awareness of her surroundings to a shrill insistence that they were overseas. It hadn't been difficult to get a psych hold on her.

What had been difficult had been leaving her there. And trying to imagine the next step.

Getting Lydia well again was the first priority. And that was the easy part of the equation. Choosing doctors, discussing treatment options . . . that could be done objectively with a clear outcome in mind.

Repairing the relationship between her and her mother . . . Cait reduced her speed as she went around a curve. That was where things got dicey.

I knew if I left you alone in the house with him more and more when he was in one of his funks that he'd plan things out. Your father came to the right decision.

A decision that had cost Cait, in one way or another, all her life.

The miles whipped by at pace with her thoughts. She cast a look at the sky. Although the pavement was dry, the skies looked like they could open up at any moment. A fitting way to cap off an already shitty day. With effort, she pushed aside the personal worries. It helped, always, to have the case to concentrate on. To obsess over something where it might actually do some good.

Her cell rang and she checked the ID. Barnes. "Yeah, Mitch."

"Where you at?"

She took a second to check landmarks to get her bearings. "About four miles out of McKenzie Bridge, give or take."

A pickup went by, tooting its horn. She realized after it had passed that the occupants were Kathy and Rick Moses.

There was an unfamiliar note of excitement in the deputy's voice. "I talked to the three resorts. Included the one Bentley had stayed at, because we're guessing he's going to end up involved in this, too, right?" He didn't wait for a response before going on. "Different names were mentioned, but one appeared at the top of everyone's list. Del Barton."

"Del?" The owner of JD's, she recalled. The slight man with the flirtatious smile and overworked wife. "Not Joanie?"

"They say there's nothing he doesn't know about computers. I've got Deputy Sutton with me, and we're out in front of his place now. Going to take him in for questioning."

"We should collect the computers from the resorts and bring them in for an examination. Maybe we'll find evidence of the spyware installation."

"I'll have Gibbs contact you. Maybe the two of you can take care of it."

"Meet you there in a few minutes." Cait dropped the phone in her purse and stepped more firmly on the gas. It shouldn't surprise her that Barton had lied to her about his wife being the computer genius, she thought grimly. Lying was the first resort of those with a guilty conscience.

But she would be slightly surprised to discover he was their UNSUB. She'd have pegged his wife as having more guts than he did.

Which made her even more eager to talk to Joanie Barton than she was to Del.

———

Cait met the two deputies walking Del out of JD's just as she pulled the rented SUV up to the curb.

"Del agreed to ride down to the station and talk to us," Mitch said blandly.

"Middle of dinner rush," Barton said ruefully, casting a glance back toward the restaurant. "Joanie's having a cow." The slight shadow of nerves in his expression could be due to just that—leaving his wife to manage the restaurant on her own. Certainly he didn't appear to be overly concerned to be headed to the sheriff's office. But there was no real reason for fear yet, she reminded herself. He wasn't in cuffs. This questioning was purely voluntary.

Unless, of course, he'd refused.

"I'm sure Deputy Barnes will have you back as quickly as possible," Cait said, standing aside as the three men headed toward the sheriff cruiser double-parked out front. She spotted Joanie Barton at the front door of the place watching her husband leave, anxiety and anger in her expression.

If Del was relatively calm, his wife wasn't.

"You!" The short dark-haired woman pushed open the front door of the restaurant with a force that sent the screen door bouncing off the opposite wall. "This is all your fault!"

Supremely aware of the onlookers on both sides of the street watching the events unfold with avid interest, Cait kept her voice pleasant. "Joanie."

"I told you nothing good would come of stirring all this

up." The shorter woman approached her like a miniature tornado. "From the minute those bones were hauled out of that cave, we've had nothing but trouble in this town. First the tourism went to pot and now you idiots have arrested Del. My Del! As if he could have anything to do with this mess!"

"Del isn't under arrest. He's answering a few questions. We've been asking lots of questions around here for the last day or so."

"He may as well be." The glare in her eyes would have been lethal if it weren't tinged with fear. "What's everyone going to think, him being seen leaving with the deputies like that? That he's a suspect, is what they'll think. What are my kids supposed to do when their friends ask them why their stepdad had to go to the sheriff's office? Do you people ever think of that? Of the innocents who get hurt while you bungle around trying to figure out what the hell happened up there in that cave?"

Despite the spike to her temper, Cait kept her voice modulated. "Some would say the people whose bones were dumped in the cave were innocents, too."

"We don't know that." Joanie was gesticulating with both arms. "Maybe they were druggies who got on the wrong side of some gang somewhere. Maybe they got exactly what they deserved, did you ever think of that? And yet law-abiding folks are getting dragged into their mess." There was a sheen to her eyes from impending tears. "Our business is hanging on by a thread, what with the drop in tourism. Now this. It won't matter what we do. The way people talk, it's probably already all over town that Del was taken in by the sheriff. Who's going to want to go to a place that's owned by a suspect in a murder case?"

She didn't lack sympathy for the woman, even if Joanie couldn't see beyond the ramifications to her family. Her business. "As I said, Del should return soon. And he told me that you're the brains behind the Internet café, so I'm certain you have a handle on that part of the business, as well."

"You misunderstood," the woman said flatly with a toss of her head. "Not surprising since you and the sheriff's department have screwed up every single other piece of your work. The café is Del's baby. I know enough to log people in and out, but he does all the troubleshooting. He's absolutely brilliant with computers. Ask anyone around here."

"We have." Edging away, Cait sent the woman an insincere smile. "They all agree. There's nothing he can't do with a computer."

And that was exactly why the man was headed back to Eugene for questioning at this very minute.

Chapter 19

It was all over town. He'd had three calls already with the news. Del Barton had been taken in for questioning by the cops.

There had been more, of course. Details factual or exaggerated, he didn't know. He didn't listen carefully past that first part. His heart had stopped beating in his chest at the words. Then had sped up like a runaway locomotive. For a moment he thought he was having a heart attack.

The sheriff's department had Sweetie.

He paced his house, ignoring the next few calls. To think prior to that first call he'd been feeling peaceful. Joyful, even. Still pumped about the plans he'd made with Sweetie—had that just been last night? With a renewed sense of purpose he'd gone to the shed and moved Barb Haines's carcass into the enclosure holding his beloved beetles. Had experienced a feeling of absolute bliss as he'd watched them cover the bones like a hungry ever-moving blanket. He'd raised them by hand, from the larva he'd acquired over the Internet. They never failed to instill a thrill of pride.

But then he'd gotten the first call.

He knew how these things worked. The fact that Del hadn't been cuffed meant he wasn't under arrest. If there had been enough evidence against him, he would have been. This part was preliminary.

But it'd also make it harder. Far harder for Sweetie to get away like they'd talked about. Fear was firing frantic bursts of panic through his veins. But he had to be calm. Had to *think*. He couldn't afford a mistake this time. It wasn't enough to take Fleming out of the equation. He had to make it clear that Sweetie couldn't possibly be involved with those bones.

And then, midstride, it hit him. The thought was so shocking in its clarity that he paused, certain there was a flaw in it.

But there wasn't. And it was so simple he laughed out loud in sheer delight.

Taking Fleming out of the equation not only removed the brains from the investigation. Killing her while Sweetie was in custody absolved him of all guilt.

He looked out the window. It was nearing dark. Swiftly, he got his pistol. Then, after a moment, also grabbed his shotgun. Extra ammo. All of the callers had given a full account of Fleming standing on the sidewalk engaged in an argument with Joanie. And he knew, because he'd been keeping tabs on her, that she hadn't checked out of the McKenzie Motel. Chances were if she'd been in town she might stay here tonight. If not . . . he headed for the back door. If not, he knew she had a room in Eugene, too. If he couldn't pick her off driving by in her vehicle, it shouldn't be too hard to make some calls. Find out where she was staying and then pay her a visit.

With Fleming dead, their problems were over.

Zach stared at the meager contents of his refrigerator and muttered a curse. The last of the bread had mold on it. He'd emptied the milk carton two days ago. And even he wouldn't eat the lunchmeat that was hard and curled up at the edges. Unless he was willing to dine on sheetrock, he'd have to go to town for something to eat.

And only hunger would have driven him to head for his Trailblazer and start for town. The prospect of a sandwich and beer was too tempting. He wasn't in the mood for company, but he wouldn't say no to a chance to kick some ass in pool.

He was in the mood to kick some ass.

The fact that the ass most in need of kicking was his own just made his mood meaner. He took the gravel faster than he usually did and heard the rapid ping of the rocks as they shot up and sprayed his vehicle. Consciously, he let up on the accelerator. Every time he thought of Andrews's expression when she'd probed about the missions he'd run in the army, he wanted to put his fist through something solid. Like she'd have a clue about scouting surveillance and counterintel. About the kind of men it took and the training it required.

All she'd cared about was whether he'd come back broken. Whether he'd used some of that training and systematically started picking off strangers and snapping their necks to get his jollies.

Damn hard not to get offended by that.

He turned on the highway, his mood grim. He'd spent the hours he should have been sleeping last night rerunning the questioning backward and forward in his mind. He'd thought at the time the sheriff had been playing it cagey. That she knew more about his missions than she'd let on and was trying to trip him up. She'd dangled Cait's involvement in acquiring the information on him in front of him like catnip. And like a damn idiot, his brain had partially shut down and all he could concentrate on was the feeling that had bloomed inside him.

A dark-colored compact passed him as he slowed for the turnoff to town. When the fog of temper had passed, it had been easier to see how Andrews had played him. How she'd used the mention of Cait to throw him off stride. And wondered now why he'd so easily accepted her suggestion that Cait had given her more, far more, than she was revealing.

The resulting burn of betrayal had been difficult to see through. But when his fury had faded, he wondered, staring blindly at the ceiling as he lay in bed, why it had been so much easier to believe Andrews, a woman he couldn't stand, rather than Cait, a woman he . . .

His mind jittered away from completing the rest of that statement. The sheriff might play games and get off by jerking people around, but Cait was straightforward to a fault. If she'd gone deeper into his military file, she'd have told him, flat out. And made no excuses for it, he thought wryly, automatically slowing to scan the cars in Ketchers's parking lot. She'd say it upfront and deal with his reaction.

He'd all but called her a liar, and he'd deserved everything she'd had to say in return. She hadn't called him a coward before leaving, but he knew that was exactly what had him drawing his hand back each time today that he'd reached for the phone.

Better to end it this way. Because the thought had his throat drying out, he swallowed. Found the act difficult given the knot in his throat. She'd be gone in a matter of days or weeks, and what was the use, really, in drawing it out? He'd never managed to keep a relationship going more than a matter of months before losing interest. Which made him a poor choice for trying a bicoastal one.

And the hollowness in his chest at that thought was surely due to hunger. He found a spot in the parking lot behind JD's. Locked his vehicle and used the back entrance.

He was a man who knew his limits. A realist who recognized that wanting something didn't mean he'd be any good with it once he had it.

And wanting Cait Fleming wasn't good for either one of them.

———————

Spending the next few hours in the company of Deputy Tony Gibbs was almost enough to have Cait wishing she'd never given up modeling.

The act of collecting the computers turned out to be more of a chore than it had to be. None of the resort owners were happy about the request. And not one was willing to deny their guests computer access for an indeterminate amount of time while the sheriff's office had a forensic cyber detective go over the machines with a fine-toothed comb.

Despite Gibbs's claim of the other night, Cait didn't notice that any of the owners were more enthusiastic given the fact they knew the man at her side.

Since their cooperation at this point was purely voluntary, in the end Cait convinced each place to give up two computers. And that had taken making a promise she wasn't sure she could keep about how long it would be before they were returned. She wondered if they needed to collect a couple from JD's's Internet café, as well, but in the end decided against it. The identified victims had been in the area long before it had been opened.

Plenty of time to pick up Del's computers after she checked with Barnes about what the man's questioning had elicited.

She slanted a glance at the man beside her. "How long has JD's had the Internet café?"

Gibbs's brow furrowed. "I dunno. Two years maybe? Something like that."

So that part of Del's conversation with her had been the truth. Cait checked the clock on the dashboard and wondered how the interview of Barton was coming. She would have liked to be present for it, but Barnes had made it pretty clear that he figured it was his territory. And in her line of work, she was more familiar than she wanted to be with cops protecting their territory.

They were coming to the town limits, so she said, "Drop me off on Main Street. I left my vehicle there."

Obediently Gibbs made the turn. "You staying in town tonight or going on back to Eugene?"

At the question, her stomach did a neat flip. In between resorts, she'd made a quick call to the hospital. Was told by a not unsympathetic nurse that Lydia didn't want to speak to her. To see her. There was no use going by the hospital tonight.

"I'll probably go back to the Landview," she said finally. "So if you want to transfer the computers to my vehicle, I can drop them by the sheriff's office tonight." It'd give her a chance to catch up on the results of the interview.

"Saves me a trip." The prospect had Gibbs sounding decidedly cheerful. "Say, did you ever give any further thought to what I told you before? About getting you access to properties around here for those soil samples?"

"That lead is probably a dead end until we nail the UNSUB and take a sample from his property," she admitted, looking out at the nearly empty Main Street. Then as memory flashed, she allowed herself a small smile. "Unless you happen to know of a place that not only possibly has hot springs but also keeps sheep. Or used to."

He pulled at his long blade of a nose as he slowed to swing in next to her vehicle. "Know a couple places like that actually. Not right in town, of course. But Kathy Gerber and Rick Moses rent an acreage and keep a few sheep. Jodie Paulsen's dad used to raise them years ago." His voice went eager. "You want me to call them?"

With a shrug, Cait said, "May as well." If nothing else, the soil samples would give Kristy a way to test the theory she'd concocted while ogling the NRCS employee. "But let's not transfer the computers until we know whether we're making more stops. I don't want to leave them in my vehicle unattended."

———

"Doesn't look like anyone's home." Cait tucked her cell into her jeans pocket in case Barnes called and grabbed the pack she'd retrieved from her vehicle before getting out of the car.

"I know he's here. I just talked to him." Gibbs scratched one large ear. Knocked on the front door again. But no one answered it. "He spends a lot of time out in his shed puttering." He strode to the end of the porch and jogged down the steps, peering around the corner of the house. "I see a light out there. That's where he's probably at, all right."

Wonderful. A fine mist had begun to fall. As if the air had exhaled, a slight wind followed. Cait trailed behind the deputy as they crossed the uneven yard, by a garden, a compost heap, and hulking shapes of old discarded machinery. Toward a wooden shed patched with bits of metal. Like he'd said, there was dim light coming from the tiny cracks between the wooden slats. But the door was padlocked from the outside.

"Well, he's not in there." In disgust, Cait looked at the deputy. She should have known this would be nothing but a time waster. "Just take me back to my vehicle. I'm going to . . ."

The wooden door splintered in front of her a fraction of an instant before she heard the shot.

She shoved Gibbs, hard. "Down, get down." They dove in opposite directions, Cait drawing her weapon from its back holster to aim at the unseen assailant. Scanning the terrain, she saw nothing moving. "Call in on your radio!"

"It's in my car!" Gibbs shouted back. She could see the outline of him, crouched low on the opposite side of the shed, only his head poking out. The shadows would give them cover, she figured, peering intently into the darkness as she dug her cell out with her free hand. As much as it did their assailant.

"Paulsen!" Cait's voice rang out in the eerie silence. "We just came to talk. You invited us, remember?" She tried to shield the light from the screen of the phone while she dialed 9-1-1. Another shot split the night, close enough to feel the heat of the bullet kiss her cheek. Hastily she crawled to the other end of the shed and around the corner, jamming the phone back in her pocket for the moment.

She focused on the direction the last shot was fired from. The looming bulk might have been an old tractor. Massive enough for a man to hide behind it. She sited, squeezed off a shot. Heard the ping of metal. There was no sign of movement.

Staying low, she made the 9-1-1 call and, afterward, ignoring the operator's direction to stay on the line, shoved the cell back in her pocket. Still no sign of Paulsen. Carefully she made her way to the opposite corner of the shed, peered around it. She needed to talk to Gibbs. Together they could . . .

Except Gibbs wasn't where she left him.

Shit.

She did a crouched run along the wall. Heard the creak of rusty hinges. And when she whirled around the corner, in police stance, the space in front of the door was empty.

But the padlock was off the door.

"Gibbs," she breathed. Looked frantically around. But the man had vanished. He was armed. At least that was a consolation. Because if they had to wait for backup to come all the way from Eugene, they just might be screwed.

She stared at the entrance to the shed again. Who had gone inside? Gibbs? Or Paulsen?

Using the door as cover, she drew it back to open it fully. Then dropped to the ground before it and rolled, coming to a halt with her weapon sited on the figure framed in its opening.

Her blood congealed in her veins when she saw not one, but two figures inside it.

Jodie Paulsen smiled beatifically. Pressed his pistol harder against Tony Gibbs's temple. "Welcome to the party, Ms. Fleming."

"You don't want to hurt Tony," she murmured, not lowering her weapon. She inched inside the shed where she could better navigate an angle for a shot. "You two are friends."

"I've got lots of friends." His voice was conversational as he dragged Gibbs farther back into the interior of the shed with one arm around his throat. "One less won't hurt. And he's not the friend that counts here, is he?"

"No, I'm guessing that'd be Del Barton." She kept her eyes trained on Paulsen's face. She couldn't afford to focus on Gibbs's wide-eyed panic. His empty holster. "He was the brains and you supplied the muscle, right? Had a nice little racket going siphoning off all those funds."

"Have," he corrected. "Nothing has changed. With you dead, Andrews will see that Sweetie couldn't have had a thing to do with the whole mess. They'll let him go. We'll be together."

Shock jolted through her. "So it's more than business between the two of you." She edged toward the left, hoping for a clear shot. But Paulsen was moving into the shadows. Away from the light spilling from a single lamp in the center of the shed.

"We're in love." Gibbs made a sound then, a choked sort of snort and Jodie lowered the barrel of the gun to shoot him in the knee. The man's cry was hideous.

"Next time it will be your brain, not that you ever had one, you stupid fuck." His voice was fierce as he whispered into the man's ear, his gaze never leaving Cait. "Drop the gun," he told her, his weapon pressed again against the man's temple. "Or he's a dead man."

"Won't be the first time you've killed, will it?" Keep him talking. It took one moment of distraction to catch him off guard. Cait circled around him so she could control his movements to some extent. Keep him away from the inner edges of the shed that were shrouded in shadow. "Which did you enjoy more? The men or the women?"

"I'm not a killer. I'm not. They were treated with respect. Given a decent send off with a fitting memorial. No one can say I was unfeeling." Gibbs's whimpers turned into a low keening sound. "I've always been too sensitive for my own good."

"So that's why you painted on the bones?" It was difficult to follow his reasoning, but that wasn't unusual. A psychopath wasn't logical.

"I commemorated their lives," he corrected. "Which is more than my mother got. And more than you're going to get."

Something in his tone warned her and she dove, rolling away as a shot echoed and re-echoed in the interior of the shed. But she realized her mistake an instant later when she heard the thud of a body hit the dirt floor. Gibbs.

There was nothing to shield Paulsen now, and she fired her weapon as he headed for the shadows. Scrambled for cover when an answering shot came her way.

Drops pattered against the metal roof in an increased rhythm. The mist had changed to full-fledged rain now. Quickly she ran for the gloomy corner on the opposite side of the shed, passing through a glimmer from the light source as she ran. And felt the blood ice over in her veins.

The beetles and larvae covered the skeletal remains in the Plexiglas enclosure beneath the heat lamp. But from the size of the skeleton, she knew it was human.

There was a ninth victim.

She ducked as he shot again, and without conscious decision, aimed at the enclosure. Sprayed the glass with bullets.

Paulsen's scream, when it came, was as agonized as Gibbs's had been. "Nooooooo!"

Coolly she waited until he came toward the toppled enclosure, to where the beetles were pouring through the shattered Plexiglas. And this time when she fired, she aimed for him.

"Youbitchyoubitch. Oh, you fucking bitch!" His voice went strangled when her bullet caught him in the shoulder. His mewl of pain was surprisingly childlike. But he didn't seem impaired when he fled for the door, firing behind him.

She chased him down. Away from the still-silent body of the deputy. Across the back of the property into the trees fringing it. And it wasn't until she ran into the dense woods for several meters that she realized he'd led her into the forest.

This time she pressed Andrews's number as she sprinted, trying to keep Paulsen in sight as he leaped over logs and dodged around stands of trees. "Gibbs is down. In the shed on Paulsen's property. Chasing suspect through forest directly east of his shed."

"I've got two cars on their way to Paulsen's house," the sheriff barked in her ear. "Estimated arrival time, ten minutes."

"Send an ambulance." She shoved the phone back in her jeans and continued running. She had a sneaking suspicion that an ambulance was too late for the deputy. But if he were alive, herding Paulsen off the property might keep him that way.

Cait wiped the rain from her face and tried to figure how far they'd gone. Spying a shadow of movement to her left, she headed toward it with renewed speed. When she wasn't on a case, she trained at home. Ran five miles a day. The way her lungs were heaving, she'd gone nearly that far. And was totally and irrevocably lost.

She slowed, scanning the area ahead for a trace of Paulsen. If he was still there, he was hiding.

Halting behind a jumble of rocks, she hauled in a breath and tried to calm her breathing. And recognized just how easily she could be trapped here. The pines stretched overhead, an impenetrable wall of timber. Rocks and logs littered the forest floor, obstacles to the unsuspecting. The rain fell steadily from an uncaring sky to saturate the ground and slick the rocks.

And Paulsen had disappeared in the midst of it.

Squinting, she tried to get her bearings, but it was useless. In the shadows, the spot looked much like every mile she'd tromped with Zach. And as she scanned the area for signs of Jodie Paulsen, she had the fleeting thought that if she could have anyone at her side right now, it'd be Sharper.

When the bullet hit the rock beside her, a jagged piece flew up to hit her face. The next one caught her in the arm as she was diving away.

The bastard was behind her.

Circled around, most likely, waiting to ambush. Gritting her teeth against the gnawing agony tearing through flesh, she stumbled toward a large pine to take cover behind. And recognized in the course of that instant that the hunter had become the hunted.

The shots were coming faster. From a different weapon now. He had a shotgun.

She dodged from tree to tree, trying to find a good place for cover. A place to linger long enough to get a shot off.

But there was nothing but trees, many of the trunks too spindly to hide behind.

"It's just you and me, Cait."

Her steps faltered as she heard Paulsen's voice. She dropped to crouch behind an outcropping of rock.

"You don't know this forest like I do. Come out and I'll tell you all about me and my sweetie."

She searched the shadows crowding her from every side. Where the hell was he?

A flash of movement caught her eye and she fired. And felt an answering shot catch her in the shoulder. A curse tumbled from her lips as the flare of heat burst into pain.

"Hurts, don't it? I won't make you suffer when I end it, Cait. None of them suffered. It's easy to snap a neck, did you know that? My father said he didn't mean to snap Mother's, but he paid for it all the same. Just like you're going to pay for Sweetie being arrested." That disembodied voice seemed to surround her. Hem her in. "I'll bet you have a beautiful skull."

There was a roaring in her ears as unconsciousness reared, was ruthlessly beaten back. And when she tried, she could hear a noise in the distance that wasn't due to rain or ragged breathing.

The faint sound of traffic.

It was hard to summon logic through the agony. But highways ribboned through the forest. Hemmed it on a couple sides, didn't it? And if she could lead Paulsen toward the highway, she had a better chance of summoning help.

She drew a deep breath. Then burst from her hiding place, spraying bullets in every direction. And stumbling in the direction she thought, hoped, would lead to safety.

Running made the pain grow jagged little fangs that gnashed at her flesh with merciless glee. Her only consolation was that he'd been shot, too. At least once.

But she knew she'd lose strength long before he did.

A bullet kicked up dirt only inches from her feet. With renewed energy, she weaved and dodged, fueled more by adrenaline than real strength.

If she could reach the stand of trees ahead, she'd have the cover she needed to return fire. If she could just . . .

And then the ground disappeared from beneath her feet. She felt herself falling. Landing in a graceless heap against unforgiving juts of rock. Her weapon bounced out of her hands as she lay there, stunned. Uncomprehending.

Darkness surrounded her. And the forest floor was cold, cold beneath her cheek. She tried to sit up, swayed. Understanding was slow to pierce the fog in her brain.

Ice on the floor. She inched over on her bottom, each movement requiring excruciating care until her searching hand made contact. Ice on the walls. It was a cave. What had Sharper called them? Sawyer's Ice Caves. And she'd fallen through the keyhole of the largest one.

"Come out, come out, wherever you are."

The ice from the walls seemed to transfer to her spine. She could hear Paulsen overhead. His whispers carrying in the darkness. She lay on her belly, spreading both arms to search the cave floor with frantic hands for her weapon.

"I'm going to feed your skull to my bugs. No time for more. Just your skull."

With a thrill of exhilaration, she picked up what she thought was her weapon. Was only a rock. Her fingers clasped around it tightly. And then she waited. Barely daring to breathe.

"Ah." She could here him moving on the forest floor of the roof of the cave. "Hurt yourself, didn't you? I warned you, but you didn't listen. They never do."

She huddled in a ball, just inside the entrance of the cave. A few feet inside so she'd have the shadows for cover. Then he was blocking the entrance, crouched down to peer inside, the shotgun in one hand.

When he caught sight of her, he smiled. "I promise I'll take the best of care with your skull. You'll be my new favorite."

She lunged. Swung the rock with all her might and struck him across the bridge of the nose. He howled, backed away frantically but slipped on the icy floor of the cave. Cait dove for the shotgun, and felt the shape of her weapon beneath her body. Reached for it.

When they fired, the two shots sounded as one.

———

Zach stared out at the damn rain moodily. The rain pissed him off. The mud he'd slogged through up the drive to his house pissed him off. His mood, not the sunniest to begin with, had taken a decided downturn within minutes of entering JD's when Joanie Barton had lasered her sites on him.

Normally the woman was too busy to toss him more than a casual hi. But despite the throng of people crowded inside the place, she'd had the time to march right up to him and read him the riot act.

About Caitlin Fleming, of all things.

Apparently his was guilt by association, and Cait's sins, according to Joanie, were numerous. Supremely aware of the avid ears and sympathetic gazes all around him, he'd tried his best to soothe the woman, who'd been as close to hysterical as he'd ever seen her.

And when he'd figured out her outrage centered on Del being taken in for questioning, he could understand her wrath.

Barton? He was a cocky little shit, no doubt about it, but he'd rank about dead last on the suspect list in Zach's book. He couldn't imagine the man climbing a boulder, much less hiking up Castle Rock in the dead of night with a set of bones on his back. And since he'd been on the receiving end of one of the sheriff's miscalculated interrogations himself recently, he'd been ready to empathize with Joanie and her husband.

Until she'd started in on Cait.

He shifted uncomfortably in the recliner. Well, hell, he could hardly stand there, could he, while the woman called Cait names he'd never heard come out of a female's mouth before? Apparently coming to Cait's defense made his a graver sin than hers had been.

He'd told her a few hard truths, and now he was banned from JD's for life. Or until Joanie got over her mad, which-ever came first. The way the woman could hold a grudge, he was betting on the former.

His cell rang and he considered not answering it at all. There wasn't a person in the world he felt like talking to.

That thought was immediately revised when he checked the caller ID.

Cait.

Resisting the urge to rub his suddenly damp palms on his jeans, he answered. "Okay, I screwed up last night, but I'm guessing after the last hour I've had, we're even."

He waited for her response. "Cait?" He knew the call hadn't been disconnected. He could hear her breathing. Thready and weak.

"Funny you were . . . the first I called. Funny, huh?" He frowned, straightening a bit in his chair. Had she been drinking? Her voice was slurred. "Should've . . . called Andrews. Told her. But wanted you. Should have had . . . you with me. Thought that. Before."

"Where are you?" He was on his feet, heading for the mudroom for a rain slicker. "Are you okay?"

"Hurts. God it hurts." Was that a laugh or a sob? Panic unleashed, galloped through him. "He's dead, though. He's dead. Both dead. Gibbs."

"Gibbs is dead?" What was going on? He ran out the door. Down the slick board that served as a walkway. Yanking the hood of the slicker over his head, his boot slipped. Landed in the mud. "Where are you?"

"Sawyer's. Ice. I 'membered." Her voice was fading. And the fear inside him roared through his system. Thundered through his veins until it was a living breathing beast. "Fell. But I thought . . . of you. Why is that, Sharper?" He had to strain to hear the words as he turned the key in the ignition and flipped the Trailblazer into gear. "Why's my last . . . thought of you?"

"You're at Sawyer's Ice Caves?" Fear made his voice rough. What the hell would she be doing there? "I'm coming to get you, baby. Just tell me. You're at the caves?"

But there was no answer. No matter how many times he yelled her name, there was no answer.

And this time he couldn't hear her breathing.

"You stay the hell clear of there, you hear me, Sharper?" Andrews sounded like she was issuing the order through clenched teeth.

Zach peered out into the night, between the swipe of the wipers on the windshield. "Fuck that. I'm going after her."

"I've got men in the area, and I redirected them as soon as you called in. But you stay put. There's an armed suspect in the region, and I don't want you in the crossfire."

"Then tell them to keep out of my way." He clicked disconnect and dropped the phone to the seat. Clenched the steering wheel until his knuckles ached. And did the one thing he hadn't done since coming back from Afghanistan.

Prayed.

———————

"Cait!" The sweep of the Maglite was little help in the utter darkness of the forest. The wind blew the rain sideways, tiny needle pricks of bone-deep chill. The canopy of trees provided little protection as he went farther into the interior of the forest. "Cait!"

He checked the biggest of the caves first. And his bowels went to ice when he saw the body crumpled in the entrance. With his heart a hard knot in his chest, he pulled the figure over. Shone his light in what was left of the man's face.

"Jesus." He took a hasty step back. Jodie Paulsen? What the hell did Jodie have to do with this mess?

"Cait. Dammit." Dread was trickling down his back to pool nastily at the base of his spine. Frantically he swept the area with the beam of the light. Took two steps away before comprehension slammed into him and he bounced the beam back to the small figure leaning against the base of a nearby pine.

"Cait!" Her lack of response was like having a spike drilled into his gut. He ran to kneel beside her, setting the Mag next to him so it bathed her in its beam. Her face was white. Deathly so. And her hands, when he lifted them to feel for a pulse, were frigid.

Her pulse was a mere flutter, but his relief was nearly overwhelming. That emotion dampened immediately when he noticed the blood covering her. Paulsen's? Or her own?

His hands shook as he ran them over her, halting when she moaned. And when he saw the blood cover his palms, he felt true fear for the first time in years.

Her eyelids fluttered. "Sharper." And miraculously she smiled a bit. "I knew . . . you'd . . . find me."

Rapidly he shed his slicker, pulled his shirt over his head and began ripping at its seams for makeshift bandages. "That's right, baby, I found you. I'll always find you."

Fear lodged in his stomach like molten lead as he pressed the cloth against her wounds to stanch the blood loss. He just hoped like hell that he hadn't found her too late.

Epilogue

"So you've got all the remains identified?"

Cait cocked an eyebrow at Adam Raiker, who was roaming the length of the lab, the head of his heavily carved cane clasped in one scarred hand. "All but one. I told you that on the phone yesterday."

He turned to look at her with his lone eye, the patch over the other making him look like a modern-day pirate. "It's been twenty-four hours since we spoke. What have you been doing?"

"Slacking off," she said mildly. "Same thing I've been doing the last four weeks."

He gave a bark of laughter, and her gaze was drawn to the jagged scar bisecting his throat. She wasn't about to complain about a couple bullet wounds to him. Not after all he'd suffered when his last case for the Bureau had gone so wrong.

"Fired a gun yet?"

"Went to a range yesterday." Against the express orders of her doctor. But she'd been driven to reassure herself that her shoulder injury hadn't impaired her ability to shoot. Raiker

WAKING THE DEAD | 321

would never allow one of his investigators into the field again who couldn't fire a weapon.

The door to the lab pushed open and Barnes stepped in. Stopped short when he saw she wasn't alone.

"Mitch Barnes, Adam Raiker."

The deputy surprised her by going up to the man for a solid handshake. "It's an honor, sir."

"Deputy. Sorry to hear about your man."

Barnes's face clouded for a moment. "It's hard to lose one."

Cait felt a hitch in her chest at the thought of Tony Gibbs. The cruisers Andrews had sent to Paulsen's place had arrived much too late to save the deputy. And it would be a long time before she'd stop second-guessing herself. Wondering what she could have done differently. If there was a way that would have spared Gibbs's life.

"Let it go."

At Raiker's quiet command her gaze flew to his. Saw the understanding in his expression. She appreciated the thought but wished it were as easy to comply with.

"The sheriff got word from the feds. They've traced the accounts Barton was bouncing the bank transfers to. They all ended in the Caymans."

Cait felt a flicker of surprise. "The travel information found in Paulsen's place was for Belize."

Mitch folded his arms across his chest. "I'm betting Barton was planning to end-run Paulsen. Promise to meet up with him in one location and split the take, but head for a different country altogether and keep the whole thing for himself. And at the rate he's going, he'll have the whole thing pinned on Paulsen before it goes to trial." Mitch moved back a step to lean against the counter. "According to him, it was all Jodie's idea, which is pure BS because Paulsen just didn't have the mental capacity to carry this thing out."

"The forensics on the computers we can link Barton to will be incriminating. His lawyer might be able to dance around the spyware installed on the computers' resorts, but finding the exact same software installed on those in his Internet café will be a bit more difficult to explain." And Gavin Pounds had explained to her, in mind-numbing detail, just how the spyware he'd installed remotely to the victims' home computers could be traced back to Barton, as well. "We don't have him for the killings, but he isn't going to be able to dodge the kidnapping charges. He hasn't been able explain his absences that correspond to the days the victims disappeared. Especially when the farmer, Tim Jenkins, is willing to swear that Jodie Paulsen was doing chores twice a day for him every day for the last ten years, with the exception of a day or two."

Barnes looked a little green at her words. She knew he was remembering her theory that after defleshing the bones, Paulsen had likely fed the remaining tissue and organs to the pigs he'd tended. They'd found the bone saw in the shed that matched the TPI measurements she'd done on the skeletal remains. Barnes had brought Kristy to the site while Cait was in the hospital to take a soil sample inside the structure.

And Cait had had to listen while her assistant crowed about being right regarding its composition. The hot springs that ran beneath the dirt floor of Paulsen's shed erupted in only one space near the end of the property line. And the shed had, at one time, housed sheep in inclement weather.

"How long do you think it will take to ID the remaining set of bones?"

"As long as it takes you to dig up Jodie Paulsen's body and get me a DNA sample."

"What?" Even Raiker was regarding her with a skeptical look.

"I've spoken to every detective with a missing persons in the database that falls within the same general description. Have compared the remains to no fewer than a dozen reference samples. Zach said something about Paulsen's father being in a nursing home in Portland, but we were unable to locate him in any of them. There was no contact information for such a place in Paulsen's home, Mitch said." She looked at the deputy. "I think his father might have been Paulsen's first kill."

Barnes scratched his head. Sometime during the last month

he'd shaved his mustache. It was an improvement. "That's going to be a tough one to get by Andrews."

"It's the only way she's going to get an ID." The other option was that the remains belonged to someone who hadn't been reported missing. That was unlikely given that the other victims all had had substantial funds transferred from their accounts.

"I'll talk to her," Barnes said dubiously.

"Where is the esteemed sheriff?" Raiker said in a silky voice Cait immediately recognized. "Holding yet another press conference?"

The deputy shifted his gaze to a speck on the floor. "I couldn't say."

He didn't have to say. Cait had long suspected that Andrews would use a successful resolution to this case and ride it into the governor's mansion. From the positive publicity the woman had garnered from this case, it looked like she might be successful.

Mitch straightened. Looked at Cait. "How much longer you going to be around? I mean"—he smiled a little—"how much longer do I have to convince the sheriff to do an excavation?"

"A week." Raiker's voice was steely. "I want my investigator back."

"It'll be two before I get a medical release to return to work," Cait said. But she avoided her boss's searching gaze. And when Barnes said his good-byes and left the lab, her heart gave a bit of a leap as the door remained open to admit Zach.

She wondered how long it would be before he stopped regarding her with that hint of worry in his eyes. She'd assured him, repeatedly over the last month, that she was fine. Had proved it, again, just last night.

He smiled and she felt something inside her soften. Then started guiltily when she caught Raiker's gaze on her, shrewd as a laser.

"Ohmygod." He looked from her to Zach and back again, an expression of disgust on his face. "Why do I have the feeling that this son of a bitch is going to cost me one of my best investigators?"

"Zach Sharper, Adam Raiker." She made the introduction mechanically. But she was focused on her employer's words. "How come you only break out the sweet talk when you think you're going to lose me?"

"A question that could be leveled to all men in your life, it appears." Zach came farther into the room, a glint in his eye warning her. "*This* son of a bitch has an invested interest in keeping Cait around."

"But I have a way guaranteed to make us all happy," she interceded smoothly. The men looked like a couple of junkyard dogs, squaring off. To her employer she asked, "Have you given any further consideration to our conversation last month about the mobile lab?"

His expression eased from fierce concern to general irritability. "I was planning to staff the labs with techs, not investigators."

"I'd be mobile, too," she said easily. Crossed the space to slip her arm through Zach's arm. "How many jobs have you turned down on the west coast because they wanted private lab facilities as well as an investigator?"

"Not enough to bother keeping track of."

"Well, now the answer would be none. And when I'm not on a case, I could fly to headquarters regularly for updated training." Raiker was a taskmaster about continued schooling for his investigators and scientists.

"Spend all your damn time in the air," he groused.

"Not all her time," Zach said pointedly.

Raiker was silent for a moment, regarding her with a fierce look. Finally he said, "I'll think about it."

Something eased in Cait's chest. But she knew better than to release the smile that threatened. "That's all I ask."

He walked toward the door, his limp pronounced even with the help of the cane. "Guess I'll have to bodily drag Andrews out of whatever media frenzy she's whipped up today to settle with her." He gave Zach a nod as he went by him. "Sharper."

"Good meeting you." Watching the man until he went out the door, Zach turned to regard Cait quizzically. "Was that good news?"

"It was very good news." The smile she'd suppressed earlier broke out. "He didn't dismiss it out of hand. And I know he wants to place mobile labs in four or five spots across the country to improve our timeliness. I might have to become a contracted worker rather than be employed directly through the agency, but . . ." She shrugged. It was a trade-off she was willing to make. Especially if it meant she and Zach would have some time to see where their relationship was leading.

"Did you call your mother today?"

The question threatened to dim the quiet satisfaction she felt after Raiker's—almost—capitulation. "She still won't take my calls." And from the guarded responses she got from Lydia's doctor, she didn't expect that to change anytime soon. Her mother's path to emotional recovery looked like it might prove to be as slow as the disintegration of her mental health.

He slipped his arm around her waist for a hard hug. As she leaned against him, she realized with a note of surprise that it was becoming easier to accept his support. They regarded each other silently for a moment. "Unfamiliar territory," he said finally.

"It is that." For both of them.

"Fortunately guiding in foreign terrain is something I do have experience in. The first trick is to go in prepared."

"Good advice, I suppose. If you know what to prepare for." He wasn't the only one who'd avoided long-term relationships like the plague.

"You don't go in alone." His hand slid down to caress her butt.

"Small chance of that." Obeying his urging, she pressed closer, feeling a little of her trepidation leak away when his arms came around her.

"You trust your partner."

She saw the flicker in his eyes. Knew he was thinking of the fight they'd had before she'd tracked down Paulsen. "Back atcha."

"I'm a quick learner." He reached up to toy with a strand of her hair, a small smile playing around the corners of his mouth. "Last thing to remember is we're in this together."

Going up on her tiptoes, she nipped at his bottom lip. "I'm counting on that."

"Then there's no reason in the world that we shouldn't expect a successful journey. Complete with enough thrills and adventure to satisfy us both."

His lingering kiss stemmed the sound of agreement she would have made. There was nothing more to add, at any rate. Cait had a feeling that teaming up with Sharper was going to be the trip of a lifetime.

Turn the page for a preview of
the fourth book in Kylie Brant's
exciting Mindhunters series

DEADLY FEAR

Coming soon
from Berkley Sensation!

Icy fingers of fear clawed through the fabric of sleep and brought Ellie Mulder instantly awake. Old habits had her keeping her muscles lax, her eyes still closed as she strained to identify what had alerted her. When she did, her blood ran as cold as the frigid Colorado wind beating against the windows.

She could hear him breathing.

It was the same snuffle snort that warned her whenever he was coming for her. He'd returned, just like he'd threatened. He'd snatch her from her bed, from her home and this time, she'd never get away. Not ever.

Her eyes snapped open as a scream lodged in her throat. The old terrors were surging, fighting logic, fueled by memory. It took a moment to see through the veils of the past and notice her familiar surroundings.

She was home. In her room. In her bed. And Art Cooper wasn't here. He would die in prison.

A long sigh of relief shuddered out of her. The bright illumination of the alarm clock on her bedside table said one-eighteen A.M. The sleep scene on her computer lit the corner of the room that held her desk. And the large aquarium on the opposite wall was awash in a dim glow. She often "forgot" to turn it off.

The items had been chosen because of the light they afforded. Her mom and dad had worried when she'd needed doors open and lights blazing to go to bed at night. But they'd been happy when she'd casually mentioned wanting a computer. Had expressed an interest in tropical fish. Had selected things to decorate her bedroom like the brightly lit alarm clock. Those things were *normal*, the psychologist said. And Ellie knew it was important that she seem normal. Even if it was a lie.

The slight noise sounded again and she tensed, her hand searching for the scissors she kept on the bedside table. But even as her fingers gripped the handle, her mind identified the sound. It was the gurgle of water in the overflow box for the aquarium. Not Cooper's breathing.

The recognition relaxed her, but she didn't replace the scissors. She kept them clutched in her hand and brought them close to her chest, the feel of the small weapon comforting. Learning their daughter slept with a knife under her pillow had made her parents cry. So Ellie had to pretend not to need that anymore. She had become very good at pretending.

So good that her mom and dad were thrilled about her new interest several months ago. She'd heard the psychologist tell them that the act of creating, of folding and cutting paper into pretty shapes would be very therapeutic for her. So there was never any fuss about the constant paper scraps on the floor. New supplies appeared on her desk without her ever having to request them.

Only she knew that the new hobby was an excuse to keep a sharp pair of scissors with her at all times. And the psychologist was right. That part, at least, was very therapeutic.

The initial flare of panic had ebbed. She listened to the blizzard howl outside the windows and found the sound oddly soothing. Bit by bit, she felt herself relax. Her eyelids drooped.

She had the half-formed thought that she needed to re-place the scissors before her mom came in the next morning to check on her. But sleep was sucking her under, and her limbs were unresponsive.

It was then that he pounced.

The weight hit her body, jolting her from exhaustion back to alarm in the span of seconds. She felt the hand clamped over her mouth, the prick of a needle in her arm and fear lent her strength far beyond her years. Rearing up in bed, she flailed wildly, trying to wrest away, trying to strike out. She tasted the stickiness of tape over her lips. Felt a hood being pulled over her head.

There was a brief flare of triumph when the scissors met something solid, and a hiss of pain sounded in her ear. But then her hand was bent back, the weapon dropping from her fingers and a strange numbness started to slide over her body. She couldn't move. The hood prevented her from seeing. A strange buzzing filled her head.

As she felt herself lifted and carried away, her only thought was she was being taken.

Again.

———

Icy needles of sleet pricked Macy Reid's cheeks as she hurried across the tarmac at the Manassas Regional Airport. The sleek black private jet sat waiting, its motors idling. It looked impatient somehow, looming dark and silent in the shadows, as if it had somehow taken on the personality of the man waiting inside it. Adam Raiker, head of Raiker Forensics and her boss, had demanded she be there within the hour. Her home in Vienna, Virginia was nearly twenty miles from the airport. Since the usual D.C. traffic was light at four A.M., she'd made the trip in under forty-five minutes.

An attendant took her suitcases and stowed them for her as she wiped the frigid moisture from her cheeks and made her way up the steps to the aircraft. Her satisfaction at arriving early dissipated when she recognized the man seated in the roomy black leather seat next to her boss. Kellan Burke. Fellow forensic investigator and all-around pain-in-the-ass.

Her stomach gave one quick lurch before she ordered it to settle. She gave Raiker a nod. "Adam." She barely glanced at the other man as she chose a seat on the other side of her boss and buckled in. "Burke."

"The inimitable duchess Macy." Kellan gave her a sleepy smile that she knew better than to trust. "Been awhile since we've been paired on an investigation. Miss me?"

"Like a case of foot rot."

"A comeback," he noted admiringly. "You've been practicing."

She could feel a flush heating her cheeks and damned yet again the fair complexion that mirrored her emotions. Almost as much as she damned the man for being right. Experience had taught her that it paid to have a ready repertoire of witty replies if she was to spend any length of time in Burke's presence. Unfortunately, those replies usually occurred several hours after they were required, leaving her at the crucial moment as tongue-tied and frustrated as an eight-year-old.

Adam pressed a button on his armrest that would alert the pilot to ready for takeoff. Then he sent them a look. "Any squabbling and you'll ride in the luggage compartment. Both of you." He leaned forward to withdraw two file folders from the pocket of his briefcase and handed one to each of them as the jet began its taxi down the runway. Macy seized it, grateful to have something else to focus on.

"Steven Mulder." Burke was studying the first sheet inside the folder, his expression thoughtful. "Why is that name familiar?"

"Maybe because he's the owner of the discount stores that bear his name." Raiker's voice was dry. "A quick Google check shows there are two thousand Mulders in the country with several hundred more operations in Europe, Asia, and South America."

The name had also struck a chord of recognition with Macy, but not for the same reason. "Steven Mulder? His daughter was one of the girls rescued when you broke that child-swap ring a few years ago." The case wasn't one she was likely to forget. Her testimony in the case helped put one of the perpetrators behind bars. It was also what had brought her to Raiker's attention.

"That's right." For Burke's benefit he explained, "Ellie Mulder was seven when she was snatched while attending a friend's birthday party. FBI took control of the case almost immediately. She was found incidentally when one of my cases overlapped a couple years later. I broke up a child auction and her kidnapper was among those looking for a trade-in. By that point she'd been missing twenty-seven months."

Macy's gaze had dropped to the opened folder in her lap, but she froze a moment later in the act of scanning the information he'd put together for them. "She's been kidnapped . . . again?"

"Abducted sometime between eleven and two A.M. this morning." Raiker's expression was grim. "Denver was having a hellacious blizzard and Ellie's mother went in to check on her. She discovered her missing from her bed and looked around the house. Woke up her husband when she didn't find her and they searched the estate. He called me an hour after they discovered her gone."

"But not the FBI," Burke put in shrewdly.

Macy caught Raiker's gaze on her and followed it to where her fingers laid against the folder. Her fingers were beating a familiar tattoo against the surface. *Tap-tap-tap. Tap-tap-tap. Tap-tap-tap.* Throat drying, she deliberately stilled them and refocused her thoughts.

"The feds failed her before." She met Raiker's stare, knew she was right. "They had over two years to find her the first time. But you're the one responsible for bringing her home to them. So Mulder contacted you."

Her employer inclined his head. "If the Mulders had their way, no law enforcement would be involved at all. They're pretty devoid of respect for LEOs after the last incident. But I convinced Steven that he has no choice but to report Ellie's disappearance. He has a personal relationship with the governor. With both Colorado U.S. Senators. He'll use his influence to bring in the Colorado Bureau of Investigation as leads."

"Elbowing aside the Denver PD," Kellan muttered, still studying the contents of the file.

"The Mulder estate is located thirty minutes outside Denver. It actually falls under the jurisdiction of the Denver Sheriff's office. This could turn into a territorial tug-of-war of monumental proportions."

Macy considered the ramifications. Being hired by a family member rather than the investigating law enforcement entity made their appearance on the scene a bit more tenuous. In a case such as this, suspicion fell first on the family and those in closest proximity to the child. The LEO would worry that their allegiance to Mulder would take precedence over their commitment to teamwork. Without Raiker running interference, they could be shut out of the investigative end of things almost completely. He was going to have his plate full handling the politics of this one.

She glanced at Burke. Found him watching her through a pair of trendy framed glasses that were new since the last time she'd seen him. "They're going to want to bring in their own people."

"Of course. But it's my job to convince them they don't have anyone who can match the experience the two of you bring. Don't make a liar out of me."

It took her a moment to realize Raiker was joking. It was always tough telling with him. "You've checked on Cooper's whereabouts?"

"Art Cooper is still in prison in Yazoo City, fulfilling his thirty year sentence for the kidnap and rape of Ellie Mulder."

"And . . . the others?" It took all her resolve not to fidget under the shrewd look Raiker aimed her way.

"All accounted for, still inside serving their sentences."

She wouldn't have asked. Couldn't have formed the words. But in the next moment he added deliberately, "Rodriguez has been bounced around some. He's currently housed at Florence in Wisconsin."

"So are we looking at the original group you rounded up

in that first case?" Burke demanded. "Do any of them have the jones to reach out this way from prison?"

"They'll have to be checked out," Raiker replied. "Every avenue will need to be explored. We can't afford to overlook the possibility that Ellie's disappearance this time is somehow connected to that first kidnapping. I'll line up the interviews for each with the prison wardens and make personal visits."

There was a sick knot of dread settling in the pit of Macy's stomach. With an ease born of long practice, she pushed it aside and looked at her boss. "And then we have to decide who the real target of this crime is. Ellie Mulder, or her father."

There were only three other cars parked in the wide drive that looped in a half-circle in front of the sprawling Mulder estate. Macy wondered if that meant Steven Mulder had been successful in limiting the scope of the LEO presence, or if others had already been and gone since Raiker received the man's call this morning. The still heavy snowfall made it impossible to tell. As it was, the trio of vehicles in the drive were already buried under several inches of wet snow that had turned the roads from the airport into thick puddles of slush. A drop in the temperature would make them treacherous.

Macy stepped out of the SUV and scanned the grounds. They'd been detained at the iron gates at the base of the drive, more than a quarter mile back until the CBI agent posted there had scrutinized their IDs and waited for permission from someone inside to admit them. That had given her plenty of time to eye the twelve-foot stone walls that surrounded the property. The discreetly placed security cameras that topped them at regular intervals. The matching stone security station in front of the gates was meant to be manned by a live operator, and looked to be equipped with full audio and video feed. Whoever had gotten in and out of the estate undetected wasn't an amateur.

The front door of the home swung open as Raiker was getting out of the vehicle, cane in hand. From the grim-faced visage of the man in the doorway, Macy knew immediately he was another LEO. Which meant he was a CBI agent.

He waited until they'd ascended the stairs to demand their IDs again. It occurred to her that the extra precautions were a bit late. Ellie Mulder was *gone*.

"Special agent in charge, Cal Whitman, is waiting for you in the study with Mr. Mulder. This way."

They were led through a marbled floor hallway that was lined with paintings and punctuated with large abstract sculptures. Macy recognized some of the artists, had no doubt the pieces were original. With Mulder's billions, he could afford just about anything. Except the one thing his money apparently couldn't buy.

His daughter's safety.

"Not too shabby," Kellen said in an undertone as he strolled along at her side, casting an appraising look at the space. "What do you figure? Ten million? Fifteen?"

"I wouldn't know." It was usually best to ignore Burke. But the man made it difficult. Even now she could feel his pale green eyes on her, alight, no doubt, with amusement. It always seemed to be the primary emotion she elicited from him.

The hallway seemed endless. They trailed Raiker and the CBI agent who had let them in. "Pretty easy to get lost in a place this huge," Burke said, unzipping his navy down jacket and shoving his hands in its pockets. "How long do you think it would take them to locate us?"

"Why don't you find out?"

He gave her a lazy grin. The prism of lights from the crystals on the overhead chandeliers shot his thick brown hair with reddish glints. She'd bet he'd been auburn haired as a youngster. She could be certain he'd been incorrigible even then.

"If you promise to lead the search and rescue party, I might consider it. I can imagine it now. Me, weak from lack of food, maybe injured. You, bending over me in concern, wiping my brow, the strap of your lacy camisole slipping down one satiny shoulder . . ."

She resisted an urge to smack him, which was the over-powering effect *he* had on *her*. "Why would I lead a search and rescue mission clad in a camisole?"

His smile turned wicked. "Why indeed?"

"Burke."

They both jumped at the crack of Raiker's voice. He was several feet ahead of them. They'd been speaking too quietly for him to have heard them. Hadn't they? "Yeah, boss?"

"Shut up."

He slid a sideways glance at Macy and winked at her, clearly undeterred. "Shutting up, boss."

And those, she considered, as they were ushered into a large dark paneled room, were the most promising words she'd heard all day.

The man who rose to his feet to step toward Raiker, his hand outstretched, was immediately recognizable. Steven Mulder. He hadn't appeared at the Rodriguez trial Macy had testified at, but there'd been plenty of news stories devoted to his family since his daughter's first disappearance. He was prematurely gray, with a long, lean runner's build outfitted in a tailored suit. Its cost likely exceeded two months of her salary. As the two men clapped each other on the shoulder and leaned forward to murmur a few words, her gaze went beyond them to the men still seated behind a long polished conference table. It was easy enough to guess which one was Whitman.

The SAC had a decade on Raiker, she estimated, which would place him in his early to mid-fifties. It was difficult to tell his height while he was sitting, but she'd bet under six foot. He had a shaved head and thick neck. He wore a suit, too, but his was ill-fitting, pulling across his beefy chest and shoulders. His flat brown gaze flicked over them, giving Macy the impression they'd been sized up in the space of an instant. There was nothing in his expression that gave away his thoughts about their inclusion in this case.

Mulder stepped away from Raiker and inclined his head

in the direction of her and Burke. "Thank you for coming. I have tremendous respect for your boss. He's performed a miracle once." There was a barely discernible break in his voice. "I'm hoping he's got another one up his sleeve."

"Where Raiker is concerned, achieving the impossible is a daily expectation," Burke assured him soberly. Macy remained silent. She was always leery about issuing assurances to victim's families. Life didn't always come complete with happy endings.

And this family had occasion to know that all too well.

Mulder turned away. "Special agent in charge Calvin Whitman," he gestured to the man she'd pegged as CBI, "and my attorney and friend, Mark Alden. He's also Ellie's godfather."

Alden was impeccably dressed, but his dark hair was slightly mussed, and his eyes were as red rimmed as Mulder's. He gave them a nod but said nothing.

"Why doesn't everyone sit down and I'll catch you up." Whitaker waited for them to take a seat at the table. As they shrugged out of their coats, he continued, "As per Mr. Mulder's request to the governor, I brought a small team of agents and we arrived around five-thirty. My people have thoroughly searched the house and are going over the grounds. An Amber Alert was issued hours prior, when Mr. Mulder contacted the governor." There was a flicker in the man's flat brown eyes at this breach of protocol. It wasn't reflected in his expression, which remained impassive. "We've found no trace of the child so far. I have an agent taking Mrs. Mulder's statement. Others have rounded up the live-in help and we're preparing to question them."

"Steven just finished completing his statement for Agent Whitaker when you arrived." It was the first time the lawyer had spoken. "We'll expect a copy of it, and of all the case notes, to be shared with Mr. Raiker's team members in an expedient manner."

The tilt of Whitaker's head could have meant anything. But it was telling, Macy thought, that he had made no verbal agreement.

Mulder obviously thought so, too. "Just so we're clear on this, Agent." He placed his palms on the table and leaned forward, his tone fierce. "Raiker's unit is here with the blessing of the governor and our U.S. senators. They *will* be a full part of this team." He gave a humorless smile. "I've been through this before. I know how it works. Althea and I are suspects until proven otherwise. So is everyone else in this house. I realize that effectively shuts me out of some of the details in this investigation. But the person I trust won't be shut out. He's here to be sure other aspects of the investigation don't stall while you're wasting your time on us." When the CBI agent would have spoken, he waved aside his protest. "I'm not waiting two years to bring my little girl home this time." He rose, and Alden got to his feet as well. "I recognize there are details to be shared that you won't share in my presence, so Mark and I will leave now. I want to be there for Althea when they've finished with her."

The room was silent as the men left, shutting the door behind them. Upon their exit, Whitaker eased his bulk back in is chair and eyed Raiker. "Your inclusion here puts us in a dilemma. You have to realize that."

"The thing about dilemmas is they always have solutions." Adam's voice was no less steely. "Consider those solutions, Special Agent. You can't afford *not* to utilize us."

The other man rubbed at the folds on the back of his neck. "I want you to . . ." He paused then, seemed to choose his words more carefully. "I'm *suggesting* that you avoid any conflict of interest by letting my people complete the search of the premises. I've got a crime scene responders going over the girl's room right now."

"And once they're done, we have free access to the property and copies of any and all reports as they're formulated." Raiker clearly knew how to play the game. "My people will be included in all briefings and task assignments."

"The information is a two way street." The agent looked at Macy and Kellen, making no attempt to mask his expression now that Mulder had gone. The man was plainly unhappy with their presence. "If I learn that you've withheld something from me, you're off the case and I'll have you detained for obstruction."

Macy noted Raiker's fingers clenching around the knob of the cane he carried. It was his only sign of temper. His voice, when it came, was silky. "Threats are the realm of the unimaginative, Special Agent. You've got some very powerful people lined up behind Steven Mulder. They were summoned because the investigation into the previous kidnapping of Ellie Mulder went nowhere."

"And you were the superstar there. Yeah, I got that." Curiously, the squaring off seemed to have eased something in the other man. "I knew your rep when you were with the bureau." His gaze lingered on Raiker then, as if taking in the eye patch and scars on his throat and hands. "Got another earful about your outfit from my director. As long as we understand each other, I think we ought to get along well enough."

His gaze traveled between her and Burke. "Which of you is the forensic linguist?"

"That'd be me."

His gaze settled on Macy then. "We don't have a ransom note. At least nothing's been found yet. But if the offender is going to reach out, I'd expect it to be within twenty-four hours. Give him time to see the girl safely situated and then turn his attention to the next matter."

"I have a few contacts in the penal department." Macy was certain Adam's words were a gross understatement. The man seemed to have to have contacts everywhere. "Everyone scooped up in that last case where Ellie was rescued is accounted for in their respective prisons."

"And there's no one else out there that maybe slipped by you guys?" The gibe was nearly hidden in Whitaker's words. "How can you be sure you got everyone affiliated with that case?"

Raiker lifted a shoulder. "You can never be positive. That's why I'm arranging another round of interviews with each suspect in that case. I've got phone calls in to each warden to set it up."

"Video?"

"In person."

The special agent nodded. "That'll save us some serious time and manpower."

"When will we have access to the scene? And the rest of the house?"

Macy caught the barely discernible note of frustration in Kellan's voice. She seconded it. As private forensics consultants, it was rare that they were ever called in on a fresh crime scene. This was one of the quickest callouts she'd ever been part of, and they were effectively being shut away from the scene for several more hours, if not days.

"When the crime scene unit is finished. It'll be evening at the earliest. Until then, you're free to sit in on the interviews of the employees. That's probably going to take us most of the day."

"How many people are we talking about?"

Whitaker glanced down at a sheet of paper in front of him. But before he could answer, Adam said, "Mulder employs nearly forty full- and part-time employees in the winter months. That would include the daughter's teacher and various instructors: piano, dance, whatnot."

"How many live on the grounds?"

"None live in the house," the special agent said, "but the teacher has a small apartment over one of the garages. A mechanic, two stable hands, and a couple groundskeepers have places above various other outbuildings. Everyone else lives off site." He consulted the notes again. "Eight security officers, six maids, four drivers, three cooks, one personal assistant—a sort of secretary to Mrs. Mulder—a hairdresser, masseuse . . . it's like a damn village around here."

"And how many of those people were here yesterday?" Kellan asked.

"Thirty-eight were on the grounds at some point." He lifted a shoulder. "A few never made it in because of the weather. Others left early. All have been notified that they're wanted in for questioning. About half have arrived so far."

"You would have looked at the tapes first," Macy noted. She wondered if the agent had been getting to that or if he wouldn't have brought it up if she hadn't asked. "They've got live video feed, right? That means a security station somewhere with someone manning the cameras. Something had to have shown up on them."

"Nothing that we've found yet. But we've only been here a couple hours. I've got some of the best techies in the agency going over those cameras. Whatever is there, we'll find it."

"How many of the security officers have arrived?"

"Six. And we've made contact with the other two. They're on their way."

Macy understood where Raiker was going with his question. She'd be willing to bet that Mulder had spared no expense on security for the estate. "What are the security specs?"

"Well, you saw the twelve foot walls around the perimeter," Whitaker said dryly. "Cameras are mounted every thirty feet. Motion detectors on the grounds. The guard station is manned twenty-four-seven. The gates don't open without keycard ID and thumbprint identification."

Raiker's voice was sharp. "But the guard out front has override powers."

"No. Only security inside can override. But we've found no record that they did so yesterday. We're looking deeper."

Exchanging a glance with Burke, Macy said, "Let's get to those interviews then. Starting with Mulder's security team." There didn't appear to be any way to get on to the estate without security knowing about it.

Which meant one of the members of the team might well have assisted with Ellie's kidnapping.

About the Author

Kylie Brant is the bestselling author of nearly thirty contemporary romantic suspense novels, including *Waking Nightmare*, *Waking Evil*, and *Waking the Dead*. She's a two-time Rita nominee and a Romantic Times Career Achievement award winner. One of her books is listed by *Romantic Times Magazine* as an all-time favorite.

Kylie lives in the Midwest with her husband and a very spoiled Polish Lowland sheepdog. Visit her website at www.kyliebrant.com or contact her at kylie@kylie brant.com.